DONNA HAS LEFT THE BUILDING

ALSO BY SUSAN JANE GILMAN

Kiss My Tiara

Hypocrite in a Pouffy White Dress

Undress Me in the Temple of Heaven

The Ice Cream Queen of Orchard Street

DONNA HAS LEFT THE BUILDING

A NOVEL

SUSAN JANE GILMAN

GRAND CENTRAL
PUBLISHING

NEW YORK   BOSTON

Copyright © 2019 by Susan Jane Gilman

Cover design by Brian Levy. Cover copyright © 2019 by Hachette Book Group, Inc.

Hachette Book Group supports the right to free expression and the value of copyright. The purpose of copyright is to encourage writers and artists to produce the creative works that enrich our culture.

The scanning, uploading, and distribution of this book without permission is a theft of the author's intellectual property. If you would like permission to use material from the book (other than for review purposes), please contact permissions@hbgusa.com. Thank you for your support of the author's rights.

Grand Central Publishing
Hachette Book Group
1290 Avenue of the Americas, New York, NY 10104
grandcentralpublishing.com
twitter.com/grandcentralpub

First Edition: June 2019

Grand Central Publishing is a division of Hachette Book Group, Inc. The Grand Central Publishing name and logo is a trademark of Hachette Book Group, Inc.

The publisher is not responsible for websites (or their content) that are not owned by the publisher.

The Hachette Speakers Bureau provides a wide range of authors for speaking events. To find out more, go to www.hachettespeakersbureau.com or call (866) 376-6591.

Library of Congress Cataloging-in-Publication Data

Names: Gilman, Susan Jane, author.
Title: Donna has left the building / Susan Jane Gilman.
Description: First Edition. | New York : Grand Central Publishing, 2019.
Identifiers: LCCN 2018048056| ISBN 9781538762417 (hardcover) | ISBN 9781549175879 (audio download) | ISBN 9781538762448 (ebook)
Subjects: LCSH: Families--Fiction. | Domestic fiction.
Classification: LCC PS3607.I45214 D66 2019 | DDC 813/.6--dc23
LC record available at https://lccn.loc.gov/2018048056

ISBNs: 978-1-5387-6241-7 (hardcover), 978-1-5387-6244-8 (ebook)

Printed in the United States of America

LSC-C

10 9 8 7 6 5 4 3 2 1

for
Ellis Avery

DONNA HAS LEFT THE BUILDING

Part One

Chapter 1

THE MORNING OF MY forty-fifth birthday, I woke up to a cop knocking on my windshield. My Subaru was parked in the dunes by a low concrete building scribbled with graffiti. I hadn't meant to fall asleep, but after driving all night—fifteen, sixteen hours maybe—crying, downing Adderall and Ativan, talking aloud to myself, punching the rim of my steering wheel—shouting along to the Ramones at one point— *Hey-ho! Let's go!*—blah, blah—you get the idea—I'd passed out in the passenger's seat, reclined all the way back like a dentist's chair. A brand-new guitar—a cheap Rogue Dreadnought—sat propped in my lap like a shotgun. I had only a dim recollection of buying it.

"Morning, Sunshine," the cop said drily. His nametag read GONZALES. When I lowered my window, he looked surprised: Clearly, he hadn't expected to see a middle-aged woman with pearl earrings in an ANTHRAX hoodie. "Everything okay in there?"

Without waiting for an answer, he took a perfunctory glance around the interior of my car. I felt a sudden kick of panic.

I'd fled in a frenzy—jamming items willy-nilly into my purse—forgetting my coat—my scarf—even my shoes. At first, I'd torn along the access roads without any particular destination in mind—driving recklessly around the grim, nickel-gray industrial parks and balding wood-lands of southern Michigan—ruminating, weeping—having just left my husband, Joey (with his sexual malfeasance and his misuse of cosmetic dentistry)—and our son, Austin—whose emoji I saw more than his face now—it was like he communicated only through hieroglyphics—and our neurotic, drooling dog, Mr. Noodles, a Labradoodle with "issues" who wouldn't stop yelping at 3 a.m.—costing us upward of $2,500 in pet psychiatry so far (a doggie shrink: really?)—and our overmortgaged house with its perennially unfinished "finished" basement—the kitchen circa 1982—our contractor, a reservist, apparently in Iraq or Kabul somewhere—so we couldn't exactly sue—wires were sprouting from the drywall like the unwanted hairs on my chin.

With the heat cranked up, my Subaru had grown increasingly yeasty over the miles, encrusted with crumbs from granola bars and gummy bran muffins purchased at gas stations. The foot wells had clogged with cellophane wrappers and coffee cups like a landfill. In the backseat lay the curvaceous coffin of my new guitar case, along with a jumble of boxes from a discount shoe outlet, and an ominous, glinting pair of industrial scissors, and some hacked-up pleather, and a bottle of Listerine Zero, and about a hundred balled-up Kleenex littered about like so many paper roses from all of my crying. There was also, I realized, a large cache of other people's prescription medication stashed in the glove compartment.

It occurred to me then that there might be a missing persons report out on me, or even—possibly—an arrest warrant.

But Gonzales stepped back from the window. "Ma'am, there's no parking here," he said wearily. "You gotta move." He motioned to a sign I'd missed when I'd arrived in the dark: PARKS DEPARTMENT ONLY. Beyond it, to my right, I became aware for the first time of the New York City skyline rising across the water like a distant fortress, the great pistons of it glittering in the morning sun. Before me stretched the vast, heaving Atlantic, tumbling and scraping...tumbling and scraping...its surf sounding like applause. As the patrol car pulled away, I glanced down at my long-dead phone—then out at the unfamiliar, mesmerizing ocean—and realized that nobody on earth knew where I was. I had literally driven to the edge of America. I was wholly untethered. I could be anyone, do anything, or completely disappear. I had nowhere left to go.

*　　*　　*

My name is Donna Koczynski, and I'm an alcoholic. A lush. A drunk.
A founding member of the Margarita Mafia, as a bunch of us on the
PTA at my daughter's middle school in Troy, Michigan, once christened
ourselves. Now, I'm a dried-out alkie. That's not how you're supposed
to say it, of course. The more correct term these days is "in recovery."
"In recovery" sounds so much more benign and generic and suburban.
But a lot of the reason I drank was to get away from being benign and
generic and suburban in the first place.

We've all heard addiction stories before. Some Bambi-eyed hopeful
takes a snort or a swallow, then another— until we watch with smug
fascination as her life spirals downward like a jet-fighter shot down over
the Pacific ("corkscrewing" would actually be an excellent verb in my
case, come to think of it). There's her spectacular plummet, but then—
of course—after the *splat*—redemption. Slowly, phoenix-like, she gets
herself clean, piecing herself back together like a gorgeous mosaic.

Yeah, well.

My life fell apart *after* I got sober.

No one expects their personal implosion to be ridiculous. Certainly,
I never did. Growing up in Detroit, I'd witnessed lives falling apart due
to big, serious events: Wars. Plant closures. Illnesses. Yet my own epic
unraveling seemed to be precipitated by a single trip to Las Vegas and a
bacon-wrapped fig.

The Las Vegas part itself actually isn't as significant as you might
think. An annual marketing conference: *bleh*. But I had been sent
there—all expenses paid—because I'd been nominated for an award.
For twelve years, I'd been one of the top "culinary ambassadors" for a
company called the Privileged Kitchen. Maybe you've heard of it: "foie
gras quality kitchenware at chopped liver prices." (Okay, I'm paraphras-
ing, but you get the gist.) Instead of a physical store, Privileged Kitchen
reps open pop-up cafés in shopping malls or come directly to your
home—and prepare an entire gourmet meal for you and your friends

using only PK products—which, of course, we pitch the hell out of to you as we cook.

So, in other words, yes: I was a salesperson. Me, Donna Koczynski, "culinary ambassador to your personal world of flavor." I can see you rolling your eyes now, shifting in your seat. It's okay. I get it. No one gets hot and bothered by some chirpy kitchen shill. No little kid grows up saying, "Gee, one day, I'd like to do cooking demos in strip malls and subdivisions." But in my own defense, working for the Privileged Kitchen enabled me to set my own hours—be home for my kids after school—keep our mortgage afloat—which, given how the financial crisis hit Michigan, was no small feat, I can tell you. And I liked the PK gig well enough. It allowed me, in my own small way, to perform again.

The honor I was nominated for in Vegas was the company's prestigious "Platinum Spatula Award." The Platinum Spatula had begun in the early 1990s as a joke, really—a giggle among sales reps: a surplus plastic spatula wrapped in tinfoil and awarded to someone based on some inane, made-up category. Best Recovery from a Kitchen Disaster. Greatest Resemblance to David Letterman in a Hairnet. That sort of thing. But over time, it had morphed into an actual trophy—an oversized pewter-colored spatula with the recipient's name engraved on the handle—accompanied by a check for $1,000. Colleen Lundstedt, the Privileged Kitchen's CEO and founder, awarded it to the rep with the highest revenue each year.

The annual conference always took place in Las Vegas—though, really, it just as easily could've been held in Disneyland, Branson, or Des Moines. We Privileged Kitchen sales reps were a stupefyingly wholesome bunch. (I suppose we had to be if we were regularly going to get invited into strangers' homes.) Most of us were women with kids, juggling all the parts. Three of my colleagues were actual Sunday school teachers. My colleague Victor and I were the only two who even swore on a regular basis. With the Privileged Kitchen crowd, there was no adultery in Vegas. There was no white powder chopped up on mirrors removed from the bathroom wall, or college funds gambled away at the craps tables at 3 a.m. My cohorts' idea of fun was karaoke ("Copacabana" and "Shake It Off," *my God*) and playing tipsy games of "Celebrity" in the lounge. With us, what happened in Vegas was never anything that needed to stay there.

Still, you'd think Las Vegas would be a dangerous place for someone like me—and you're right. Except that I'd developed little strategies. I brought jumbo bags of sugarless gummy bears from Costco and carried Austin's Traveler Guitar with me. I'd gotten it for him for Christmas after he'd complained that my old Stratocaster was too "bulky" to practice on. "Why should I have to, like, stand and hold a guitar, when I can just compose on my iPad?" he'd said. His shrug of indifference was like a blade in my gut.

The Traveler Guitar was lightweight, just a truncated neck and frets, essentially. It was nearly as portable as a laptop, and I'd held out that misguidedly optimistic, idiotic parental hope that Austin would be thrilled by its novelty, that this new-generation hybrid would magically inspire him to want to keep practicing. (And let's face it, make him love me more!) Obviously, though, I'd missed the memo: Almost by definition, no sixteen-year-old boy wants to play the same musical instrument as his mother.

And so, the Traveler Guitar that I'd ordered specially for him sat propped in his room behind his hockey equipment until I'd finally decided to liberate it for my trip to Las Vegas. The afternoon I arrived, I sat on the edge of my hotel bed, tuning it, strumming through a few light riffs as they came to me. Random stuff, stuff I hadn't played in decades: "Should I Stay or Should I Go?" "In Between Days." Inexplicably, the theme from *The Munsters*. It was odd what I recalled, what I seemed to channel, the muscle memory in my now-uncalloused, stinging fingers. But it felt surprisingly good; it kept me occupied.

When I ran out of songs, I went into the bathroom and undressed. I told myself that I was just going to bathe, yet inevitably, I scootched down in the tub so that my pelvis was directly beneath the faucet and spread my legs. As the water tongued against me, I imagined Zack, my boyfriend from when I was sixteen, and then the cute, bed-headed guy who'd assisted me at the Hertz counter earlier that day at the airport. Okay, I'm not proud of this. But what can I say? Joey and I, we'd been married twenty-three years already. And since hitting forty, my hormones? Well. Nobody tells you that perimenopause is like puberty in reverse. Just a snow globe of emotions all over again, and some days, I was in so much sexual heat, I was sure it was boiling off me in a vapor. Other times I was just, well, *sweaty*.

The Platinum Spatula was awarded on the second day of the convention during the final plenary session—a time chosen, I suspected, to allay that hypoglycemic funk of late afternoon, when everyone started yawning and stretching and secretly checking their phones. Two other sales reps had been nominated alongside me: Amelia McCorkle, a high-strung dog breeder from Boston; and Brittany Chang, a twenty-seven-year-old fireplug of a girl from Corpus Christi who'd once broken her ankle auditioning for *The Next Food Network Star*.

Colleen Lundstedt called us all up onto the stage. We had to stand there like beauty contestants as she chimed from the podium: "Don't they all look great, folks? Big round of applause, please, for the top culinary ambassadors of 2015!" With great fanfare, she introduced each one of us (finally pronouncing my last name right. Koczynski—*Koh-zhin-skee*—it's not that hard, people). Then, she held up the "secret envelope"—which was just plain silly, really, because everyone knew that Colleen herself selected the winner. "A drumroll, please!"

The only time I'd ever been awarded something was for my sobriety—the one-year token, then two, and most recently, five. Joey and the kids had attended each ceremony and hooted and applauded. The first year, we'd had a sheet cake afterward at home, studded with candles and buttercream roses. The kids had made cards: Austin's a crayoned picture of me holding a big glass with an arrow pointing to it saying "Diet Coke" and *Congrats, Mom on 1 year sober!!! Thank you for not getting drunk!!! I am so proud of you!!!* (Good God, that alone nearly killed me.) The next year, we'd gone to dinner at a Mexican restaurant the kids loved, with an insipid mariachi band and virgin strawberry margaritas all around. Yet in the end, we were always celebrating, in effect, something I'd *stopped* doing, not anything I, myself, had ever managed to achieve or create.

Colleen paused dramatically, her head thrown back, her spray-tanned wrist pressed against her forehead. Playing along, Brittany Chang clasped her hands together and jumped up and down campily and squealed "ohohoh!" There was a smattering of laughs from the other reps—though I didn't think Brittany was fooling anybody. It seemed obvious to me that she really wanted to win.

So did I, frankly. A thousand bucks—with one kid in college already, and us finally dug out of bankruptcy? Plus, I deserved it. I'd been with the Privileged Kitchen longer than either Amelia or Brittany. I'd worked harder than either of them, too. I know that selling kitchenware sounds like a joke, but do you know how stressful it is to prepare an entire three course meal (tuna crudo with avocado mousse, ginger-glazed duck breast; pineapple panna cotta) while shouting like a carnival barker inside a shopping mall—trying to capture people's attention as they meander aimlessly from Yankee Candle to the Sunglass Hut, their eyes glued to their phone screens? It's not easy to cook in front of thirty skeptical invitees, either, in some stranger's kitchen—pets, toddlers, hostesses clattering underfoot—their ringtones playing snippets of "Born to Run" and "La Cucaracha"—all while you're chopping and sautéing and smiling and keeping up the friendly patter as the oven overheats and olive oil spits up from the skillet, freckling your wrists with tiny first-degree burns.

As a PK rep, I'd gone to places on weekends that no one else ever bothered with. My hometown, the ruins of Detroit—whole neighborhoods sitting burned out and discarded like shell casings in weedy fields. I'd driven with my wares past miles of ghost gardens, collapsed factories, abandoned skyscrapers, meeting on Saturday mornings with young artists and hipsters striving to revive the city with little farm-to-table restaurants in the trashed storefronts of Corktown. Joey hated when I went downtown—he insisted on accompanying me whenever possible—it was still one of the carjacking capitals of the US—but sometimes, I braved it alone myself.

I drove over to Dearborn regularly, too. There was a huge Arab-American community out there—completely untapped. They tended to lie low, especially since September 11—twice they'd had to cancel their heritage festival because of protests and threats—and a lot of folks tended to be leery of them, but I'd figured: Hey, they cook, right? And so I taught myself how to make labneh and kibbeh and pilafs—easy enough—really delicious, actually—and the women were appreciative and welcoming—they even taught me a few words in Arabic, though I think this was just for their own amusement—most of them were American-born to begin with—and even *I* could tell my accent was a nightmare—and they tended not to buy a lot of stuff in the end. But still. Royal Oak, Inkster, Sterling Heights, Livonia: I did them all. No potential customer within a fifty-mile radius of me went unpitched. Utensil by utensil, I moved that inventory. I was intrepid.

"And the winner is..." Colleen Lundstedt's voice chimed like a nursery school teacher's. In spite of myself, and my desire for total nonchalance, I felt my heart catch and my face smile as I heard her say my name—my name!—in the echo chamber of my head. "Brittany Chang. Brittany," Colleen Lundstedt announced, "you have not only had some of the highest revenue for 2015, but also, the highest ratings on our website's 'customer satisfaction' survey *and* the most followers on Twitter and Instagram!"

And suddenly, perky Brittany was jumping up and down, clapping and posing for photos with Colleen Lundstedt, and waving the spatula victoriously above her head. Amelia and I stood there with the good-natured smiles plastered across our faces that we salespeople are such masters at—then we, too, congratulated Brittany, shook hands with Colleen Lundstedt—it was an honor just to be nominated—*blah, blah*—before getting the hell off the stage. "Hey, at least we got a free vacation, right?" Amelia sighed, biting her lower lip. "Though, dammit, I'm missing my dogs."

"Yeah, well..." I said vaguely, and my voice trailed off. And I realized, on some level, I'd been expecting this very outcome all along. It seemed inevitable, somehow. Nowadays, the world valued velocity and spectacle over anything genuine. Or maybe I was just getting old.

Afterward, there was a cocktail reception we were all obligated to go to as well. It was held in one of Vegas's swanky new restaurants, on a mezzanine overlooking the main dining room. The gimmick of the place was a giant glass "wine pyramid" that rose up through the center of the dining room like a three-story volcano. Waitresses in acrobatic harnesses rappelled up and down inside it, plucking bottles of merlot and sauvignon blanc from racks fifty feet overhead. It was meant to be elegant, I suppose (the menu said the design "recalled the French tradition of the Louvre"), but Vegas can't help itself, can it? It was far more Ringling Brothers than Le Cirque, so literally over the top.

Me, I ordered a cranberry and club soda—one, then another, then another—God, I would've loved something stronger. At AA, a fellow alkie once said, "I feel like I've got this voice inside me crying all the time, *I need. I want. Fill me.*" This was my reality exactly: *I need. I want. Fill me.* At the reception, I wandered around sucking on my gummy bears nonstop, accepting jokey condolences from my colleagues, posing gamely with them for group selfies, smiling until my face hurt. I had a vague sense that hors d'oeuvres were being passed—platters of mushroom tartlets, baby lamb chops, some sort of deconstructed spring roll but my stomach was in knots from the ceremony—and anyway, all of it was just loaded with calories. And so I didn't eat, and the party began to blur around the edges and, suddenly, the atrium below me was rotating. I excused myself to the ladies' room, performed some human origami trying to wrestle myself out of my Spanx, gave myself a good talking-to in the bathroom mirror, then doused my face several times with cold water. By the time I emerged, I was surprised to find the last of my cohorts already downstairs by the coat-check, struggling to punch their arms through the straps of their complimentary Privileged

Kitchen 2015 tote bags. The servers were clearing away the dishes, disassembling the bar.

I felt a stab of abandonment. A postparty melancholy started to seep in. Twelve years of hard work, and *zilch* in the end.

I stood alone on the mezzanine, unsure of what to actually do with myself now (call Joey? text the kids?)—certainly, I should be doing *something*—what was my life, after all, without responsibility and productivity and guilt? Turning my phone back on, I saw I'd missed several alerts. My screen read:

Ashley Kozcynski tweeted:

@BernieSanders should ban GMO's. They're killing the bees! Sanders 4 Prez. #FeeltheBern #noGMOs;

Charleston massacre pain scene lingers. Check your White Privilege, people!!!;

Russian airstrikes rumored to start targeting Homs!! ☹

Ashley, our daughter, was studying abroad in London for the year. She was majoring in—God help us all—something called "Social Theory and Practice"—living in a group house full of homemade hummus and recycled toilet paper. When she'd first told us about the exchange program in Britain, I'd pictured her sipping tea in some grand Victorian drawing room, being waited on by a butler—okay, I'd been binge-watching *Downton Abbey*—yet whenever I Skyped, she appeared in a grungy kitchen with an electric kettle plugged into a green wall and a Union Jack tacked over the sink like a stage prop—her own declaration of independence, I supposed, though geographically backward.

In our family, her earnestness and sense of justice were legend. Always, she had been the rescuer of stray cats, injured birds, the keeper of lost caterpillars. Once, when she was four, she'd asked tremulously as I was giving her a bath, "Mommy, what happens to all the soap bubbles when they go down the drain?" When I told her they popped and dissolved into the sea, she'd cried inconsolably. "All the bubbles die? And the sea gets full of dirty water? But then who washes the sea?" Her empathy, to me, was stunning—and admirable—and poignant—but, also, good God, exhausting. At one point, Joey had a standing offer of $20 to the first family member who could make Ashley laugh hysterically (an extra ten for milk-out-the-nose!).

Now, occasionally over Skype, she'd mention going to the British Library or the Tate Modern. But mostly, she seemed consumed with tweeting her moral outrage over the world's injustices to her 39,672 Twitter followers. I squinted down at my phone: What the hell were Homs?

So often, I felt like I didn't have an actual brain anymore; now that I was into my forties, my mind seemed to have been reduced to a sushi train at a cheap Japanese restaurant: nothing but tiny plates circling around on a conveyor belt, offering little substance, only reminders about PK demos, doggie tranquilizers, weight gains—Good God, I'm putting myself into a coma just thinking about it—but there on the balcony, all my internal chatter came to a halt. Dumbly, I stared at the airborne waitresses in their glass pyramid. It was like watching exotic fish undulating in a giant aquarium.

"That takes guts." A man in a rumpled suit jacket emerged from the men's room. He stood planted in the path between the reception alcove and the kitchen, rattling the ice cubes in his glass, eyeing the girls.

He was heavyset, baby-faced, perspiring. A forelock of grubby blond hair fell into his eyes like a comma. The smudgy lozenges of his eyeglasses gave him a slightly robotic look. He seemed to be one of those men in their thirties who, due to indulgence, work, and junk food, were not aging well. A wedding band winked dully on his left hand.

As a waiter passed between us holding aloft a tray full of ravaged hors d'oeuvres, the man held up his hand like a stop sign. "Hey. Hang on a sec." He motioned to the platter. "Got anything good?"

Surveying the leftovers, he plucked an untouched mushroom tartlet from the debris and popped it into his mouth. "Mmm. Not bad." Pulling out a napkin that appeared to be clean, he nimbly piled on it two remaining triangles of spanakopita, a congealing baby lamb chop, and the last pancetta-wrapped fig.

I felt a prickle of irritation. Freeloading hors d'oeuvres was something my husband would do. Whenever we found ourselves at a restaurant buffet, Joey piled up his plate multiple times with crab salad, pasta, miniature pizzas. "Go back for seconds," he'd instruct the kids. "I want everyone eating our money's worth." Anytime we stayed at a motel on our way to Mackinac Island, Joey wrapped up danishes and mini-muffins from the breakfast bar in paper napkins and smuggled them out under his shirt along with single-serve boxes of Kellogg's cereals. "What the hell are you doing?" I always said. "You hate Fruit Loops. You tell your patients this crap rots their teeth."

"And let it all go to waste?" he'd say. "We paid for it!"

Scavenging food was something I believed only starving actors, musicians, or homeless people should do. It was the very behavior I'd once hoped I'd left behind for good.

"Are you an entertainer?" I said to the man on the balcony.

If he detected any acidity in my voice, he ignored it. "Sure. Absolutely," he said cheerily. "I'm a magician." Dangling the bacon-wrapped fig by its stem, he tilted his head back and opened his mouth exaggeratedly. "See? I make food disappear."

In spite of myself, I smiled. "Cute." I raised my club-and-cranberry salutatorily in his direction, then turned back to watch the girls. They were as dizzying to watch as window washers, suspended above the dining room like human mobiles. Their mothers would have heart attacks, I thought, if they could see their babies like this. It was night-time now, and the ambient music in the restaurant had been turned up; a techno version of "La Vie en Rose" throbbed across the dining room. The walls themselves seemed to pulsate.

In my peripheral vision, I saw a birdlike flutter. The man eating hors d'oeuvres was beside me now, performing what could only be described as a pirouette, his face flushed. Bowing gallantly to the airborne waitresses, he whipped around—his large body moving with unexpected agility to the backbeat—his hands pressed poetically to his heart. He threw himself against the brushed aluminum railing of the balcony, trying to attract their attention. He did this once, twice, then a third time with operatic passion, clutching his fists to his solar plexus, as the women continued to levitate past him indifferently. He bowed again, torqued halfway around with his arm flung out, then collapsed on the tiles.

It was only then that I realized he hadn't been dancing for the girls at all.

He had been choking on the fig.

I screamed, but my voice was vacuumed up by the clamor of the restaurant, the amped-up music, the raucous parties at the bar downstairs.

The man lay beached on the parquet. His glasses were mangled and hung off his ear at an odd angle, his skin was turning an alarming whitish-lavender, pallid and waxy as a guest soap. "Somebody!" I shouted. But the landing was deserted.

Instinctively, I dropped to my knees, yanked open his mouth, and jammed my hand down his gullet. I fished around in the swamp of the man's epiglottis but couldn't dislodge anything. I pounded his chest. His torso was clammy, tufted with a frisée of hair that crunched beneath my palms like steel wool. Through his layer of baby fat, I could barely palpate his ribs, his heart. He smelled of astringent and, ominously, of mushroom tarts and bacon. "Help!" I shouted. The life was seeping out of him: I could feel it. Trying to remember my first aid from a class at the Y, I pinched his nose, clamped my mouth over his—our teeth knocked violently—and blew as hard as I could. When that didn't work, I raised myself up on my haunches and slammed my entire body weight down onto the man's belly. I'm not a big woman—five foot three at best, 138 pounds in my underwear, if I'm being honest—but I pounced on him with all my mass, straddling him as if he were a mechanical bull. It was savage—I landed hard right on my pubic bone—the pain was excruciating—but the force of my landing finally pounded all the remaining air out of the man's lungs, and the half-eaten bacon-wrapped fig flew out of his mouth like a champagne cork.

I collapsed against him with relief. "Oh my God," I murmured into his pale, grayish ear. "You're okay. It's okay. Breathe."

But he remained prone, motionless.

I straddled him again, my hands like bellows against his chest. Someone who sounded oddly like me was screaming, "Help! Help! Breathe, goddammit!" and then, finally, there were legs and feet scrambling around me, and the manager was wrangling me to a standing position, and another person—a burly Hispanic man in a chef's apron—was now astride the man performing violent compressions, and I heard a waitress sob, and someone say: "I just thought they were having sex, otherwise...," then two figures in EMS windbreakers pushed through with a stretcher and an apparatus, and red-blue lights were rotating feverishly over the far walls of the restaurant from the street like an insane disco ball, and someone was talking frantically into a walkie-talkie, and someone else was saying, "The rear elevator is best," and someone else said: "Table nineteen needs more bread"—*Oh my God! What?* I felt my legs give out and a busboy, I think, helped me into a chair by the bathroom. Then a cluster of people moved past like a carnival float—sprouting equipment, rubber tubing—with a tablecloth draped over a supine form with a pouf of blond hair—and I was gripping a glass of melty ice water and staring straight ahead. After a moment, I heard myself whisper: "Is he dead? Did he die?" A hand landed on my shoulder. A voice said: "I don't think so. They said they got a pulse. You okay? You need a drink? You did good, ma'am."

I started to shake. Another voice said: "Do you think she should maybe go to the hospital too?"

"No," I heard myself say. "No hospital."

"Ma'am," said the voice gently, "you're bleeding."

Only then did I notice that my palms and my knees were serrated with tiny cuts, sticky with blood. Apparently, when I'd first realized the man was choking, I'd dropped my club soda; I could now see shards of glass sparkling on the floor and in the weave of my skirt like frost.

"I'm okay. I'm okay," I said.

I stood up abruptly and wobbled into the bathroom. It was hard to dab away at the cuts through my pantyhose, which had begun to mat to my skin. Yet I was too shaky to remove my stockings. I thought of myself, straddling the man on the floor. How had it even occurred to me to do that? My heart was still punching frantically; I could still feel the man's damp chest beneath my palms.

After I cleaned myself up as best I could, I stepped back out into the restaurant. The mezzanine had been cleared of all debris, and a pair of waiters were now shaking a fresh tablecloth out over the buffet table. Beyond the balcony, the wine angels kept moving silently up and down in their glass encasement, laughter billowed up from the bar area, the hiss of filet mignon and duck breast from the grill came in piston-like gusts as the kitchen doors swung open and closed, open and closed, punctuating the music throbbing through the recessed speakers and the rattle of the cheese cart stuttering from table to table.

I gingerly gathered up my belongings and made my way down the stairs. A large, unruly party had herded into the restaurant, and the maître d' and a waitress were hunched over the computer, trying to sort out the seating.

"Hey," I shouted over the music to the hostess. "That guy — do you happen to know if he's okay?"

"What guy?"

"The one the paramedics wheeled out. Upstairs, on the mezzanine."

"EMS was here?"

"He choked or had a heart attack?"

She regarded me narrowly, shrugged, then motioned to a group of diners behind me to step forward. Pushing my way through the glass doors, I plunged into the blaze of the Strip and took a deep breath. After the climate control inside, the night air of Las Vegas came as a shock, and the overload of lights and traffic and crowds on the street was even more chaotic. I navigated in a daze through the casino in the lobby of my hotel to the karaoke bar in the back. Sure enough, a group of my fellow sales reps had commandeered a couch and a low table in the corner. Someone had ordered a pitcher of frozen strawberry margaritas that was quickly separating into striations of red slush. A rep named Traci stood on the little blue-lit stage, holding a microphone plagued with feedback. "No, I mean, the *other* Adele song," she was saying to someone behind a laptop.

I sat down stiffly. Both my knees felt scraped up, and my legs were trembling spasmodically the way they did after too much yoga. I had a strange, metallic taste in my mouth. Had I really just clamped my lips over a stranger's?

My colleague Victor was perched on the arm of the couch, swiping the screen of his phone. Normally, we were karaoke buddies together; get us warmed up, and just watch what we did with the Human League's "Don't You Want Me." Sometimes it was easy to forget that Victor was almost twenty years younger than me—though, sometimes, it wasn't. He constantly referred to the Red Hot Chili Peppers and Run DMC as "that '90s music."

"Buona sera," Victor said showily, standing to give me an air kiss over each shoulder. "Girl. You were *robbed*, is all I can say." He looked me up and down. "Clearly, that ceremony was rigged. Here. Liquid consolation." He dumped the remainder of the frozen margarita pitcher into a sweaty glass mug, handed it to me, then fluttered his hand at Traci. "Bitch gets one more minute to choose her song, then I'm taking over."

I looked deep into the margarita—it smelled like a juice box—and set it down.

"Victor," I said quietly, tugging his elbow. "Victor, I just saved a man's life."

"Shut up! What?"

"At the restaurant," I said incredulously. "He was choking on an hors d'oeuvre."

"Oh my God!" Victor slapped his hands over his mouth and laughed throatily. "Oh, I'm sorry. I'm sorry. I shouldn't laugh. But wouldn't that be, just be, like, the worst way to go? 'How did he die?' 'Oh, you know. He choked on an *hors d'oeuvre*. In *Vegas.*'"

The margarita in front of me was lurid and melty, a noxious pink. "He was down on the floor, and—I had to straddle him—and I pounded," I said.

"Where was the staff?"

I shrugged. "Nobody helped." Suddenly, noiselessly, I started to weep. I kept seeing the man, writhing in all his terror and desperation, fighting to breathe, while tables full of diners tucked into steaks and heaps of truffled fries below. He had a wife back home, possibly children. What if it had taken me just a few seconds longer to react? Even so, at this very moment he could be lying rigid on a metal hospital gurney—*snap!*— gone—just like that—while somewhere his wife was receiving the most brutal phone call of her life.

Bringing my hands up to my face, I stared at my palms, running my thumbs lightly over the tiny cuts and creases where the rivulets of blood had run, like a reverse Lady Macbeth, reliving the sensation of the man's chest beneath my hands as I tried to force the life back into him, the myoclonic jerk as his body expelled the fig.

"Well, did you at least get it on video?" Victor sniffed.

"Excuse me?"

"Next time that happens, you have to totally, like, film it. And put it on YouTube. I bet you'd get, like, a million hits."

Traci sang two bars of "Rolling in the Deep," then stopped plaintively.

"That does it." Victor tucked his phone into his pocket and made his way toward the stage. "Somebody needs an intervention."

I stood up. I glanced down at the sugary margarita, then over at the gaudily lit stage. *How*, I wondered, *how could I ever have looked forward to this?* All I should be doing at this moment was wrapping my arms around Joey's solid, meaty shoulders in our bed back in Michigan, and feeling him breathe, and telling him how much I goddamn loved him. I should be Skyping Ashley in London, waking her, making her talk to me while she sat in her flannel cow pajamas clutching a bowl of fair-trade coffee with soy milk. I should be sitting on the barstool in our kitchen as Austin got ready for school the next morning, watching as he straggled in and yanked open the fridge and gulped his low-fat chocolate protein drink directly out of the bottle like he wasn't supposed to—after which, I should be rumpling his sweaty hair and insisting that he let me, his momma, kiss him, hold him, soak him into my pores.

Instead, I was in this artificial fun house in a desert.

"That's it," I said aloud to no one in particular, setting my feet down on the floor like two gavels. "I'm out of here."

I always hated red-eyes—actually, I hate flying, period, especially without booze—I've got a fear of heights, claustrophobia, the works—yay— me and my damn dog, two peas in a pod—but I paid the $200 change fee directly at the check-in counter, then raced across the concourse of McCarran in my blood-flecked stockings and rumpled blouse, my roll-on jerking and jiggling behind me, the evening's adrenaline sloshing through my veins. Once I was finally settled into my seat on the last flight to Detroit—and we were certain it was actually going to take off despite an hour spent sitting on the tarmac—(how the hell could there possibly be air traffic at 1 a.m.?), I texted Joey all my revised travel info. I also emailed Colleen Lundstedt: **Heading home immediately. Family emergency.** For it was an emergency, wasn't it? Then I composed a text to both of my children: **Ashley & Austin, I love you more than the universe. You are two beautiful souls & the greatest blessing in my life & I am so proud of you.** I knew it was overkill, but so what? I was done with being Cool Mom, tiptoeing around their adolescent moodiness, "respecting" their "boundaries." Each of my children should have some record of my fathomless love for them before this flight departed. Just in case. How easily—how *willfully*—we forgot: All it took was a fig.

As I braced for takeoff, I had the joyous, irrational urge to shake my fellow passengers' hands and introduce myself: "Hi. I'm Donna. Guess what? I just saved a man's life!" But the traveler on my right had outfitted himself like a termite—bulbous, noise-canceling headphones, eye shades, fat neck pillow—and the one on my left was hooked up to an action movie on his iPad, each of them radiating that territorial disdain other passengers always seem to reserve for the person in the middle seat.

I finished off the package of gummy bears and tried to catch the eye of an attendant for a cup of water.

Back home, with the time difference, it was almost 5 a.m. when my flight finally lifted off, rocketing up, up—and I clutched the armrests and peered down through the window at the hallucinatory Vegas skyline with its electrified fake Venice, its fake Paris, its fake New York—all brilliant and toy-like against the dark canyons at the horizon. As I watched it grow smaller in my wake, I exhaled—a complicated breath of loneliness and urgency and a little inexplicable dread—relieved to be heading back to the one place I knew that was truly, grippingly real.

While I was gone, I'd let Austin use my Subaru, so when I finally did land, I had to take a car service, which was just as well. I hadn't been able to sleep on the red-eye, and in my fatigue, I had no business driving.

The town car threaded and lurched through the traffic across the flatlands of southeastern Michigan. Cidery morning light glinted over the marshes beyond the airport, burnishing the billboards and the gas tanks rising above the grasses like moldering cakes. Enormous jets levitated, hovered above the horizon. Sometimes they swooped in so low, I could see the logos painted on their tails: Delta. Southwest. Electricity zapped across the power lines bisecting the landscape.

My iPhone was in my purse, which I'd thoughtlessly placed in the trunk. *Dammit.* My phone. The moment I'd brought it home from the store, I couldn't stop fussing over it—was it still on? Was it beeping and vibrating? Did it have enough juice? To Joey's chagrin, I had it sleep beside me in our bedroom so I could answer it as soon as it sounded. I even bought little outfits for it, too—first a clear plastic "skin," then one by a designer made of quilted fabric.

Now the whole world around me was abuzz, while I alone remained quarantined, insulated in a bubble of silence. I thought about asking the driver to pull over so I could retrieve my purse, but there wasn't any- place safe to stop. He didn't even have the radio on. I tried to convince myself this was just as well. There was rarely any good news coming out of Michigan these days. At the moment, it was all Flint Water Crisis—all these little children poisoned from lead in the water, citizens calling for Governor Snyder's head—24/7 of heartbreak and outrage— punctuated by occasional other breaking news about mass shootings, white policemen killing black teenagers, massacres by ISIS. While my daughter followed these stories obsessively, I myself could only take so much. News was always depressing—it sucked something out of you without giving anything back—and yeah, sure, absolutely, the great injustices of the world troubled me, but what, exactly, was I supposed to do about them? Before she'd gone to London, Ashley had wanted to take a semester off to go support the Black Lives Matter movement. "Your job isn't to save the world," I'd told her. "It's to finish college."

"But Mom," she'd protested, "how can I just sit in some classroom while the world is imploding?"

"You think you're going to best serve the world as a college dropout in a drum circle outside the state legislature?" I'd said. "Nuh-uh-uh-uh. You get your degree first. It's like on the airplanes. You put your own oxygen mask on before you help others with theirs."

My daughter: the tweeting, the pinging! To find myself in the taxi now listening to only the thrum of the car engine without all those screen alerts: Well, I had to admit, it was oddly relaxing.

Our house, too, was as tranquil as a temple when I finally arrived. It was past 9 a.m., so I'd missed Joey and Austin in their tumultuous rush out the door. For a moment, I listened for Mr. Noodles before remembering that he was at some new psychiatric clinic for dogs over in Auburn Hills. *How the hell*, I wondered, *did we wind up with an inpatient for a pet?*

Usually when I went away, I returned home in the evening after Joey and the kids had had full run of the place all week. Before Ashley left for college, I'd likely find her in bed with her headphones clamped to her head, four days' worth of cereal bowls, workout clothes, paperbacks, chargers, bath towels, shoes, and art projects covering the floor. The family room would be reeking of fried chicken and farts, Joey and Austin in their undershirts hunched before the enormous flat-screen, their thumbs working away furiously, their bodies lurching with each insane explosion, shouting, "Gotcha!" "Watch out!" "Aaah! DIE!" I'd have to fish the remote out from between the sofa cushions and aim the Mute button at the screen before they even registered that I was home. Dumped in the mudroom by the recycling bin (but not actually *in* it) would be a landslide of empty pizza boxes and chicken buckets and pulverized cans of Mountain Dew. "Hey Mom," Austin would say, his gaze still grommeted to the screen. "Dad showed me how to make a single pair of underwear last four days. So guess what? Less laundry."

But now, I'd scarcely been gone forty-eight hours, Ashley was on another continent, and the ravages of boy-ness hadn't had time to take hold. How oddly serene the house felt. I was usually out the door myself by this hour; the late-morning light was not something I was used to. For a moment, I was afraid to make a noise for fear of shattering the hush. Slipping off my coat, I hung it over the others piled on the wrought-iron hooks by the door. Above the clutter of rain boots, gym bags, and skateboards clogging the entranceway, portraits stared down from the wall. Joey and Ashley at homecoming outside the stadium, maize-and-blue M's grease-painted on their cheeks. Austin, age six, solemnly lighting our menorah on the coffee table before the Christmas tree, dressed in his *Star Wars: Return of the Jedi* pajamas. Joey and me flanked by his fraternity brothers in matching tuxedos, deep moss-green with gold cummerbunds, my wedding dress a fountain of ruffles. *Dear God, what on earth had ever possessed me to choose all that?* I supposed I was being ironic.

I padded through the empty family room back toward the kitchen. My back ached. *A drink*, I thought suddenly, rolling my shoulders— *No. Stop that.* Instead, I should put in a call to Joey, shower, throw in a load of laundry. I wanted to call the restaurant in Vegas, too, to see if there was any news of the choking man, but it was still too early there. How funny: I didn't even know his name. But first, I was craving something indulgent and breakfasty and hugely caloric, like waffles with maple syrup and bacon. A low-fat yogurt with frozen blueberries would have to do—though I'd put whole milk in my coffee instead. Certainly, I'd earned that. Hell, I'd saved a man's life.

Oddly, the lights in the kitchen were still on. As I entered the lemon-painted room, with its warped, sliding glass doors leading out onto the deck, I was overcome by an eeriness. I felt it: the sudden atmospheric shift, a disturbance of molecules, a shiver of fear.

Then I saw.

Ten feet away, a strange, slatternly woman was down on all fours on our laminate floor with her head in the oven.

I screamed.

The woman's body jerked. A horrible metallic clatter issued from inside the oven, followed by a muffled cry as she struggled to get out. Her fleshy body was clad in a pinafore that had traveled up her thighs to unveil an enormous rump covered in white ruffled bloomers. Her wide, lumpy legs were encased in nubby pink ballet tights, and her feet were spilling out of old-fashioned black patent-leather party shoes with delicate ankle straps. I screamed again. The woman's head popped out of the oven, a lunatic tumble of dark sausage curls. She appeared homeless, demented. Frantically, she shook and yanked at her hair to get it out of her face. Her mouth was a wild smear of candy-pink. Her cheeks were streaked with garish red circles in a grotesque approximation of rouge. Oversized clip-on pearl earrings knocked against her jowls.

She staggered to her feet, and there was a singular moment of suspended disbelief before comprehension set in.

This huge, crazed woman panting before me in a ridiculously frilly cap? I knew her crinkly, espresso-dark eyes. The aging, mawkish lips obscuring a year's worth of bridgework. The grayish beard-stubble bracketing her mouth. I knew the bulky chest whose dark thicket of hair was curling over the cotton-eyelet edge of her pinafore.

"Jesus Christ!" Joey shrieked. He dropped a can of Bon Ami oven cleanser and it rolled across the floor and under the table.

I stepped backward. And for a moment—and I'm ashamed to admit this—I wasn't sure what shocked me most: the sight of my husband standing before me dressed like a deranged Little Bo Peep—or the simple fact that he had actually been *cleaning* something.

Just then, from the powder room by the pantry, came the sound of a toilet flushing. The sliding door rolled back and a young woman emerged. She was wearing black laminate, impossibly high stiletto heels, and a velvet mask like a cartoon bandit's. She stood in the doorway like a strange bird, a heron dipped into oil, her two small, pert breasts like the bells you use to summon a desk clerk. "Is Zsa-Zsa having trouble following orders?" she cooed. Then she saw me and stopped. Her black-gloved hand went up to her mouth. "Oh," she said plainly.

Oh.

Like a gunshot.

For a moment, I just stood there, regarding the two of them, who were now regarding each other. There was that curious delay between the shock of the impact and the walloping onset of pain. For a moment, I wasn't quite sure that any of this was actually happening.

The young woman pivoted slowly to face Joey. "Zsa-Zsa, is this part of our session?" she said carefully.

Almost imperceptibly, his devastated eyes now fixed on me, Joey shook his head. "Regis Philbin," he mumbled.

"Okay. Shit," said the woman in the catsuit. "Well then." Her voice turned perfunctory. "I think I better go." With whippet speed, she disappeared into the guest bathroom again and quickly reemerged in a cheap, plum-colored trench coat, a large, ruched metallic bag slung over her forearm. Her mask was still on.

"Um. We'll settle up later, I guess?" she said quickly, frowning, rifling through her handbag. "I mean—"

Joey turned toward her. "Please. Mistress Tanya."

It was then that I found my voice—sickened, lethal, almost unrecognizable: "Are you fucking kidding me?" I said. "Are you insane?"

"Donna—" Joey's voice cracked. He looked beseechingly first at me, then at the woman in black.

"Get the fuck out of my house," I said.

The young woman held up her hands as if in surrender and took a step back.

"Okay. No disrespect."

She was so slender, she looked like I could snap her in half.

Her stilettos clacked as she hurried to the side door. (She used the *side* door? She *knew* my house?) As she yanked it open, she glanced back at me. "Hey, look," she said awkwardly. "I know this seems weird, but, like, try not to judge too much? Really. Your husband's a very nice guy."

The door to the mudroom slammed. A moment later, I heard the garage open and shut.

Her departure seemed to suck all the oxygen out of the kitchen. I felt that I should shriek—hysteria was definitely in order—but my whole body suddenly felt like wet sand. I stepped back and slid down against the refrigerator door onto the tiled floor.

Joey paced before the sink-island now like a caged animal. "You were supposed to be in Vegas," he shouted. His wig was torn off. It lay on the counter like a dead animal. His spiky, salt-and-pepper hair was matted against his skull. Though caked with ghoulish pancake makeup, his face was red with fury. A rope of fake plastic pearls encircled his neck, the toy kind that I used to have as a child, where one bead snapped into another. On his wrist was a matching bracelet where his watch usually was. His pink pinafore had a satin bow on the bodice, his puffed sleeves trimmed with little pink rosettes. I noticed his apron for the first time, white satin with black lace and pink heart-shaped pockets. A lot of thought had gone into this outfit. A wave of nausea came over me.

"You brought a prostitute into our home, Joe?"

"She's not a prostitute. She's a dominatrix," he snapped, as if this explained everything. "You just show up? Unannounced?"

"Excuse me? This is my house! Plus, I emailed. I texted. That's not the issue here."

"Eight p.m. you said, not eight *a.m.*"

"What?"

"You know I can't read those tiny fucking letters—"

"Joey, you were with another woman. You're wearing a *dress!*"

"Well, if you didn't just sneak up on me—" He slammed his fist down on the countertop. Instantly, he winced. His face turned into a nimbus of pain.

I was on my feet now. "What are you saying, Joseph? You're in a dress with a prostitute and your head in the oven, but I'm the bad guy here, because I didn't use a bigger FONT?"

"I told you: She's not a prostitute. She's a dominatrix!"

A fat ceramic Privileged Kitchen utensil holder in the shape of a pineapple sat on the counter by the stove. I grabbed it and hurled it against the pantry door. Terra-cotta and cooking implements exploded across the room. I seized a caddy of fancy olive oil and balsamic vinegar and threw that, too. Condiments and glass splattered everywhere; the kitchen began to smell like a salad.

Joey yanked off his apron and pinafore, threw them on the counter, and stood there, hairy-chested, in an enormous medical-looking, rubberized white bra and falsies, panting. "You're being insane," he shouted.

"*I'm* insane? You're in *drag!*" Then I stopped. I doubled over, gripping the counter. I felt suddenly whiplashed. "Oh. My. God. Joey." Another thought had occurred to me. "Is this, like, a Bruce Jenner thing?"

"What?"

I cupped my hands around my eyes and started to rock back and forth. Horrible enough was the adultery—but was Joey himself a lie?

He'd been president of his fraternity in college; he'd grown up hunting with his brothers in the U-P and fixing cars. Was all of this just a disguise—an elaborate act of overcompensation? We'd watched *I Am Cait* a couple of times, plus that TV series on Amazon, where the father transforms himself into a mom. Back in the '80s, when I'd done the club circuit with my band, I'd certainly seen my share of cross-dressers: cruising the parking lots, flinging french fries at each other at 4 a.m. at the Motor City Diner. But now there were all these conversations in the media about people being born in the wrong body. My book club had even gotten sidetracked for an entire evening discussing it; Heather Mickleberg was convinced transgenderism was a chromosomal anomaly caused by gluten and Wi-Fi.

Was this *Joey*?

"Oh, for fuck's sake, no! I don't want to be a girl!" he cried. "Christ, Donna. I just, I just—" He plopped down heavily on one of the barstools.

Hugging myself, I started to shiver violently. My teeth were like castanets. All of it, *all* of it, was so surreal and outlandish, so utterly *wrong*. "That girl. Do you love her? Do you not love me anymore?"

"What? Yes—no! Yes, of course. Of course I still love you. No, I don't love Mistress Tanya! Please. This has nothing to do with you, Donna."

I swallowed. "Oh," I said bitterly, my eyes welling. "Oh, I think it does, Joey. This has everything to do with me. You're fucking another woman. And you let her into our house—"

He put his hands up. "I'm not fucking her! We're not having sex! I told you. I swear. That's not what this is about."

"Really?" I said. "Because I gotta tell you, that's certainly what it looks like to me." I yanked a gingham dish towel from beneath the sink, blew my nose in it. "Some sort of perverted, fucking affair right under—"

My husband did something then I hadn't anticipated. Crumpling, he began to weep. He wept the way our children did when they were very small, with abandon, his bulky, hairy shoulders heaving, making *bwuhuhu* sounds, his whole body given over to sobs. In all the twenty-six years we'd been together, Joey had almost never cried—in fact, I could list the number of times he had (births of our kids; gallstone; Tigers losing the World Series).

His wailing continued relentlessly, abject in its pain and rawness. When he cried aloud to the ceiling, "God, what's wrong with me? I'm sorry, Donna, I'm so, so sorry—" I walked into the powder room and grabbed the box of tissues. Returning to the stool next to him, I thrust it at him and motioned toward his nose. I didn't know what to think anymore. I just sat there.

Joey snuffled and blew.

There was a pause. "I never meant for you to find out. I wanted to protect you," he said hoarsely.

His makeup was all streaked now, a spray-painty wreck. "It's just, I have these urges, Donna. I just—sometimes—" He blinked up at the ceiling, fighting back the tears again. "Sometimes I just need to dress up, and be feminine, and have somebody tell me what to do. I just want to be a slave for a little while."

He must have seen the repugnance flash across my face, because he added quickly: "Not for real. Just role-playing. Just make-believe." He massaged his cheeks forlornly. "Sometimes, I just need to be Zsa-Zsa, the Sissy Maid. French. A perfectionist. If Zsa-Zsa doesn't scrub the toilets or the oven correctly, she gets punished. Humiliated. It's like, it's a game is all." When he saw my face was not changing, he shook his head. He stared down at the linoleum tiles. His face grew palsied. He pressed his fists to his smudgy eyes. "It's a compulsion, Donna. It's like something I just have to do. It's I can't I can't help it. Can't you, of all people, maybe understand this a little?"

I looked at him. "Oh, don't you dare," I said viciously.

"Okay, okay... But, I just—I figured, if I hired a professional dom, it would be like, I don't know—therapy?"

"So you pay her just to act out these scenarios?" I said slowly. "No sex?" My mind began to pinwheel with questions: *How long? Where? What did she charge? How did they meet?* I wanted to know, and yet, I didn't want to know anything.

"Actually, I don't pay her at all." A tinge of satisfaction crept into Joey's voice. "We worked out a trade. Service-in-kind. In return for each session, I give her free dental work." He blew his nose again. "Her semiannual cleanings. A root canal." He added proudly, "You know, she's even thinking about getting veneers?"

Chapter 2

WHAT MAKES US LOVE whom we love; what makes us choose to do what we do?

The night I met Joey, I was playing a gig at the Blind Pig on South First Street. He and two of his fraternity brothers came in selling raffle tickets to benefit a children's literacy program in Flint. My set was bad—disastrous, really—my band, Toxic Shock Syndrome, wasn't the type of music the Blind Pig had originally booked for that night. The place had a regular Bluegrass Tuesday. They'd called us in last-minute after someone's truck broke down. It was a shit-show, really. Drunks in flannel wanting to two-step, howling at the stage: your basic ritual humiliation. Afterward, my asshole bandmates abandoned me in the parking lot. Joey volunteered to drive me back to my place. I was tearstained, I was upset, I was calling the bass player a "tone-deaf motherfucker." This was back in the days when I tried to do everything like Kim Gordon from Sonic Youth—or at least how I *imagined* she'd do things—of course, I'd never met her—it was all adolescent posturing and conjecture. Still, I'd spent my last $7 doing tequila shots and tearing around the place: Absolutely not at my best. But Joey dutifully escorted me back to the grim student apartment I shared with my friend Brenda, even carrying my amp up the stairs for me. He was dressed in a golf shirt and khaki shorts that hung like bells around his knees. His hair was so closely shorn, I could see the moon of his skull through the fuzz of it. He had that goofy, scrubbed look that mothers always seem to find attractive. Generally, I was not impressed.

When he spied my CD collection and milk crates full of *Love and Rockets* comics, though, he fell to his knees. "Hey, check you out," he said, thumbing excitedly through the plastic sleeves. He was so clearly enthralled, it touched me. I had a psychology paper due the next day, but we ended up sitting on my bed drinking warm Kahlúa and milk in Styrofoam cups, listening over and over to the Pogues. Joey had never heard them before. After certain songs, he'd stop and scooch down the bed toward my stereo: "Wait. Can we listen to that one again? Do you mind?" When he talked, a gentle intensity accumulated behind his eyes that I liked. At his urging, I took out my Taylor acoustic and played a couple of songs I'd written. This was not something I normally did. He told me with pride about the cars he'd remodeled back home. About his survivalist father living in a shack up in Marquette with wife number three. Both of us, it turned out, had lost our mothers—mine to cancer when I was fifteen, his to a car accident when he was six—which I believed was far worse. At least with mine, I'd gotten to say good-bye.

Close to daybreak, Joey stretched extravagantly. "Yahhyahh," he yawned, cracking his back. He patted me on the knee. "Yep. Well. Great hanging with you."

Zipping up his sweatshirt, he lumbered toward the door.

I was surprised by how insulted I felt. "Wait," I heard myself say. "Just like that?"

He turned on the threshold. "Huh? Oh." Reaching over in almost a brotherly fashion, he took my chin in his hands.

He gave me one kiss. It was soft, but obliterating.

My previous boyfriends had been: hot, crazy Zack, who slept on the railroad tracks...preening bass players, "spoken word" poets with "sexuality issues"...a philosophy major who sold his Kierkegaard paperbacks to the used-book store for drug money...Joey, by contrast, was a bricklayer. An oak tree. A human levee. He drank milk with his meals and painted his face half blue, half yellow (excuse me, half *maize*) on game days, then drove through Ann Arbor in his pickup with a grill in the back, inviting along anyone who wanted to tailgate with him. His fraternity brothers nicknamed him "Koz" and treated him like the mayor. He was so *clearly* not-my-type, I told Brenda: I was merely trying him on like a costume.

But oddly, I found I liked him. I liked his easy, muscular decency, his burliness and stability, his uncomplicated happiness. I'd needed it. I'd sought it out.

Joseph Vincent Koczynski.

Nobody ever tells you, nobody ever prepares you for marriage *really*. Nobody ever shows you yourself after the wedding: matted with sweat, cursing, howling like an animal in a hospital gown, strangling your husband's hand, snorting and sucking air, girding yourself, bucking, until finally, hours into raw, bestial misery, it feels like a membrane inside you is ripping, and this husband of yours, ghoulishly pale in minty-green scrubs, is summoned to crouch between what are now your disembodied thighs, where he sees blood and mucus, and—yep—a little bit of shit—squeezing out of your gash (good God)—as you finally push your tiny, perfect 7-pound, 9 ounce daughter into the world—and he catches her in his disbelieving, latexed hands—after which you both pretend that you were never splayed out like that, that he never saw what he saw. It is only miracles and joy and beauty now. That is what you will photograph, what you will enshrine and report.

Your husband: running behind this very same daughter, his belly jiggling, fingertips barely touching the back fender of her new tangerine-colored two-wheeler as he cheers, "That's it! That's it! Keep pedaling!" and watching him, you feel a bolt of love, but also a secret bit of jealousy because he's always the Fun One, the Hero—and she harbors a special, sparkling adoration for him alone. Your husband, keeled over on the toilet, his pants around his ankles, weeping from the pain of what will turn out to be a gallstone. Your husband, pressing you to him on the deck, stroking your hair, murmuring, "Hey, you just woke up on the wrong side of the bed is all," after you've just lost it with your kids—

in a tsunami of PMS and insomnia, you grabbed Ashley by the wrist and swatted her for pushing Austin's stroller into the parking lot outside Kroger's. You and your husband, lying in bed together, realizing that time is eroding your bodies, your responsiveness. Appendages are sagging; the two of you are becoming limp, landed fish. It is dispiriting and ominous. A vapor of shame thickens between you until, finally, you say to the ceiling: *Well, this sucks*. And he snorts: *Not that that would even help at this point*, and then, improbably, you both start to giggle. No one ever lets you know that one day, your husband is going to come home from a dentistry conference, talking a mile a minute about some boorish colleague he had to sit next to, and you're going to have to interrupt him, and make him come sit beside you on the couch, and put both your hands around his and gently say, "Joey, honey. Your brother just died." No one tells you how murderously bored you'll feel—could he please stop picking his damn cuticles?—or how stupidly tickled your husband will be that you were once in an indie-punk band, bringing up your demo CD from the basement to play for people at your first Christmas party in Lakeshore Manors, saying, "Can you believe she once had pink and purple hair?" unwittingly humiliating you and making all the other guests stare uneasily down into their cups of eggnog. No one tells you how the investment properties you bought will go into foreclosure— and you'll sit up nights together trying to figure out the Rubik's Cube of your finances. Or that one afternoon, your husband will hold your hair back as you vomit in the ladies' room, handing you his handkerchief afterward, then gently ushering you back into the mall area where you are doing a Sunday brunch demonstration, all the while making jokes and apologies to the customers ("Too much cooking wine, folks! This is why our 'The Drunken Chef' TV-show idea never took off!"), until one day—one day it becomes too much—after which, he will stand before you solemnly in the family room and say: *I love you, but this has got to stop. I've made an appointment*. And that for the next five years, he will refuse to even keep beer in the cooler in the garage for his buddies. No one will tell you how, when you sleep, even when you are no longer touching, even when you are feeling sick or irritated or indifferent, you will turn over in unison like dancers.

No one will tell you that after more than two decades of marriage, this same husband will begin to secretly dress up like a giant baby doll and think nothing of letting another woman into your own home to humiliate him—and you—in exchange for free dental work. That you will suddenly face this man across the counter of your own kitchen on a sunny Wednesday morning at the end of September—surrounded by all the cheery trappings of your life together—and have absolutely no idea who the hell he is.

"Cancel the rest of your appointments. Have Arjul cover for you," I told him. I'd be damned if I'd let my husband retreat into his office or a hotel somewhere, leaving me to face the wreckage alone.

Arjul Banerjee, DDS, was Joey's partner. He was an excellent dentist, if a little too gung ho. He'd crafted a social media presence for himself, Dr. BanerTeeth, through which he tweeted out oral hygiene advice to some 2,749 followers. Other times he Instagrammed pictures of gum diseases or the molars he'd just pulled. He claimed it helped attract new patients.

"Of course. Of course." Joey nodded weakly. In his frilly bloomers and absurd brassiere, he looked utterly defeated, a chubby Miss Havisham. He picked up his cell phone, punched a button, murmured something to his receptionist about food poisoning. Then he stood before me like a penitent, staring at the floor. "Um, I guess— Should we talk?"

"Jesus Christ, Joey. Take that stuff off first."

He fled up the stairs, his Mary Janes clumping on the runner. In the empty, salad-smelling kitchen, photographs from our vacations to Disney World slid and dissolved across the screen on the family computer in the desk nook. A coffee mug reading WORLD's #1 DAD sat beside it, jammed full of assorted pens. Magnets on our refrigerator held grocery receipts and pizza coupons. All of it so banal, so *normal*.

You never expect your own life to become something tawdry, so lifted-from-the-pages-of-a-supermarket-tabloid, so laughably awful. *This* was so far off the spectrum of anything I could wrap my head around. I was dying for a drink. Perhaps, I thought desperately, if neither Joey nor I said anything more, if we did not address what happened out loud, perhaps all of it would just dissolve somehow and prove a mirage.

Unpacking my suitcase in the mudroom, I threw in a load of laundry, then climbed upstairs to the kids' bathroom. Only once I was in the shower did I realize that I was still wearing my clothes. I dumped the sopping mass of fabric into the dryer back downstairs, then frantically set about righting the kitchen, sweeping up the shards of pottery, mopping up the vinegar. Joey hovered in the doorway, dressed now in his old chinos and a T-shirt.

As I was frantically finishing up, Austin wandered in from school, clutching his skateboard, his face obscured by two lank curtains of hair. When Ashley left for London, Austin seemed to have disappeared into a foreign country of his own. Overnight, it seemed, my sweet, solemn, contemplative boy had taken up residence in Glowerstown. Surlyville. The Walled City, Joey and I called it sometimes. He'd barricade himself in his room—or return home from school hours after it let out—petulant and closemouthed, sometimes with stains on his clothes, scrapes on his hands, smelling of chemicals I couldn't quite place—turpentine? Adhesive? I was worried, of course: Drugs? Was he huffing? Or, worse still, was he one of those kids who was secretly building an arsenal in his best friend's garage? Joey and I had agreed not to keep guns in the house— but a lot of people we knew did. Was I smelling gunpowder on my kid? Crystal meth? Yet when I confronted Austin, he narrowed his eyes and looked at me with utter contempt: *Jesus Christ, Mom. What kind of a psycho-moron do you think I am?* Then, he boycotted me: nothing but stony-faced silence for days. He was home but not home.

I knew it was a phase—I kept telling myself it was a phase—I kept waiting for his frontal lobe to develop more, for him to grow out of it— just as he had after what Joey and I now referred to as "The Minecraft Years." But what if Austin never did? This is what they never tell you about parenthood: that it leaves you bereft, in a perpetual state of yearning, secretly, for your child to revert to their newborn state—to smell again of that wonderful baby-smell of fresh cream and talc—for them to be as miraculous as they were the first time you held them—to that way you loved them and they loved you right back—that pure, fierce, clobbering joy. *Come back to me; let me love you again without restraint.* And yet, what if your kids never leave home? Well, then you're really screwed. Parenthood was either failure or loss, it seemed. It was no-win.

"Oh. You're back early," Austin said impassively. Loping into the pantry, he emerged with a bag of Tostitos clenched between his teeth, seemingly unfazed by the fact that both Joey and I were home, standing in the kitchen in the middle of the afternoon. Outside, the sun was coppery on the lake. Grabbing a Pepsi out of the fridge, Austin finally pulled out his earbuds and regarded us. "Yeah, um. For English class, we're supposed to, like, do this project on this book called *The Odyssey?* So can I use the computer in your office?" He flashed a large, quick smile—sixteen-year-old boys were never so charming as when they wanted to borrow something. Joey and I nodded numbly. Normally, I'd waylay him before his retreat: *Excuse me. Not so fast. Tell me about your day, please. And since when are you allergic to hugs?* But for once, I was grateful for his total self-absorption and remove. "Go," I said, waving. And then our son tromped upstairs, and the house was eerily quiet again, and I went back to the mudroom, alone, to continue doing our laundry.

That night, Joey lingered in the doorway of our bedroom. "Should I sleep on the foldout?"

The question hung in the air.

After a moment, I shook my head.

Almost formally, he walked around to his side of the bed and stood there like a footman. He waited and drew back the covers only when I did, as if on cue. For years, of course, we'd been going to bed in sort of a haphazard fashion. Joey might head up to sleep before me—I'd get caught up with some test recipe in the kitchen or folding the last load of laundry—but half the time, when I finally did climb upstairs, I'd find he was awake anyway, watching *Game of Thrones* on his iPad or playing *Candy Crush* or half asleep with the TV still on, his reading glasses sliding down his nose.

Now, however, we lay in our bed, as stiff and alert as two virgins in an arranged marriage. I could almost hear us blinking in the darkness, the soft clicking of eyelashes. Only the red pinpoints of the television and the cable box glowed on the bureau. When a car pulled into the Brodys' driveway next door, a broad parabola of light swung over the ceiling, carrying with it a gust of music that halted when the engine was cut. I heard the crunch of gravel, then a ruffle of wind, then silence. Just air and molecules again.

After a while, there came a gasp, then a sniffle. The mattress shuddered lightly, the sheet tugged. "Donna?" Joey said, his voice scarcely more than a whisper. "Please, Donna. Don't leave me?"

All night, and well into the next morning, my mind revolved like a rock polisher, sifting over the fragments of my marriage, trying to smooth the edges, make them something I could grasp. *So, okay: Joey liked dressing up as a girlie maid. Really, was that so terrible? Wouldn't it be worse if he'd wanted to dress up, as, say, a Nazi?* I was actually beginning to feel more sanguine about it until, after breakfast (largely uneaten) I went to get the "12x = 1 Free" card for the dry cleaner. Shuffling through Joey's assorted fidelity cards, it dawned on me that he was more faithful to the local car wash and frozen yogurt stand than he was to our marriage. "You bastard!" One by one—in perhaps the most pathetic act of wifely vengeance in history—I tore the cards into confetti.

But then again, I thought grudgingly, *had he really committed adultery?* Joey claimed he wasn't paying this dominatrix for sex—and that no bodily fluids had ever been exchanged between them (except, perhaps, during teeth cleanings). So how unfaithful had he been, exactly? Was it not that different, really, from paying a shrink, as he claimed?

I honestly didn't know. Why weren't there different degrees of cheating, say, like there were with murder? First-degree, second-degree, premeditated, and so forth?

Inevitably, of course, I blamed myself. Those ten pounds, which came off, then back on, like a tide. And our sex life? Sometimes, getting Joey to give me an orgasm was like teaching a teenager to parallel park. *A little more to the right; now slow down*... Once, in the middle of it, I noticed our bedroom ceiling had a crack in it shaped like Florida.

Also: *How could I possibly not have known?* I'd found a few websites in the cache of our old computer: Frisky French Maids with peek-a-boo décolleté and white lace panties, bending over with feather dusters to expose pert little buttocks. But I'd assumed Austin had been looking at them (Had I even mentioned them to Joey?); I'd never dreamed they'd been a how-to manual for my husband.

"How long?" I asked as I emptied the dishwasher.

"How long what?"

I tried to sound casual. "How long have you had, you know, these *urges* to dress up?"

Our basement still held all the equipment from Joey's Brew-Your-Own-Beer phase, including four cases of unused 12-ounce brown glass bottles that he kept insisting he was going to sell on eBay. There was the foam mat and his extensive Bruce Lee DVD collection from his kung fu period. His *Star Wars* models (the Millennium Falcon! X-Wing Starfighter! Still in the trophy case). His teach-yourself-Polish kick (in which he stuck Polish vocabulary stickers all over the house. I was still finding little labels reading *filiżanka do herbaty* or *sos łodzi* taped to the underside of our good dishes). Over the years, Joey had acquired fishing poles, night goggles, an archery set, bird-watching magazines, an infra-red camera, rock-climbing gear, and how-to books for his disastrous foray into day-trading: mercifully short-lived. Wasn't it possible that his desire to dress up as a chambermaid was just another hobby?

Joey shrugged. "I don't know," he said plainly. "Years. Maybe always? Ever since I was a teenager, I think. But in the past few years it's gotten harder to ignore."

This was not, of course, the answer I'd been hoping for. It was starting to dawn on me: My husband *was* the Other Woman.

"You know," I sighed, running a clump of steel wool around the sides of the sink to scrape off bits of congealed oat bran. "We've spent over two grand on a puppy shrink, Joey. Shouldn't we maybe see a marriage counselor ourselves?"

Joey set down his coffee mug and looked at me, his face arranging itself into an amicable grimace. "Sure," he said, his voice cracking. "If that's what you want."

It wasn't what I wanted, of course. I'd spent enough time, it seemed, sitting on folding chairs in church basements with strangers, discussing my neuroses and cravings and fears in great detail. But I just didn't know what else to do.

There was exactly one couples' therapist covered by our health plan who could see us the next day. Her name was Cheri Marciano; she looked to be about twelve. "I know, I know, my name. It's like maraschino cherry in reverse, right?" She laughed, waving us toward a large Naugahyde couch across from her swivel chair. There was a dying ficus in the corner and a small rock fountain plugged in on the windowsill. The constant burble of water made me instantly want to pee. "So," Cheri said cheerily, "Mr. and Mrs.— Wow." She moved the clipboard closer to her eyes as if trying to get it into focus. "That's a mouthful. How do you say it?"

"Koczynski," Joey said murderously. I looked at him. He was staring at her teeth. They were crooked and unusually large for her small, pointy jaw. She also had a pronounced overbite. Once I noticed this, it was hard for me to stop staring, either.

"So tell me, Cheri," I said, glancing quickly away at her bookshelves. "Are you married yourself?"

"Me?" She laughed, tossing her head back. Her voice was as light and watery as her electric fountain. "Oh, God no. God no. Why?" She grinned. "Do you know someone who's single?"

I glanced at Joey. He was still staring at her enormous teeth.

"Yeah, well," I said, standing up. "I don't think this is going to work for us."

In the parking lot, Joey gallantly opened the car door for me, helping me into the Subaru as if it were a limousine, his hand on the small of my back.

"Have I told you lately how beautiful you are?" he said when we stopped for lunch at a Panera's. He leaned across the table to brush a lock of my hair out of my eyes. Neither of us was eating, but we hadn't known what else to do with ourselves for the rest of the hour. I reached for my phone, but Joey stayed my hand. It was midday, and around us, families shuffled back and forth squinting at the menu over the counter, trying to decide what to order. An elderly couple collected two paper containers of soup and a turkey sandwich they were sharing. Watching the husband help his wife into a booth, I felt a bolt of grief. "Especially right now?" Joey continued, "with all the lights in your hair?"

I set down my sandwich. "Stop it. Just stop," I said.

"But it's true," he said, reaching over to give my hand a squeeze. "You've never looked more beautiful, with your hair all tousled—"

"Don't be so goddamn nice to me," I said in a low, vicious voice. I withdrew my hand from his. "It's insulting."

The only reason he was flattering me now—as we were both too well aware—was for penance, for absolution. It only underscored how strained and unnatural everything between us had become. The Joey I'd known for twenty-six years was jocular, never courtly. Seeing him so suddenly eager to please, so obsequious, repulsed me. The more he showered me with love and compliments, the more petty and vindictive and nasty I felt. We were becoming grotesqueries.

"But it's the truth," Joey insisted. "You have never been more beautiful, Donna. I love you, you know."

I couldn't help myself. I looked him dead in the eye. "Oh, suddenly, we're all about the truth here? Truth and love?"

His face crumpled. I pressed my fists against my temples and squeezed my eyes shut. "Goddamn therapist," I said. "Who the fuck names their kid 'Cheri Marciano' anyway?" I started to cry. I felt Joey's hand grip mine, though I still didn't open my eyes. After a while, I whispered, "I just want things to go back to normal."

Joey looked at me, pained. "I know," he said miserably.

Yet my words, as they hung there in the air, seemed childish. *I just want things to be normal?* Since when had I become so besotted with, so dependent upon normalcy? *Kim Gordon*, I thought suddenly. *Joan Jett. Siouxsie Sioux. Patti Smith. Debbie Harry and Suzi Quatro.* I hadn't thought of my idols in years—not in the iconic, shamanistic way I had as a teenager—but it suddenly occurred to me: What would Kim fucking Gordon do? More to the point, what would *I* do? Not the me right now—the married, mother-of-two, kitchenware saleswoman, weeping pathetically in a chain restaurant with a soup-and-salad "heart smart" lunch special before her on a plastic cafeteria tray—not the Botoxed woman in the suburbs with her brain stuffed with to-do lists and two disgruntled teenagers—but my long-ago, punk-rock, best badassed self? Joey had clearly transformed himself into some alter ego buried deep within him. What if I did the same? How would the younger, renegade, nineteen-year-old me have responded to all this?

My adult life pinwheeled around me. Our children, our idiot dog, our bills, our mortgage, all that we had endured and built together, everything we owned and owed in this world. I saw suddenly, too, that man in the restaurant in Las Vegas, turning to paraffin as the life drained out of him. All of us were just cells and bones and circuitry, as fragile as lanterns sheathed in Japanese paper. I'd loved Joey for twenty-six years—longer than I'd loved anyone else in my life. Our situation was ridiculous beyond belief. But maybe he was right about something. Maybe I, of all people, had to understand compulsion, the dark and twisted ways we all tried to mask and channel our pain. Joey had gotten me sober. He had once helped save my life. Surely, I at least owed him now some compassion, some generosity of spirit.

I blew my nose and balled up my napkin. I took a deep breath. I didn't like what I was going to say—I had not really warmed to it at all—but I'd be damned if I folded so easily. Surely I was made of tougher stuff than this. It seemed like the best I could possibly manage.

"Okay, Joseph." I swallowed. "Show me. Show me what you like. Show me what to do."

Chapter 3

THE PLEASURE CHEST WAS located toward the end of a strip mall between a Quiznos sandwich shop and a dry cleaner on the outskirts of Pontiac. I must have driven past it a dozen times taking Mr. Noodles to his puppy shrink without ever noticing. Three mannequins in the window were posed as a French maid, a tarty nurse, and a Chippendales cowboy holding plastic jack-o'-lanterns, their limbs draped with cottony bunting meant to approximate cobwebs. At first glance, it looked like any other Halloween display; the only giveaways were the candy-colored dildos with stick-on bat wings bouncing overhead on fishing lines. Otherwise, the sign reading TRICK OR TREAT!—well, it could've meant anything.

"Oh, very tasteful," I said, motioning with my chin. "Especially those bat vibrators."

I was determined to be a good sport. The Halloween decorations were actually a relief. God forbid, if Joey and I ran into anyone we knew, we could always claim we were shopping for costumes.

Over the weekend, in preparation, Joey had shown me various websites (BDSM for Dummies; Wiki: How to Act Like a Dominatrix). "Sissy Maids" were a subculture within a subculture; some men simply liked to cross-dress as ultrafeminine maids and wait on people hand and foot; others wanted to be emasculated, punished, debased. Joey, unfortunately, leaned toward the latter. "Are you sure you're okay with this?" he kept saying. "I know. It seems really freaky."

The truth was, I *wasn't* sure—it did seem freaky—but the alternatives were infinitely worse. Being a dominatrix was simply a type of theater, I told myself. It would be like glam rock, no different from, say, Bowie's Ziggy Stardust, Marilyn Manson, the band KISS. You dressed up, slipped into a persona for a performance—the parameters were well defined—and here, of course, I'd be playing to an audience of only one, who'd be playing a role as well. All I'd have to do was boss him around for a bit—he'd clean the oven, maybe mop up the floor—I could spank him with a wooden paddle if I thought he was being "bad"—okay, whatever—then, *tah-dah*. We could take off our makeup together with cold cream and order in a pizza. It would be a new kind of "date night." Outside the box: yes. Preposterous: absolutely. But manageable.

In the years since I'd given up drinking, I'd worried I'd grown dull. Yeah, sobriety was healthier—it made you more "present," "alive," "in touch with your feelings"—*blah, blah*—we all know the benefits believe me, I don't need to be convinced. But sometimes, when I was having one of those 4 a.m. existential crises when your eyes snap open in a panic and you start inventorying all the deficits of your life, I worried that by giving up booze, I'd forfeited the last of whatever had made me really interesting and edgy and effervescent.

Well, if I'd wanted some iconoclasm back in my life, I was about to get it.

Besides, from what I'd seen on the internet, a dominant was supposed to "control each aspect of her submissives' lives, forcing them to obey her, disciplining them when needed." Frankly, the skills this required didn't seem that much different from those of being a wife and a mother. So much of my time was spent nagging, cajoling, threatening: *Austin, feet off the table, please. Joey, would it kill you to actually put your cereal bowl in the sink? Ashley, did you get the money we sent you? If so, could you please let me know?*

I'd never asked to become a shrewish, banal person (the "enforcer," Austin sometimes called me). It made me unrecognizable even to myself. But if I didn't oversee all the daily detritus of our lives, who would?

It had gotten to the point where every time I opened my mouth, my kids began texting and pointedly putting in their earbuds. "Okay, okay," Joey would say without looking up from his iPad. I couldn't remember the last time Ashley or Austin had called me Mom, in fact, without stretching it out to at least three syllables. *Mo-o-om*. The verbal equivalent of an eye-roll.

The one difference between being a dom and a wife seemed to be that when you were a dominatrix, people actually *listened* to you. So, okay. If my donning a bustier and a cat mask was what it was going to take to get my husband to fold the damn laundry and empty the dishwasher: Fine. Sign me up. Surely other women must have become dominatrixes simply because they wanted some help with the goddamn housework.

Joey pulled open the door of the Pleasure Chest. "After you, mistress," he said merrily. In his corduroy hunting jacket, his U-M baseball cap, his relaxed-fit jeans, he looked like any other Midwestern dad en route to Home Depot. Ever since the night I'd agreed to try out the lifestyle, though, he had been as adoring as a groupie. We even made love with an urgency and a passion (and okay, with the help of a pill—Joey was nearing fifty, after all—let's not kid ourselves here—time happens) that we hadn't experienced since the earliest days of our relationship, since before we'd had kids—hell, since before we'd had *jobs*.

I'd be lying if I said I'd never been in a sex shop before. Back in high school, there was a sordid little boutique on the outskirts of Ypsilanti called the Pink Pussycat. It catered mostly to gay men, but my friend Ann-Marie and I once drove there on a dare, pretending to be completely blasé about it. We were just browsing, we told each other, of course we weren't turned on or grossed out or fascinated whatsoever—we just *happened* to be in one of the most decrepit areas outside Depot Town. And we'd glanced cursorily at the vibrators, cock rings, and lubricants trying to absorb as much as we could while feigning disinterest.

The Pleasure Chest, by contrast, had the cheery, drafty feel of a discount supermarket. Joey and I walked through a black velvet curtain cloaking the entrance and found ourselves in a reception area equipped with a zebra-print love seat and two hot-pink tulip chairs. A glass case on the wall behind them had a series of dildos arranged sequentially like musical notes; they were so painfully enormous, I assumed they were for display purposes only. They didn't look like anything you'd remotely ever want to use to have sex with—unless, perhaps, you needed to inseminate a horse.

"Well, this gives the phrase 'big box store' a whole new meaning, doesn't it," I said.

Joey barked with laughter. "You did not just say that! Wow." He shook his head. "Come. Let me introduce you."

He led me past the reception desk to the main floor; it was lined to the ceiling with racks of clothing like a costume warehouse: frilly lingerie in all sizes and colors, catsuits, more French maid outfits, sexy medical uniforms, a whole leatherwear section. Mannequins suspended overhead were completely mummified in patent leather with only zippers for mouths. The sheer volume and tidal garishness of it all was decidedly unerotic. See enough rubber vaginas and latex dildos and squeeze bottles of lube displayed in bulk, and it starts to look like what it really is—just so much plastic crap likely manufactured in China. If you squinted your eyes, it didn't look any different from the junky accessory stores that I used to take Ashley to for Hello Kitty backpacks and rhinestone birthday tiaras. It made me curiously melancholy. Clearly, there was a market for all of this. So many people needed all these props in order just to love each other. Now, I was one of them.

Canned music played just as it did everywhere else: some Bruno Mars, then some awful, toothpasty song that turned "Marvin Gaye" into a verb. Being a child of Motown, this seemed like perhaps the most obscene thing in the store so far. *Let's Marvin Gaye and get it on.* Really? Nearby a young couple was fondling a few different pairs of faux-fur handcuffs by the SALE bins. The boy still had acne and a rabbity face; he kept yanking at the cuffs to see how much resistance they offered.

The girl was glancing around self-consciously, saying loudly, "Well, these could be good for our HONEYMOON."

"Let me see if I can find Vicki." Joey scanned the aisles. "She's the one I usually deal with. You'll like her. She's from New York, actually."

On the ride over, Joey had briefed me about the Pleasure Chest. Since I was what was known as "vanilla" in BDSM parlance, he worried that I'd be turned off by the more hard-core aspects. But really, it was the store owners I was most worried about: Vicki and Diane were a former porn star and a stripper who'd been privy to a side of my husband I'd never known existed until a few days ago. I pictured them fawning over Joey with their melony breasts, their asses plumped with injectables. I imagined when I was presented to them to be outfitted, it would be like one of those British makeover shows I used to watch on BBC America, where they took a dumpy woman with bad English teeth and osteoporosis and dressed her up in a silk coat from Top Shop.

Joey assured me the store owners were discreet "and totally cool." They ran a weekly Bondage-Discipline/Sado-Masochism support group and would even give me private dominatrix training, if I was interested.

"Yeah. Right. With all my free time." I snorted.

"Zsa-Zsa!" a voice sang across the aisles. "How you doin'? Long time, no see!"

A stocky, middle-aged woman threw her roast-beefy arms around my husband. She had spiky, electric-pink, cactus-needle hair and funky geometric glasses on a chain around her neck. Otherwise, she was dressed head-to-toe in black—some sort of asymmetrical smock, black leggings, black Converse high-tops. Releasing Joey, she turned to me. "Hi. I'm Vicki. So, you're the adoring wife, I hear, yes?" Her Long Island accent was so heavy, for a moment I assumed she was putting me on. She said "yawh" instead of "you're"; "adaw-ring" instead of "adoring." The entire town of Syosset lived in her voice.

"Uh, yeah. I guess. That's me," I said, smiling haplessly. "Miss Vanilla."

"Well, not to worry," Vicki said, unfolding her glasses, sliding them on, motioning for us to follow. "Joey's told us all about you, and we're going to get you a nice outfit and make sure you're comfortable. Show you the ropes, as we like to say, ha ha—no pun intended. You're going to have fun here, okay?"

"Sure, okay," I said gamely, though I just could not get past her voice: My God, it was like a sex shop run by Fran Drescher. Yet, more than anything else, it was the pink hair that threw me; it was the very same shade I myself had had when I was sixteen. Pink hair on a middle-aged woman, I'd always told myself, was grasping and pathetic. But Vicki managed to pull it off. I felt a great callowness—a sudden need to prove and endear myself to her. I wanted her to understand that I was actually "cool" and not all *that* vanilla, either.

"So," I said, trying to sound casual as I followed her back through the clothing, "Joey said you used to do porn?"

"Oh, sure, a long, long time and about fifty pounds ago," Vicki said breezily, leading us past circular racks of lingerie. "Back in the '70s, you know, before AIDS, before digital. I did a few titles. *Starsky and Crotch* was the big one. But then I had my kid, of course. And let's face it: Gravity is nobody's friend." She stopped at a section where rows of various riding crops, whips, and cat-o'-nine-tails hung from display racks like umbrellas and handbags. "Do I wanna start you off here?" she said aloud to herself. "Nah, let's get you outfitted first." She waved at us to keep following her as she changed direction. "You keep walking, I'll keep talking. I tend to talk a lot," she said. Joey shot me an encouraging look and mouthed: *Isn't she great?*

"The thing with porn is," Vicki continued, "you can only do that stuff for so long. I'm really a people person, you know? Like, I did Myers-Briggs, and I was way out on the extrovert scale. EMIT, EMIS—something—I forget exactly. You'd think porn would be very social, but actually, not so much. On the set, it's you and five, maybe six people, tops. And then you do the shoot, and that's it. Maybe a zillion guys jerk off to you, but me? Most of the time, I was just going home to eat KFC and watch *Love Boat*. It was depressing."

I felt my handbag vibrate. A message from Colleen Lundstedt appeared on my phone: **Is everything all right? When you get a chance, please check in. We've gotten several sales queries for you regarding the "Via Vecchio" earthenware.**

Vicki was leading us through a section now devoted to blow-up dolls. "So when my kid got into U-M, Diane and I moved up here and opened the store instead. Detroit, Flint—already they were a mess. But as I've learned, basically anything to do with sex is recession-proof."

Not a good time, I messaged back to Colleen. **Still dealing w family emergency.**

Vicki looked me up and down. "For a bustier, I'm thinking you're what? A size eight?"

"Uh, sometimes. Sometimes ten, depending on the cut."

"Anyway, I get to meet tons of people now. Plenty of vanillas come in. Bachelorette parties, couples looking to spice it up. Though most of our regulars are hard-core. The BDSM community is a very lovely, very down-to-earth bunch. Really, you'll see. You should come to our workshops. I told Joey, if you're going to be doing this regularly, you should get some training so that all your play is safe and aboveboard. We so-called 'perverts' look out for each other. Let me tell you, my sister? She lives over in Peoria, where she does the Junior League?" Vicki gave a low, disbelieving whistle. "Those women are nasty with a capital N. The backstabbing? The viciousness? *That's* real abuse. That's the *not-okay* type of sadism you've got going on over there. But for some reason, *we're* the 'deviants.' Go figure."

Vicki stopped at a case full of nipple clamps: not much different from the Privileged Kitchen's assortment of clips for potato chip bags. "Here, we're all consenting adults. Oh, I love selling sex toys. It's so much easier than doing porn. Let's face it, nobody gets a bladder infection from showing customers how to use restraints properly, am I right? As I always say, 'There's no VD in the word 'retail.'" Vicky checked back to see if I agreed. I must have looked a little stunned because she said, "TMI? Whoops. Sorry. I never know. My therapist says I 'overshare.'"

We'd reached a section full of shiny bustiers now, fire-engine red, black, faux patent leather, real leather, satin, some with intricate boning and ties, some with aggressive stitching, some with lace, others with spikes. For some of my gigs with Toxic Shock Syndrome, I'd actually worn a black lace bra, a leather dog collar, studded cuffs. It sounds so clichéd now, but at sixteen, I'd really thought I was being edgy.

Vicki sized me up, then whipped out a tape measure and motioned for me to raise my arms so she could measure my bust. "Yep. Thirty-two. Zsa-Zsa," she said to Joey. It was the first time she'd addressed him since we met. "You got a price range?"

Joey had a broad, happy smile plastered across his face. Shaking his head, he flicked his hand at the ceiling as if to suggest that money was no object: The sky was the limit. It occurred to me that so far, this was actually the most shocking thing I'd witnessed all day.

"Hey! Zsa-Zsa, how are you?" another woman said as she emerged from amid the clothing racks. She was pixieish with sheared gray hair and a crinkly-eyed smile behind small, rectangular glasses. She wore strawberry-colored dungarees and—what charmed me immediately—a vintage Runaways T-shirt. She gave Joey a brittle, bird-like hug, then pushed her glasses farther up her nose with her finger. "Vicki said you'd be coming in today."

"Diane," Vicki said, steering her over to me.

Diane's head bobbed up and down as she shook my hand vigorously. "Oh my God. You must be Donna, yes? Hi, hi, so pleased to meet you. Really. Truly."

"Pleased to meet you, too," I said. *This was the former stripper?*

"Can I just say?" Diane's face shone with an almost evangelical enthusiasm. "We are so thrilled to have you here. Zsa-Zsa is one of our favorite customers—if I'm allowed to say that—if we're allowed to have favorites. And what you're doing here? I need to say this: It is really, really *brave*. And *kind*. I wish more spouses could be as open-minded as you are. A lot of wives, frankly, they find out about their husbands' lifestyle, and they just get all judgy and freaked out—"

"Yeah, well—" I said.

"Though we have gotten a lot more vanillas in here since *Fifty Shades of Grey*," she said. Reaching over, she pulled a black vinyl bustier off the rack and handed it to Vicki. "I think this one'll work well on her." She turned to me. "Have you read it?"

"What? *Fifty Shades*?" I said. "Not really." My book club had chosen it one month, and I'd gone so far as to download it. But the truth was, I wasn't much for fiction—or books in general. Oddly, even though I'd ended up majoring in English Literature at U-M, these days I just had no patience for reading. Mostly, I'd joined the book club for the socializing. My first sponsor had invited me, and I was desperate to spend time with people who didn't spend *all* their time talking about not drinking.

"Well, good. Don't," Vicki said with surprisingly vehemence. "That idiotic book totally misrepresents the lifestyle."

Diane looked like she was about to disagree, but Vicki shot her a look. Clearly, this was an ongoing point of contention between them.

"So, Donna, is there anything you like?" Joey said quickly, motioning to a rack of bullet bras. Put him in as many crinolines and bloomers as he wanted, but my husband was still a guy. *Stop chitchatting, ladies*, his tone said. *Move it along here.*

Vicki and Diane helped me into fishnet stockings. A snakey-tight Spandex miniskirt that retracted like a bungee cord and shone like dark syrup. A spiked collar. A black patent-leather corset that jutted and curved like a piece of architecture. It was heavily boned, bolstered with struts, a dozen hook-and-eye closures running down the back, criss-crossed by intricate stays. As Diane yanked the laces tighter and tighter behind me, I felt like Scarlett O'Hara. My waist went from twenty-three inches to nineteen. My breasts rose two inches, mashed together; for the first time in my life, I had serious cleavage. I had to admit, I felt creature-like, exalted, eroticized—utterly transformed. I had not felt this unabashedly sexy in ages—if ever—though how I was going to manage to put on this outfit again at home, by myself, was another story.

"That's exactly what slaves are for, Donna," Vicki said. "Zsa-Zsa will dress you, bathe you, do anything you tell her to." I had to say, I was warming more and more to this dominatrix idea. I hadn't been this fussed-over since my wedding day.

Diane knelt before me and scooped one of my feet, then the other, into stilty, lipstick-red stiletto pumps. She handed me a riding crop.

"Whoa," she said as she and Vicki stepped back to assess my finished look. "Va-va-voom."

"Come." Diane offered her hand. "Let's introduce you, shall we?" She parted the curtain. "Zsa-Zsa?" she called to Joey. "Come and meet your new mistress."

I posed in the doorway, hands on my hips, trying to look as fierce as possible.

Joey rose from the stool, dumbstruck.

"Donna," he said. "You look—"

"She's a natural, isn't she?" Diane said with satisfaction.

"Killer," Vicki agreed.

"Donna," Joey said again.

"I gotta say," said Vicki, shaking her head. "We get alotta doms in here. But you? You really got the look. You got the attitude."

I stood planted there, smiling, basking in their admiration. Slowly, I raised my riding crop once and sliced the air with it.

"Oh, baby." Joey laughed.

In the mirror across from the dressing room, I could see myself. I didn't look ridiculous at all. I didn't look like a woman just about to turn forty-five. Vicki and Diane knew exactly what they were doing. I looked like an Amazon, a superhero, muscled and glossy and indomitable. I could bestride the globe, force men to kneel before me. Serve me. Love me, motherfucker. I am Donna, the Dom.

There was only one problem.

I couldn't breathe.

Or walk.

The corset was crushing my ribs; it seemed to cut off the blood from my waist down. And those luscious, pornographic-red heels were so high, I'd keel like a felled tree if I took a single step. Everything felt like an iron lung.

"Mistress Donna," Joey said encouragingly, curtsying a little before me, "what can I do for you?"

"Go on, command him," Vicki instructed. "Order him to do something. Make him serve you."

All I could do was stand there, immobilized in my costume; all the muscles in my face suddenly felt paralyzed, too. I may have looked powerful, but I felt as if I'd contracted Guillain-Barre syndrome.

"You want to serve me?" I said. "Then please. Get me out of these fucking shoes."

On the way home, Joey and I stopped for lunch at Applebee's. My feet and ribs no longer ached, and as we ate our burgers, we smiled at each other as impishly as teenagers. In the middle of the meal, my phone vibrated once, then twice. I was tempted to ignore it, but it was Ashley, tweeting from London: **Merkel 2-faced? Rumor that Germany might close Austria & Hungary borders! Croatia overwhelmed!** ☹ ☹

Then: **EU calls for hotspot in Lesvos & Chios. Refugees now must register? Camp will be detention facility? Horrible!!!** ☹ **#refugeecrisis**

I passed it to Joey. "What the hell is she talking about?"

He glanced at the screen. "I have absolutely no idea."

It was the first time in a long while that our kids were not center stage in our lives. Joey leaned across the table until his face was just a few inches from mine. "Hey mistress," he said, tipping his head in the direction of the Subaru parked beyond the window, its trunk full of brand-new fetish-wear. "Wanna go home and play?" Austin had hockey practice; we'd have at least four hours to ourselves in the middle of the day. The next evening was my birthday dinner—at our regular Italian place—and then I had PK demos scheduled for the rest of the week. It was now or, well, a long time from now.

I reached for the check. "Okay. Let's do this." By now, I admit, I was eager. I was primed. Like anybody with a brand-new purchase, I wanted to try it out.

Nothing in a marriage will ever be as nakedly intimate as childbirth. But watching your husband dress up in his Sissy Maid uniform while he, in turn, laces up your dominatrix corset, was, at least for me, a close second. Joey was unnervingly adept at donning his bra, girdle, bloomers, et cetera. To be so up close and personal as he effected his transformation—the makeup, the wig, the frilly cap and bits of pearl jewelry—even perfume (Fantasy by Britney Spears? Really?)—well, it was something.

Then it was my turn. Of course, putting on any outfit at home is always anticlimactic compared to trying it on in the store—and as Joey struggled to fasten all the hooks and eyes of my corset (first he needed his reading glasses, then he claimed his fingers were too fat, then we started bickering over how the laces were supposed to tie. It was likely the least sexy transformation in all of erotic history), my apprehension began to return, and I began to think that what we were doing was pure folly—that in agreeing to be Joey's dominatrix, I was just aiding and abetting a mutual descent into insanity.

In the end, though, we got there. Joey became Zsa-Zsa, and I—because I'd been told it was best to have a special "dom name" to help further delineate the role-playing from reality—was now Mistress Moyet, a moniker I'd chosen after the lead singer from the '80s New Wave group Yaz.

Joey and I regarded each other with the same dawning astonishment we'd had on our wedding day. In my bustier and rubber skirt and fishnets, I looked cocksure and fearsome. And Joey? He looked surprisingly vulnerable. All the grizzly lines of him had been softened by the flounces and lace of his pink dress, and in his great desire to climb out of his muscle-bound, hairy man's body, well, he was almost poignant.

"Okay. Now what?" I said. Just getting dressed was a massive undertaking. Already, I felt exhausted. I wondered if, as a dominatrix, I could just order both of us to take a nice afternoon nap. "You're going to have to give me instructions until I get the hang of this myself."

"Well, sure, sure. Of course. Yes, mistress," Joey said. His voice, suddenly, was no longer Joey's but a high, puppety falsetto—the kind men always seem to adopt whenever they're trying to mimic women. "Why don't you snap your riding crop and *order* me to tell you what to do?"

I frowned in my leather collar. "What riding crop?"

A look passed over his powdered face. "The riding crop we just bought at the Pleasure Chest, mistress."

"We didn't buy a riding crop."

"Yeah we did. Vicki wrapped it up with your collar and shoes."

"Nuh-uh."

"Are you sure? I thought we got the riding crop. And the paddle."

"No. Remember? You said they were too pricey."

"What? No. I said they were too expensive *together*, so I said to just get the riding crop."

We rummaged through the bags from the Pleasure Chest. Just to be sure, Joey checked the credit card receipt in his wallet. It seemed we had, in fact, forgotten to purchase any riding crops or paddles. "Shit, I can't believe this," Joey said, in his regular voice now. "Mistress Tanya always brought her own."

Just hearing that name got my back up. "Hang on," I said. Twisting my feet out of the stilettos (How was it, I suddenly wondered, that I was supposed to be the powerful one here, but Joey, in his Mary Janes, still got to wear the comfortable shoes?). Rifling through the closet in our home office, I emerged with the new Privileged Kitchen "nonstick, slotted, flexible fish spatula" ($16.95, if you care); a red silicone batter-scraper ($8.95); one of our beechwood long-handled kitchen spoons ($5.85); and the new PK stainless burger-flipper ($18.95 on sale). "Will any of these work?"

Joey picked them up one by one, assessing their weight, slapping them each a couple of times against his opened palm as if to test them.

"Wow. You could have a whole new side business here." He laughed. He placed the fish spatula in my hand, angled my wrist, and guided me though a swing like a tennis instructor. "Straight through, like that, with a flick at the end. Not too soft. You don't have to hold back."

Bending over, he pulled down his ruffled bloomers and tights to expose his pinkish, gelatinous buttocks to me. "Give it a shot, mistress," he said.

I remained motionless. "You've got to be kidding me, Joey."

"C'mon, I'm not Joey right now, okay? I'm Zsa-Zsa, the bad little girlie French maid."

But why would I want to spank a little girl?

"I'm not doing this." I crossed my arms.

"Please, mistress. Just try," Joey urged in his simpering falsetto. "I'm Zsa-Zsa. A girlie-man, a big sissy, who's submissive and helpless. I need to be disciplined, mistress. I've been a very bad girl."

I suppose because his femme voice irritated me so much, I drew my hand back and hit him on the ass with the fish spatula. When the non-stick stainless steel connected with his skin, I flinched, but Joey didn't seem to even feel it. "That's it. You can go much harder. You're not going to hurt me," he said affably. "Don't worry, if anything gets too intense, I'll say our safe word."

Right. *Regis Philbin.*

I spanked him two or three times with the fish spatula, then the batter-scraper, then the wooden spoon, then the burger-flipper. What can I say? It was one for the record books, though nothing I was ever going to mention in our annual Christmas newsletter. A few times, it was actually hard to keep from giggling. In the end, though, Joey and I agreed that the fish spatula was the best. It handled well, and my husband said the slotted surface distributed the pain nice and evenly. There was something satisfying about having a little consensus between us. Finally, we could get down to business.

"Mistress Moyet," Joey said in his girlie voice. "I'm Zsa-Zsa, a prissy little Sissy Maid. How can I serve you today?"

This, I had prepared for. I called up a list on my iPad. A lot of it was lifted directly from my own to-do list, but why reinvent the wheel?

Pick up dry cleaning.
Buy self birthday present & wrap.
Flea collars for Mr. Noodles.
Renew car registration.
Prescription refills.

Since these required Joey to go outside, I focused on the next item on my list:

"Okay, Zsa-Zsa," I said. "Today we're—I mean—*you*—you're going to bake gluten-free brownies for my book club."

I could see his smile waver a bit behind his makeup; it seemed this might not be what he'd initially had in mind. Yet I told myself to ignore it: How much time did I spend cooking each day? Now, it was his turn.

"Yes, mistress," he said obediently.

"Here's the recipe," I said, tapping it open on my screen. "Take a look, get a sense of it, okay? First, let's assemble all the ingredients here on the counter in a *mise-en-place*, so we don't have to keep running back and forth, all right? We're going to need some brown rice flour and some brown sugar to start, so if you could go to the pantry, please, and—"

"Regis Philbin," Joey said abruptly. I stopped. Switching back to his own bass voice, he said, "Donna, as my mistress, don't be polite, okay? Don't say 'let's,' or 'if you could,' all right? Say, 'Read that recipe. Fetch the ingredients.' The whole point is to command me to do stuff. Take control over me. And don't have me walk to the pantry. Remember what the websites said about emasculating me? Make me skip—or, better yet—crawl. Really humiliate me."

I looked at him dubiously. "Okaaay."

"Look, wave your paddle around if you need to." He gestured toward the fish spatula. "And call me Zsa-Zsa. I think that'll help you get into the role-playing more."

We tried it again. "Zsa-Zsa, read this recipe for gluten-free vegan brownies," I shouted, slapping the side of the counter with the fish spatula.

"Yes, mistress." Dutifully, Joey studied my iPad.

"Now, recite it back to me," I ordered.

"Yes, mistress." He recited it back to me.

"Now, skip into the pantry and fetch the ingredients." I added, "One by one. Rice flour first."

Joey skipped into the pantry; in his flouncy petticoats, he reminded me of the little pirouetting elephant in *Fantasia*. Skipping back, he placed the rice flour on the counter with a mincing, exaggerated curtsy.

"Don't look so pleased," I said. "You've got nine more ingredients to go. This time, crawl."

It was odd. As a saleswoman, I'd never say to a customer: "Chop the cilantro." It was always: "I'm sorry, Arianna, but while I start sautéing the onion and ginger, would you mind cutting up some cilantro for me? Great. Thanks so much." Being direct now felt strange and counter-intuitive. But also: liberating.

As soon as I said "crawl," my husband dropped to his hands and knees and started crawling into the pantry, wiggling his ruffled behind back and forth cowishly. It was starting to feel like bona fide make-believe, the way you play when you're a child—*Everybody pretend to go to sleep now!* your friend says, and then you all roll over onto your sides and snore exaggeratedly. And having Joey jump at my every command? I had to say, it was thrilling.

Yet a moment later, he called out, "Regis Philbin." Then, in his regular voice: "Donna, where's the brown sugar?"

Oh, you're shitting me, I thought. *Really?* "It's right there on the second shelf," I shouted.

"I'm looking. It's not here."

"Yes, it is. Check behind the baking soda."

"Is that the stuff in the orange box?"

"Does the orange box say 'baking soda' on it?"

"I dunno. I can't see. I don't have my glasses."

I yanked off my stilettos again and stomped into the pantry. "The brown sugar is right there," I said with annoyance, pointing. "In the big brown box that says 'Brown Sugar' on it. Right behind the little orange box of baking soda that says—wait for it—'baking soda.'"

"Oh," he said defensively. "I could've sworn it wasn't there a minute ago."

"Jesus Christ," I muttered. How exactly was I the one in power here? I didn't want to have to walk him through baking the damn brownies: I just wanted it *done*.

Joey ratcheted his voice up two octaves and resumed his exaggerated, feminine gestures. "I'm so sorry, Mistress Moyet. It's just so hard for a bad little Sissy Maid like me to read these teeny-tiny letters. Following a recipe is just so complicated for a little girlie-girl. I'm so weak and helpless and at your mercy. And I've displeased you, I can see. So I need to be punished."

With that, he turned around on all fours, pulled down his bloomers and tights, and exposed his ass to me, again. "I will submit to whatever horrible and degrading punishment you think this bad little girlie-girl deserves," he chirped.

What?

"You can spank me and tell me how naughty I am," he prompted. "You can make me drink water from Mr. Noodles's dog dish and tell me what a pathetic little sissy I am in my lace panties and my sissy dress and my girlie bra. You can pour the brown sugar all over the pantry floor and make me lick it up with my pink sissy tongue. Punish me, mistress, until I learn to cook and bake and clean and do everything exactly the way you do."

He went on suggesting different punishments and humiliations, but I had stopped listening. *Exactly the way you do?* Excuse me? Was this what my husband really thought "being a woman" boiled down to—wearing lipstick and lacy panties? Being frilly and silly and helpless? *Baking?*

Was this how he saw *me?* In the twenty-first century?

Drawing my arm back, I slapped him as hard as I could across the ass with the fish spatula. He visibly shuddered. "Yes, Mistress Moyet. Thank you, mistress," he said. "I'm a bad, bad Sissy Maid, aren't I?"

Why was being "girlie" and "sissy" so synonymous with shame anyway? I thought suddenly. What was so inherently degrading about housework? For all the years I'd managed our household—even while working full-time myself—had he secretly thought it was a joke? That what I'd been doing was actually somehow infantile and shameful and beneath him? With a swoop, I spanked him even harder with the fish spatula. "Thank you, mistress," he yelped. "Do you want me to pull up my girlie panties now, or am I deserving of more punishment? Should I lick your feet?"

My God, I thought suddenly, *do you really want to experience being humiliated as a woman, Joey?* Then cut your damn paycheck by thirty percent! Have a guy drug you at a party in college—but have an administrator tell you you're overreacting when you want to report it to the police. Take your Subaru into the shop; have the mechanic ignore you for twenty minutes while he flirts with some big-titted seventeen-year-old—then have him talk condescendingly to you about not riding the clutch—even though you've been driving longer than he's been alive. Have men at barbecues that *you're* hosting interrupt you every time you try to contribute to the conversation. You want to really be humiliated as a woman, Joey? Be like my mother: die from ovarian cancer because the male doctor at the VA won't take your complaints seriously and the insurance companies won't cover "women's health." Hell, Joey, perform CPR on a man to save his life, but have a waiter ignore your cries for assistance because he assumes you're *just* a Las Vegas prostitute.

The air cracked with the sound of the spatula landing sharply on Joey's exposed flesh, again and again. And then I saw something I hadn't seen, really, for years: a giant, tumescent hard-on, purple-pink like chewing gum, poking out through Joey's bloomers like its own animal. He hadn't needed a pill for this—and I realized with a sickening rush that for years, he hadn't needed me at all to get turned on. *This* was what he'd been doing with Mistress Tanya—and whether she'd finished him off or he'd taken himself into his own hands—that was immaterial. This fetish of his had always been sexual—I'd probably known this on some level all along—my husband had been getting off with another woman—with the help of a whole community that knew him more intimately than I did, in fact—that outfitted him, that supported him—he'd been getting his rocks off routinely despite me—in spite of me—by pretending to be a grotesque exaggeration of *me*.

I swung the fish spatula across Joey's ass with all the force I had.

"Ow! Shit. Mistress!" Joey shouted. "Whoa! Hey! Regis Philbin!" The blows caught him on the backs of his thighs, the sides of his pinafore, in between his meaty shoulder blades where his bra was fastened. A couple of times, the side of the spatula hit him on his biceps and little perforated lines of blood began to rise on his skin. "Is this giving you a hard-on?" I shrieked. "Is this getting you off?"

Snatching up the stainless-steel burger-flipper, I swung at Joey's head, his face.

He was crawling away beneath the lacerating smacks as fast as he could; he was huddled on the floor in the corner of the kitchen now, his arms wrapped around his head protectively as I swung the kitchen utensils at him at close range with full force. I hit him on his puffed-sleeved shoulders, his frilly maid's bonnet, his upraised hands. He yowled in pain. "Regis Philbin! Donna, please! Stop! Don't you hear me? I'm saying 'Regis Philbin'!"

"Regis Philbin? So what! Do you think this is some kind of joke?" I smacked him again. "For over twenty years, I've been cleaning the goddamn oven! For over twenty years, I've been doing all the baking and cooking for you, Joey! You think it's funny? You think it's degrading?"

"No, I don't! I don't!" he cried, trying to fend off the implements and stay my hands at the same time.

I don't know what came over me. I was crazed. I was feral. I just couldn't stop. "You cheated on me, Joey!" I shouted, taking another swing at his shoulder. "You did! And now, you're just mocking me, and your daughter, too."

I was crying now. "You let someone else into our house—into our marriage—and you're mocking me—" With a swing of the burger flipper, I slapped him across the face as hard as I could. The cracking sound was unmistakable. Suddenly, there was an explosion of blood—blood pouring out from between Joey's fingers and running down his wrists as he clutched his nose. Blood dripping onto the linoleum, mixing with his lipstick, with his makeup. Blood on the kitchen implements. I hurled them at him—one after the other—they missed, hitting the wall above his head—then I picked up the lurid red heels I'd taken off and pummeled him with those, too, on his head, his shoulders, before throwing them down at him like two bright grenades. One landed beneath his thigh, the other hit him on the wrist—he flinched—and as I stood there panting, I saw the terror in his eyes. He was weeping and choking; I was weeping and choking—his blood, it seemed to be everywhere—his pinafore was soaked with it. "Oh my God," I screamed, jerking back. "You did this, Joey! You did this to us!" even as I knew, somewhere deep in my lizard-brain, that I was feeling murderous—that I was volcanic— that I had detonated and something had just gone horribly, horribly wrong. With my feet finally freed from their torturous heels, I turned and I ran. I heard some kind of deep, animal-like panting: *Leave! Get the hell out! Go!* I pounded up the stairs to our bedroom, grabbed the first shirt I could find—yanked it on—grabbed my purse, phone, wallet— and shoved my netted feet into a pair of flip-flops by the bathroom.

The next thing I was aware of, I was in my Subaru, an old VIRGINIA IS FOR LOVERS T-shirt thrown over my bustier, car key shaking in my fist. There was a growl, a jerk, and a spray of gravel.

Chapter 4

FOR A WHILE, I simply zoomed over the back roads in my flip-flops. I sped past rusting water towers, overgrown railway depots, grain elevators shaped like bundles of dynamite. The autumn trees along the roadside flickered and leapt like flame.

I found myself barreling toward Flint—with its toxic river, its poisoned children. When I came to a traffic light swinging overhead like a noose, I swerved right. I was seized by the idea of going to Pontiac—directly to that damn shopping mall—and driving straight through the front window of the Pleasure Chest. *Trick or treat!* I could already picture the ejaculatory shatter of glass, the mannequins toppling, the hideous crunch of their fiberglass torsos and limbs beneath my tires as I floored the accelerator and surged forward, bouncing onto the display floor amid fumes of plaster, mowing down racks and racks of lingerie—black lace and pink satin negligees catching on my hood and windshield until my Subaru looked like some insane, X-rated, sorority-girl homecoming float. I could smell the stench of gasoline mixed with strawberry lubricant. Best yet, I could hear Vicki screaming—Vicki with her electric-pink hair, who'd never played a guitar a single goddamn day in her life—and I pictured myself coolly emerging from the driver's seat, still fierce in my bustier: *Who's happy now, bitch, selling sex toys? There. I've just destroyed your life as casually as you've destroyed mine.*

But instead, I gunned the car onto the ramp for Interstate 75 heading south, circumventing Pontiac entirely, joining other cars in a flood of velocity. I craved speed—speed and distance—I was hoping, stupidly, to outrace my fury and wretchedness and nausea. I grabbed my phone. I needed desperately to talk to someone. But who? Since getting sober, most of my "closest" friends had fallen by the wayside. My colleague Victor was clearly out of the running now. And my sponsor, she would only drag me to a meeting, which was the last place on earth I wanted to be—trapped in a basement, listening to other alkies bellyache. Besides, lucky me: the most depraved episode of my life, and I'd somehow managed without a single drink.

Oh, but I wanted tequila!

If I wanted to stay sober, though, I needed *someone*. Struggling to keep an eye on the road, I scrolled quickly through the names in my phone. My book club: the two Laurens, Mindy, Heather, Arundi, Abigail. Yet even in my hysteria, I knew: When I first confessed, the members would clasp my hands and fix their gazes on me bathetically. *Oh, honey*, they'd say. *That's awful!* Yet as soon as I excused myself to go to the bathroom, their faces would go slack with shock and amazement and just a flicker of titillated glee. *OMG!* Overnight, I'd become the urban legend they told all their other friends: *If you think your life is bad? Wait'll you hear about this woman in our book club who beat her cross-dressing husband with a fish spatula!*

I knew this because if somebody else had just botched a do-it-yourself S&M session with her dentist husband in drag, I'd be on the phone to Joey in a heartbeat myself, recounting every salacious detail, smug with the relief that *this was not us*. I wasn't proud to admit this, but it was true.

The financial crisis of 2008 alone had nearly demolished Joey and me. If word got out now? No one would trust us with their teeth or their kitchens again.

I threw down my phone. Until the very moment I had caught him in his frilly cap and apron, the one person I would've sought solace from was Joey himself.

My eyes watered. Perhaps if I went fast enough, I could break the sound barrier, burst through my own skin, propel forward into another dimension entirely.

I hadn't planned on driving to Detroit, yet, suddenly, I was headed to the epicenter—past mile after mile of scorched houses, bashed-in storefronts, shuttered factories. The late-afternoon sun torched the skyline. The Renaissance Center gleamed like the barrel of a revolver aimed straight at the sky.

During my first weeks at the University of Michigan in Ann Arbor my freshman year, I was amazed to meet out-of-state kids who proudly said they were from "New York," "Boston," "DC." Only once they were heading home for Christmas did I discover that the New Yorker actually hailed from a suburb called "White Plains." The Bostonian came from "Newton." The kid from Washington lived in another state entirely: Chevy Chase, Maryland. Yet, ostentatiously, they claimed these cities as their own, eager to bask in the reflected light of them. But we Detroiters? Where were we from? Oh, Livonia. East Dearborn. Sterling Heights. Grosse Point, we said. Between the riots, crime, and plant closures, our families had hightailed it out of the city center like the crowds in old *Godzilla* movies; even Motown had packed up and left. Despite its recent so-called renewal, much of Detroit was still a modern-day Pompeii, an entire city abandoned in a stampede, the ruins of its previous life standing ghoulishly—empty factories with hooks still dangling from the ceilings; deserted restaurants with dusty barstools still riveted to the floor; burned-out Cadillacs still sitting where owners had last parked them; playgrounds overgrown by weeds; boarded-up mansions whose gardens had grown savage after their caretakers disappeared, so that they were now explosions of wildflowers and rodents; broken glass on the sidewalks glinting through the overgrowth. As for Austin and Ashley—I didn't think they'd been downtown more than four or five times in their entire lives. Mostly for Tigers games at Comerica Park and coneys in Greektown. And we lived only thirty-five minutes away. Recently, Austin had begun asking Joey and me about what Detroit had been like in the "glory days," and we honestly couldn't tell him.

The highway spit me out onto East Jefferson. I turned right, then right again, until, suddenly, a few blocks from the river, I was free of the traffic. Yet as I tore down East Larned, out of nowhere, a woman with a baby carriage stepped into the crosswalk. I slammed on my brakes. The Subaru made a tearing sound. It was not a woman at all, but an elderly, hunched man pushing a rusted shopping cart. His feet were bandaged with duct tape. He never glanced at me. When the light turned green, I let my engine thrum, but I didn't budge. I watched the man lumber down the block, then turn a corner and disappear. Still, I sat there. There were no other cars behind me. I could make my own rules.

Overhead, the "People Mover" skated eerily along the elevated track that looped its way in and out among the empty skyscrapers. It stopped with a ghostly hiss at a platform where no passengers waited. The doors opened. No one got on. No one got off. The doors closed. Something about watching the train hoosh and hiss, hoosh and hiss, and the hypnotic blinking of the traffic signals, and the quiet husk of the city, calmed me, finally.

Then, the scene in our kitchen hit me anew.

My God. What had I done?

Perhaps, I told myself, it wasn't as horrific as I'd imagined. A misunderstanding, a marital spat—okay, with a no-stick fish spatula—*and* a stainless-steel burger-flipper—but surely I wasn't the only woman in history to do such a thing? Surely, there had been some cavewoman taking swings at her caveman with a mastodon bone—and plenty of nineteenth century housewives in bonnets, brandishing rolling pins and cast-iron skillets, chasing their husbands around the chicken coops? Surely, legions of women had clobbered their philandering men with kitchen implements over the ages—couldn't this be a trope, a meme, a *thing*?

Quickly, I turned into Greektown. A diner called the Acropolis was open for business, so I pulled up in front of it, made sure my doors were locked, and stared at the little glowing rectangle of my phone. Not a single message. My heart thrummed. Slowly, mechanically, I punched in my passcode and called Joey. I couldn't have done too much damage, I reasoned—unless—there had been so much blood.

When he picked up on the second ring, my breath caught.

"Yuh," he said flatly.

"Hey," I said, sniffling uneasily. "It's me."

"I know." And then for a while, he was quiet, though his breathing was loud. I could hear the deflation and wheeze of it. "What do you want?" he slurred.

"Are you okay? You don't sound so good."

Another pause followed. I could hear the static of traffic in the background.

"I'm with Arjul. He's driving me to the emergency room."

"What—?"

"You broke my nose, Donna."

"Oh God."

"Yeah. And my bridgework. And I can barely see, cuz my cheeks are so swollen. So yeah. That's why I don't sound very good, Donna. Arjul's got me on 600 milligrams of Vicodin."

He gave a mirthless laugh, which sounded like an engine stalling. "You're lucky I don't press charges," he lisped. "Or sue you."

It wasn't clear if he was kidding.

"Oh my God, Joey. Look, please. It was crazy—"

"Austin came home *early*, Donna. His hockey practice was canceled."

I closed my eyes, pressed my forehead against the steering wheel. A whole sickening tableau unspooled before me. I said, "I think I'm going to throw up."

"Luckily, just luckily, by the time he came in Arjul had already helped me into my sweatpants, and my old jean shirt, with the snaps."

"So he didn't see?"

"Well, I had an icepack on my face. And Arjul was there. And there was blood all over the kitchen."

"Oh God. Did he freak? What did you tell him?"

A man in a leather coat sauntered out of the diner just then. He aimed his fist at a dented gray Ford parked in front of me. A car alarm began whooping insanely.

"I told Austin you went on a bender," Joey said. "I told him you called my office stinking drunk, so I came home to try and sober you up, and we had a fight. I told him that while we were fighting, I slipped and bashed my face on the kitchen island. And you just stormed out."

"Jesus Christ, Joey! Why on earth would you tell him that?"

"What was I supposed to say, Donna? That you beat me?" Joey gave a sort of hiccup.

"You said I was drunk?"

"Austin saw my face, Donna. He saw the blood on the floors and the wall. Your stuff was strewn everywhere. Your car was gone. Arjul was there with an icepack. It was the only thing I could think of at that moment."

I sat panting. I felt cornered. But Joey was right. What other explanation could he plausibly have given? Certainly not the truth. Hell, our kids got squeamish once when Joey and I simply sang along to "Crazy in Love" in the car—just goofing around—bopping in the front seat. Ashley had leaned forward and announced, "If you guys don't stop, Austin and I are hitch-hiking to Grandpa's."

The light beyond my Subaru was ebbing, turning the sky the color of cognac. I shook my head. "No, you're right, Joey. You're right," I said weakly. "Of course. It makes sense." Then something else occurred to me. "So wait. Arjul is with you? Joey, he won't say anything to anyone, will he? Or tweet stuff? Or post photos? I mean "

"Christ, Donna. Is that what you're worried about? C'mon. Arjul's known about Zsa-Zsa for years."

"Excuse me?" I felt a fresh jab of betrayal, yet before I could say anything else, a muffled, seashell roar poured through the speaker: Arjul in the background, saying something faintly, then Joey murmuring, "If you want."

Arjul's voice was suddenly loud in my ear. "Yes. Hi, Donna," he said breezily. "Let me tell you. You have no worries with me at all. I have explained to Joey that in India, we have something called 'hijra.' It is actually a very ancient tradition. Hijra are born men, but they feel and dress like women. In our culture, they're considered a third gender. They can even have this on their passports now. So really. People have impulses to be another sex or to dress some other way from time to time. Who knows? There is endless variety. Maybe it is something left over from their past lives. And I have said to Joey, there is nothing for him to feel embarrassed about. Clothing is all just packaging in the end, is it not? We all come into this life naked. We leave naked. So what does it matter what we wear in between, whether it is satin or cotton, a big man's pants or a little girl's skirt?"

"Yeah. All right, okay," I said. I wasn't sure if Arjul expected me to engage him in a philosophical debate at this moment, though I sensed he was intending to reassure me. "Listen, the thing is—" I tried to arrange my thoughts into some coherent order, but the prospect of having to explain what had upset me so much suddenly seemed overwhelming and exhausting. I felt a bolt of despair. All I could murmur was "I didn't mean to hit him like that, Arjul."

"Oh," he chuckled. "You have a temper like nobody's business. But between dentistry and India, I have pretty much seen everything," he said, almost happily. "The human condition, it is endlessly fascinating. No two dental records are exactly alike. People talk about snowflakes being unique. But I always say, 'Have you ever truly looked at somebody else's teeth?'"

"Yeah. I guess. Okay. Thanks," I said. I was absorbing less and less; the notes and cadences were just washing over my anxiety.

Joey came back on. "We're just pulling up to the emergency room. Shit. The lot's full. I don't know how long this is going to take."

"Where's Austin? He's at home?"

"Yuh. I told him I might be a while. I told him to order a pizza." I heard gravel crunching, then the squeak of a brake. Joey said, more calmly now, "Okay, we're heading in. So where are you anyway? Are you on your way home yet?"

"Just driving." I sniffled. "Greektown. Where are you? Beaumont?"

"Yeah. Once I know how long the wait is, I'll text. Actually, Arjul will." And then, for the first time, something close to tenderness crept into his voice. "You and me, Donna, we don't seem to do so good with messages lately, do we?"

"No," I said. And my eyes started to fill with tears. "No, Joey. We don't."

"Shit. It's getting dark. Hey, I'm inside now. They're going to make me shut off my phone."

"Okay." I exhaled. "Look, if you're going to be there awhile, tell Arjul that I'll come relieve him as soon as I can. I just want to check on Austin first."

"Thanks. That'd be great. Arjul's going to have his hands full for the next few days covering for me. Hey, Donna? One more thing?" Joey's voice was growing more muffled as he walked. I could hear the clatter of the ER around him.

"Yeah?" I swallowed.

"On your way over, can you stop at Smashburger and pick me up a chocolate milk shake? Not the Oreo one. Just the regular."

We hung up. I breathed in and out, staring at my screen saver. I'd customized it with a photo from our family vacation three years ago in Petoskey. Ashley stood squinting, dressed in a beach tunic glinting with little sequins. Her face had a glassy, feverish look from sunburn and her arms were roped playfully around her brother. At thirteen, Austin's scrawny frame was just beginning to elongate—his smile was a metallic blaze of orthodontia—but big and wide and unabashedly happy.

Austin. I knew better than to call. He and his friends didn't regard "talking" as a function of a telephone at all—in his mind, I supposed, talking on a telephone was as ridiculous as talking into a typewriter—if he even knew what a typewriter was. Good God, I was old—but if I called him, I knew it'd simply go straight to the Black Hole of Calcutta known as his voice mail. Squinting at my screen, I doggedly pecked out: **Hey. R u ok? Be there in 40 min.**

It blurped into the ether, and there was no answer, until I started up the car and my phone pinged with his response:

Awesome! Totally psyched! Miss u!

For a moment, I felt sweetly perplexed until, in a separate bubble, a string of emojis appeared: three phallic ears of corn, three eggplants, a bikini top, several pairs of lips, and a smiley face with hearts bugging out of its eyes.

This was immediately followed by:

NO! IGNORE LAST TXT!!! That wasn't 4 u MOM!!!!

My kid was sexting? Just yesterday he was learning to say "ba-ba" and "cup." Was he inviting a girl over to our house behind my back? Before I could even begin to fathom how to respond to this, another text arrived, this one clearly for me:

Mom r u drunk?

Then another:

Dad sez u r drinking again.

This was followed by a string of emojis: three glasses of wine, three angry red frowny faces, and a giant thumbs-down.

Then he texted: **Y come home? U left so leave. Go 2 AA meeting instead. B w other drunks.**

I sat back heavily in my seat. After a moment, I started to type out: **Am sober & coming home** when my phone vibrated and *whooped* insanely and my daughter's name flashed on the screen. Ashley. Skyping from London. She never, ever initiated calls; always, I'd had to email and nag just to set up a phone date.

"Ash?" I said, pressing the "S" repeatedly, hoping I was connecting. "Hey Ash, can you hear me? Honey, are you all right?"

"I can't believe it, Mom!" her voice shouted so loudly, I nearly dropped the phone. "YOU'RE DRINKING? YOU'RE FUCKING DRINKING AGAIN?"

"What?"

"Austin just WhatsApped me. He says you drunk-dialed Dad? And Dad had to come home from work to keep you from passing out?"

"Wait, no. Hang on. Ashley—"

I could hear her panting and gasping over the phone; she was in tears. "HOW COULD YOU DO THIS, MOM? DID YOU NOT PUT US THROUGH ENOUGH HELL THE FIRST TIME? All those burned meals—and the time the cops came—and my thirteenth birthday THAT YOU TOTALLY RUINED—was all that humiliation JUST not enough for you? Is life so fucking hard that you can't say no to a fucking cocktail?"

For a moment, I went mute; I'd never heard my daughter like this— I was unprepared for her fury, the raw hurt behind it, the explosive profanity. Clearly, it had been stockpiled for a long time. She seemed like an entirely different person.

"Ash," I said.

"How many of those meetings did we have to go to with you, Mom? Clapping and celebrating every time you got a fucking token—"

"Ashley, it's not—"

"And now, today, you beat up Dad? You BEAT him?"

"What?" I felt all the breath knock out of me. "Ashley, who on earth said—"

"Oh, please, Mom! Austin's sixteen now, not six. He's not stupid, you know. He said there's no way someone gets their face bashed up like Dad's was just from 'slipping' in a kitchen. He said Dad had welts all over the place. But, oh, of course, Dad's still sticking to his story, still trying to protect you, still being the great enabler—"

I set down the phone, letting her rant on. Her thirteenth birthday party. The memory bobbed to the surface like a cork: Joey preparing the grill for the make-your-own pizzas. Our yard stippled with light. Ashley's new clique of pretty seventh-grade friends sipping pink lemonade from plastic martini glasses.

Carrying out the tray of pizza toppings, I stumble on the decking. Circles of pepperoni and bacon bits and flecks of mushrooms turn to confetti. As I mix myself another vodka-and-lemonade in the kitchen, I write "Happy Bithday" on the red velvet cake by accident, scrambling to disguise it with candles.

Kelsey, the most popular girl in Ashley's class, announces they're giving her a group gift. All the girls crowd around, bouncing as Ashley opens the box, pushes back the tissue paper. "Oh my God," she starts to shriek. "Oh my God! Is this—?"

The other girls start squealing, clutching one another, jumping up and down in unison like teammates, exploding with glee: "It's Juicy Couture! It's Juicy Couture!"

"We all saved up! We've been saving up for months! Megan was even babysitting!"

"You guys! You guys!" Ashley cries tearily, hugging an armful of hot-pink velour. She has been campaigning for Juicy Couture from Joey and me all year. "Mom, look!" she shouts, dashing into the kitchen. "They got me an entire outfit!" She holds up a fuzzy hooded sweatshirt and matching pair of lurid pink sweatpants. Across the butt, written in big gold block letters, is the word JUICY. "Isn't this awesome? All the celebrities wear this. Paris Hilton. Britney Spears. J. Lo. Madonna. It costs, like, $300!"

"More! $359!" Kelsey announces proudly. "But my mom found it on sale online for $329 and we all chipped in!" In a barrage of overlapping stories, each girl details her role in the secret operation; it sounds positively military.

A cloud comes over me. Joey and I are fending off foreclosure. "You paid $329 for a *tracksuit*?" I spit.

Ashley's smile freezes. "Mom, it's not a tracksuit. It's Juicy Couture. For *real*. See?" She turns down the waistband.

I feel myself sway slightly, the kitchen starts to bifurcate. "Well," I say. "Who needs a label inside, when you've got the name plastered across your ass like a billboard? 'Juicy.' What's that supposed to mean exactly? You're a fresh piece of meat? An underage hooker?"

"Mom, please?" Ashley presses my hand to the fabric. "See? Just feel how soft that is?"

The pink velour is liquidy, silk-like. "Good God," I murmur. Then I start to laugh, really laugh. "You know what they feel like? You remember that stuffed pig you used to have when you were about four? They're made of exactly the same fabric! Oh my God," I say, laughing. "It's Pinky Pig! They're dressing you up like Pinky Pig!"

A drowning look passes over my daughter's face. Her friends shift about uncomfortably, stare at the floor. I sense I've gotten off track somehow. "Oh, c'mon, you guys, I'm kidding!" I say garrulously. "It's a joke, okay? I mean, okay, so it's three hundred bucks for a tracksuit—for a thirteen-year-old—during a recession. That's an absolute riot! God, what does it take to get a laugh around here?" Snatching up the pink hoodie, I begin animating it like a puppet, poking it in their faces. "Hi, everybody, I'm Pinky Pig, I'm Juicy Couture!" I say in falsetto. "Oink, oink! Here, piggy, piggy, piggy!"

I stared up at the roof of my Subaru, my eyes growing wet. The things I wished I could go back and undo. Ashley was nineteen now—legally an adult—living half a world away in one of the more sophisticated cities in the world. I could tell her the truth about Joey. But I knew better. I sensed it in my gut: If one of Ashley's own multiracial, bisexual friends dressed up as a Sissy Maid, my daughter might think it was "the coolest thing ever." But not if it was her own father. Teenagers were like that—hell, all of us were. My daughter loved her daddy so. If I told her, there'd be no rolling it back. I just could not do that to her. I had ruined enough things already.

"This fight with your father and me, Ash," I said carefully. "It's complicated."

"What's so fucking complicated, Mom? You're white and privileged and First World— You don't, like, even have a real job."

"Excuse me?"

"I mean, it's not like you're full-time, or a wage-slave coal miner or a seamstress in some Bangladeshi sweatshop—"

"Well, here's a news flash," I said more angrily than I'd intended. "Neither are you."

"You go around selling this overpriced crap—and then getting drunk—"

"Oh really? How the hell do you know?" I shouted. "When was the last time you ever worked or cooked, you spoiled little brat!"

Who hung up first, I could not tell. That was the thing with cell phones—they just cut off suddenly—there was no satisfying, definitive click.

For a few minutes I sat there shaking, fighting the urge to call back. I felt whiplashed, nauseated all over again. Kids: They knew exactly where to plunge in the knife, how to twist it precisely between your ribs to gut you with the most damage.

The fastest route home would've been to go back the way I'd come, north on I-75. But in my upset, I made the wrong turn and ended up heading south instead, which immediately snared me in the traffic for the Ambassador Bridge that arced across the river to Windsor, Ontario—Canada—just minutes away. I had my passport in my purse—I carried it with me as a matter of routine now, because I sometimes did demos over in Windsor—and since 9/11 you suddenly needed ID to cross the border—sure, okay, you could get a special license now, so you wouldn't need a passport, but that meant dealing with the Department of Motor Vehicles, which I was convinced was the sole reason people became anarchists and libertarians and antigovernment survivalists in the first place—it wasn't air-pollution regulations or the finer points of the First Amendment in the end—it was having to sit in the jaundiced light of the goddamn DMV for hours just to get your tags renewed while some soporific clerk sat behind a NEXT WINDOW PLEASE sign drinking a Big Gulp—so I always had my passport with me—though it was stampless and nearing expiration. And it occurred to me—just for an instant—that instead of driving west, I could just slip across the bridge and disappear entirely into another country.

No sooner did I think this, of course, then I knew I wasn't going anywhere. My husband was in the emergency room now with multiple facial abrasions and a splint on his nose, no doubt. My horny, surly, wounded child—whether he realized it or not—was in need of reassurance. And Ashley? Somehow, I would have to fix this. I was due home.

Yet, oddly, heading south, after I crossed the Rouge River into Lincoln

Park, I missed the exit for Outer Drive, which would have taken me west, then passed the next turnoff, for Route 39. Without realizing it, I'd plugged my phone into the sound system, and the Cure's "In Between Days" thumped deafeningly through the car.

Why was I the only bad guy here? I wondered. *M-o-o-o-m*, the drunk. *M-o-o-om*, the enforcer. How had I ended up the sole villain in all of this?

How could Joey say I'd relapsed so casually?

Sure, I made jokes about AA, rolled my eyes. But that sobriety token on my key ring was living proof of each excruciating hour I'd actually managed to master a craving that ravaged me. Sometimes I fingered the warm metal disc like a talisman. All those days I'd counted, surrendering to a Higher Power I doubted wholesale, reciting a Serenity Prayer that brought me no real serenity—just a sense of futility, really—faking it until I made it, as they said in the parlance. All those nightmarish Koczynski family wakes and Thanksgivings and Christmases I'd managed to endure sober—calling the potato pancakes *placki* instead of *latkes*, the cabbage rolls *golumpki* instead of *holishkes*—allowing their Polish-Catholic heritage to prevail over my Jewish one—sipping Diet Vernor's while my sisters-in-law waylaid me: how I'd smiled and nodded and pretended I was listening to their chitchat when all I could really focus on were the lurid glasses of red Zinfandel they balanced so casually in their manicured hands? At night sometimes, I actually dreamed about alcohol the way other people dreamed about sex.

A sign flashed past, welcoming me to Ohio. I'd have to turn around near Toledo. On my iTunes now: the Clash. "Straight to Hell." "Oh my God. You know what? You know what else?" I said aloud to the empty car, pounding my fist against the steering wheel. "Not only don't I drink, I don't even eat, either!" Once, when Ashley was eleven, we were walking across a parking lot in the sunshine. "Mom?" she said fretfully, motioning to the dark silhouettes of the two of us elongating on the pavement. "Do you think my shadow looks fat?" And instead of saying to her, as I should have: "Ashley. Don't be ridiculous. You're perfect and beautiful," I had stopped in my tracks and replied, "Well, Ash, if you're so worried about your weight, don't eat so much. You're not a little kid anymore. You can't just put anything you want in your mouth without consequences." (Good God, was it a surprise she'd become a vegan? She ate nothing now, my beautiful daughter. Only coffee with soy milk, raw root vegetables, joyless mashed beans. I felt a wave of shame.) I couldn't remember the last time since my own middle school days when I myself had eaten a second slice of pizza. Every single thing I put into my mouth, I knew the calorie and carbohydrate count of, and I kept a running tally in my head like a meter. This was simply a reflex: The numbers had been drummed into me like music.

But Joey? I thought with sudden fury, leaning on the accelerator. Mr. President of Phi Delta. Mr. Dentist. Where was his sense of self-restraint? *He* clearly felt no compunction about indulging his most prurient desires *in our own home*. His pornography, his personal dominatrix! Hell, he had a whole store—a whole community—entire industries, in fact—dedicated to helping him "be his authentic self" and fulfill his darkest, most primal appetites. He had a friend he could confide in—who'd never breathe a word—because their business practice and their fates were intertwined—and probably because, as men, everything for them seemed to be excusable under the banner of "HORNINESS." How goddamned lucky for him! For a moment, I wished I'd had a fish spatula in my hand and he was close by so I could beat him bloody all over again.

I'd had an Arjul once, I thought miserably, defiantly—a friend I'd lived with, worked with, trusted completely with my deepest, most shameful secrets, whom I felt I could be my most "authentic" self with. My housemate at college, Brenda.

I thought of who I had been back then, when Brenda and I used to drink cheap jug wine and make ramen noodles for dinner, dancing around to Prince and Tone Loc in our communal kitchen—pulling all-nighters together—writing papers for *The Modern American Novel*—me helping her run lines for her part in a campus production of *Antigone*—

her coming to my gigs—all the confessions and parsing about boys and sex and mothers and fear—our late-night tarot card readings and political debates. I'd had my guitar and my pink hair then—all that ambition—the songs and poetry pouring out of me sometimes—I was a rock chick—I was going to be famous!

And we'd remained best friends for years after, until? Well, I wasn't sure, exactly. Her career went white-hot, my time got taken up by the kids—blah, blah—until now? Suddenly, I was about to turn forty-five in a Subaru. Look at me. It was pathetic.

By accident, I turned onto the highway running east of Toledo instead of I-75 going northwest. A horn blared—I'd almost strayed into the lane of an oncoming tractor trailer—I jerked the wheel to the right. The highway rose slightly, the land splayed beneath it at a remove. I was fully beyond the border in Ohio now. The sun was setting. The edge of the highway was beaded with bluish-silver lights against a purpling sky. Joan Jett had come on rotation on my iTunes, then Patti Smith, Echo and the Bunnymen, Prince, early U2. I became aware now of a throbbing by my armpits, crescents of pain beneath my breasts. Only then did I realize that underneath the T-shirt I'd thrown on, I was still wearing the corset. I had been encased in it for hours now. My waist felt garroted. My lungs felt compressed. I needed to take it off *immediately*.

At the first exit, I pulled over onto a darkened roadside, undid my seat belt, removed my T-shirt. I looked down at the shiny pleather contraption restraining me. How the hell was I supposed to get this off by myself? Groping around my back, I was able to unlace the stays halfway, but the intricate hook-and-eye closures between my shoulders were impossible. After a great struggle, I tried desperately to tug it around, so that the back of the corset was in my front, but after all those hours encased in the airless plastic, my flesh had grown sweaty and swollen, and the garment stuck to me like adhesive. Yanking and grunting, I managed to move it only an inch or so before giving up. The underwires and boning were now misaligned. While the places they'd been gouging began pulsating with relief, new points on my breasts and my ribs were getting jabbed. It felt as if my skin might puncture. I realized, too, that I still had on the fishnet stockings—and the miniskirt—which had crept up into my lap like a rubber band, the hem of it squeezing my thighs, cradling my belly, revealing just the smallest little mound of my underwear. Everything from my neck down bulged and hurt and throbbed.

Given the traffic, I was at least two hours from home now. I looked deranged. There was no way I could make it back to Michigan in this state. Where could I possibly go for help dressed like this? Then a single word came to me. It came to me like a religious epiphany.

Walmart.

Quickly, I googled it. Praise be to God, the nearest one was just twelve minutes off the Ohio Turnpike in Fremont. Ashley was not a fan of Walmart—she often berated me for getting her prescriptions filled there because of its horrible labor practices—and a few years before, the company had done knockoffs of several Privileged Kitchen products. But at this moment, Walmart shone to me like the City on the Hill. Walmart was my salvation.

By the time I arrived, I was nearly incandescent with pain. Just limping across the parking lot in my stockings and flip-flops proved a challenge, as my toes had broken through the netting, which now sawed into the tender flesh between them every time I took a step—and my skirt, which bound my legs as tightly as a tourniquet at this point, kept riding up. The only mercy was that my VIRGINIA IS FOR LOVERS T-shirt was so oversized—it had actually been Joey's—that it fell to mid-thigh. By the time I reached the automatic glass doors, however, I'd given up on the flip-flops entirely. I was now essentially barefoot and appeared to be shopping in nothing but a giant souvenir T-shirt. Even for Walmart, it must have been appalling, because the other shoppers quickly jerked aside with their carts as I approached.

I grabbed a pair of yoga pants off a rack, a shirt, a bra, a pair of granny underwear. A sweatshirt with some daisies on it off a SALE rack. I found a cheap pair of canvas ballerina flats in the shoe department. Though Joey would disapprove, I used my teeth to break the plastic wire that conjoined them and slipped them on right there in the aisle. Padding as quickly as I could through the housewares section, I found a pair of industrial scissors that looked like they would do the job. I paid for the lot with a credit card, then tromped quickly into the ladies' room. With my now-shaking hands, I ripped the scissors free of their packaging, then sliced into the corset, first into the peplum fanning around my waist, then carefully through the thick plastic encasing my swollen, throbbing torso. When my flesh was finally unleashed, it was like emerging from a chrysalis. My breasts and lungs seemed to spread out like wings, expanding in the air. I groaned with relief. Then I hurriedly went about hacking off the rubbery miniskirt, then the waistband of my fishnets, stuck to my belly with sweat. In the narrow metal stall, impeded by the urine-sprinkled toilet and the metal receptacle overflowing with discarded feminine hygiene products, it was hard to maneuver. But I finally managed to peel everything off, layer by layer, and for a moment, I stood completely naked, my bare feet tiptoed atop the ballerina flats—the only thing between me and the grimy tiled floor—letting my flesh cool and breathe and fill its own space. The boning and elastic had left deep, angry red welts all over me—I could see the imprint of the entire corset on my torso, in fact, as if a surgeon had drawn on me with red marker, mapping out incisions—and as I tried to shake out my limbs they began to tingle with that pain that comes when your foot's fallen asleep. It was an intense, concentrated ache, followed by a flood of relief—the relief that, by its very nature, read as pleasure.

As I stood there in the bathroom at Walmart—listening to other shoppers tromping in and out, kids whining, plastic bags ruffling, jeans unzipping, the hiss of pee hitting the bowl, stalls slonking open and closed—I finally began to understand S&M. This tide of endorphins after so much accumulating pain: *This* was the endgame, the great erotic payoff.

But so fucking what? Why should I have had to suffer like this at all in the first place? It was just way too much work.

The hacked-up fabric looked incriminating somehow, so I squirreled it away in my shopping bag. I was loath to reharness myself in any sort of bra or underpants, but one can stand naked and shivering in a bathroom stall at Walmart for only so long. Snipping the tags off my purchases, I put on my cheap, new chemical-smelling clothes and headed back into the blaze of the store.

By now, my whole body was sore and I had a splitting headache. In the pharmacy section, I got a jumbo bottle of ibuprofen, then some toothpaste for the downstairs bathroom because we were out, and then— because I was there anyway—I got in line for the kids' prescriptions I was supposed to have gotten filled that morning—the Adderall Austin took for his ADD was running low; Ashley needed a three-month supply of her antianxiety medication, Ativan, shipped to her soon in London— and I stood there, still wanting a drink and wondering why Walmart didn't have open bars in their mega-stores along with everything else— tell me there wasn't a parent in America who didn't crave a cocktail while shopping there with their kids—if they'd just let you wander the aisles with to-go cups full of margaritas or open bottles of Budweiser— the corporation could pay its workers twenty bucks an hour and still make a killing.

As I waited there for my order, all these families around me were getting on with their lives, cattling past me with shopping carts, buying jumbo bottles of shampoo and laxatives and cheap Halloween decorations, one little girl begging her mother *OhpleaseohpleasepleaseIpromise*, clutching a gallon-sized carton of malted-milk balls—all around me, people were shopping and buying and paying and eating—in a carnival of consumption, everyone trying to get something nice, something a little better, for themselves—and then the pharmacist handed me the clear, fist-sized, burnt-orange vials stapled tidily into the white pharmacy bags—and I could feel my phone vibrating in the zippered pocket inside my purse, and the idea of getting into my Subaru and turning around and walking back into that blood-spattered kitchen suddenly felt repellent and physically impossible to me—and I thought: Everyone thinks I'm on a bender anyway. So get your own damn milk shake, Joey.

Part Two

Chapter 5

WHEN MY BROTHER, TOBY, and I were little, the sodium lamp over our garage filtered into our window at night, casting an eerie salmonish glow over our bedroom. We liked to convince each other it was oozing and bacterial. Squealing with fear, we'd scramble to barricade ourselves against it. Toby would pull our beanbag chair on top of him; I'd tuck my covers in so tightly around me I was practically mummified. Beneath them, I could see only blackness, an absolute, infinite void. It was, I imagined, what floating in outer space must be like—or death. My whole body would tingle with the exquisite terror of it.

Now, as I barreled blindly through the Rust Belt, the sensation I felt was not dissimilar. Tract houses and then commercial strips flashed by like comets—Dunkin'DonutsShellDenny'sPetco7-ElevenHomeDepot— ribboning together in a smear of color and light that quickly slid backward into an obliterating darkness. I was there, but not, exhilarated by my own audacity, hurtling in my rocket full of gasoline and music.

However—I don't know if it was the Diet Cokes or the Adderall (I'd taken just one pill, *one pill only*, as a precaution, so I'd be sure to stay alert)—I kept needing to pee. In Norwalk, Ohio, I found myself having to swerve over and stand outside in a silty wind behind a gas station, fumbling with a restroom key that the owner had chained to a block of wood to keep people from stealing it. What seemed like only minutes later, I was sixty miles farther east inside a Starbucks, bouncing from foot to foot behind a beleaguered mother weighed down with a toddler and a baby and a giant quilted diaper bag—both of us trying to ignore the suggestive, watery hiss of the espresso machine—hoping to God that the teenager who'd gone into the one toilet stall with her rhinestone phone and makeup bag would hurry the fuck up already. In my adrenalized fugue, I urinated my way through Medina, Akron, Youngstown, Ellwood City: a bitch marking her territory, I supposed.

All the while, my phone vibrated insanely and ignored in my handbag. I should have shut it off all together, but what can I say? I found myself growing giddy with Joey's frantic attempts to contact me, the mounting "missed call" alerts, the urgent bubbles of text. He'd wanted me to punish him for being a Bad Sissy Maid?

Well, now. Here you go, pal.

Yet somewhere near Pittsburgh, in a town called Cranberry—how the hell I got there, I don't quite even know—my exhilaration started to curdle. *Good God. What was I doing?* My hands grew icy on the steering wheel; all I wanted to do was wriggle out of my skin. *You know what will take the edge off,* I started to think. I slammed the accelerator. *C'mon. Certainly, you can handle it by now. It's not like five years ago.* Some walnut-sized part of my brain knew that now was exactly the right time to pull over and google the nearest AA. But the serpent within me kept hissing louder and louder: *Hey, you deserve this.*

On the road up ahead, an Applebee's materialized. I could just go in and order a cheeseburger, I decided. A cheeseburger and, okay, a single drink. As of midnight, after all, I was turning forty-five. Certainly, a forty-five-year-old woman was entitled to *a single fucking drink* on her birthday. Certainly, a forty-five-year-old woman could handle that much.

As the homey, red neon apple came into full view, though, it occurred to me that if I went into an Applebee's, I'd be surrounded by the exact same decor and the exact same menu that I'd been surrounded by eight hours earlier, three hundred miles away, at lunchtime. Such generic, metastasizing cheeriness suddenly struck me as all wrong, even sinister. I began to worry that if I went inside Applebee's, I would find myself caught up in some bizarre time loop, where I'd step through the glass door and find myself with Joey back in Michigan at the other Applebee's, exactly where we'd left off earlier, doomed to relive the same horrid chain of events over and over.

Turning blindly, I found myself bouncing down a narrow strip of asphalt. Only veiny bushes were visible in the yellowish cast of my headlights. A few low branches clawed and scraped at the sides of my Subaru. It was the kind of rural road where cars always broke down in horror movies—I half expected a man with a meat-hook to emerge—or, the more I thought about it, some mutant life-form from Applebee's— but after a few minutes, it merged with another access road and I came upon a town. For a moment, I felt a bolt of relief. There on my right, on the side of the road, illuminated ghoulishly, was a sign.

JOHNNY'S.

Beyond it, up a little rise, was a low, shingled building with two neon logos sputtering in blackened windows. It sat there awaiting me. Like a reward.

The planked floors inside crunched sandily with sawdust; Bachman-Turner Overdrive's "You Ain't Seen Nothin' Yet" played on an antique jukebox at a volume high enough to cause arrhythmia. A few steps down past the pool tables (*kwok kwok!*), a large, horseshoe-shaped bar rose up from the center of the room like a shrine, the illuminated shelves behind it displaying bottles as if they were artifacts, glowing amber, citrine, topaz in the light.

The air had that wonderful bar perfume of wood varnish and hops. Competing televisions blazed from the paneled walls around me: replays of a Pirates game was being televised at full volume, Fox News on another screen, a video of Nicki Minaj and Beyoncé feeding each other french fries and twerking in a kiddie pool. On CNN, Donald Trump and Ted Cruz were yelling at each other above a digitized swoosh reading "America Decides," before the camera cut to a clip of a bombed-out high-rise in Syria. As nonchalantly as I could, I sauntered down the steps, my eyes fixed on the screens. I pretended not to notice I was making a beeline for the bar. It was like visiting the Pink Pussycat boutique as a teenager again. *You just happen to be here*, I told myself. *You're just taking a break from sitting in your Subaru so you don't get that deep vein thrombosis they warn you about in airplanes.* But my dirty little heart was kicking like a horse. *Just one. Just one.* I could feel it already: I was nothing but a parasympathetic nervous system now. *I Want. I Need. Fill Me.* I could already feel the satiating heft of beveled glass, the pillowy crescent of lime giving way between my thumb and forefinger.

"Sorry, ma'am. We've got a private party here tonight." A man in a flannel shirt stepped in front of me and flicked his thumb at two velvet ropes cordoning off the bar. "It's table service only now." He tilted his chin toward the jukebox. A young waitress slumped against it, absorbed by something on her phone. When he summoned her, she looked startled to find herself in the middle of a roadhouse.

"Just one?" She barely glanced at me. Pivoting sullenly, she scanned the dining room. "The thing is, it's Happy Hour, so, like, there's not really any places free right now?"

"You've got nothing?" I said. "Look. Please. I've been driving for hours. I just—dammit! This shouldn't be rocket science!" I glanced around, embarrassed by my own shrillness. I was certain the whole bar was turning to stare at me. I forced a laugh. "I mean, what do I need to get a drink around here?" I tried to sound playful. "A special user name? A password?"

"Well?" Knitting her fingers together, the waitress squinted back toward the kitchen. "Are you, like, okay, just having wings?"

"Wings?" Good God: That was exactly what I needed. Great wings of violet and peacock green and gold. To soar above all disappointment and pain.

Then I realized: No. She meant *chicken*.

"Because if you want to join the table over there," she said, "the deal is, tonight, for twenty bucks, you get all-you-can-eat hot wings and a 'bottomless' Bud. That's, like, five bucks more than normal? But the extra money goes to Kiwanis? For, like, these kids with hiatal hernias or something?"

She motioned to a banner hung above a banquet table by the blacked-out windows: "WINGIN' WITH KIWANIS 4 KIDS." It was already crowded, I could see; the table was piled with discarded red plastic-mesh baskets and half-empty pitchers.

Hot wings were one of Joey's favorite foods—not mine. In fact, whenever possible, I avoided them. They were oily and messy, impossible to eat with any sort of élan. Plus, because they were chicken, you might think maybe they weren't fattening, but they were! One serving of six had 616 calories—not even counting the blue cheese dressing (another 230)!

And beer? Why would anyone order Budweiser when you could have tequila? Or a martini?

But the room was starting to constrict around me—and the prospect of walking back up the steps and climbing into my Subaru felt suddenly unbearable—my heart was throbbing with longing—and once my eyes fixated upon the foam-streaked pitchers dotted up and down the long table, well, it was done. Already I could feel the mug sweating in my hand.

The Kiwanis diners had large paper napkins tucked into their shirt collars like bibs. They were laughing with their mouths wide open, tossing wetwipes at one another, slapping each other's backs with exaggerated bonhomie. They were in the early stages of inebriation—the best stages, flush with goodwill, when everybody's still your friend, even the strangers. I'd forgotten how much I missed this camaraderie. Drinking together was like being in a band.

There was only one empty chair left, next to a biker with a gray ponytail and a walrussy mustache. He was wearing a red baseball cap with WING MAN embroidered across it in white. "Hey. Welcome to team Wing Nuts," he said as I wedged myself in. "Glad to have you aboard. We're already one man down. Let's get you set up."

An older, cadaverous woman passed me a stack of napkins and a fresh plate. She had hair dyed the color of paprika and a neck-load of beaded necklaces. "Hi. I'm Leanne," she said in a rusty voice. She nodded at the biker. "This here is Lenny."

"I'm Brenda." I don't know why I said this—it was just the first name that popped into my head. I glanced around for a waitress.

"So," Lenny said, "are you a speed freak or a fire eater?"

"Excuse me?"

"Marty over there, man, our 'Wing Leader'? He ate forty wings in under three minutes this year at the annual festival in Buffalo. Tina?" He motioned toward an Asian girl in a Ball State sweatshirt seated to my left. "Almost the same. They're aiming to be inducted into the 'Chicken Wing Hall of Flame.' Now me? I'm a 'fire eater' myself. For me, it's all about the burn, man."

He leaned in and gazed at me with the intensity of a war veteran. "You ever eat wings made with the sauce from the Trinidad Moruga scorpion pepper? Or ghost peppers?" He shook his head, drained his beer. "Hottest things on the planet, man. They'll fuckin' kill you—pardon my language. But I find it's a very spiritual experience, you know? The pain is very purifying."

Good God: Why is everyone so besotted with self-inflicted pain? I wondered. Was this now a *thing*? I scanned the dining room again. "Do you see the waitress?" I said. "I don't have a mug."

"Oh, honey, you don't want to start with the beer," the redhead said. "It'll fill you up too quickly. You won't be able to stomach more than four or five wings. We always save it until after."

"Sorry?" I said over the din.

She raised one penciled-in eyebrow and grinned. "You know this is a wing-eating contest, right?" When she saw my face, she patted my arm and chuckled. "Oh, wow. A first-timer. Don't worry, honey. We gotcha covered. It's all in good fun. Just eat what you can, fast or slow. It's a team effort. They count up how much we eat *as a group*. Otherwise, those professional speed-eaters over there, heck, they'd win every time. Here." She passed me a cruet bowl of flecked whitish dressing and a fistful of celery sticks. "Just remember: Blue cheese is your friend."

"Oh, wait. No, listen. I'm sorry." But as I pushed my chair back, it got caught in the legs of the others.

"Everybody ready?" Marty shouted, picking up his phone. "Now, for round three, we've kicked it up a notch. It's 'Hell's Kitchen' level now, folks. For those of you just joining us, over here, in the yellow T-shirts, all the way from Akron, is the team Wings and a Prayer. Next to them, from Bakerstown, winners of round one, is the team Hot Lips. Beside them, going for their second win of the night, I bring to you the Kiwanis chapter president himself, Sammy Ballon, and his lean, mean, chicken-eating machine, Lords of the Wings!"

Other customers were woo-hooing and whistling and climbing up on their chairs, aiming their phones in our direction. I felt that same cold panic I used to feel in high school when a test that I hadn't studied for landed on my desk. I just wanted a beer, dammit. But as team Wing Nuts was announced, Leanne grabbed my hand and shook it in the air above our heads as if we were a pair of boxers entering a ring together, and then a basket heaped with greasy, gleaming wings appeared before me. "Don't worry," the biker said and winked at me. "You got this. You're good."

"Okay, folks," Marty called down the table. "I'm setting my timer."

"Excuse me," I called after the harried waitress doling out more chicken. "My beer? Or a shot of Cuervo? I'll pay extra."

Tina, from Wings and a Prayer, and her teammate Bruno were both Instagramming pictures of their chicken. "I hashtagged it 'mouthkiller,' 'toohottohandle,' and 'wingwoman,'" Tina announced. "Dude," Bruno said to his phone. "Already, mine's got, like, forty likes?"

"All right, folks," Marty said, holding up his phone and squinting at it, trying to approximate the button on the touch screen with his thumb. "On your mark ... get set ... Go!"

Suddenly, heads bent down all around me and moved back and forth over the chicken drumlets like the chassis of old typewriters and dot-matrix printers. They chewed and swallowed, chewed and swallowed, tossing the stripped bones into the baskets with robotic speed, not once looking up, each one singularly absorbed, their puffy, sauce-slicked fingers delicately pinching the ends of the lurid wings as they sucked and devoured and tore at the flesh. "Go, go, go!" a few onlookers shouted, crowding closer.

In the plastic basket, the chicken wings awaited me, deep-fried and radioactive in their tangerine-colored gloss. They were all that stood between me and a mug of Budweiser. "More Than a Feeling" was now blaring over the jukebox; the television mounted above us was running an extended commercial for diabetes medication. The air around the table was pungent with the fungal, slightly vaginal smell of blue cheese. How the hell had I gotten myself into this?

Suddenly, I thought of Joey with an odd pang. He'd have loved all-you-can-eat hot wings—I could see him chowing down with his old fraternity brothers, licking his fingers sequentially, covered in napkins and sauce. Then I thought, *Fuck him*. Unlike my husband, I'd spent an entire lifetime suppressing my appetites. Well, that would end right here, right now.

Tonight, I would be the one to gorge myself on chicken and drink pitcher after pitcher of Budweiser. I would revel in gluttony and abandon until I was obese and shit-faced and incoherent and sated. My debauchery, it would be savage. It would be epic. Better yet, it would be for charity. I wouldn't be surrendering my sobriety so much as *donating* it—for all the poor kids of western Pennsylvania with hiatal hernias.

Seizing a drumlet, I leaned in and bit down wolfishly. Almost instantly, my lips ignited. It was as if someone had lit a ribbon of gunpowder along my tongue and down my throat, directly into the pit of my stomach. I nearly choked from the assault of it. Dropping the chicken, I blew rapidly from my mouth the way I had in childbirth. Fanning the air before me, I stabbed a celery stick into the blue cheese dressing and smeared it over my lips like balm. "Oh, God," I gasped, though it came out sounding like "Aw Gaw."

The audience now was cheering: "Eat, eat, eat! Faster, faster!"

I willed myself to take another bite. Beneath its coating of heat, the chicken was infused with a sort of horrible, tangy deliciousness, oily and succulent, the tender meat near the bone offering a fleeting reprieve from the incinerating chili. I pulled at the wings delicately with my teeth, trying to avoid touching the sauce directly to my tongue. *Beer, beer, beer*, I thought like a mantra. *Just keep chewing, just keep swallowing.* The physical distress I began experiencing was dizzying: sweating, tearing, sniffling, all spigots opening, a sort of profound, intense drainage. The biker was wrong; The pain did not feel spiritual, except for the fact that I soon felt myself praying: *Dear God, let this be over.*

"Whoa! Check it out! Look at that Asian girl chow down! Totally sick!" I heard a guy shout. "Yo, are you getting this?"

The rest of the competitors bent over the table as if it were a trough, emitting suction sounds punctuated by the clinking of discarded, gnawed bones hitting the plates. There seemed to be endless heaps of chicken, of fibrous, graying celery. I felt a stab of nausea. My lips felt as if they'd been split open and pumped full of Novocain.

Marty raised his gory hands high in the air. "Time! Time! That's it!" he shouted as his phone began bleating. "Hands up!"

It was over. There was a tide of applause. Around me, people were slumping back, fanning themselves, saying, "Whew, I'm sweating now!" and tearing open lemony wetwipes and twisting them over their hands. Marty was moving from place to place, tallying up the number of bones on each plate. My mouth, however, was still full of flesh from the last wing. I couldn't quite bring myself to finish chewing or swallow it. I tried to keep the meat tucked in my mouth until Marty passed, then looked around frantically for a napkin to spit in.

"By only three wings, the winner of this round is team Wings and a Prayer," Marty announced.

"We won!" Tina shouted. Pointing to her plate, she stood up and did a little wiggle dance with her fists pumping the air.

She slid her phone toward the biker awkwardly with her elbow. "Lenny, do the honors? I can't do a selfie with my hands sticky. Get me with—here—" She picked up her plate of bones and tilted it toward the camera while flashing a thumbs-up. "Make sure they can see how many. Hashtag 'Speed Queen'! Hashtag 'We kicked Sammy Ballon's ass'! Hashtag, 'Winners,' people!"

At last, the waitress banged a mug of beer down in front of me, an entire, shimmering vortex.

"Aw, don't worry. We'll get 'em in the next round," Leanne whispered to me. "The hotter the wings get, the more Lenny eats. He's our secret weapon. Plus, you'll see. You'll start to build up a tolerance to the heat. In the next round, your endorphins'll kick in. I tell you. These things are addictive."

I nodded robotically, my eyes fixed on my beer. As I grabbed it, though, my hands were so slick with grease, the mug slid into my lap. The contents spilled down the front of my sweatshirt and splashed across the crotch of my pants, down my leg, and onto the floor.

"Aw, fuff," I cried.

It took everything I had not to reach across the table and grab someone else's mug. In fact, I was just about to lunge for Tina's when she swiped it up and held it aloft like the torch on the Statue of Liberty. Someone had placed one of the red plastic baskets on her head like a crown. "All hail the Wing Woman! Can you believe it?" she squealed. "Wewonwewonwewon!

"Get another picture?" she pleaded to Bruno. "For my mom?"

I stared at the beaming winners. Except for raising our two children, getting sober was the biggest achievement of my adult life. In fact, it occurred to me suddenly, except for our kids, it was my only achievement, really. Two dozen copies of Toxic Shock Syndrome's unplayed demo sat in a dusty carton in our basement beside a tumbleweed of Christmas lights. Somewhere in my closet was a laminate file full of old xeroxed flyers for our gigs, clippings from the now-defunct *Ann Arbor News*, as fragile as eggshell, profiling us for their ARTS section. A few black-and-white contact sheets for the "official" band photos taken on a rooftop in Ypsilanti—me closest to the camera, in a ripped tube dress and muddy eyeliner—which my kids, years ago, had studied like an artifact, hooting, "I can't believe that's Mommy!"

What else did I have to be proud of? Joey's and my now-failed real estate ventures? My earlier stint, just after the kids were born, doing women's "colors" at Marshall Field's Department Store? (*Well, Jennifer, you're clearly an autumn. The problem is, you've been dressing like a winter.*) My years spent pounding out chicken breasts with a mallet in the middle of a shopping mall? Cooking meals for women perennially on diets—policing one another, groaning *Ohweshouldn't! Girlswe'rebeingsobad!*—so that my culinary demos often became mere food porn—more voyeurism than eating—with the bulk of what I cooked getting scraped into the trash afterward?

I thought of myself back in Vegas, standing on that stage beside Colleen Lundstedt like some clueless, middle-aged show pony—with that stupid, hopeful smile on my face—so proud to be there in my brand-new pencil skirt I'd worn for the occasion—because I'd actually thought—my God, I'd actually *believed*—that I might finally receive some recognition.

"I'm sorry," I lisped, pushing back my chair with such violence, it nearly fell over. I rubbed my hands on my pants furiously and tossed two $20 bills onto the wreckage. "For the kids of Kiwanis."

Back in the Subaru, hot sauce glistened on my cheeks like blood, my sweatshirt stank of beer, and I looked like I'd wet myself. After mopping up the mess as best I could with some hand sanitizer, I felt around under the backseat for the old can of Febreze I kept in the car for when I transported Mr. Noodles to his doggie shrink. I sprayed it over myself like cologne. The fumes of "Hawaiian Aloha" tropical air freshener didn't mask the beer nearly as much as I'd hoped—rather, it competed with it—and for a moment I thought I might vomit.

Yanking open the glove compartment, I took out the vial of Austin's Adderall and stared at it. Just one more. For clarity. To keep from having an accident. Why, it might even help me understand my son better, to experience what he did chemically. Pills, I knew, were technically as verboten as beer—hugely risky behavior, a giant AA no-no, but I simply couldn't let the perfect be the enemy of the good—especially while night-driving—for the purpose of *fleeing* a bar—besides, didn't desperate times call for desperate measures? Choking down the pill, however, proved more challenging than I'd thought. My throat was scorched; I might not be able to swallow normally for days.

Slowly, finally, I did what I realized I was supposed to have done all along. My sponsor's name was Jenny. Jenny Jaroluch, I had to remind myself as I scrolled through my contacts. I actually hadn't spoken to her since Ashley's high school graduation, it had been that long.

After about twelve rings, an automated sequence of electronic notes came on informing me that the number I had dialed was no longer in service. Oddly, I felt only relief. In fact, to my great shame, I found myself hoping the number was no longer in service because Jenny Jaroluch herself had started drinking again and was sitting in a parked car somewhere, even more deranged than I was.

I was a horrible person. And pathetic. Look at me: My one great act of rebellion had consisted of eating hot wings for three minutes, then wiping my hands on a pair of stretchy pants from Walmart. Who was I anymore?

Yet, I felt ravenous. The monster of my own bottomless appetites had been poked awake with a stick; if I didn't do *something*, I was certain I would implode.

With a *bing!* of the ignition, I tore down the road again, hunting, hunting. *I want. I need. Fill me.* In a town called Monroeville, I zoomed past a giant discount designer shoe outlet—then made an illegal U-turn.

Women and our damn shoes—it's such a cliché—but the warehouse was warm and bright with its insipid, Cinderella promises, and I just didn't know what else to do with myself. Hurrying down the grim, industrial aisles, I pulled out boxes marked "6," stuffing my feet into silver high-top tennis shoes and ankle boots studded with biker buckles and kittenish heels. It was the end of the day. The outlet looked ravaged, picked over: I found myself actually stopping along the way to put all the random shoes people had discarded back into their proper boxes—

but finally, I made it to the checkout. Somehow, I'd acquired nine pairs of new shoes (none more than $19.95! Buy 2 get 1 free! What a deal!), and as the cashier rang them all up, I actually felt suffused with pride, as if I'd achieved something enormous. (Wait 'til they saw these at my book club—especially the jeweled kitten heels—and heard how little I'd paid!)

But no sooner was I outside in the parking lot again with my purchases than I was overcome with a nearly debilitating sadness. The high heels: They reminded me of Joey. I didn't even bother opening the trunk; I just threw everything in the backseat.

I still felt seized with hunger, by great internal claws of craving. The shopping malls were now on the verge of closing for the night—I could see security guards rolling the metal lace down over the glass doors. There was a Sporting Goods Outlet—and Austin did need new shin guards for hockey—but then, at the end of a strip, like a beacon, I saw the sign GUITAR CENTER. The only brand-new musical instrument I'd ever purchased had been that Traveler Guitar—and not for me, but for my son.

"Ma'am, we're closing in twenty minutes," a goitered manager informed me.

"Nuh-nuh-nuh, please!" I raced past in my papery ballet slippers. "I'll be quick."

Now in the mirrored showroom, hundreds of shiny new guitars sat propped in their stands like curvaceous, up-ended lollipops, butter and rosewood and onyx and royal blue—acoustics and electrics, double-cutaways, basses, guitars with chrome fingerboards and wireless capabilities. I wanted something insanely amped-up, a top-of-the-line, kick-ass electric—blazing red, shining like maraschino syrup—with effects pedals that would make the sound howl and distort and rip flesh from bone.

But beneath a Day-Glo 20% OFF sign was a basic Rogue Dreadnought acoustic. Cheap, lightweight. Something I could afford (sort of) that would go easy on my unpracticed fingertips. I grabbed a case as well, plus a strap, a couple of colored picks, and then, at the cash register, I saw a bunch of clearance "vintage" sweatshirts with band names on them. Since my hoodie from Walmart was now soaked with beer, I grabbed the only one they had left in my size. It wasn't until I was back in the Subaru that I saw it read ANTHRAX. An awful band—just yelling without politics—but then, I thought miserably, isn't that what Ashley would say about me? Besides, it was getting increasingly colder now, and the sweatshirt was fleecy and warm.

And then I was driving, and driving some more, plunging deeper and deeper into the darkness, way past where I'd vaguely imagined I'd finally stop and turn back. Instead, I was bouncing up and over the curvaceous hills of Pennsylvania, with my new purchase beside me. I kept sneaking happy little peeks at it. My brand-new guitar. I thought of B. B. King. How he'd called his Lucille. I named mine, inexplicably, Aggie.

As the reflective emerald signs floated past me overhead, with their pointillist letters and arrows, and the road unspooled before me, I was overcome with a strange, prickly feeling of déjà vu. A rest stop, a gas station off I-78. The mini-mart. I had once stood in line there—I was sure of it—drinking a bottle of Diet Pepsi in the punishing, bleached lighting, breathing in the same fumes of floor cleaner and coffee and boiled hot dogs. And at the turnoff, I knew without checking my phone that there would be a weigh station for trucks.

How did I know this? Had Toxic Shock Syndrome ever been on tour here? No. We'd never played anyplace farther east than Cleveland. I was certain. "Aggie, this is freaking me out," I told the guitar. Maybe I really was caught in a time loop—or brain-damaged from all that hot sauce. Traffic had thinned; a slight fog had descended. The interstate was wide but dark and ghostly now with vapor and glitter; to steady my nerves, I had Elvis Costello playing, the entirety of *My Aim Is True*—a brilliant album, still holds up to this day—but suddenly, in the middle of the song "Allison," he cut out. Just like that. "Al-li—" he was singing. Then nothing. At first, I thought it was a trick, a tease recorded by Costello himself—which was just stupid, of course—I'd only listened to the album about five zillion times. But it scared me. It sounded like a sudden amputation. Keeping my eyes on the road as best I could, I reached for my phone. It had run out of power.

I swerved over onto the shoulder, put on my hazards. I fumbled through the glove compartment, then my purse, then the storage compartment in the armrest. While I'd managed to purchase entire outfits and boxes of shoes and snacks and beverages and even a brand-new musical instrument, I did not, anywhere, have a charger.

My electronic umbilical cord to the rest of the world had been effectively cut. "Whoa," I said aloud. "Shit." The clock on the dashboard said 12:07 a.m. On a phone, somehow, the time never seemed like a pronouncement to me so much as a cute numeric glyph, part of the decorative, digital wallpaper. But now I stared at the blank rectangle of onyx. The hour sank in. "Well, that's it," I said. It was too late to veer off the highway again in search of a store. What's more, I realized, I didn't want to. Not now. Not yet. For the first time in years, for better or worse, I was completely off the grid.

Switching on the radio, I drove on blindly now. No GPS, no map app. "We're on our own, Aggie," I said. "Just us and the stars. We'll have to navigate the way seasoned pilots and mariners have for centuries." Of course—who was I kidding—there were road signs all over—I was hardly Odysseus or Magellan or Harriet Tubman—yet I was plunging forward unassisted, not knowing where I was heading—only that I was not ready to turn back.

Now it was just me and my cheap new guitar and whatever the music gods transmitted over the airwaves. The rock station I'd located seemed clairvoyant. *All your favorites from the '70s, '80s, and '90s!* Iggy Pop and Alanis Morissette and Grace Jones. I became convinced that their songs were coded messages to me. *I am the passenger...All I really want is deliverance...Won't give in and I won't feel guilty...* God—if there was one—was speaking to me directly through the hit singles of my past. I began rehearing, relistening to them with the same reverence that I'd had at sixteen, singing along with total abandon, and at the same time, in my own way, praying: *Please, don't forsake me. Please, forgive me. Please, tell me what to do.*

Somewhere outside Harrisburg at around one o'clock in the morning, the Ramones song "Blitzkrieg Bop" filled the Subaru. And as I gingerly sipped a Diet Coke from a drive-thru McDonald's—my mouth was still blistered but almost painfully dry—for some reason, I was weeping again, too—I was runny-nosed, shivery, my voice fracturing—it came to me. The Ramones. The first song of theirs I'd ever heard had been "Rockaway Beach," and as a teenager, I'd always imagined I'd go there one day to pay homage and see it for myself. Rockaway Beach. Why, just that past weekend, I'd read an article about how Patti Smith had bought a little bungalow there, her first bona fide "room of one's own." Of course. Rockaway.

I would make a pilgrimage. A great rock 'n' roll pilgrimage in honor of my best, former self—hell, I already had a guitar! I'd feel my way in the dark, driving without a map—you couldn't get more punk rock than that. Surely, there had to be road signs leading me through to Rockaway, to the Atlantic Ocean, which I had never in my life seen before. I would figure it out. I'd make my way to the birthplace of the Ramones, to the ruins of CBGB, maybe even to Patti Smith's house. Why not? It seemed oddly ingenious.

What they never tell you about the iconic American road trip, though, is how mind-numbingly dull so much of it can actually be—especially at night—especially alone—with only a guitar to talk to—the miles and miles of pavement and wan lights and nothing much doing—until, suddenly, you're in New Jersey on the Turnpike, feeling sorry as hell for the tollbooth clerks, who—no matter what's gone on in your own pathetic, shattered life, have got to inspire pity—all that carbon monoxide, the endless hours on your feet, the claustrophobia, the loneliness—and where the hell do you pee? After passing through the tolls and spending insane amounts of money to enter turnoffs and tunnels, I found myself barreling through the night streets and expressways across Lower Manhattan, down into Brooklyn, too tired to see anything beyond what was right in front of me, turning and following and hoping and stopping a couple of times to shout/ask directions from a couple of winos by a gas station—until, in a dream, I saw I was near, or there, or close enough—I was sure I could hear the ocean—certainly, I could smell it—and with less than a quarter of a tank of gas left, I pulled into what appeared to be a parking lot by a low building at the edge of the shore, perhaps the very edge of the earth, nothing beyond it but black. *You've made it*, I told myself. "Aggie," I said, "we're here! In Ramone-land!" And I put the Subaru into park and somehow hauled myself over the gear-shift in the dark to the passenger seat, and tilted it back and collapsed. But I needed someone to hold, something to love, to commemorate the occasion, and so I hugged Aggie. And I popped an Ativan now, too—just to balance out the Adderall—Ashley would hardly miss *one* pill—and I needed it now, because even though I was beyond exhausted, my heart was still percussive, and I was scared, and I didn't want to think too much at all. "I'm just going to shut my eyes for a few minutes," I told Aggie. "I'm just going to unwind so that we can start our great rock 'n' roll adventure properly. This is awesome, isn't it? Rockaway Beach?"

It was only later, in the bright, stinging light of morning, when the cops found me asleep in the Subaru and woke me up that, well, I had to admit: The tableau I'd created was beyond pathetic— too fucked-up, in fact, for words.

Chapter 6

A PSYCHIC ONCE TOLD me that in my very first life, I was a slave in ancient Babylon. My existence was short, filthy, and brutal—as were my next dozen or so, which she summed up as: peasant, baby, concubine, serf, vassal, goatherd, peasant. I seemed not to have been reincarnated over time so much as inbred. "Oh my God," I'd groaned. "I'm like karmically retarded."

"Nah," she said breezily. "Folks always imagine we were great historical figures in the past. But most of us were just poor." My own lives didn't get remotely interesting until the late eighteenth century, she said, when I was a royalist flunky beheaded by Robespierre in Paris, then a medicine woman in Borneo, then an ill-fated surveyor of the Panama Canal, whose shoelace got caught in the gearbox of a tractor. However, the life I was currently living, in the United States of America, straddling two millennia, *this one*, she announced, would be infinitely better. I would enjoy unparalleled comfort, health, and freedom.

"Hm. But, wait. You'll have to be careful around your forties or fifties," she warned.

I shifted uncomfortably on her futon. "Why? Does something terrible happen?"

She stared at the cards. "I'm seeing a sudden crisis. Some sort of collapse? Maybe marital strife? A financial problem?" She drew another from the deck. "Oh. Now, *this* is odd. If you can *stretch* yourself—"

"You mean, like a contortionist? Oh my God. Am I supposed to join the *circus?*" I started to giggle. The psychic started giggling, too. She was my college roommate Brenda, and we were both stoned out of our minds. Before she'd offered to perform a "regression reading" for me as a graduation gift, we'd smoked an entire bowl of Peruvian hash with my Philosophy TA in the basement.

Brenda read tarot cards from time to time, and she'd often alluded that she'd inherited some "psychic sixth sense" from her great-aunt Eliza in Trinidad. But Brenda seemed to have an endless parade of aunties whom she was always inheriting things from, which made it doubly hard to take her seriously now.

The idea of me ever being forty—or God forbid, *fifty*—one day was ridiculous. Though I planned on living forever, I certainly did not plan on aging. "You and I, Brenda, we will always be fabulous," I proclaimed on her futon. "And I will never have a midlife crisis because I, for one, will never be 'middle-aged.'"

Decades later, however, after the police woke me up in Rockaway, it was a struggle to simply climb out of my damn Subaru. My ankles had swollen. Every joint in my body felt like a rusted hinge.

Blinking at the hypnotic tumble of the waves, I was hit by a longing for my mother, gone so many years—then my daughter three thousand miles away in London, burrowing into the wind with her umbrella. I saw the spatula *thwack* across Joey's face, blood spattering on the kitchen tiles. Hacked-up pleather in the Walmart bathroom. Heaps of gnawed chicken bones. Ghoulish halos of fog along the New Jersey Turnpike as I tore through them in a fugue.

"Oh, Aggie," I said aloud, blowing my nose in a paper napkin. "What the hell have I done?"

And my mind snagged on Brenda's prediction from twenty-five years earlier. Was I actually caught in the beginning of some personal apocalypse?

No, no, I told myself. I was being ridiculous: It was just the Adderall talking. The adrenaline rush of it was much stronger than I'd anticipated. I'd merely gone for a long drive, was all. So what? Didn't everybody do that from time to time? Ashley even had a theory that Americans were addicted to road trips because none of us were really rooted here. "Our country is one giant displaced persons camp," she'd insisted. "Even the Natives have been kicked off their lands and marched someplace else." (When I pointed out that Troy, Michigan, was hardly—Where exactly were those tent cities? Africa someplace? The Lebanese border?—she'd responded with exasperation, "I mean in the scheme of the *world* and *history*, Mom.")

Yet try as I might, I could not shake my own terrifying suspicion that I'd done much more than simply put my car into gear. Alone on a beach, it was difficult to keep lying to myself. Maybe every marriage came with secret, niggling doubts—maybe this was an intrinsic part of *forsaking all others*. But long before I'd caught him in the kitchen with his mistress, I'd known, in the deepest recesses of my heart, that I hadn't fallen in love with Joey so much as *willed* myself to love him. He had seemed so sturdy. So loving and *normal*. But ours had not been a great, volcanic romance. Rather, we were a partnership forged as practically and deliberately as a bridge. Like a piece of steel, I had bent myself to fit it.

Now, I was buckling. I felt the very core of my soul crack open. The thought came to me with such violence, it dropped me straight to the sand. *Was my marriage over?* Look at what had happened to us over the years. To me. I never thought my life would turn out like this. Suddenly, I was forty-five. Suburban and manic. As beige and lumpy as oatmeal. Was this it? Were my best years all gone? And if so, who would ever take me seriously—or love me—or even look at me again?

In the past, I'd kept such wretched thoughts at bay by drinking. Here, all I could do was get back in the car and lean my forehead against the steering wheel and weep. I wished I had a mother, a road map, someone wise enough to reassure me and tell me what to do.

I tried to remember: What had Brenda said exactly? Something about stretching? A circus? Nothing was making sense anymore. I started to shiver. Sniffling, I slowly eased the car out of the sandy lot and lurched onto the road.

Patti Smith. Once, my punk-poet idol had set aside her own musical career to be a mother in suburban Detroit—just like I had. In fact, when I was feeling particularly frustrated, sorting through my children's dirty laundry in the mudroom, I'd console myself sometimes by thinking, *Well, Patti Smith is probably sorting through her children's dirty laundry in her mudroom right now, too!* It began to dawn on me: Was there anyone better in the entire universe for me to talk to right now? Surely, Patti Smith could advise me about what the hell to do with a cross-dressing husband. I could track her down—right here on Rockaway Beach. Okay, yeah, absolutely, it was a long shot—but the more I thought about it, the more convinced I became that it was, in fact, possible. Why not? Weirder things had transpired in the past twenty-four hours.

I began to envision meeting Patti Smith so clearly, I could taste it like the salt off the Atlantic. Her house would be a sleepy little clapboard bungalow alone on the edge of the sand just beyond the boardwalk. She'd be sitting out on her porch, bare feet propped up on the railing, an acoustic guitar in her lap—practically waiting for me.

Yet on the main strip of Rockaway Beach I was surprised to see concrete high-rises towered above the Atlantic. Aluminum-sided row houses sat crammed together between telegraph poles. Slowing down, I squinted out the window. Shouldn't there be signs posted for rock 'n' roll landmarks? Where, exactly, were the bungalows? A driver behind me leaned on his horn. "Hey Michigan," he shouted out his window. "Stop taking your car for a goddamn walk."

I pulled up beside a group of construction workers repairing a garage.

"Excuse me." I rolled down my window. "Would any of you guys know where Patti Smith's house is?"

A look of amusement ping-ponged between them.

"Patti *who*?" one of them said not to me, but the others. "Why's she asking me? Do I look like fuckin' Google?"

More cars started honking behind me. "Hey asshole. That light's not gonna get any greener!" I turned the wrong way down a one-way street, then up onto a curb, nearly hitting a guy on a bike. "The *fuck* you doing?" he shouted.

"Good God, Aggie." I stopped abruptly.

What the fuck *was* I doing? If I did find Patti Smith, did I really think that, instead of calling the cops, she'd actually put her arm around me—and invite me inside—and say in a warm, sisterly fashion, "Well, Donna Koczynski, my fellow musician who's come all the way from Michigan. You're obviously a kindred spirit in need of marital advice, so please, have tea with me, and then we'll read aloud from Baudelaire together"?

Miserably, I put the Subaru into reverse and tried to backtrack my way through the crowded streets. But I was a lab rat now caught in a maze. Lurching to a stop again, I leaned my head back and let loose a lone, dry sob. It was finished. I was all out of ideas. I wondered if I should find a police station somewhere, turn myself in. I was just about to roll down the window to ask for directions when I saw, winking in a storefront, a blue neon outline of a hand. Above it, in tomato-red letters, flickered two words: PALM READER.

There it was. There was no more denying it now. In fact, it was so glaringly obvious—so literally a *sign*—I wondered why it hadn't occurred to me sooner—or why I'd been resisting it for so long. She alone might hold the key as to how to fix my fractured, idiotic life. *Of course.* She'd seen it already, in fact. Immediately, before I did anything else stupid or destructive or insane, I had one last lifeline to try—one last person to call—right there in New York.

Inside the Laundromat rows of washers and dryers rotated like gears. A Hispanic man sat reading the *New York Post* beneath a sign that stated NO DYING ALLOWED, which struck me as oddly reassuring. Bolted to the wall by a vending machine was the only working pay phone for miles.

It had been years since I'd used one; the receiver felt unnaturally heavy in my hand. Raising it to my ear, I paused. There was someone else I had to call first, even though I was loath to do it.

However, I had no doubt that the police were pacing our living room by now, studying framed photos of me on the mantelpiece, asking Joey if I'd been acting strangely beforehand and jotting down what I'd been wearing when I first disappeared. (Good God, would he actually tell them? I could picture him hemming and hawing.) Austin would be hunched over on the couch clutching his stomach, rocking slightly, trying to appear indifferent. But I knew my son. Despite his carefully curated swagger and hair, some mornings before a chemistry test he'd dash into the bathroom, filling it with a gastric stench. Once, I found him in a fetal position on the bath mat. Now, he and Joey would've spent a night tortured by sleeplessness, imagining worst-case scenarios, frantically calling our friends, local hospitals—perhaps even morgues?

As I fed my handful of quarters into the metal slot, my heart punched.

My plan was, as soon as Joey answered, to say simply, *"Hi. I'm alive and well and sober, so don't worry,"* then hang up. That would suffice.

Yet a different, croakier voice answered. "Uh, hello?"

"Austin?"

"Yuh huh," it came plaintively. "Mom?"

My kid. My kid was actually answering a phone?

"Austin. Honey." My voice broke in my throat like an eggshell. "Are you okay?"

"Mmm-hmm. Yuh. Just, uh, waking up." There came the elongated, winded sound of him stretching, followed by a crack of bone. He'd slept? "Uh, Dad's in the bathroom. Do you want me to bring the phone in?"

"No. No. Look, I just want you to know, Austin," I said as steadily as I could, blinking at the ceiling, "I'm absolutely fine, okay? I haven't been kidnapped. I haven't had any sort of accident—"

"Okay. Hey Mom?" he said. "Were you really in a chicken-wing-eating contest?"

"Excuse me?"

"This guy at the bar? Lenny? When we called—"

The receiver slipped; I caught it by the metal snake of its cord as it swung back and forth. "Wait? What?" I said, returning it to my ear. "How did you know where I was last night?"

"Uh, your 'Find My iPhone' app?"

"My what?"

"That tracking thing? I set it up for you, after that time in the super-market? Uh, Dad has me use it to follow you sometimes. Like, when you're going downtown."

I'd been twisting the drawstring of my hoodie around in my fingers. I stopped.

"Your father has you put me under surveillance?" I said. "Like with a drone?"

"No, jeez. It's just an app, Mom," Austin said. "Last night, when Dad got home and you still weren't here. And you weren't answering texts or calls or anything? He started getting freaked, you know, like maybe you'd been in an accident or something. So I went online and did the trace and we saw you were, like, in this tiny town in Pennsylvania. At this place called Johnny's? So, like, just to be sure that you hadn't been, like, robbed or beaten or carjacked or anything—and, you know, like, some criminal was using your phone—Dad called the place to check. And the manager said to call some other guy there on his cell phone, and to maybe text him your photo because the bar was, like, packed, and though while he didn't *think* he'd seen you based on our description, he couldn't be sure? So I ended up talking to this one guy, who passed me to this other guy Lenny, who was like this Hell's Angel—he was pretty cool, actually—and he said you were doing this big chicken-wing-eating contest with them. But then he couldn't find you. He thought maybe you'd gotten sick on the wings, so he sent this woman to check to see if you were, like, throwing up in the bathroom. And in the meantime, while we were waiting, he asked me if I'd ever known anyone who'd been in Nam, so I told him about Grandma and Grandpa, and oh, hey—"

Suddenly, there was a muffled sound. For a moment, I pulled the receiver away and actually stared at it to verify what I was hearing: This was the most I'd heard Austin talk in months—in years, possibly. Yet then I heard him say, "Yeah, it's her," and there came an abrupt, violent shift of air, and Joey was suddenly yelling into the phone: "You went to a bar, Donna? A roadhouse in Pennsylvania? Are you out of your fucking mind?" and before he could say anything else, I hung up the phone so hard it seemed to ring back on itself.

"Fuck!" I shouted at the pay phone. Grabbing the receiver, I slammed it back onto its cradle once, twice, three times, as if I were bludgeoning it, each time making it give a metallic cry of reverberation. Impressively, the man reading the newspaper and the other Laundromat customers never even glanced at me.

I paced, panting. The nerve! The unfairness of it all! They'd slept soundly while I'd been in my *car*? They'd been *monitoring* me? Was there no real escaping, no anonymity *anywhere* anymore? And yet no one at Johnny's had even noticed me? How had I managed to remain under constant surveillance, yet utterly invisible at the same time?

And Joey had just instantly assumed I had fallen off the wagon? This unleashed a whole new wave of fury in me. *He* did not trust *me*?

I glanced wildly around the Laundromat, its washing machines all vibrating in unison, the dryers thrumming and chugging out a bass line: a narcotizing orchestra of appliances. For a moment I felt the perverse, overwhelming desire to yank all the clothing out of the dryers and rip it to shreds. I looked back at the pay phone. I picked up the receiver again.

As I fed more quarters into the slot, I was shaking. I knew Brenda's number by heart like a melody: Back in the days before smartphones, I'd dialed it repeatedly for years. Still, my fingers could barely punch out the digits. I wasn't sure if the number still worked—or even where Brenda was living nowadays: New York? LA? the Caribbean? But the beeps of the keypad beat out her name with a hopeful, nostalgic, pneumonic singsong: *Bren-da, Bren-da.*

If you were an insomniac with basic cable anytime between 1999 and 2008, chances are you might have known my friend Brenda, too. Except you'd have known her as Madame LaShonda Peyroux, the celebrated

Jamaican clairvoyant on the "Channeling Channel" who did past-life regressions and tarot card predictions on-air for $1.99/minute.

Whatever's ailin' ya, darlin', whether it's love, money, or health problems, Madame LaShonda Peyroux would say, her head wrapped in a Rasta kerchief, her enormous hoop earrings bobbing as she spoke, *I'm gonna do a reading for ya an' fix ya up right. Just call me here, darlin', right now, at 1-900-CHANNEL.* All the while, a phone number flashed insanely below her in big purple numbers. Madame LaShonda Peyroux's infomercials became so iconic, at one point they were parodied on *Saturday Night Live.*

Long before she'd been recruited to play this flamboyant cable TV soothsayer, however, I'd known her as Brenda Lena Peebles, my freshman roommate at the University of Michigan. She'd swanned into Ann Arbor straight from Miss Porter's School for Girls in Fairfield, Connecticut. My first day of college, I'd arrived at our dorm to find her mother, an impeccably coiffed woman in a floor-length chinchilla, fussily smoothing a coverlet over the choicer of the two beds.

"Oh, hello. You must be Donna, yes?" She paused long enough to proffer a hand weighted with rings. "I'm Dr. Peebles, Brenda's mom. Brennie's gone downstairs for more boxes."

"Oh. Hey. Hi." I stood clutching my guitar case and my father's old army duffel; I smiled awkwardly. Doctor Peebles's skin was like dark syrup. Until that moment, I hadn't realized Brenda was black.

Her mother regarded my fuchsia hair and my leather jacket gouged with safety pins. Her eyes stopped at the padlock on the thick chain around my neck.

She fixed me in a sterilizing gaze. "Tell me you're not in one of those skinhead bands," she said.

Only then did I realize what a gross misjudgment my outfit had been when I'd assembled it that morning, hoping to establish myself as a punk renegade. I felt my face flush.

"What? Oh God, no," I cried. "I'm Jewish. My grandparents fled the Nazis. My band's alternative, is all."

Dr. Peebles frowned. "So. This is all just for effect? Dramatis personae?" She returned to smoothing out the bedspread in a soldierly way. "Well, that's a fine fettle," she murmured. "Peas in a pod."

As if on cue, a girl sashayed in dressed in riding boots and a suede bolero jacket glinting with dozens of little gold buckles. She was nearly liquid in her motions the way a ballerina or an ice-skater might be, carrying a billowy ficus as if it weighed nothing at all. A trail of emerald leaves lay strewn in her wake. "Hey, are you Donna? Bienvenue," she said. Her face was wide and flat, with high cheekbones that made her look slightly Asian. Her dark hair was sculpted in a theatrical swoosh over her left eye. As she smiled, a small, distinct gap between her two front teeth gave her a mischievous, saucy look. She shifted the plant to her hip to free her hand. "Obviously, I'm Brenda." Behind her, a darker-skinned young man in a tie and sunglasses lumbered in hauling a trunk. "And this is Roland," she said breezily, "my attaché."

Roland snorted. "Yeah. Keep dreaming." Dropping the trunk with a thud, he exited, then returned carrying a Macintosh SE computer, a complete set of the *Encyclopaedia Britannica*, several crates of CDs, a tennis racket, ice skates, and last but not least, an entire case of microwave popcorn. "Mom," he said to Dr. Peebles, who was now hanging white eyelet curtains over Brenda's side of the windows, "Dad says to hurry up. He's blocking the fire lane." Dr. Peebles nodded but proceeded, unhurriedly, to begin lining Brenda's dresser drawers. "Now, Brennie, be sure and register for Organic Chemistry first thing," she said, slicing a roll of parchment with an X-Acto knife. "Those courses fill up quickly, you know. And don't forget to call your grandmother and thank her for the electric blanket. And Reverend Putney should get a call, too. Maybe even a note. He's expecting you."

When her family finally departed, Brenda flopped across her bed and pressed her wrist dramatically to her forehead. "Oh my God. Fifteen hours in the car with all of that. I was getting ready to hang myself with my seat belt." Propping herself up on her elbows, she gazed at me. "Wow. Pink hair. That's *genius*. I should totally do that, too." She shook her head in a whinnying way. "Please, tell me. Is your mother anywhere near as overbearing as mine?"

I shrugged and looked down at the bare tiles on my side of the room. "I don't know," I said. "She's dead."

Brenda clamped her hands over her mouth. The stark awfulness of my words hung in the air between us like an enormous fart. "Oh my God," I said. For some reason, I started to laugh. "Oh my God. I'm such an asshole! Who the hell meets their roommate and is like, 'You think your mother is bad? Well, mine is dead'!"

Brenda started laughing, too. She laughed the way I did: honking and deep-bellied and loud. The sound of our laughter made us laugh even harder. We bent over ourselves, gasping, fanning the air. "Oh, please. Stop. Stop!"

"Ow, my lungs."

Finally, we collected ourselves.

"Well." Brenda grinned, dabbing her eyes. "You certainly know how to make small talk."

Brenda's parents were insisting she become a doctor, though she herself longed to be an actress. Already at Miss Porter's, she'd played the inspector in *Arsenic and Old Lace*, Tatiana, and Ado Annie. "I think I was the first black girl in *Oklahoma* ever," she said.

We were both artists, she and I understood, each a rebel and an outsider in our own way, brimming with aspiration. All semester long, she'd sit on her bed late at night with a textbook on her lap, kneading peach-scented moisturizer into her elbows as she memorized alkene basics, while I sat in my desk chair, plucking out notes on my Stratocaster and jotting lyrics on a notepad. Inevitably, I'd set aside my work and grab two Bartles & Jaymes Light Berry wine coolers from our mini-fridge. "Your cocktail, milady?" I'd say, bowing, and she'd say, "Oh, how ever so thoughtful of you, milady." Much to the annoyance of our hall mates, Brenda and I were constantly addressing each other in British accents—hers cribbed from *My Fair Lady*, mine from the Sex Pistols.

When a guy next door remarked loudly that Brenda "didn't sound black" and that I "didn't look Jewish," we began calling ourselves "Shylock and Dreadlock" just to fuck with him—Brenda speaking with a Yiddish accent, me like a Rastafarian—cracking ourselves up with our wit. Brenda did wrinkle her nose at my punk albums ("If I wanted to hear white people yelling all day, I could just go back to Philly"), while I groaned whenever she put on her show tunes ("God, Bren, *Pippin* is enough to give you diabetes"). We also gravitated toward different groups on campus. (She began sitting at the "black table" in the dining hall, experimenting with braids and natural hair. "Which has the added benefit," she explained to me one night, "of pissing off my mother.") Nevertheless, at the end of each day, we were always each other's trusted after-party. An enthusiastic intimacy took root that perhaps only occurs when you're eighteen—and wide open to the world—and the words "hanging out" are still a verb, not a description.

After college, when Joey and I got married, Brenda flew back from the Royal Academy in London. We exchanged mixtapes, birthday cards, long-distance phone calls as she hopped from LA to Chicago to Williamstown. But the year I got pregnant with Austin, Brenda called from New York to tell me she'd been offered her own cable TV show. She'd been asked to perform psychic readings and past-life regressions for the Channeling Channel based on a Jamaican alter ego she'd crafted for herself in an improv troupe in Lower Manhattan.

"Can you believe they want me to do this?" Brenda said. "Madame LaShonda Peyroux is a parody, for Chrissakes! She's like that bit we used to do in our dorm! Does anyone really believe Jamaicans talk this way?"

"Your own TV show? Brennie, that's awesome," I said.

"Yeah," she said vaguely. "I suppose. My agent says I need more TV credits. Plus, the show would go on live from 9 p.m. to 11. So I'd still have my days free to audition. Plus," she said with a sigh, "it's not exactly like anyone's breaking down the doors to hire classically trained black actresses." And then, of course, there was acting lesson *numero uno*: Never turn down a steady paycheck.

Oddly, I seemed more excited than Brenda did. Okay, so it wasn't Shakespeare. But more people, I told her, would probably sooner watch a fake Jamaican psychic than *Troilus and Cressida*. "Don't think of it as a parody so much as a tribute," I suggested.

Brenda had based her character, of course, on her great-aunt Eliza. Tellingly, Great-Aunt Eliza had been the only member of the Peebles family who had not cut Brenda off after she turned down medical school.

"I suppose," Brenda said. "Though she'd be pissed as hell that I made her from Kingston instead of Port of Spain."

Late-night cable was hardly Hollywood or prime time. In the beginning, faced with two hours' worth of "dead air" on live television, Brenda had her friends call in pretending to be clients, the station waiving our per-minute fee. Once, I was "Roberta Wozniak," a lovelorn Amway saleswoman. Another time, "Lulabelle Ludlow." When Joey's old fraternity brothers came over for a barbecue, we put on the Channeling Channel and took turns dialing the 900 number to have her channel our dead pets.

"Thank God nobody really watches. Talk about 'theater of the absurd.' But I have to say, artistically, it is a gold mine," Brenda confessed one day. We spoke every few weeks, late at night, when I finally got Austin to sleep. Brenda would usually just be getting back from the studio, Joey would be snoring away. I'd tiptoe down to the kitchen, pour myself a tumbler of chardonnay, dial her home phone.

"I'm getting so many ideas for characters from my callers, I could write a one-woman show," she said. "My contract is up just before Thanksgiving. So I'm going to hand in my notice, buy a new laptop, and *voilà*."

Five days later, two jet planes torpedoed the World Trade Center.

The night after September 11, Madame LaShonda Peyroux's on-air hotline was inundated: *Please, can you channel my Danny? He was with Ladder Company 3 in Lower Manhattan.*

Madame LaShonda, my daughter was a flight attendant on United Flight 93. Can you tell me? Did she suffer much?

My boyfriend, Guillermo, he is, like, only fifteen months in this country. He is busboy at Windows on World. Can you tell me if he is still alive?

Days of it, weeks, months. Even the FBI called. Sometimes, it turned out, the bureau quietly used psychics to help them develop leads in investigations. Madame LaShonda Peyroux, it seemed, had developed quite the reputation by then. For all of her theatrics, Brenda had proved startlingly adept and accurate as a medium. Two agents wanted to know: Did she have any sense as to who might have mailed envelopes full of anthrax to Senator Tom Daschle's office and NBC News?

In its panic, in its grief, in its insomnia, a reeling nation turned not just to its vast cache of pharmaceuticals and booze, but to its psychics—particularly, to the serene Jamaican woman with the caramelized voice who reassured them that their murdered loved ones, did, in fact, live on in another realm.

The Channeling Channel anointed Brenda its "national spokes-psychic" and emblazoned her face on billboards high above freeways in Chicago, Miami, and Los Angeles. Newspapers across the country began running a syndicated column with Madame LaShonda Peyroux's picture and byline. She appeared (always in character) on several late-night talk shows. QVC, for a brief period, carried an "exclusive, limited" line of Madame LaShonda Peyroux's "authentic" Jamaican hot sauce and "homemade" jerk seasonings. Joey and I saw her gap-toothy photo on the front pages of supermarket tabloids: "Madame LaShonda Peyroux's Psychic Forecast for 2003! Make the Most of Your Personal Past Lives!"

"Wow," Joey said, staring at her pixilated grin, "She's really making a killing off that bit, isn't she?"

The fact that I was friends with such a celebrity eventually became my children's favorite and most-respected thing about me.

Not surprisingly, however, the more famous Brenda got, the less we saw of each other. I told myself it was because she had grown so busy—

we were now worlds apart—what could she possibly want with me anymore—blah, blah. Though in my dirty little heart, I knew better.

The last time we'd gotten together, Brenda had been in Chicago for a talk show; I'd driven five hours from Michigan to spend the evening with her afterward. Brenda arrived at the Drake looking slightly unreal in her television makeup, apologizing profusely for her lateness, clad in a leopard-print coat and saucer-sized black sunglasses that at once redacted her face yet marked her unmistakably as a celebrity.

"Mon Dieu, I'm so happy to see you," she said, hugging me tightly. "Finally. What do you say we go to Gibson's for steak? Courtesy of the Channeling Channel, of course." While we were waiting for our table, I swallowed one Hennessy, then another. She turned to me on her barstool and clasped my hands warmly in both of hers. "So, milady. Talk to me. How are you? How's Monsieur Joey? The kids?"

"Oh, Brennie." Her coat alone, I suspected, cost more than our monthly mortgage payments. "You don't want to hear about my boring little life." That morning back in Michigan, a shelf in our pantry had collapsed. Three jumbo jars of marinara sauce from Costco had smashed into thousands of little pieces of glass, splattering and staining everything. While I'd been down on my knees scrubbing up the jagged, acidic mess, Austin's kindergarten teacher had called to say she was concerned that he was having trouble forming letters.

I signaled the waiter for a refill.

"Please. I'm not here to be entertained," Brenda said. "I'm here for the real. Seriously. Talk to me, Donna."

Reluctantly, I started to explain about Austin being tested for dyslexia. A large blond woman charged over. "I'm so sorry. I am so sorry," she said breathlessly, honing in on Brenda. "But I have to ask. I just bet my girlfriend over there. Are you Madame LaShonda Peyroux?"

Three more times during dinner, we were interrupted at our table. With an apologetic sigh, Brenda set down her fork and dutifully signed autographs. Politely, she listened to fans recount word-for-word how she'd predicted something that had subsequently come true for them

(*And just like you said, he got accepted to Purdue University the very next week! Two years later, I was promoted to manager!*). She'd ordered an astonishingly expensive bottle of Silver Oak Cabernet, and I poured myself one glass, then another, then a third. I refilled Brenda's glass, too, as she nodded and smiled. "Please," a fan pleaded with her. "Do the voice! Do the voice!"

Finally, Brenda sighed. "Hey, do you mind switching?" Awkwardly, we traded seats so that I was now sitting on the banquette. Once she had her back to the room, the interruptions ceased. It came as an enormous reprieve. "Okay, so. Listen," Brenda said finally, leaning in. "I've got some big news. News you, in particular, will appreciate. Now, it's very preliminary—and it might not happen—but. You know the one-woman show I wrote, based on all the different characters who've called in to the hotline? Well, I'm currently in negotiations with HBO. The Steppenwolf Theatre here, they've got this New Plays Initiative? The plan is to perform the show here first as a sort of trial run, then adapt it for television."

"Wow," I said. "That's really something." I smiled at her intensely. I was very drunk, I realized.

"And I'll be playing all the characters myself, Donna. Writing, producing, starring—all of it! An entire one-woman enterprise!"

"Well, wow again," I said. "Yes. Yay for you." Even though my glass was half full, I poured some more wine into it.

"I mean, Donna." She pressed her hand to her throat. "This is huge. This is what parlays me into *serious actress territory*. And as a black woman? Usually, it's, like, there's a quota. 'Well, we've already got Anna Deavere Smith.' This is *it*, sweetie! My proverbial big break! We have to celebrate!"

I signaled the waiter for a second bottle of Silver Oak Cabernet, though I found I could barely taste it. As Brenda elaborated on the details—what her agent said, the concept, the money—I found myself engaging a little trick that I used to do as a child where I tried to hear words merely as collections of phonetics, peeled away from all meaning.

Once...once, I had been up onstage, of course, writhing ecstatically in the white-hot spotlight; once, audiences had applauded for *me*. And the more Brenda smiled her dazzling smile, and gripped my hand across the tablecloth, and informed the waiter, "Yes, we're having dessert!" the more I found myself feeling sickened and reeling. As soon as Brenda excused herself to the ladies' room, I swallowed the rest of my wine in a single glug, wobbled to my feet, and staggered over to one of the tables where her fans were finishing up their steaks. "I'll just have you know," I announced, "that Jamaican accent of hers? *I* did it first. In college. And her first callers on her show? All of those characters, all of them were *me*. Look at you, fawning over her. You're pathetic. Pathetic fucking nobodies, that's who you are. Nobodies and fucking sycophants."

The minute I stumbled back to our booth and slammed myself down onto the banquette, I was overcome with shame and self-loathing. I was a terrible, ugly person. When Brenda returned from the restroom, I told her I thought I had food poisoning and needed to go back to the hotel. Grabbing my purse, I polished off the remainder of the wine and handed my glass to a busboy on my way out. After that, my memory was sketchy: a town car, a piano bar, lights binging above a gilded elevator.

Back in Michigan afterward, I could barely watch HBO for fear of coming across some news about Brenda's show. Like a baby who thinks that if she covers her eyes, the world disappears, I secretly hoped that if I simply ignored Brenda's success, it might just go away. When the phone rang late at night sometimes, I found myself tensing, though, invariably, it turned out not to be her.

Nobody ever talks about the breakup of a friendship. It can feel as haunting and painful as the end of any romance. For months, I was relieved not to have contact with Brenda. And yet, she was also a phantom limb. The echo of her presence—and my longing for her— never fully vanished, either.

Now, in the Laundromat, Brenda's old home phone number rang and rang. Outside, a garbage truck ground by. A jackhammer started. I was just about to hang up when there came a sudden click: "Hello? Mom, is that you?"

"Brenda?" Though I hadn't meant to, I hesitated. "It's me. Donna. Donna Koczynski."

"Wow. Birthday Girl. I don't believe it." I heard a snap. "I was just thinking about you."

"You were?" *Well du-uh. What did I expect? She was psychic.*

"Well, sure, when I saw it was October 6 this morning. Joyeux anniversaire, mon amie. Wow. Donna. Talk about a blast from my past."

In my head, I'd rehearsed an opening. Adopting a light, generous tone, I'd planned to say, "Shylock, it's Dreadlock," or "Bonjour, milady." Yet the moment I heard Brenda's familiar, Brahmin voice, it was like the saddest violin chord plucked within me. "Oh. Brenda. You're there. I am so glad. God—I'm so sorry, Bren—I didn't mean to call you like this. It's just—hey, guess what? Guess where I happen to be? New York City. The Big Apple. All by myself."

"You're here? Right now?"

"Just footloose and fancy-free. A girl's weekend. Just for one. I don't really have a plan yet—you know me, all wild and spontaneous. Rock 'n' roll! God, I can't fucking believe you remembered my birthday, Bren. You know you're the only one who did?"

"Donna?" Brenda interrupted, not unkindly. "Sweetie, have you been drinking?"

I felt a wallop of shame. Of course, Brenda had only ever known me as a drunk. A vague memory stirred like a fish beneath the surface from our evening in Chicago.

"No, no, Bren. I was just out driving, you know? Just going along in the car, and the Ramones came on the radio—'Rockaway Beach'?—or a different one, but it was so funny—it was like this message, you know? To go to New York—and I was thinking of you, Bren, the entire time— It was like you were there beside me, for some reason—and I just really wanted to see you, you know? I mean, oh, God, Bren. I'm sorry that I've been so out of touch, I've been a bad friend— It's just, I slept in my car—and I ate all these chicken wings—"

"Okay, okay. Hang on a minute," Brenda said distractedly. "Donna, I want you to do something. Take a deep breath. Can you do that for me? Inhale?"

Over the phone, I nodded. I took a deep breath.

"Okay. Good. Now, exhale, slowly."

Again, I obeyed.

"Now. Tell me: Where are you?"

"You mean, literally?"

"Literally."

I glanced around. A woman in a hairnet and flip-flops was bent over a dryer, shoveling hot clothes into a mesh cart.

"A Laundromat. Somewhere near Rockaway Beach? I don't know what it's called. Wash'n'Dry, I think?"

"Yeah. Okay." Brenda exhaled. "There's no way we're meeting there. Can you access Google Maps or a GPS?"

"I'm at a pay phone. My cell died. I'm sorry, Bren. I know it's last-minute."

"But you've got a car?" For a moment, she seemed to put the phone down and I heard some whispering and a faint clicking. "Look, I've only got an hour or two this morning," she said when she returned. "I'm going to give you directions. Waze is telling me that with traffic, it'll take you about an hour. Do you have something to write with?"

I yanked a flyer off the bulletin board, dug in my purse for a pen. The one time I'd visited Brenda in New York, years ago, she'd been living in a luxury condominium on the thirty-second floor at the very tip of Manhattan. I could see the Statue of Liberty from her living room. The interior was bone-white, all clean lines and stark, modernist furniture. Although I'd joked to Joey that it looked like it been decorated by a Swedish gynecologist, I was secretly awestruck how elegant her life was. Now, Brenda had moved up even farther on the success ladder; her new address was on nothing less than Park Avenue.

When I arrived, she instructed, I was to double-park and ring up-stairs. She'd come down to direct me to the garage herself. "Okay. *This* is workable. We'll have a birthday breakfast," she said. "Sorry, but you've caught me at a really crazy time."

"Oh, Bren. Thank you. I mean it. Thankyouthankyouthankyou."

In the background, I heard sirens. "Okay then." She took a deep breath. "Godspeed, milady."

Hanging up the pay phone, I cleaned myself up as best I could in the ladies' room. I looked terrible. My face was like melted putty, my eyes the color of lox. Maybe the Muslim women were really onto something, I thought: Just throw a big piece of cloth over yourself and be done with it. Maybe there was something truly liberating in that. I was ashamed of how disheveled I was going to appear to Brenda—of how little I had to show for myself after all these years—how wide the gap in our fortunes had continued to grow. I kept ruminating over that reading she'd done for me in college—she'd seen something significant in those cards—I was sure of it now—but she hadn't been able to elaborate on it because I was too fucking stoned—Oh, I was a fool! Would Brenda remember what she'd predicted? She had to—Brenda *was* psychic. For all I knew, she'd known all along the radical missteps I was going to make, how far off course I'd been straying from myself.

She had done so well for herself, Brenda. Despite all my past jealousy and begrudgery, I was enormously proud of her. She had, in fact, made it *big*; she was living out her grand, artistic dreams. Certainly, one of us should. *Root, root, root for the home team*: What else was there in the end? Maybe *this* was getting older. Maybe *this* was sobriety.

My fabulous, famous, long-forsaken best friend. Long ago, she'd predicted a critical breakdown in my life. Now, I could only hope she'd remember what she'd foreseen for me—and maybe, just maybe, how I could fix the mess I had made.

Chapter 7

DRIVING THROUGH NEW YORK CITY was like electroshock therapy. I'm sorry, but who the hell decides to push a burrito cart diagonally across a four-lane expressway while wearing headphones and talking on their cell? By the time I reached Manhattan, I was shattered. I passed an office building resembling a giant chunk of rebar, then a battery of brutalist high-rises. An elevated track loomed overhead. It was obvious I'd written down the wrong house number entirely because when I arrived at what was supposed to be Brenda's address, there was only a liverish tenement, old air-conditioning units hanging out its windows like tongues.

A heavyset woman trundled by, pulling a large vinyl suitcase behind her. "Excuse me?" I called out. "I'm trying to find Park Avenue?"

She glanced at me with tortoise-like indifference. A gold plastic crucifix hung around her neck on what looked like red yarn. "You on it."

"But—" I'd seen Park Avenue before in photos, in movies. "Is this, you know, *the* Park Avenue? Is there, maybe, another one someplace?"

"Hmph." A look of contempt settled across her face. "You hear that?" she announced to no one in particular. "White lady here wants to know if there's *another* Park Avenue."

Finally, I put on my hazards and climbed out of the Subaru. A train rumbled and clanked somewhere above. I didn't know what else to do except look in the building to see if it offered some sort of clue, but the front door was locked. Peering into the vestibule, all I could see was a narrow greenish corridor, subaquatic-looking in the murk. A horrible thought struck me: Had Brenda given me a fake address? In college, we used to give out bogus phone numbers all the time to guys we weren't interested in. Then I noticed a line of buzzers by the doorframe. Beside 5C was a piece of masking tape reading PEEBLES.

A sense of foreboding came over me. Ringing the bell, I half expected the building to detonate. Instead, a voice crackled over the intercom: "Donna? Hey, I can't come down right now. Go two blocks farther north, hang a right, and you'll see a garage called CJ's."

CJ's Body Shop wasn't a garage so much as a lot fenced with razor wire. After I parked, I gathered up my drugs and my Walmart bag full of underwear and stuffed them into my guitar case—though I left the nine boxes of shoes in the backseat. Fuck it. Let somebody steal them. Happy Halloween.

When I arrived at the fifth floor of the tenement (a walk-up), Brenda's door was propped open with a tennis shoe. In a high-ceilinged living room, a pull-out sofa bed lay open and unmade, a pile of dirty sheets clumped on the floor. A wall of shelves was crammed with books, extension cords, coffee mugs, piles of old *Vogue* and *O* magazines, little wooden puzzles in the shapes of fantastical animals, stained glass candles, intricate sculptures of body parts: mandibles, kidneys, ears; clear-plastic storage containers stuffed with office supplies and bungee cords, a faded blue-and-maize felt flag reading MICHIGAN. Most disturbingly, a life-sized replica of a human skeleton hung suspended from a hook in the corner like a cadaverous mobile. Someone had draped a Harry Potter cape over it and an old gold-and-violet Hermès scarf that I recognized as Brenda's from our college days.

"Hello?"

"In here." I found Brenda standing in a tiny kitchen the color of old teeth, furiously scraping the last dregs of mayonnaise out of an enormous glass jar onto a slice of bread. A coffeepot hissed on a hot plate in the corner. A Bluetooth earpiece glowed against her cheek like a sapphire bullet. The kitchen was so cramped, the refrigerator door banged against the countertop every time she opened it. "But I *did* pay it." She pivoted over to the sink and twisted on the faucet. "It's set up as an automatic withdrawal. Straight from her account." Glancing at me, she winked, then pantomimed shooting herself in the head.

"Check the account again," she said sharply. "Not seven-*eight*. Seven-A. As in 'Apple.'" Nudging the refrigerator open with her hip, she leaned in and took out a bag of miniature carrots, a tangerine, and a clump of something meat-ish, then dumped them all on the counter.

Ten years had been a long time. Still, I was shocked. Brenda's face was husk-like now, as if all the juiciness had been suctioned out of it. Her hair was shorn close to her scalp, giving her a piebald look. And her frame, at least fifteen pounds lighter, was overwhelmed by a shapeless, lavender smock and slate blue, industrial-looking pajamas. Day-Glo plastic clogs, the color of parking cones, were jammed on her feet.

I'd never been big on social media—truth be told, I used it mostly to network for the Privileged Kitchen and, okay, to spy on my kids—I had a fake account for that—Kayla McMullins, age sixteen, obsessed with One Direction and bubble tea—but in the years since I'd gotten sober, I'd occasionally worked up the courage to google Brenda, hoping to reconnect. Yet nothing had ever come up for her personally— no Facebook page, no LinkedIn. Until this moment, that hadn't struck me as terribly significant. But clearly, I had missed something big.

"Sorry," Brenda said to me. "This is the third time they've put me on hold. And some sadist put 'That's What Friends Are For' playing on a loop." Her eyes registered my own disheveled appearance. Was I imagining it, or was there a flicker of pity on her face? "Why don't you put that in the corner?" She nodded toward my guitar case.

Turning around, I nearly tripped over a little boy barreling into the kitchen. He was darker-skinned than Brenda, dressed in a gray school uniform and laced oxblood-colored shoes; a young Hispanic woman hurried behind him, fussing with an *Avengers* backpack. She had a belted coat thrown hastily over what looked like pajamas, wild dark hair falling into her face. "I know, we're late. What do you think? Should I Uber it?"

"Hold on." Brenda clicked off her earpiece, swept the food on the counter into a vinyl pouch, and knelt before the boy. "Eli, I want you to remind Ms. Halperin that you get lactose-free milk today, okay?"

The boy reached into the bag and took out a box of raisins. He shook it like a castanet. "Hey. Morse code. I can send a message. S-O-"

"Eli, did you hear me? Sweetie, put those away."

"Do you read me, roger? Copy over and out!" he announced in that earnest way children have when they're testing out a new phrase.

Noticing me, he grew quiet. His eyes, as they scrutinized me, were dark and liquid; they seemed to take up the entire top of his face. I could see whole worlds alive and afloat in them, molecules, tiny galaxies. He was, I thought with a pang, around seven or eight, at that age full of ricocheting energy and wonder, when I'd enjoyed my kids the most.

"Say hello, Eli," Brenda nudged.

Kids are like dogs; if they dislike or distrust you, they let you know it immediately. Sidling over to Brenda, he glowered at me. "Are you a doctor?"

"No. Sweetie, Donna is an old friend of Mommy's. Now, go with Marisol. And hurry. It's already ten to nine."

"Come on, Eli," the Hispanic woman said in a singsong, coaxing voice designed to mask her irritation. "Otherwise, I'm going without you."

Brenda herded him toward the front door. "Now, you're going to be good today, yes?" She kissed him on the forehead. "You've memorized your times tables? Okay. Au revoir, mon petit chou-chou."

"Au revoir, maman."

She stood on the threshold beaming and waving until the sound of their footsteps receded down the stairwell. Then she locked the door with a definitive series of clicks.

"Brenda," I said, stunned. "You have a kid."

"Surprise." She plopped down across the sofa bed and massaged the bridge of her nose. "Alors. Sometimes I feel like I have three of them."

I sat down heavily beside her at her feet. "My God. How did I not know that?"

"Ten years is a long time, sweetie."

I felt profoundly disoriented. I did not know where to even start. "And that woman?" I tried to sound casual, though my mind was pinballing: Was she a nanny? A lover? Brenda had not been a lesbian in college, but after Joey, who the hell knew what people really were.

"Marisol?" Brenda said breezily. "Oh, I met her at the hospital. I let her crash here between her shifts, and she helps out with Eli whenever I just can't move anymore." Heaving herself up, she shuffled over to the coffee table and began stiffly gathering up discarded food containers.

The hospital?

In the daylight of the living room, I could now see how sunken Brenda's eyes looked when she was not smiling. Little patches of ashy skin dotted her hairline and jaw. Her hair hadn't been trimmed at all, it occurred to me. Rather, *it was growing back.*

"Oh my God, Brennie," I said. "You're sick."

Brenda stared at me, her face morphing from disbelief to bemusement. "No, sweetie," she said after a moment. "I'm just exhausted. I've been on call for sixteen hours straight."

"What? I thought you left the Channeling Channel?"

"Not there." She nodded toward the buildings just beyond her window. "Mount Sinai."

I stared at her and she stared back, willing me to comprehend. Finally, it clicked. "No!" I barked. "Shut up!"

Brenda grinned. "Can you believe it?"

"Oh, my God! You're DR. PEEBLES now?"

A prim, triumphant look came over her face.

"Oh my God," I said again. "But I thought you hated medicine."

"Well, I never *hated* it."

"But when? How? Brenda!"

She made a *pppfffftttt* sound. "Let's get you some coffee, shall we? I need tea. I'm exhausted and wired at the same time."

"Dr. Peebles!"

"Yeah. I know." She shook her head disbelievingly as I trotted behind her back to the kitchen. "I had to retake three semesters of undergraduate science first because everything I'd learned at Michigan was about fifteen years out of date." She filled a kettle with water. "Let me tell you. Organic Chemistry is a helluva lot harder in your thirties than when you're nineteen." She set a box of Kashi cereal hastily on the table and a carton of rice milk and a bag of craisins. "Sorry about this 'birthday breakfast.' Fresh Direct hasn't come yet."

"But?" My brain felt like a collision. "Brenda. You were rich. You were famous." A muscle in my left calf began to spasm. I started jiggling my leg, trying to get it to stop.

Brenda twisted on the gas with a *tick-tick*. A ring of purple-blue flame whooshed on the stove. "Madame LaShonda Peyroux was a joke, Donna. You knew that." She set the kettle down on the burner. "But somehow, I went from delivering the punch line to being it. No matter what I tried to pitch, all the networks were interested in having me do was a *reality show*. 'LaShonda Peyroux' back 'home' in Kingston, cooking jerk chicken. Telling fortunes. Auditioning reggae singers in talent contests. Tell me that's not the most insane and insulting thing you've ever heard?" She yanked open a drawer.

"Well," I said. "I guess."

"All this 'reality television.' Donald Trump. The Kardashians. Soon people won't be able to tell what's real or fake *at all* anymore." With a clatter, she rooted around for a strainer.

Her phone vibrated. She glanced at it. Yanking the kettle off the stove, she poured boiling water into a china teacup.

"Once I adopted Eli?" She tossed two spoons onto the table. "Oh, I was just done. I thought, 'Barack Obama's running for president; Oprah has her own media empire. But I'm playing some sort of psychic mammy on cable? This voodoo Aunt Jemima?'" She shook her head with surprising violence.

"Oh, Brennie, no," I said quickly. "You really helped people. I saw."

"One evening, I was in my dressing room, tying on my 'Rasta' kerchief, and I saw a stamp on it: 'Made in China.' And I looked at myself in that big, movie star makeup mirror, trimmed with all those blazing white bulbs. And I heard a voice as clear and as loud as if I had channeled it myself: *YOUR. MOTHER. WAS. RIGHT.* And I thought: There has got to be a far better way for me to serve humanity than *this*. Right then and there, I called my lawyer. 'I'll pay whatever's necessary to break my contract,' I told him. And I did." She pried open a tin on her little table. "Biscotti?"

I shook my head, trying to absorb it all. "Yeah, well," I said after a minute. "I certainly know what it's like to be a shitty role model for your kids, Bren." I gave a mirthless little wave. "Drunky McDrunkenstein here. World-famous kitchenware shill. Voted 'Biggest Embarrassment' by not one, but two teenagers."

"Ha." Brenda looked at me—not pityingly but with deep, knowing appreciation. And there it was. Our old connection. Shylock and Dreadlock. The years falling away, but also fattening us, giving us heft and deep, renewed reserves of love and goodwill. She cocked her head. "It's good to see you, milady."

"It's good to see *you*, milady."

"You know, I can't tell you the last time I had a real conversation with someone my own age that wasn't medical." Stirring her tea, she smiled sadly. "Not a lot of people understand where I'm coming from, Donna. A black, single mother in her forties doing a medical residency? I'm like a unicorn. That's what I was thinking this morning when I realized it was your birthday. I was remembering how we'd just pour out our hearts to each other and laugh our asses off. How we just 'got' each other, you know? And then, twenty minutes later, voilà! You called out of the blue."

"Oh, Bren. I was driving, and I saw this sign for a fortune-teller. A *literal sign*! And I was just, like, 'I have to call Brenda *immediately*!'"

Yet deep inside me was that insistent throb, like a bass line: *I need, I want, fill me.* "But you don't do readings at all anymore? Not even for, like, friends?" I took a big gulp of coffee, which was a mistake, because my throat was still scorched from the chicken wings; I coughed and tried to smile. "I mean, Brenda, I know you did it all very tongue-in-cheek, but you do have a gift."

Brenda pulled out her earpiece and tossed it on the table.

"Donna. Tell me. Why are you here, exactly?" She twisted her tea bag around on her spoon and garroted it with its little string. "Did you really just decide to go on a drive?" Before I could answer, she continued, "Because I've got to tell you. You smell of beer. And piña coladas."

"Oh, no. That's just Febreze. 'Aloha Hawaii.' I sprayed it on my pants." She raised an eyebrow.

"After, okay, I spilled beer on them." I set down my coffee. "I was this close to drinking, Brenda." I held up my thumb and forefinger. "I even had a mug in my hand. But I dropped it. And I took this as a 'divine intervention.' Ha-ha."

My teeth were starting to chatter, I realized. The coffee was bolstering the Adderall. "Yeah. I wouldn't believe me, either. It sounds ridiculous. It *is* ridiculous. I am a ridiculous person, Bren." Suddenly I started to tear up. "I've been sober five years, six months, and sixteen days now. But it just doesn't get any easier, you know? I hate going to meetings because everybody, they're always like, *Oh, my sobriety is the best thing ever* and *Oh, life is so much better!* But me?" I wiped my eyes on the back of my wrist. "You're never supposed to say it, but I loved being an alkie. I felt funny, and alive, and like I had some of my old edginess back. Now, I'm just in pain all the time. I feel insatiable, Bren. Why is that so great? Why is that such a virtue?"

She looked at me. "So," she said carefully, "you left Joey?"

"What?" I set down my mug and sat upright. "So you do remember! I knew it!" I pounded the table. "You foresaw this whole thing!"

She looked at me oddly. "Sweetie. You just drove nonstop from Michigan to New York City covered in room deodorizer. Alone, on your *birthday*. It doesn't take a genius."

Her phone vibrated again; she glanced at it. "Shit." Snatching it up this time, she typed something rapidly. "Dammit."

"Brenda?" I leaned forward. "Our last night at U of M, you did this really big, past-life regression for me, going all the way back to ancient Babylon? And you told me that in the middle of my life—I would have, like, this big, sudden crisis—but you also saw something I was supposed to do, maybe to avert it or to fix it—though you never got around to saying exactly what it was—okay, I think we were high at the time— but now, I know it sounds crazy, but I was just wondering if maybe you remembered any of it—"

Her phone pinged again. "Donna, look," she said quickly, her eyes on her screen. "I'm sorry. But I do not do that stuff anymore." Grabbing her phone, she said into it, "Yeah, I just saw. Tell him not to worry."

"But, can you recall even just a little?" My voice was rising. "I mean, just to even humor me? Or, didn't we record it?" Vaguely, I remembered a red Panasonic tape player. "Wasn't there a tape?"

Brenda set down her phone and looked at me, dead-eyed. Her annoyance was suddenly palpable. She pushed back her chair. "Look, I'm sorry, D., but this is my one day off in like, months, and I've got fifty thousand things to do." She picked up her phone as if it were evidence. "And now, I've just gotten something else added to my list."

"Oh God." Suddenly, I realized how repellent I was being, how presumptuous it was to think I could just show up on her doorstep like this. "I'm so sorry. I have no business doing this." Struggling to my feet, I picked up my dirty cereal bowl to put it in the sink, then saw there was no room. "I'm just a massive wreck, is all." As I whirled around looking for someplace to set it down, my spoon clattered to the floor and

I banged into the table. "Shit, shit. I am such an asshole." I looked at her plainly. I was shivering again for some reason. "Oh, Bren. Can you forgive me?" I fanned myself with one hand. "Goddamn perimenopause. I'm, like, waterworks here."

Brenda cocked her head. Slowly, she reached over and pressed her hand to my cheek. "Look, Donna. I'm sorry I never wrote back. I always meant to. I just got completely overwhelmed with medical school, and Eli." She sighed, not unkindly. "It was obviously very difficult for you to write. And it meant so much to me. It really did, Donna. I *did* understand. Our lives *had* become such opposites."

I squinted at her. I'd missed a segue somewhere.

Then, it came to me: Step Nine: *Make amends to the people I'd harmed.* When I'd first started in the program, I'd actually written Brenda a letter. How had I possibly forgotten? My brain seemed to have a damaged hard drive—or had sobriety wiped it clean?

Brenda knit her hands around the back of her neck and stretched extravagantly. "That last time we were hanging out together, in Chicago? You were talking to me, Donna, about your kids. And you said to me, 'I would die for them, Brenda. Who the hell would you die for in your life?'"

"Good God, I said that? That's horrible. That's a horrible thing to say to someone." I recalled again that nightmarish evening, my jealousy drenching everything like a knocked-over martini. I winced as I saw myself barking at a patron who'd politely asked me to please lower my voice. Brenda finally announcing, *I think we're done here*, and me saying, *Not me, sister.*

"Well," Brenda said carefully, "it was memorable. But. It did get me thinking, Donna. Who *would* I die for in my life? Who would *I* ever love or want to protect so fiercely? Maybe, sure, the 'biological clock' kicked in. But I think, frankly, you're the one who first planted the seed."

"Wow." I leaned back, considering this. It was the first time that any of my drunken behavior seemed to have amounted to any good.

Brenda yawned again. "Look. Where are you headed next? Do you have a plan?"

Embarrassed, I shook my head. I realized that up until that moment, there was still a little part of me that was hoping against hope that I might stay with Brenda a little while—that she still had a luxury condo with a guest room where I could squirrel away and clear my head for a little while. Oh, I *was* a fool. "Is there maybe a cheapish hotel nearby?"

She made a *ppffftt* sound. "Not really."

"I guess, all I was hoping for, Bren, was some sort of a clue. When you did that reading for me? Maybe, okay, it was a goof—but your prediction, it really did stay with me. And I keep thinking, why? There has to be a reason, right? And now my life has pretty much imploded, just as you'd said it would one day, so I was just hoping to find out. Is this actually part of some greater plan that you might have foreseen—even by accident? Is my marriage salvageable? Am I supposed be on a path to something better now? I mean—I just *feel*, Brenda, that piece by piece, I sort of bargained myself away over the years. And now, I don't know what to do. Literally. Once I get out of the parking lot here, I don't even know if I turn left or right."

Brenda and I regarded each other. It was like a shared old song between us, sweet and mournful and symphonic.

"Look, sweetie. I can give you actual directions. Like, how to get onto I-95. But your *life*?"

"You know me better than anybody. Bren, you couldn't just do a reading—maybe just to humor me?"

Sighing, she glanced at her phone again. "Okay. Look. You have a car?"

I nodded.

"Are you still up for driving a bit?"

"Yeah. Sure, sure. Absolutely." Though, secretly, I hoped she didn't want to go too far. I was beginning to feel light-headed.

"Eli's teacher just texted. He forgot to bring in his big social studies project this morning. A model of Nevado Sajama. Don't ask." She massaged the bridge of her nose. "I've also got to go over to see my mom and bring her some stuff."

"Your mom's here?"

"Yeah. I moved her up last year. The commute was becoming impossible."

"Oh no. Is she okay?"

Brenda frowned. "When she's lucid."

"Oh, Brennie."

"Yeah, well." She threw up her hands.

"Look, if you need me to drive you to see her, I'm more than happy to do it."

"That would be a huge help, actually." Brenda's eyes met mine. She smiled weakly. "And after that, if you want to crash here this evening, we can make up the couch. I'm sorry I can't put you up for longer, but I let the other residents crash here between their shifts when I'm on night rotations so I have someone to look after Eli. Hotel Peebles has been booked for weeks."

"No, no. I totally understand." I tried to hide my disappointment. "But we can have a girls' night, Bren! Like back in college. Ramen noodles and Diet Pepsi—play 'Purple Rain' fifty times in a row—"

"Wow. Does that ever seem like another lifetime." She smiled wearily. But she must've sensed my desperation—because she added guardedly, "And then maybe—just maybe, we'll see what kind of shape I'm in after Eli goes to sleep. But this is not something I'm inclined to do for *anyone* anymore, you understand? Absolutely no promises."

I tried not to betray any nascent hope. "Sure. Sure. Yes. I totally get it."

"And if my fellow residents do stop by to shower or nap, you don't mention anything about cards or predictions or Madame LaShonda Peyroux at all, okay?"

"They don't know?"

Brenda rolled her eyes. "One of them, this white girl, the first week of our residency, she goes, *Oh my God. You look like somebody totally famous. You're not Maya Angelou, are you?* As if I'm, like, eighty. But I've gone to great lengths to scrub my profile and keep my two identities apart, and I want to keep it that way." She shook her head. "You know, until I shaved my head, people were still coming up to me, begging me to tell their fortunes? At the supermarket, the dentist's. Even in an airport bathroom once. I do not want that at my workplace.

"Besides." She grinned at me in her old sly, ironic, Brenda-ish way. "Trust me. No one ever wants to learn that their spinal tap is being performed by a former television psychic."

As I drove Brenda around Manhattan, every time I glanced over at her belted in the passenger seat, my insides stopped quivering. I felt better somehow.

When I pulled up to where her mother lived, however, a sign over the entrance read THE HEBREW HOME AND HOSPICE.

"You've put your mom in a home with the Heebs?" I tried to make a joke to hide my uneasiness, though Brenda didn't pick up on it.

"It's one of the benefits of working at Mount Sinai," she said, looping her arm through mine. Clearly, I was expected to accompany her inside.

I took a deep breath.

The lobby was bright, hung with Chagall prints—someone was making an effort. But still. I could smell it immediately. That euphemistic, chemical stench of industrial cleanser and floral air freshener designed to mask human decay. Same as it had been thirty years ago.

Brenda twisted and untwisted her plastic bakery bag around her index finger like a tourniquet as we waited for the elevator. She chewed her lip. I could not abandon her here. *Just breathe through your mouth*, I told myself, though my leg was spasming again furiously.

As we moved hurriedly along the carpeted hallway, just as I had as a teenager, I tried to focus on the ceiling tiles and pretend I was in an office. But the plaintive moans emanating from the rooms, the blare of televisions as we passed the dayroom, the sound of a woman rambling loudly, *Morris, he said he put it in the valise!* and the occasional beep and wheeze of respirators were inescapable. When I nearly tripped over a medicine cart, I saw two West Indian nurses pushing a pair of shriveled white women in wheelchairs down the corridor. A bulletin board by a watercooler announced the activities for that day: bingo and a lecture about the Holocaust.

The door to Dr. Peebles's room was only partially ajar.

"Are you sure I'm not intruding?" I said. "Really. I can wait downstairs if you want."

Brenda squeezed my hand. Hard. Then she straightened her blouse and took a deep breath herself.

"HI, MOM. IT'S ME. YOUR DAUGHTER, BRENDA." Her voice was suddenly higher-pitched, full of artificial cheeriness as if she were talking to a small child. I stepped in behind her miserably and looked around. The room was no bigger than the dorm room Brenda and I had shared as freshmen. A few homey touches had been brought in to soften the standard-issue furniture provided by the home: a Danish floor lamp, plum-colored throw pillows, a brocaded blanket.

Photos were everywhere. In frames, on the walls, printed out from a computer and hastily taped up. Beneath many of them were labels on large, Day-Glo Post-its. ROLAND, YOUR SON. MICHAEL ALBERT PEEBLES, 1934–2011, YOUR HUSBAND. DANA, WILLIAM, AND ROLAND JR., YOUR GRANDCHILDREN (ROLAND'S). I recognized the print as Brenda's. I could see family reunions, people smiling on a beach in Trinidad, nephews and nieces and grandchildren graduating from schools, her father's memorial service. A whole chunk of her life I'd missed.

I tried to fix all my attention on the photographs. The bed, however, was in the center of the room, putty-colored and unmistakably mechanized and unavoidable. So, too, was the bedpan. And the tray full of pill vials.

"LOOK, MOM. I BROUGHT YOU A PRESENT," Brenda said.

Dr. Peebles sat stone-still in the corner by the window in one of those newfangled "gliders" that didn't rock so much as slide back and forth on a set of wooden skis. A show was blaring on the television across from her, though she didn't appear to be watching it: On-screen, a real estate agent was trying to convince a couple of prospective home buyers that a large closet was really a "bonus room."

Dr. Peebles turned her head, slow as a turtle. I got a shock. Although she now wore thick, plastic-framed glasses and was dressed in wine-red velour "activewear" and slippers, she otherwise looked almost exactly as she had twenty-four years ago at Brenda's and my college graduation. Her thick, dark hair was still impeccably styled, her cheekbones high, her jawline taut. Even her long, slender doctor's hands were devoid of any of the knobbiness or gnarled veins that usually come with age.

Reaching up, she slowly took off her glasses as if removing a mask. She looked at us with utter blankness, a milky scrim of incomprehension.

"Kimberly?" she said in a papery voice.

Brenda snatched up the remote and hit the Mute button on the television. "NO, MOM. KIMBERLY'S YOUR DAUGHTER-IN-LAW. I'M BRENDA, YOUR DAUGHTER."

Dr. Peebles leaned closer and peered at her. "You turned off my program. They were hunting for a house in Baltimore." She blinked at Brenda. "Kimberly?"

Brenda set the bag from the bakery in her mother's lap and placed a new pair of Isotoner slippers on the table. "I BROUGHT YOU THE PEANUT BUTTER COOKIES YOU LIKE, MOM. SEE?" Reaching over, she undid the bag and dug out one of the big cookies, crisscrossed with tine-marks, proffering it in a slip of filmy paper.

Dr. Peebles frowned. "Stop trying to feed me! I'm not hungry. I want your husband."

"ROLAND ISN'T HERE. HE LIVES IN WASHINGTON, DC. I AM BRENDA, YOUR DAUGHTER, AND WE ARE IN NEW YORK."

"Eli lives in New York City. My grandson." She looked over to the wall with the photos and the Post-its. "Oh," she said. "Of course. Brenda. Here you are."

"That's right, Mom," Brenda said, her voice quieting.

"I was just testing. I have to test you, you know, or you'll get lazy." She pointed to the television. "You were on television."

"That's right, but I'm not anymore, Mom."

For the first time, Dr. Peebles looked over at me. She seemed to decide I was some innocuous bystander. "That was terrible. A terrible, terrible show," she said. "I was so embarrassed. So ashamed."

I saw Brenda's mouth twitch. "I'm a doctor now, Mom. A doctor just like you."

Dr. Peebles stared at me. "I don't want to eat. Where's my daughter?"

"I'm right here, Mom." Brenda knelt down in front of her so her mother could see her in full.

"Is Eli coming?"

"No, Mom. He's in school."

Dr. Peebles looked at me. "He's not a real grandson. He's adopted." Brenda stood up. Her mother added quickly, "But we love him just the same. Don't we?"

Brenda had begun unwrapping the slippers, yanking apart the plastic tie that bound them with her teeth. She motioned for me to take a seat on a hospital stool I'd been avoiding.

"Mom, I brought an old friend. Do you remember Donna?"

"Hi, Dr. Peebles." I waved foolishly, the same way I did the very first day in the dorm room as an awkward seventeen-year-old.

Dr. Peebles leaned forward and squinted at me. She had it, too: that same Mercurochrome-y hospital smell that my mother had had. Just a whiff of it made me recoil.

Ovarian cancer had desiccated my mother physically; in the end, her flesh seemed to have dehydrated around her bones. Except for her distended abdomen, she'd looked vacuum-packed, homuncular, gray. Now, I wasn't sure which fate was harder to take: losing the body or losing the mind. Dr. Peebles had been so formidable and elegant. It was like seeing a great civilization gone to ruin.

"DR. PEEBLES. DO YOU REMEMBER ME?" I said like an imbecile. "BRENDA'S OLD ROOMMATE?"

Unsteadily, Dr. Peebles pointed to my neck. She said shakily, "Padlock."

"Ha!" Brenda gave a bark. "That's right, Mom."

"Oh, good God," I said. "*That's* what she remembers about me?"

"Hey, you're the one who showed up wearing shackles to meet your black roommate." Brenda snorted.

"Yeah. Well." I guessed there was no living that down.

"The driver," Dr. Peebles mimed.

"That's right, Mom." Brenda nodded vigorously. "Donna drove me."

"The funeral," Dr. Peebles said. "You came in the snow."

I brought a hand to my forehead. *Of course.* That was why the drive through Pennsylvania had felt so familiar. Freshman year, Brenda's grandmother had died. It had been during a massive snowstorm. All the airports in the Midwest had shut down, so I'd borrowed Toby's four-wheel drive. At some point during the thirteen-hour trip, we began referring to me as "Smedley," joking that I should show up to the funeral in a chauffeur's uniform. All we'd brought along to eat was a jumbo box of Double Stuf Oreos and a few bags of sour-cream-and-onion potato chips. One of Toby's tapes had gotten stuck in the cassette player, so we'd had to listen to *The Very Best of Conway Twitty* the entire way. It had been near-whiteout conditions. Whenever the truck fishtailed across the snowy highway, we shrieked with laughter as if we were on a roller coaster. If my own kids did anything like that now, I'd kill them.

Dr. Peebles's memory was like a shortwave radio. "We buried my mother in her pale purple silk dress. Roland, he took some of the money she left him and bought that Pontiac, didn't he?"

A knock came on the door; an orderly in flowered scrubs came in. Her nametag read ROSADO. "PAULINE, I COME TO TAKE YOU TO PHYSICAL THERAPY, YES? COME." She tapped her watch.

Brenda's mother got a wild look on her face. "Where are you taking me? I don't want to go anywhere. My daughter is here."

"I'm sorry, Pauline." The orderly glanced at Brenda with a conspiratorial frown. "But it's time. We have to take you, remember? It's Tuesday."

"Physio is good for you, Mom," Brenda said encouragingly. "You know that. *You're a doctor.*"

"I don't want physio! I don't want to move! Who turned off my television?"

"Pauline, we need you to go to physical therapy now so they can come in to clean your room."

"Why are you people barging in here? Why are you harassing me like this? Turning off my television! Forcing me to eat!" She flung the bag of cookies Brenda had brought her onto the floor. "Get away from me! I want my children! Where's Kimberly? Where's my husband?"

She started to flail. "You're all going to hell! You know that! You know that!" She stabbed the air repeatedly at Brenda with her finger. "Don't act like you don't know! Don't be ignoring the signs! You see the world! You read the Bible! You see the end times coming! You want to suck me down with you! Get away from me!" she screamed. A buzzer rang and another aide arrived.

Back in the Subaru, I didn't turn the ignition on right away. I sat quietly, staring out the windshield, giving Brenda time to collect herself.

Finally, she tugged on her seat belt and clicked it in place and cleared her throat.

I looked over at her. "You okay?"

She stared out at the street. "How did you do it, Donna?"

"What?"

"Watch your mom die."

"I don't know," I said. "Oh, wait. I drank like a fish."

"Why does she still make it so difficult for me? I mean, you heard her, right? Even with her mind half gone? Eli isn't a 'real' grandson; I've been a total embarrassment."

"Oh, Brenda, you are an amazing daughter. Seriously. She's a sick woman, is all."

Brenda looked down at her hands, knitted in her lap. "What kind of horrible person gets furious at her helpless, dying mother?"

"Uh, everyone. Being left is the worst."

Slowly, I turned the key in the ignition.

Brenda blew her nose again. She leaned toward the radio. "I'm going to find some Conway Twitty just to torture you."

After a moment, she glanced over. "So hey. What happened, exactly. With you and Joey?"

I took a long sip of water from the bottle I'd left in the cup holder. During my midnight drive across the country, I'd constructed elaborate, prima facie arguments for myself like an attorney. But sitting across from Brenda now, I suddenly felt foolish presenting myself as any sort of victim, as someone whom things *happened* to.

"I caught him cheating, dressed up as a French maid with a dominatrix in our kitchen, and I beat the shit out of him," I said plainly. "With a Privileged Kitchen stainless-steel fish spatula."

Brenda's hand went up to her mouth. The corners of her eyes scrunched. "Sorry," she said after a moment. "You still have that way of saying awful things that just makes them sound really, really funny." She shook her head. "Wow. Okay. I did not see that one coming."

She blinked at me. "Is he seriously injured? Pressing charges?"

"No, no. It was an accident. It was—" I looked out at the street in front of me, hoping some succinct, ready-made explanation might present itself amid the cars and trucks and pedestrians hurrying back and forth before my windshield. We were stuck in traffic. I took a deep breath and spit out the whole sordid story. Recounting it, I felt increasingly queasy. Joey hadn't just wanted to be humiliated as a woman, of course, but also as a slave. "It's unbelievable, isn't it?"

Brenda sighed. "Unfortunately, no." An ambulance whooped past, throwing fistfuls of red light across the interior of the Subaru. "Fifty percent of men over forty have regular erectile dysfunction. Apparently, some of them need to go more and more hard-core just to get off at all. And I wish I could say it was news to me that men have all these fantasies full of sexism and racism, but nope."

"Fifty percent?"

"Yeah. You learn a lot in medical school. Between that and being a psychic..." Her voice trailed off. "I'm only sorry it's happened to you. You know I always thought Joey was fundamentally decent. The big doofus."

I felt myself tear up.

"What almost shocks me most, though," she said as she shifted around in her seat toward me, "is that he lied to your kids about your drinking. And all the disrespect."

"Exactly! Thank you!" I pounded the dashboard. "I tried telling him, 'It's not so much about the dressing, Joey.'" We were at a red light. I turned to face her. "He broke the deal, Brenda."

"You made a deal?"

"Well, *I* did. Okay, maybe without telling him. But Joey was supposed to be stable and trustworthy, Bren. *You* know that. I traded 'hot' for 'reliable' with him. Hell, if I'd known he was going to cheat on me, I could've just stayed with Zack—or any number of those toe curling bass-playing man-whores I used to fall for. Now look at me." I snorted. "Medea in a Subaru, married to a philandering dentist."

"Sorry." Brenda chuckled. "That's also really funny."

We sat blinking at each other. A taxi behind me honked.

"Bren," I said after a moment. "Do you ever miss it? Even just a little?"

"What? Being young?"

"No, a celebrity."

She shrugged. "I miss the clothes." She considered it a moment. "I miss the help. Having a cleaning woman come in every week. A doorman, sure. And the town car sent over by the studio was nice."

I grinned. "Well, at least you're getting Smedley back for a day."

"'Oh, Smedley, dahling,'" she said in her old, parodic British accent. "'Thank you ever so terribly for retrieving my dry cleaning.' Listen," she said, switching back. "Donna, this whole Joey thing—this is serious shit. So can I give you some advice?"

"So you *will* do a tarot reading for me?" I said a little too quickly, a little too enthusiastically. "Oh, thank you, thank you, thank you, milady."

"What I was going to say is: Sweetie, I think you should go to a meeting."

"Oh. C'mon, Bren. I hate those things."

"Look. You showed up reeking of alcohol, Donna. You said yourself you came *this* close." Reaching over, she squeezed my hand. "I want to help you. But *you* know you've got to help yourself first. Start with the tried and true. And then, okay, I'll break out the cards."

Chapter 8

"HELLO. MY NAME IS DONNA. And I'm an alcoholic."

"HI, DONNA."

It was always a shock to hear so many strangers bellow my name as if it were a surprise party. In my cheap pants and ANTHRAX hoodie, I felt like a bumpkin. I was sure I *looked* like one.

"It's been five years, six months, and sixteen days since my last drink. The first time I got drunk I was eight."

I glanced at the roomful of faces turned toward me like sunflowers.

"One night, while my mother was at work, my dad and one of his buddies were blasting music in our basement. I came downstairs in my nightgown, crying because it had woken me up. It was smoky, I remember, and the music was really loud. Hendrix or something. My father was slumped down on this old couch we used to have. 'Daddy, I can't sleep,' I said. He had this weird, sloppy look on his face, and he pulled me toward him and said, 'Here, baby girl. Try this.' And he tilted this can to my mouth. Ballantine beer, I remember, because, you know 'Ballantine' rhymes with 'valentine.' I swallowed as fast as I could, but a lot of it spilled down my chin. His friend was laughing insanely, saying, 'Jerry, man, you're crazy.' But my father, he kept pouring it, and he was winking at me as if we were performing this magic trick together. And he was my father, so I just kept gulping it down. It was really bitter, but I liked the way my father's large hand felt cupped at the back of my head. He so rarely touched me. And he smiled down at me from beneath the tangle of his beard and mustache, and his eyes were pink and dreamy and approving. Almost instantly, I felt floaty. 'You like that?' he prompted. 'You want another sip?' Since I had the idea he wanted me to say 'yes,' I nodded.

"By the time I was eleven or twelve, I was partying with him in secret and also with some kids from my middle school," I told my fellow alkies. "I used to steal six-packs from the 'backup' cooler in our basement, thinking no one would notice." I cleared my throat. "By the time I finished high school, my dad had been committed. My mother had died of cancer. My brother and I, we'd become legally emancipated. We were probably already alcoholics, too, though who knew—when everyone else was partying." I shrugged. "I know it wasn't just how booze made me feel physically. Anytime I drank, I know it made me feel subconsciously closer to my father. Duh. It's Freud 101. Whenever I took that first sip, I felt that one twisted, blissful moment of his love."

Abruptly, I sat down. A few people glanced over at me sympathetically and nodded.

"THANK YOU, DONNA."

But all I felt was numb. And callow. Because the story I'd told was a set piece. Yeah, technically, it was true. It had been my dad who'd first gotten me drunk when I was eight years old. It had been our secret: chemical incest. But I'd recounted that sordid episode so many times as an adult at so many meetings that it felt stale and rote and leached of all emotion by now. As I'd recounted it, I'd even sensed exactly when to pause for maximum impact. I was like a one-hit wonder performing my top-ten hit for a tent full of nostalgic fans. I hadn't said a single truth about my sobriety now, of course, or my stash of pills. But why should I? In my dirty little heart, I felt a perverse need to thwart the whole AA enterprise. Yeah, it had gotten me sober, likely saved my life—blah, blah. But still, I resented it. Couldn't I be defined by more than what I'd given up?

Being with Brenda was a far more valuable use of my time than emotionally prostrating myself before a roomful of alkies.

As soon as the group finished chanting, "Work the program, it really works!" I dropped the hands of the people on either side of me and fled.

Brenda was waiting for me on the steps of the church. She was typing on her phone, a half-eaten waffle cone clamped between her teeth; Eli jiggled up and down beside her, his mouth bracketed with remnants of vanilla ice cream and colored sprinkles, his backpack hanging off his shoulders as he animatedly related how a kid in his class was double-jointed (*His thumb, it goes all the way back! Like this, Mom! Look! Like this!*).

Her eyes fluttered over me as I emerged. "How'd it go?"

"Good. Great. Wow, did I ever *wow* the crowd." I attempted a laugh. "And. Tah-dah. Still sober."

But I was thinking that just one day earlier, I had been teetering in a pair of red stilettos in my pantry back in Michigan, shrieking and beating Joey with a spatula. And now, here I was with Brenda, running around picking up dry cleaning and visiting hospitals in a parallel domestic existence. What the hell was I doing? The Adderall was making my veins vibrate beneath my skin. *I need. I want. Fill me.* What I needed was clarity: What I needed was a plan.

Back at the apartment, Eli and I uneasily bided our time together in the living room while Brenda ordered dinner online. I tried asking him what his favorite Harry Potter book was and who was better, Spider-Man or Batman—a subject of lengthy and impassioned debate when Austin was that age—but Eli's eyes remained fixed on an Iron Man action figure he kept walking along the edge of the sofa—no mistake, I was being boycotted—thanks, kid—though what finally engaged him was when I asked if he knew how to disable the "Find My iPhone" feature on a phone. Immediately, he picked it up to demonstrate. "What's your passcode? No. Don't say. It's secret. Do you know what's the most popular password in the entire world?" Without waiting, he announced. "1-2-3-4. Never, ever, do 1-2-3-4 as your secret code. It's like giving your information away."

I thought of my passcode and winced: 6-2-9-2. Joey's and my wedding anniversary. In fact, all of my passcodes were variants on our wedding anniversary, plus his birthday, or those of our children. The *we* of us was everywhere.

"Okay, so. You go here." Eli swiped my screen. "Where it says 'Extras,' then open this icon—"

When I was seven, I didn't even know what the word "icon" meant. I could barely plug in a night-light; I was scared I'd get electrocuted. My generation was constantly accused of being "helicopter parents," and ceding too much of our power to our kids. But how could we not? They were the only ones who knew how to operate the damn electronics.

As dinner arrived, I slipped into the bathroom. Okay, okay, I told myself. Just one more Adderall, so I don't pass out in my plate. Austin would not miss it given the vast supply. Yet I probably shouldn't have taken it on an empty stomach, because throughout the meal, I felt shivery and accelerated and unfocused. Beyond all else, I felt my dirty little heart beating: *Brenda, would you please, please, please perform a psychic reading for me—travel back with me in time—give me a clue how to survive this mess of my marriage, repair the wreck of my life.*

When she finally stood up and stretched and announced to Eli, "Okay. It's someone's bedtime," my pulse fairly exploded.

I'd forgotten how baroque it could be coaxing an eight-year-old to go to sleep. The epic teeth-brushing, the precise arrangement of stuffed animals, the negotiated number of stories. Finally, finally, Brenda and I were sitting cross-legged on her bed, facing each other atop her duvet cover just like we had back in college. Trains rumbled by in the street below, rattling the bedroom windows in their casings. The city seemed to bear down on us. Brenda spread a triptych of cards before her. "Sorry," she murmured as I stared between her and the Tarot anxiously. "I'm a little rusty.

"I feel compelled to offer a disclaimer. All of this is merely a tool for interpretation, sort of a Rorschach test, okay? Nothing more."

"Of course. Of course." I nodded vigorously.

She flipped over two cards with intricate stained-glass designs, rods and pentacles, and a figure in a boat, and studied them. "Well, I am seeing a betrayal here. A broken legal contract or a pact."

I scootched closer. "Yuh-uh. Absolutely. That makes total sense. What else?"

Fwup, fwup. Three more cards. Her pursed lips twitched from side to side. "You have a guitar with you. Any particular reason?"

I shook my head. "I just bought it last night." Was it possible to still become a rock singer at age forty-five? "Oh my God. Why? Do the cards say I should start playing again?"

"Nuh. Just asking."

She could see I was disappointed, because quickly she turned over two other cards and pointed to them the way you might to distract a toddler on the brink of a meltdown. "Now, these suggest a journey. A serious one. To places you've never been before."

"So I won't be going back to Joey?"

"Why am I seeing water?" Brenda murmured.

"This journey, is it good? Or dangerous?" My heart was going wild in my chest now.

She flipped over another card and placed it definitively on top of the others. Two beautiful figures on it were intertwined erotically. Even from where I sat, I could see the words "The Lovers."

Brenda stared at it for a long time. A pigeon alighted on her windowsill for a moment, dark wings flapping.

"It says 'the lovers' there, Bren." I pointed.

She squinted intensely, shaking her head. She turned over another card, wholly absorbed. "Hmm. Well, this journey does seem to take you toward a new love—"

"So, *not* back to Joey?"

She frowned. "I'm getting a new love, but with an old face—but it's not what you'd—"

"Like, someone from my past? Or just, like, literally, someone old?"

"Give me a minute, Donna, will you?"

"'Past' as in past-life past, Bren? Or someone here, now, who I've already known?" Already, I had an idea. In fact, the clarity of it gripped me like a seizure. I was certain exactly who it was. "Oh my God. Bren. I'm supposed to go find Zack, aren't I?"

"Now, hang on. I haven't said—"

"But you see it! It's right there! Oh my God. Maybe I wasn't even meant to marry Joey at all, Bren, was I?" I leapt off the bed. "That's what you saw the first time you did a reading for me, wasn't it? Remember how you froze all of a sudden? Oh my God. It was! It was! I know it! You saw it, Bren, *way* before! Joey was never my greatest love—it was Zack—and you knew this in your heart, and you saw it in the cards— this 'midlife marital crisis'—and how I'd have to 'stretch'—that was your word—but you thought Joey was a better guy—and he and I had signed that lease already—so you didn't want to say—either you were afraid— or protecting me—or, I don't know—jealous—"

With a sudden motion, Brenda swept up the cards.

"I'm sorry. I am not doing this anymore, Donna."

"But you've just confirmed everything you once predicted for me, Brenda. My life coming apart? Between forty and fifty? And now, you're telling me to go find Zack."

"Donna, like I've said. This is just a reading."

"But you're a psychic, Bren. You have a gift."

"Look, Donna. Sweetie. You need help. Get a marriage counselor. Call a life coach. Keep working the program. Call in the reinforcements."

"That's exactly what I'm doing here, Bren."

"Oh, no, Donna. I will not be your shaman or your enabler or your shrink."

"But you said it yourself, twice now, Bren, that my life would fall apart when I was middle-aged. And now, that's exactly what's starting to happen. And the cards are saying right here that I'm destined to embark on this journey to find my great love. 'An old love in a new face.' It makes total sense! So I just need you to confirm, please, is it someone I've actually known in the here and now, or in the 'past-past,' like

ancient Babylon? Or eighteenth-century Paris? Or, didn't you once tell
me I died in Panama? But he wouldn't be Panamanian now, would he—
that just doesn't make sense. I mean, my 'past'—it has to be someone
from high school, right? I mean, Dry Lake, Michigan, makes a lot more
sense than Borneo or Central America."

"Donna, do you hear yourself?"

"It's Zack, Brenda. It has to be! It has to be. I mean, c'mon. First,
I reunite with *you*—then, next, *him*! It's a *pattern*! Don't you see? You
know that *he* was my great love of all time. But when we met, we were
way too young, and—"

"Donna, I need you to listen to me." Brenda stood up. She finished
knotting up her tarot cards in a silk scarf. She dropped them in a sandal-
wood box and slammed it away in the drawer of her nightstand. "This is
exactly what I don't want to be doing."

"I think that, no—I'm not supposed to just turn back around and
try and patch things up with Joey—I am supposed to go out there and
find Zack. It's my destiny, Bren. All the signs are pointing to it. Maybe
every single crazy thing that's been occurring has been just to set this in
motion—like, if that guy in Vegas hadn't choked on that fig, I wouldn't
have come home early, and if I hadn't come home early, I never would've
caught Joey—And maybe the whole reason Joey himself was cheating
on me, it wasn't ultimately for himself, but for *me*, to free *me*, to help
me find *my* great love."

"Donna. Do I have to throw this glass of water on you? STOP."

Contritely, I sat back down on the edge of her bed.

"Now look. I'm going to tell you this, and then, we are done here, do
you understand?"

She waved the air around me. "This"—she made an airy-fairy-spell
motion with her fingers—"is not going to get you what you need. Comb-
ing back over the past, running around looking up some ex-boyfriend or
driving off to meet him, or whatever—"

"But you told me, Brenda. I'm not making it up. Twenty-five years
ago—"

Brenda shut her eyes.

"Okay," she said loudly, "since you're so stuck on cards and predictions and psychic powers, I'm going to give it to you straight. You want me to tell you what I really see as a psychic, Donna?"

She made a wide, circular motion with her hand. "I don't see *any* of this going well."

"You mean with my trip? Or Joey?"

"No, Donna, with the world. With things far bigger than you, milady."

"Okay. Now you're just scaring me."

"You wanted the truth, Donna? You wanted a prediction? Well, here it is. I see a lot of ugliness out there. Extremism. Divisiveness. Obama being our president—I'm sorry, but that has not ushered in a golden age of equality."

She stared at me. "You know, when I was on the Channeling Channel, all the time, I'd get these white callers—I'd do a reading for them, and just as they were hanging up, they'd say, 'I love all your predictions, Madame LaShonda. Just as long as you don't tell me that Barack Hussein Obama's gonna be our next president, ha-ha.' Or they'd start mimicking my accent, or trying to talk like a rapper. I had one guy ask me to channel his dead mother just to reassure her in the afterlife that he'd never marry 'a Jew, a black person, or a Mexican'—though you can bet, he didn't use those words. We had to bleep him. Live, on-air. I was, like, 'Excuse me? Can you not see me right there on your television screen?' It is out there, Donna. Real hatred and ignorance and fear. And I'm talking, like, right outside my front door in Manhattan. The way I see Eli get treated at his school? Where he is the smartest kid in the class?" She threw up her hands.

"So *you* want a prediction from *me*? I see us, Donna—*all* of us—needing to get our houses in order. The world is going to need grown-ups. Gardeners and builders and healers. People who stand up, fight for real justice. Not some middle-aged white lady driving around in her Subaru chasing down an ex-boyfriend based on a tarot card."

"Wow," I said, with more than a little anger and hurt. I glanced away.

"Look, I'm telling you this, Donna, because I'm your friend. I know you're going through something emotionally brutal right now. But you need to be your strongest, best self—and this? This is not it. And who knows. Maybe you and Joey will work your shit out. There's been a lot of love there between you, for a lot of years. People have reconciled with far less."

"I can't trust him, Brenda! You said so yourself." My eyes were wet and hot now with tears of frustration and anger more than grief.

"Okay, and that's a biggie." Brenda exhaled. "But tell me, Donna— have you yourself been so perfect? Have you never betrayed someone, even a little, because of your own bullshit?" She looked at me, hard.

Her phone pinged and buzzed. I wanted to smash it with a hammer. She glanced at the screen.

After a moment, she said wearily, "Listen, we're both exhausted. I've got to get some sleep. And so should you."

I nodded faintly. Yet I found myself unable to look at her. A fissure had formed between us, two tectonic plates cleaving. We each stood there, on opposite sides of her bedroom, me staring at the floor, Brenda out the window.

"Brenda, I'm sorry. This is not how I'd hoped to reconnect with you," I said quietly.

"Well, look. You're in a bad situation, Donna. And my life is just a cyclone." She sighed. "It's a lot more complicated now than it was at eighteen."

Her saying this, I knew, was an olive branch. She was smoothing it out for us a little.

"I really appreciate your letting me stay here tonight," I said.

"Sure, sure. Do you need help making up the bed?"

"No, no. I saw the sheets. I'm good."

She made a feeble attempt at a smile. "You realize we're both going to bed now at 8 p.m.?"

"Oh. Wow. Well, I won't tell anyone if you don't."

"Deal. Definitely." She smiled at me grimly. I tried to smile back.

"Hey, go easy on yourself with your mother," I said. "You're living through a heartbreak with her. Just feel whatever you feel."

"Yeah. Well."

We shared a brittle hug. "Joyeux anniversaire," she said. But when I left her room and padded down the hall to the sofa bed, I knew both of us were relieved to have me gone.

I need. I want. Fill me. As soon as I heard Brenda shut the door to her bedroom, I scrambled over to the bookcase and seized the only drug I had left: my phone, finally recharged. My heart pounded as I scrolled down the screen. There seemed to be dozens and dozens of new messages. I swiped through them furiously. There was an entire series from Ashley. **While you were away,** the first one began, **THIS happened...**

It opened up to an AP photo of a rubber raft on an island somewhere in Greece. **While you r drinking, some people have real problems, Mom,** Ashley had written. **#standwithrefugees.**

Her next message had a photo of smokestacks polluting the air and a link to an article on climate change. Another had an update from Ferguson. **Like YOU'RE really a victim, Mom? #blacklivesmatter #checkyourprivilege.** She seemed to have sent me one every hour. I felt assaulted now from all angles: The horrors of the world, yes, they were horrible—doom and gloom, everywhere—but how the hell was I supposed to deal with it here pretzeled and heartsick on a friend's fold-out couch? I had barely *slept.* My pulse grew so loud in my ears, it was like a backbeat. Finally, I texted back. **Enuff, Ashley, okay? I haven't been drinking, just in fight w. your father. #checkyourfacts #imstillsober #givemeafuckingbreak.**

The moment I hit Send I regretted it hugely, even as I also felt a tremor of glee.

There was a message from our bank **(alert: you have a series of out-of-state charges on your VISA)**; from Colleen Lundstedt **(Subject: Where are you? Donna, we got a call from mall in Inkster saying you** missed your demo today...); book club; and finally, amid the spam and PK requests, several texts from Austin.

Hey Mom. Sorry we got disconnect earlier. Glad u r ok.

Hey Mom, R u still ok?

Hey Mom, Where r u?

My thumbs moved frantically over the keyboard. **Austin. I am fine. Phone died. Had to recharge. Don't worry.** Immediately after I sent it, I added. **R u ok? Love & miss u.**

Almost instantly, to my great relief, I saw a gray bubble pop up on-screen filled with ellipses. He was typing a response:

Where r u?

In NYC w Brenda.

??? Who???

The psychic.

The famous one?

As if I knew several. **Yes,** I typed back. **R u ok? How was yr day?**

Ok. Math test + Odyssey.

He continued typing. **When r u coming home?**

I sat there for a moment blinking up at the ceiling. **Not sure,** I finally responded. **Just need a little vay-cay.** That seemed like an honest and neutral answer.

We can talk if u want.

Wow, I thought. I should take a screenshot of that.

Would love to. But don't want to wake B or her kid. Tomorrow?

K

I love you, Austin.

Glad u r ok, Mom.

As I was about to close the app, another message from him blurped up: **p.s. Don't drink, ok?** With this were emojis of a thumbs-down and a beer.

Sniffling, I scrolled through the rest. There were a few emails from Joey. Oddly, I felt a bubble of hope rise as I opened the first message. It had to be a missive of love and contrition. But it said only:

For laundry, one tab of soap or two? Also, bleach???

Then: **Visa alert re: out-of-state purchases. You bought a guitar, Donna? Seriously? Plus nine pairs of shoes?**

And then: **Now reviewing ALL charges. Walmart too? ALL the kids' pills, D? Tell me you're not on a bender.**

Tell me you're not on a bender? Really?

"Oh, that fucking does it," I swore under my breath. As if I'd needed any further prompting.

Of course I'd googled my ex-boyfriend Zack before—c'mon, who doesn't check out their exes on the internet? Six thousand years of human technological development have culminated mostly for *this* very activity—okay, second only to porn—and okay, maybe shopping. But in the past, I'd always googled Zack furtively, in a flood of conflicted emotions. When the hundreds of thousands of results popped up for Zachary Phelps—none immediately and obviously linking to *him*—I'd grown overwhelmed and panicked and quickly closed all the tabs.

What's more, this had inevitably compelled me to look up my other former bandmates from Toxic Shock Syndrome, who proved infinitely easier to find. Alfie Montana, once our skinny, gravel-cheeked bassist, was now a top "go-to" studio musician touring with Lenny Kravitz and Ronnie Spector. Danny Thurman, whose only redeeming musical quality back in high school had been his ownership of a Fender Twin Reverb Amp, was now known as DDT, a house deejay in Toronto. His YouTube video remixes had *millions* of hits. Seeing these, I'd felt sucker-punched by jealousy. "Him? He's a no-talent. He couldn't play guitar for shit back in high school." I'd quickly descended into a tailspin of regret and dissatisfaction. Googling people from my past was just setting myself up to be ambushed.

But now?

Z-A-C-H-A-R-Y P-H-E-L-P-S. Methodically, I scrolled through the results. Of course the Olympic swimmer kept popping up, even though his first name was "Michael." (Thanks, Google.) Yet, otherwise, there were people named Zachary Phelps everywhere. Over four hundred thousand of them, in fact. There was a Zachary Phelps bowling competitively in Australia; a Zachary Phelps newly born in a maternity ward in Macclesfield, England; a Zachary Phelps serving as treasurer of the Elks Club in Wilkes-Barre, Pennsylvania; a Zachary Phelps filing for a patent for a gel-based stain remover; and a Zachary Phelps fund-raising for a kennel for rescue dogs in Christchurch, New Zealand. There was even a Zachary Phelps doing time for grand larceny in a federal correctional facility in Talladega, Alabama (I clicked on the photo to make sure it wasn't my Zack, and it wasn't, unless my Zack was now part-Asian and thirty-eight years old with dyed-blond hair).

When it became clear that I needed to winnow my results, I logged on to Facebook. This yielded hundreds, rather than thousands, of individuals with the name Zachary Phelps. But even scrolling through all of these quickly seemed like folly. Then I remembered that in high school, Zachary, ever the showman, had once started spelling his name Zakk and calling himself, only semi-ironically, "the Zakkolator." The chances were slim, but I tried it.

And there he was.

Zakk "the Zakkolator" Phelps.

And he actually did not look that different. His public page was sparse, but he'd added a profile picture, which I immediately enlarged as much as I could and began scrutinizing.

He had aged, yes, but only in that eerily indefinable way where you keep looking at someone and wondering what, exactly, is different. All I could see was that his face had lost that cherubic, untested lushness of youth. It was more angular now, the skin itself coarsened and dulled. His smile lines were more pronounced so that they now formed triple parentheses around his mouth, and the flesh around the folds by his nose and lips had weathered, creating the impression of beard stubble, even though he was clean-shaven. His hair, though, was still a wreath of dark, distinctly rock 'n' rollish curls, if slightly thinner, and his eyes remained hazel and warm and full of mischief, even as crinkles fanned out from their corners. He was staring directly into the camera with an amused, triumphant look that said proudly, unabashedly, *Come and get it*. And I knew he'd been aiming for exactly that look, too, because I knew Zack in his very essence, and I could actually picture him posing (he seemed to be standing on a scaffold of some sort, with a blurry sky behind him; it was a close shot, from the shoulders up) and directing the photographer (his buddy? a girlfriend?): *Get me like this! No, wait, hang on. Here, man. Ah, yeah. This is totally a better angle.*

The Zakkolator.

Seeing him now, in all his charismatic, utter Zakk-ness, felt like a full body blow. And I might as well have been sixteen again, because I actually squealed aloud and clamped my hands over my mouth and started jiggling like a pair of cheerleading pom-poms before I could calm down enough to type. **ZAKK!!!!!** I punched into Messenger. **OMG!!! It's YOU! HOW AND WHERE THE HELL ARE YOU???**

All caps and triple exclamation points. Just like in high school, too.

And my heart began pounding frantically as I saw the three gray ellipses appear in the corner of the screen as Zack, wherever he was on this planet, began typing in response. Without waiting, I resumed typing, **I WAS JUST TALKING ABOUT YOU!!! AND THINKING ABOUT THE OLD DAYS!!! YOU R STILL CUTE!!!** And then, I couldn't help it. I actually added an emoji. The smile sticking its tongue out.

And no sooner had I hit the arrow to send the message than Zack's response appeared: **Who the fuck is this?**

And I laughed and typed back: **OMG. YOU STILL HAVE A DIRTY MOUTH!!!**

And he wrote back: **No. Seriously.**

And then he added: **Is this a prank (v. funny, LJ)?**

And then: **If u r one of those undercover online cops, I have a teenage daughter. I don't date them. Go fish somewhere else.**

At first when I saw this, I thought it was Zack teasing me, flattering me that I still looked like a teenager in my profile picture. But then I glanced at my profile picture again. And I saw that, out of habit, I'd logged in not as myself, but as Kayla McMullins, the sixteen-year-old One Direction fan I'd invented to spy on my kids. And Zack: Wow. He had a daughter now?

Zack, no, it's Donna Koczynski (formerly Cohen) trying to contact u. I typed frantically. **SO SORRY. Logged onto wrong FB page to message u. The one I use to spy on MY teens!**

This last line was crucial if Zack himself was married with kids now. Best to roll it back a little, establish myself as the same.

After I hit the arrow icon, however, the screen seemed to freeze. There were no more ellipses, no sign that Zack was still typing at all. I pictured him, tossing aside his phone in disgust. A wound grew in my stomach: Had I just blown it? Completely humiliated myself and chased him away?

But my phone vibrated and a Facebook alert appeared. *Donna Koczynski has new Facebook friend request from Zakkolator.* Immediately, I accepted, and as soon as I did, I saw a brand-new IM awaiting me on Messenger.

It read: **DONNAAAAAAAA!! BELLA DONNA! OMG, IT'S U!!!! HOW THE FUCK ARE YOU? BWHAHAHAHAHAHA!**

Chapter 9

ZACHARY PHELPS.

My sophomore year in high school—before my mother got diagnosed and everything *really* went to shit—I was part of a small clique of eye-linered, combat-booted malcontents. We'd hang around the bleachers at the far end of the football field after class, smoking pot and listening to the Cure on a boom box. When the weather grew lousy, we convened at Ann-Marie Larkin's house instead. Set in a weedy lot by the Jiffy Lube, it had the teen dream trifecta: paneled basement, ear-busting stereo system, and no parents around whatsoever.

Ann-Marie's boyfriend, Alfie Montana, had an electric bass. Danny Thurman, a kid from my homeroom, was tone-deaf but owned a top-of-the line Fender twin reverb amp. Ann-Marie's older brother, Dwayne, had a drum kit, and when he and his girlfriend were finished fucking upstairs, he'd saunter down and pull off the plastic tarp and start jamming with us while his girlfriend sat on one of the dilapidated couches in the corner, smoking Virginia Slims and glowering.

Calling ourselves "Toxic Shock Syndrome," we entered Dry Lake High School's 1984 Talent Show. We performed a shrieking three-minute punk rant called "Talent Shows Are for Losers"—and were oddly surprised (and embittered) when we lost.

One afternoon as we were rehearsing, Rooster appeared in the doorway. "Hey-ho. Dwayne around?" Rooster was almost nineteen but still hung around our high school, driving up in his lowrider with the motor chugging. I'd seen him at our school dances sometimes, too, staggering around the parking lot, hurling empty bottles at the field house.

In the Larkins' basement, Rooster unzipped a gym bag and tossed us an ounce of weed bandaged in plastic wrap. "I've got some coke and E, too, if you're interested." All of us scrambled upstairs to help Dwayne and Ann-Marie ransack the utility drawers for their mother's "rainy day" funds.

In the mudroom, a guy my age stood lookout. Lithely built, only a head taller than me, he was dressed, I saw, in a grubby, fleece-lined denim jacket and heavy boots. His shaggy chestnut hair fell to his shoulders, and his eyes were hazel and long-lashed, giving his face a look of perplexed sweetness. He paced around humming to himself—pausing from time to time to pantomime a little air guitar—his fingers flickering by his shoulder and his crotch. Spying Dwayne's assorted baseball caps, he began pulling them off their pegs, trying them on one by one, then putting them back randomly. When he saw me, though, he stopped, a Tiger's cap limp in his hand.

We stood there dumbly for an instant, regarding each other. "Oh," he said grinning. "Hey."

His voice, hoarse but somehow silky—the way it is with people who've just woken up—lingered on the "ay" part of "hey," so that he sounded not at all surprised, or indifferent, or studiedly cool, but eerily familiar. He said it as if he and I already knew each other intimately—as if we'd perhaps just been chatting at Burger King, and I'd gotten up to get more ketchup packets, and now we were resuming the conversation mid-sentence.

"Oh. Hey," I said back. In the exact same way. And I experienced a vertiginous sense of déjà vu. *I know you. I know you*, I thought—my certainty unshakable and profound, and inside, I felt an odd sort of sunrise.

Rooster tromped back into the mudroom, jamming a wad of money down the front of his pants.

"Okay, dickhead, you're up." He tossed the shaggy-haired guy a set of car keys. "Just try not to shear off the side-view mirror this time, okay?"

Before I could say anything else, Rooster clamped his hand on the boy's back and pushed him out toward the yard. The boy glanced back at me. He called out laughingly: "I don't know what the hell he's talking about, man. I'm like Dale fucking Earnhardt!"

"Yeah." Rooster snorted. "Dale Earnhardt with a learner's permit."

As I watched the van lurch and screech down the driveway, I felt strangely undone.

"Who was that?" I asked Ann-Marie.

"Him? Oh, that's Zack. Rooster's stepbrother or something."

"Oh," I said, trying to sound as nonchalant as possible. And then I uttered that insipid but most deathless of all teenage girl phrases: "*Oh. He's cute.*"

The day after Thanksgiving that year, my mom sat Toby and me down in our living room in a very formal, unsettling way. She told us that she had not merely been working double shifts at the hospital. She'd been receiving treatments, and they hadn't been working. The muscle in her jaw twitched as she explained that she was scheduled for some surgery. But the prognosis was grim. There was little more the doctors could do: It was likely a matter of months.

Is this a joke? Is this a joke? I remember Toby leaping up, his fists pressed to his temples.

"But Mom," I heard myself say, "you're a nurse." In Vietnam, she'd stitched up men with their limbs blown half to pieces, with their intestines falling out like jellied ropes—*they'd* lived.

"I'm a nurse, not a miracle worker, my pet."

In a very clinical way, she elaborated upon the details of what was happening to her and what was likely to happen—she seemed driven to impress upon Toby and me the precise scientific terminology of it all, the Latin names of body parts and diseases, the minutiae of the surgical procedure—as if she herself were not the patient but rather an instructor—or a teaching cadaver—at a medical school. As she spoke, all I could do was stare unblinkingly at the mantelpiece above her right shoulder. On it was an ornate, ridiculous gold clock that her parents had managed to carry with them all the way from Berlin when they'd fled. It was encased in a glass dome like an exquisite pastry. If you looked closely enough, you could see little pastoral scenes painted on porcelain panels on either side: a rosy-cheeked farm boy with a sheaf of wheat, a milkmaid with a yoke on her shoulders, the two buckets swinging as jauntily as her breasts. As my mother talked, I remember thinking, *How can anyone die if such a tacky clock exists?* It didn't seem possible that cancer and kitsch could occupy the same universe at the same time. *As long as you keep staring at this clock, and it's here,* I told myself, *this really isn't happening.*

In the next weeks, my mother took us to the Detroit Art Institute to see Diego Rivera's mural. All I was cognizant of was my throat hurting and a grotesque riot of color and us getting caught in a downpour. She took us to the movies in the middle of the day—films neither Toby nor I really wanted to see—and bought us troughs of popcorn and jumbo-sized boxes of Raisinets that went largely uneaten. Pep rallies at school, a fusion-jazz concert up in Ann Arbor, a lecture at the public library on Kurt Vonnegut: She had us embark on a whirlwind of activities together. Yet the fun was forced and miserable. The more we did, the less I saw. The less I felt.

And then, too soon, she lay inchoate in a mechanized bed, with all its tubes and cords and pulleys. Its rubbery smell of ether and urine.

The whole rest of the school year was a blur. To this day, I have no memory of the geometry I studied, any novels I read for English class, if I was excused from my finals or not the week of her funeral. That summer, I got a job waitressing at Bob's Big Boy. I'd wake up for my breakfast shift and find my father sitting in his recliner in the dark, his hand gripped murderously around the neck of a 16-ounce Pabst, his gaze a million miles away like a sniper's. When I came home later in the afternoon, he was usually gone, leaving only an ashtray and a cache of empties. Sometimes he would disappear for days, oily skid-marks glistening in our driveway, his uncashed disability checks piled on the kitchen table. Toby and I wondered aloud sometimes if we should maybe contact someone—our estranged grandparents in Detroit, the VA, or the authorities—but we worried that if we did, they'd call CPS because at fifteen and sixteen, we were still underage.

I stopped hanging out with my crowd. I stopped playing guitar. I stopped reading books. I took on more shifts at Bob's Big Boy. Since I didn't have my driver's license yet, I could mostly work only lunches. Afterward, I'd bike home, then steal half a six-pack or so from my dad's cooler and walk along the back roads—drinking one can, then another, the plastic collar looped around my wrist like a bracelet, the beer cans dangling like a giant, aluminum charm.

At the edge of town beyond the water tower was a single set of railroad tracks and an abandoned brick signal house. It was on a slight hillock rising gently above fields of wild grass. From it, you could see across southeast Michigan toward Ohio.

Trains never stopped in our township. They just barreled through. I sat beside the signal house and stared at the vectors of silver vanishing into the horizon. I wished they would carry me off to another dimension in time and space entirely, or that the fields themselves would part like the Red Sea, then swallow me up in their loam until I biodegraded like cardboard. Sometimes, I looked at my hand, and it didn't even seem to be a part of my body anymore. "This is your hand. This is your hand," I'd tell myself, feeling even more disembodied as I said this, seeing it not as a hand at all but some weird appendage. When I heard a train whistle, I'd place the empty beer cans on the track, watching them crush and flatten beneath the blur of the train.

One day, I decided to lie down on the tracks myself.

It was July; the air was thick and sultry. The ground between the railroad ties glittered with broken glass. You could always hear the approaching trains from miles away and feel the rails begin to vibrate long before they drew near. I lay in the crickety quiet among the weeds with my shoulder blades and my coccyx pressed against the rails like some cartoon damsel in distress. Closing my eyes, I imagined a locomotive bearing down on me—the spirit of my mother watching as I was pulverized.

"Whoa. What the fuck?"

I sat up abruptly. A guy hovered over me in jeans and boots, his hair a dark corona. With the sun behind him, I had trouble seeing his face, but as he shifted above me, I recognized him as Rooster's brother, Zack.

Nobody likes getting caught in the throes of their own private fantasy. And this was like masturbation in reverse, a willing myself to pain. And of all the people!

"Jesus, I'm just chilling." I shrugged, trying to hide my embarrassment.

Zack cocked his head. He was wearing a T-shirt reading BUDDY'S B-B-Q, and his grimy jeans hung so low on his hips, I could see the struts of his pelvic bones. "On the railroad tracks?" He seemed to consider this. "Wow."

"Hey, it's a free country." I sounded more defensive than I wanted. Then suddenly, I was overcome again by an eerie sense that we knew each other from somewhere else. "This is my spot, okay?"

He grinned. "Well, I hate to break it to you, but this is *my* spot, too, actually. In fact, I'm, like, the mayor here. No, better yet, I'm, like, ha, the *king*."

I gave him a look.

"I am, I am." He motioned grandly to the abandoned brick signal house with its tiny rusted, paneless windows. "Check it out. I've got a whole setup. Sleeping bag. Boom box. *Refreshments*." He was holding a half-empty pint bottle of Bacardi, I saw now, and he raised it proudly in a toast. "Hear, hear." As he smiled, his hair fell into his eyes again. He wobbled a little.

"You sleep out here?"

He snorted. "Only when my stepfather's being an *asshole*. No, wait, wait. *Excuse me*. Allow me to rephrase that: Only when I get sick of my stepfather's bullshit, and him beating up my mom, and her taking his side even after I fucking stand up for her and get my nose busted for giving a shit."

"Your stepfather broke your nose?"

"What? No! Of course not. No way. Not broken. Jeez." He flexed his bicep. "Look at me. I'm totally pumped. I'm practically the Incredible Hulk." Frankly, his muscle did not look that impressive to me. But there was something boyish and poignant and transparent about his braggadocio. I found it enormously touching.

"You know, *my* dad—" I started to say.

"Okay, Move over, missy." Zack nudged me playfully with the toe of his boot. "Whoops." With some difficulty, he lowered himself down beside me. The warm skin of his upper arm pressed lightly against mine. We were sitting side by side on the rail now, our backsides balanced on the strip of metal. Reaching behind him, he pulled a handful of petals off some blue asters bobbing beside the track and threw them over me like confetti. "We're havin' a party," he sang. "Ow." Patting his ass, he shifted around. "Okay. These are even more uncomfortable than they look. These are not designed for human recreation."

I giggled. "You're drunk."

He glanced at the fresh beer cans lying beside me. "Oh. Ha-ha. And you're not?"

I motioned to his pint. Handing it over, he let his eyes rest on me. I could sense his desire registering. Grabbing the bottle, I threw my head back as sensually as I could, closing my eyes, swallowing luxuriantly in long, confident gulps. When I finished, I dragged the back of my wrist as slowly as possible across my lips.

"Wow. The lady knows how to drink." Admiringly, he took another swallow, then sputtered and coughed. "Whoa"—he pounded himself on the chest—"So, do you have, like, a name?"

"Donna."

"No kidding. Is that short for, like, 'Belladonna'?"

"Nope. Just 'Donna.'"

"Nuh-uh." He shook his head vigorously. In the sunlight, his long, thick hair glistened like ale. "You should totally have people call you Belladonna instead. 'Belladonna' is way better. It means 'beautiful woman,' you know? And also, I think, poison, ha-ha. Or wait. Maybe a flower. Something, though."

"So what are you telling me?" I said teasingly. "That I'm beautiful? Or that I'm deadly?"

He squinted out across the fields. "Donna is just so—blah. So dishwater." He must have realized how insulting this sounded, because he added quickly, "And you are so *not* a Donna. You're a total *Belladonna*." In a deliberately cartoonish way, he looked me up and down again and wiggled his eyebrows. "Totally. I mean, look, it's the same for me, okay? 'Zachary'? Fuck. That sounds like some farty old car dealer. 'Zack' is way, way cooler. 'Zack' is a saxophone player. I've even started spelling it without the 'c' and, this is the best part, a double 'k.' Just Z-A-K-K! One note, one syllable, superfast. Like, pow! Whap!" He mimed cracking a whip. "Bam! Shazaam!"

"Shazaam has two syllables."

"Oh my God, ha-ha, you're right!" He bent over and slapped the ground beside him. "Two syllables! Two syllables! That is so funny! Pow! Bam! Zakk!"

The rails beneath us began to vibrate softly like an electric toothbrush. We could hear a mournful faraway owlish *hoooooooohoooo*.

"You play the saxophone?" I handed him back the bottle. I wasn't used to drinking straight rum. We'd always mixed it with Coke.

"Oh, big-time. And I'm good, I'm telling you. Really innovative. I'm like, what's-his-name. That black guy."

"Charlie Parker?"

"Yeah. Like him. Totally."

Another prolonged train whistle echoed in the distance, louder this time. Zack glanced down at the space between his legs, the railroad ties beneath them. His jeans, I saw, were shredding at the knees. "Once I get my sax out of hock, I'll play you something."

"I play guitar," I volunteered.

"Yeah? Are you, like, a Stevie Nicks chick? Ha. I can totally see that! The black lace. With a shawl. The boots."

"Ugh, please. Stevie Nicks? Hell no. More like Joan Jett, baby."

"Ooh." He said appreciatively. "So you're hard-core."

I grabbed the bottle and took a swig. "I am hard-core, baby," I announced. "I am punk rock." I don't know why I kept saying "baby" all of a sudden. I'd never used it when I spoke. But I liked the way it sounded now coming out of my mouth, shiny and hard like enamel. I liked the way it made him grin at me.

"So where's your pink hair, then?"

"Where's *your* pink hair then?"

A dark speck appeared in the distance. A whistle bleated.

"I'll dye mine if you dye yours." Zack's breath smelled like candy: rum and licorice and something citrusy. Beneath us, the rails were shaking now, the whistle hooting more insistently.

"So, what do you think?" He glanced at the black pinpoint growing steadily bigger. "You inclined to move?"

He flopped his arm chummily around my shoulder and drew me closer. Switching the bottle from one hand to the other, he took another sip, then pressed the rim to my lips. I gulped dutifully. I could smell his warm skin, feel his hair against my forehead. Blinking at him, I no longer saw one of him anymore, but two, the original and another misaligned copy, as if on tracing paper that had shifted. I felt emboldened now, invincible. He'd said it himself: Belladonna. I was no longer Donna, but a far more sophisticated, desirable creature, a deadly, dangerous flower.

I gave him my most provocative smile. "How low can you go?" I sang—I don't know why, it made no sense. I said coyly, "You scared?" My heart was pounding furiously now, and some tiny part of my sober brain tucked away somewhere—what had they taught us in Biology class?— was it the amygdala? The hypothalamus?—was frantically transmitting to me in a distorted, fuzz-box voice, *What the fuck are you doing?* But

I wanted to impress him, dare him, challenge him; I wanted to be the wildest girl he'd ever met.

His hooded eyes were fawn-colored, impossibly tender. He leaned into me. "Okay, then." He took a deep breath. "All right. Wow. So then we're doing this, then."

Drawing me even closer toward him, as if to kiss me, he jammed his hand beneath my armpit, waggling his fingers. "Tickle, tickle!" he shouted.

"Jesus!" I leapt up, flailing. "What the fuck?"

"Bwhahahahahaha!" He lay half over the edge of the rail, hunched over, laughing so hard he was gasping. I don't know why, but I swiped at him then, catching him under his chin with my fingers. "Tickle, tickle!" I yelled back. Laughing insanely, he rolled over the rail to escape me, bits of dried grass matted to the back of his T-shirt. As he tumbled down into a shallow ditch, the ground shook volcanically. A whistle shrieked, "Oh shit!" I jumped back into what felt like a wind tunnel and fell into the grass.

The train tore past, a violent blur of metal, its velocity whipping the air so fiercely it felt like repeated slaps to my face. The blood pounding in my ears merged with the thunder of the engine. An endless smear of clacking boxcars, blood-brown and rust-red and dark green flashed by and by and by for what seemed like a very long time. When it finally receded, the silence in its wake was jarring. All I could hear by the side of the tracks was my own breath, coming in little yelps.

I was almost surprised to see Zack still standing in the thicket on the other side of the track, his legs rooted wide apart now, his arms thrown back as if he'd just relinquished something heavy. He was panting so hard, I could see the logo on his T-shirt, BUDDY'S B-B-Q, rising and falling.

"Whoa. That was fucking intense."

I laughed. "Oh my God. That was awesome!"

He stepped across the rails toward me. "Jesus Christ, my heart, it's going like—feel that." Yanking my hand, he mashed it against his chest beneath his T-shirt. An electric shock shot through the plates of muscle and skin directly into my palm. He felt pulsating, animal. I did not want to remove my hand. I did not want to stop touching him. Ever.

"You feel that? You feel how fast it's still beating? Fuck." He gazed at me in astonishment. "Woman, you are *insane*."

Soon, it was like drugs. Maybe that first teenage love always is. Soon, seeing Zack was all I wanted to do, and when I wasn't with him, I felt bereft and jittery and crazed with hunger. I'd be in Trigonometry or practicing guitar, but all I could think about was Zack Phelps. Checking the clock every five minutes to meet by the lockers. Calling him on the pay phone at the gas station during his break. Sleeping in his BUDDY'S B-B-Q T-shirt with its intoxicating Zack scent. Doing ecstasy with Zack, cracking each other up making "monkey mouths" with orange slices, daring each other to leap up on the hood of a stranger's Buick or to kick in the windows of a derelict shed in Inkster just because we felt like it. Zack wheeling me crazily around Safeway in a shopping cart, terrorizing the elderly shoppers, eating an entire bag of Doritos before reaching the cashier. Him holding up the phone to the radio and singing along with Billy Idol to me, "Gonna spend my life makin' love to you." Catty girls at school telling me, "You know Zack's been hooking up with, like, three other girls," and Zack and I fighting, then laughing and deciding that everyone else was just jealous of us: How could they not be?

Us kissing, his fingers raking through my hair, the sleepy way his eyelids dropped as he got aroused. The two of us tangled on his puffy sleeping bag in the thicket by the signal house, his head between my legs, then his pelvis, the way he'd writhe above me like a lion caught in a trap. Good God: Nobody ever told me how beautiful boys could be, how leonine and sculpted. You were supposed to be reticent and coy with them, but I'd love to run my hands over the brackets of his hips and grab the indentations where his thighs met his ass. Also, he was the first guy I ever came with—which I'd never thought possible—it usually seemed to take so much patience and stamina, even by myself—plus the precision, really, of a safecracker—and with the few boys I'd hooked up with before—it had just felt like so much lurching and tearing and I'd always faked it. But Zack's wildness, his abandon—coupled with his appetites, his willingness to do *anything*—"Goddamn, Bella, I love the way you taste!" he'd sometimes howl. "You feel fucking amazing!"—made me forget about worrying whether anything about me was icky or gross—and gave me permission to wholly unleash myself.

Oh, I was *such* a teenage girl. It was textbook: Every time we had sex, I marked it with a little purple heart in the corner of my datebook. A pink star, too, for all the times he went down on me.

And the daydreams.

Tina Turner. Annie Lennox. Patti Smith. Debbie Harry. Kim Gordon — blah blah. Almost every great rock chick has been coupled with someone in her band. It's just the way it happens. Playing music is such a mind-meld—your central nervous systems fuse. In my fantasies, I started to picture Zack and me as this great rock romance.

For his birthday, I took all my tips from Bob's Big Boy that I was supposed to be saving for a car—or college—and used them to retrieve his saxophone from the pawnshop in Inkster. "I'm sorry this is not, like, new," I said. When he saw it, though—well, I'd never seen a boy weep before. "My God. Belladonna," he whispered hoarsely, pressing his thumb and forefinger to the bridge of his nose, his slender shoulders heaving.

Unfortunately, Zack played the saxophone as if he were trying to inflate it.

"You like that? You like that?" he'd say, blowing a series of discordant, earsplitting notes.

"Wow," I'd say after a moment. "That's really, um, different, babe."

"I know, right? At first, I thought needed a new reed, but then the sound was just, like, totally raw and real, right? It's like, *heavy metal saxophone*! I'm inventing, like, a whole new genre!"

Still, when I rejoined Toxic Shock Syndrome in Ann-Marie's basement that autumn, the others welcomed him without comment. I supposed it was because we were a punk band: Who cared if Zack sucked? (Though more likely, it was because Zack's presence meant that Rooster came around more and gave us free drugs.)

Zack was quickly as besotted with the idea of us as this hot rock couple as I was. We liked to lie on my bed sometimes and stare up at the dusty ceiling fan and talk about how famous we were going to be. We even practiced poses together in the mirror for whenever Annie Leibovitz came to photograph us for the cover of *Rolling Stone*.

"What do you think?" Zack would say, gathering his long hair. "Back like this, or loose in my face? And shirtless, right?"

And I would come up beside him, in nothing but my lacy little pink panties, and he'd yank me around in front of him, and wrap his newly tattooed forearm around my waist, and push my hair aside, exposing my pearly neck, and devour it, his hands cupping my breasts, until I began to moan. And then he would freeze us there, right there, young and muscled, entwined on the brink of ecstasy, and point to our reflection in the full-length mirror on the back of my bedroom door and say, "That's it. Just like that. Look how fucking hot we are."

For three years, Zack and I were on-and-off, on-and-off, like a faulty neon bar sign. We'd break up in that awful, recriminatory, manic-depressive sort of way—full of screaming scenes in Burger King and parking lots, public accusations and CDs being flung out car windows and late-night sobbing from pay phones—real class acts, both of us. But then I'd find some lame excuse to call him (*Hey, I was just wondering, do you happen to have that bootleg New Order album we once talked about?*) or he would lurk around Bob's Big Boy, waylaying me at the end of my shift. It spooled on and on, even after I went away to Ann Arbor for college— nearly right up until the time I met Joey, in fact.

And yet it was that image of us in front of the mirror that remained most distilled in my memory, that I always came back to and lingered over in fits of nostalgic longing. The two of us, so young and blossoming, nearly feral with sex, believing we alone had invented the orgasm (an eye roll, please—but we'd believed it!), delighting in our own exquisiteness, poignant in our desperation, convinced we were destined for greatness—such intense surety! (I'd had so much less, but felt like so much more!) How wild and commanding I'd been with him.

And that singular kiss. Zack's lips crushed like a rose against the cool of my neck just above my clavicle, one hand gripping my bare hip and pressing me urgently against him, the other cupping my breast. Somehow this, more than any other act in our vast repertoire, never failed to arouse me and fill me with an aching desire, no matter how many years had passed. That moment was like my secret, most favorite old record that I turned to whenever I felt my greatest despair, and played over and over again in my head.

And now, over a quarter of a century later, here he appeared, out of the ether. Zachary Phelps.

Belladonna Cohen!!!!!

OMG.

How the FUCK are you????

Reuniting with your first love online: Whether it's risqué or cliché, one thing is certain—it makes for absolutely banal reading. Our hourlong exchange sounded not like torrid lovers reconnecting so much as a transcript of a job interview between two fourteen-year-olds. **OMG: How r u? Where r u? U have kids now? U married??**

Me: **2 Kids! Girl,19 & boy, 16. Married?...It's complicated. U?**

Z: **Am checking out yr photos on FB. U r still hot!**

Me: **Is that NO?**

Z: **LOL. No longer married 4 sure. 1 daughter, total badass 15, lives w her mom in Ohio.**

Me: **Where r u now?**

Z: **Nashville. Got some big gigs this week. Then LA, Texas, Baltimore. Miami. I'm all over the place, baby!**

My heart caught. Though I'd braced myself for the possibility that

Zack was married now, I'd never considered that he'd gone into a career in music. Not him, too! I felt a sudden knot of envy.

U r a musician? I typed.

When he replied, **No. A rigger**, I was embarrassed by how much relief I felt, even though I had absolutely no idea what the hell a "rigger" was. Something to do with sailing? Welding? I pictured him shirtless, in faded jeans, wielding some sort of artillery-like equipment. I felt myself warm to it.

Sounds HOT.

It is!!!! I put together the whole show. Lights, tech, stage. Everything. Nothing can go on w/o me, baby! ☺

Texting: It should be left to rot with other misguided trends like bloodletting and 8-track cassettes. It was the death of all poetry and nuance and true human connection. It was Zack's actual voice I was craving, the sleepy scrape of it, and the throbbing heartbeat behind his lunatic laugh—not proxy in boldface. When he typed out **No longer married 4 sure**, what exactly did he mean—that he himself was unclear of his marital status? Or, "Not married! For sure!" like a happy definitive? The goofy emoji that he used to punctuate this with—a smile with one bug-eye—was only more obfuscating. What cartoonish symbol could possibly sum up or illuminate a Shakespearean range of feeling?

Working fish fry @Fontanel this wkend, Zack texted. **KID ROCK!!! Totally Awesome.**

Fish fry? Fontanel? Wasn't that the soft gap in a baby's skull when it was first born? And Kid Rock? Clearly, I was missing something. **WTF?** I typed.

Big outdoor concert, he wrote. **Music-fest.**

This is torture, I typed. **I Hate IM & txting. Want to hear your voice instead. Can we speak 2moro when I can actually talk? Wish I could c u in person. So much better!**

DEF! Wish I could c u 2! 2 bad u r not on the road with me, B. U would totally love it.

Me 2, I typed back. Then I stared at his message.

Too bad you are not on the road with me. Was there any sentence in the English language more pregnant with longing and romance?

I thought about Brenda's cards. The Lovers. I'd seen it right there, firsthand. It was out there for me, waiting. This message from Zack could not align more perfectly with it—it was here now—a reunion out of the ether, a sequence of opening doors. It was coming together so exquisitely, in fact, it was ridiculous. I took a deep breath.

Actually, I typed back, **I happen to be heading to Nashville this week—For some music biz. I could come down early & join u.**

As I watched the screen without any new text appearing, my heart began pounding insanely. But finally, a response materialized.

R U Kidding? When?

I can drive down tomorrow.

Seriously???? he wrote.

SERIOUSLY.

Do I even need to say that once I finally logged off, there was absolutely no way I could calm down and sleep? My skin was clammy with adrenaline. I thrashed about wretchedly on Brenda's sofa bed until nearly midnight, tempest-tossed by the incessant rumble of trains below on Park Avenue and the whoop of sirens. The "City That Never Sleeps" never shut up.

More than anything else, of course, my brain was on the spin cycle: Zack Phelps. Zack Phelps. Zack Phelps was in Nashville. According to Google Maps, it was just a fourteen-hour drive from Brenda's. Of course, I'd have to make a few stops along the way: I'd need my roots touched up, a quick trim, some makeup—and, certainly, fabulous clothes! The maps showed designer outlets and a Bloomingdale's off the highway in New Jersey—fuck it, I was done economizing, done buying clothes at Valu-Village while Joey plunked down good money for size-twelve Mary Janes and custom-made sissy outfits. There were salons at the malls, too—I could book an appointment online—good God, I loved the internet! I got sidetracked reading all the Yelp reviews, then looking at photos of bad celebrity haircuts, then bad celebrity plastic surgery—but finally I made an appointment for cut, color, the works. By the time I arrived at the Delaware border, I'd be an entirely new creature. The only problem was getting my car out of the garage in the first place; CJ's Body Shop, I saw, didn't open again until 6 a.m.

Not knowing what the hell else to do with myself, I found myself starting to clean Brenda's kitchen: washing all the dishes as quietly as I could, putting away the silverware: spoons cradled in spoons, forks in forks, knives perfectly aligned, their tips like compass needles pointing north, Tupperware nesting according to size *and* color! I was creating rainbows! What was that mnemonic device from elementary school? "Roy G. Biv"? I scoured all her appliances, then began scrubbing her floor with Lysol I found under the sink. My back burned and my knees got scraped, but it felt good to do something physical and taxing and transformative—the linoleum was starting to glow—why, cleansers were like magic! Really, I could be a spokeswoman! Or write a song! Why were there absolutely no songs about housecleaning?

When there was absolutely nothing left in the kitchen, I couldn't resist starting in on the living room with silent ferocity. I'd forgotten what a whirlwind kids were: how stray plastic game pieces (tiny boots, light sabers, wheels) and oily stubs of crayons wound up buried between chair cushions and in the piles of the carpeting. I cleaned and stacked and dusted and polished; I even straightened the Harry Potter cape and the scarf on the Skeleton, completing the look with a pair of Brenda's sunglasses I found underneath the radiator.

Some women would hate anybody else touching their stuff. But I knew firsthand what a neat freak Brenda secretly was. Her chastisement had clearly hit a nerve with me, and I cleaned in a stew of guilt and contrition, determined to show her that I was sorry and that I loved her and, also—that I was not nearly as much of a narcissistic asshole as she'd made me out to be.

Finally, there was nothing left but the bathroom. It had an old-fashioned tub with a scorch-mark of rust beneath the faucet. As I scoured the grout between the tiles, I could hear a garbage truck below making some predawn rounds. A plastic cup by the sink was jammed with a candy-cane assortment of toothbrushes with different initials and names scrawled on the handles with black marker. *AJ. Marisol. Jordy. Petra.* I could picture all the young medical residents tromping in and out in their scrubs, showering hurriedly between shifts, discussing prognoses with Brenda over lukewarm coffee in the kitchen. She had a whole community of colleagues now—no more sitting alone in a studio, taking on the problems of the world—and for a moment, I felt a fresh wave of envy and love and heartbreak for her all at once, and I felt myself tear up again. Good God: I was a mess.

I stripped and showered as quietly as possible, scrub-scrub-scrubbing myself with her organic lemongrass bodywash. I toweled off and re-dressed, studying myself in the mirror. And then, well, old habits die hard. Quietly—*shhhh*—I eased open the medicine cabinet. Just to peek. I was astonished at how many prescription bottles were inside. A forest of amber. Grabbing one closest to me, I shoved it into my bra, nestling it between the cups. It was an instinct, a sudden hunger. I didn't even bother reading the label. I just needed to feel a vial pressing against my heart.

As I stepped out onto the street at daybreak with my guitar case, I felt like a fugitive, but I had to keep moving. To kill time, I headed south on Park Avenue just to satisfy my curiosity until I was standing on the gardened median ten blocks from Brenda's apartment, at which point the entire neighborhood did, in fact, transform into that *other* Park Avenue—the one I'd seen in all the movies—a broad boulevard full of grand, luxury high-rises with liveried doormen standing sentry beneath the awnings. An omen, somehow. As the sky blued from night to dawn, the windows above me slowly illuminated with gold lights as the rich woke up for breakfast and their 6 a.m. workouts and their waiting town cars. I watched the city awaken, then headed back uptown to East 102nd Street, where I stood on the sidewalk shivering as a Hispanic man in a tweed cap unchained the gates, quieted the dogs, and allowed me to reclaim my Subaru.

When Brenda awoke and saw my note propped up against the peppermill in the kitchen ("I couldn't sleep and didn't want to wake you...love to you & Eli..."), she'd likely see through it immediately and know where I'd run off to. Maybe it was cowardly, my slipping out like that. But I didn't want to face any more of her disapproval. She herself couldn't deny what she'd seen in my cards—and while she might have loftier ideas about the world, I told myself, I had my own little romantic destiny to follow. I'd wasted enough time as it was.

Chapter 10

IMAGINE ALL THE LOVE letters penned throughout history, all the wet dreams, all the desperate prayers, all the stolen glimpses and winks and kisses in marketplaces and temple grounds and school cafeterias. All the hearts leaping at the sight of the postman, the obsessive replaying of ballads and answering machines. The crotches waxed, eyebrows plucked, wrists anointed with perfume. If we could distill the great tidal wave of human desire into its purest, chemical form, it could fuel civilization for the rest of our days.

Me, I found it was even stronger than my son's Adderall in keeping me focused on driving one thousand miles of brain-numbing highway. When I'd Skyped Zack from a hair salon in New Jersey, his voice had sounded just as it had when we were teenagers, scraping over the vowels like velvet over sand. It had triggered a Pavlovian, sexual reaction in me. As I drove south through Delaware, Maryland, and the Shenandoah Mountains along the spine of Virginia, I kept anticipating that first lightning-bolt moment when we would actually set eyes on each other again: Would the attraction still be there in full force? Would we still click as much in person as we had seemed to online and on the phone? How much would he have changed? I imagined Zack standing in the hotel lobby, anxiously checking his watch and clutching a cellophane cone of pink roses like he used to bring me from the gas station.

Yet when I finally arrived at the Comfort Suites Motel in Goodlettsville, Tennessee, a television bolted to the wall flickered soundlessly overhead in a deserted lobby, broadcasting the *Tonight Show* to no one. A chubby, brown-skinned night clerk (Indian? Pakistani?) sat on a stool behind the reception desk, playing Sudoku. She had thick glasses and wore a LADY ANTEBELLUM T-shirt.

Twice she asked me to spell my last name. Zack had promised he'd make a reservation for me, but there was nothing in the system. I asked her to check under his name, too, but that only yielded more clicking, more frowning.

I could feel my shoulders drop in defeat, my handbag slide to the ground with a heavy *thwump*. I imagined how pathetic I looked, standing there all primped and hopeful, close to midnight, flanked by my guitar case and a flashy purple roller board stuffed with new clothing.

"Okay then. I'll just book a room myself now, in cash," I said.

"I'm sorry, ma'am. But we are all full already."

"You don't have a single room? But how can that be?" Goodlettsville was a tiny blip on the map, a full twenty minutes away from Nashville.

"Kid Rock's having a fish fry over in Fontanel this weekend. Every hotel in the county is booked." She motioned to a poster tacked above a water cooler. It showed a picture of a bass in a cowboy hat playing a guitar.

Anxiously, I dug out my phone.

"BELLA," Zack shouted over a dull thump of bluegrass and traffic, "WHERE ARE YOU?"

"Where are *you*? I'm at the Comfort Suites, just like you said."

"I'm just across the road. Do you see that sign out the window? On the right? Bailey's Sports Bar? Come on over. I'm with some of the guys from work."

"You said you made a reservation for me, Zack. They're telling me there's nothing."

"You're fucking kidding. No way." In the background, I heard a clatter of dishes. "Hang on. I'm calling it up on my phone. Okay. Right here. 'Donna Cohen. Reservation number 567095K.'"

Cohen. Of course. He'd made it my maiden name. He'd never known me as anyone else.

"We're just grabbing some drinks," Zack shouted. "Come on over. In fact, tell me what you want and I'll order for you. Hang on a sec. Hey!" I heard him shout across the din. "What time's the kitchen close?"

I felt myself prickle. I'd just driven nearly a thousand miles. I didn't want to meet in a sports bar. I didn't want to meet any of Zack's work buddies. Was it too much to ask that he just cross the fucking street?

"Look, I've been driving since dawn," I said wearily, and though I didn't want to, I added, "so maybe I'll see you in the morning instead?" Hugely deflated, I hung up.

I grabbed my room key and my free breakfast coupon from the receptionist, stuffed them into my bag, and yanked my belongings into the elevator.

Inside my room, the light flickered on spastically, revealing a bone-white kitchenette and an enormous flat-screen television bolted to the wall. A king bed flanked by two serviceable lamps. In its sterility, it looked like a controlled-living experiment in a psychiatric hospital.

I plopped down miserably on the edge of the bed and kicked off my boots. Unbuttoning my blouse, I pulled out the one thousand dollars in twenties I had stashed in my bra and tossed it on the bureau. The wad had grown damp; the tight fist of paper had irritated my cleavage. *You fool*, I thought.

Glimpsing myself in the mirror, I saw how wilted and drained I looked, despite all my best efforts in a ladies' room twenty minutes before. I flopped back across the mattress, clutching my phone. Messages from Joey and Colleen Lundstedt and the Privileged Kitchen and our bank and Visa had accumulated all day. From Colleen: **Donna, you missed another sales demo ... Donna, the mall in West Bloomfield says you haven't confirmed ... Donna, irate call from woman about Via Vecchio Earthenware you were supposed to deliver? ... CALL ME PLEASE ...** Oh, shit: I'd had alerts set on my phone for all my PK appointments, dinners I'd ignored. From Visa: **Security Fraud Alert activated ...** From Joey: **Donna, Austin keeps asking me when you're coming home.** Also: **Did you forget Mr. Noodles? Pickup today?** I felt a jab of guilt. Quickly, I texted my son: **Hey A. Your momma loves you.** But then another from Joey read: **It doesn't need to be like this, Donna. We can get you all the help you need. Am looking into rehabs for you.** I swiped away the alerts and tossed my phone onto the pillow. I breathed in and out, staring at the popcorn ceiling with its little emergency sprinklers, its red-eyed smoke detector. *Just one minute*, I thought, closing my eyes.

The banging on the door was so urgent that for a moment, I thought there was a fire. I scrambled up, not knowing where the hell I was. "Bella! Belladonna! You in there?"

I yanked my shirt back on, my hands shaking as I rebuttoned it. "Hang on!" Tripping over an ottoman, I fumbled in my purse for my comb, scalloped lipstick over my mouth, popped an Altoid.

"Room service, room service!"

"My fucking God," I said as I pulled open the door. "It's after midnight."

And there he was. Deliberately posed. One hand pressed high against the doorframe, the other hooked through his belt loop, his legs spread wide apart like a cowboy's. At his feet sat a shiny white plastic bag. He was wearing a jean jacket and boots and some sort of utility belt slung low on his hips like a holster. He tossed his head back, clearing a curl of hair from his eyes, and grinned. He was showing off for me—and he knew that *I* knew he was showing off—his exaggerated bravado like an old, inside joke between us. "So, gorgeous." He winked. "Somebody here order a midnight buffet?"

"Well, aren't you still the peacock."

"Bwhahaha. Oh my God. You're still so funny. And wow. Look at you! Yep. You still look totally the same." Snatching up the bag, he sauntered inside. I smelled a whiff of beer, of fruity shampoo. "No, seriously. I am not fucking kidding. Jesus, Bella. It's like you've barely changed." He gazed at me, up and down. "Well, okay. Now your hair isn't pink."

"You are out of your mind." He'd been drinking, I realized. I also realized that I'd expected this—and also, that I didn't care. Seeing him, I was so instantly turned on, it was like having a seizure.

Showily, he held up the bag. "As soon as you hung up, I thought, *Hey, asshole. She's just driven, like, a zillion miles to see you. Get over there.*"

"Yeah, well, I gotta say." I tried to keep the annoyance out of my voice. "I kind of thought that you'd be waiting for me."

"Oh? You were worried? You missed me?" He seemed to enjoy the prospect of this a little too much. He set the bag down on the little white table in the kitchenette. "Well, maybe I did take a moment to watch you arrive from the parking lot."

"You what?"

"Just for a minute—that's all, I swear. You know, I just wanted to take a moment. Take you all in." He poked around in the plastic bag. "I hope you like hot wings. They gave me, like, two dozen cause the kitchen was closing."

"Oh. Good God."

"I wanted to bring over a pitcher of margaritas, but of course, they won't let you take drinks off the premises. But I had a six-pack in my truck." He waggled two bottles of Heineken at me. Grabbing a bottle opener from his belt, he uncapped one with a dramatic flourish, letting the top drop on the floor. "Want?" He took a swig.

I reached for it, then stopped. "Nuh-uh. I'm good for now." I tried to sound casual, though my heart kicked up a notch.

It was only then, when Zack paused and stared at me, that I realized just how nervous he was. This touched me to the core, somehow. "Wow. Donna Cohen. It's really you."

We just stood there for a moment, grinning at each other stupidly. I forgave him for watching me from the bar. Twenty-six years. It was a lot to deal with.

He had a light scar under his left eye now, I noticed, and in person, he was bulkier than he'd been in high school. I could see the crinkliness around his eyes, the slight erosions on his brow. Yet, in a way, he looked even better than when we were teenagers. The coiled skittishness had disappeared from his face. He was sturdier. I cringed slightly imagining how I, in turn, must really look to him, now that he could see me live, in full, from the neck down. Softer, rounder, my lushness diminished, no doubt: I was more powdered jelly donut than ripe peach. My hair was askew, my new clothes rumpled. Certainly, this was not at all how I'd planned it.

From down the hall came the belch and rattle of an ice machine.

"Wow, okay," Zack said awkwardly. "This is weird, isn't it?"

"I know." I laughed nervously. "I've never seen you speechless before." After a moment I added, "Look, if this is all wrong for you, you know you can go. I'll understand. No harm, no foul." I tried to sound gentle and generous, though, in truth, my heart was burning.

"No, no. Not at all," he said quickly.

"So what do we do now?"

He took another swig of beer and set the bottle down beside him on the counter. "What does the lady want?"

"I don't know. Should we hug maybe?"

A hug seemed safe, all-in, but skewing heavily toward affection. I opened my arms. Zack pushed off from the counter toward me. We hugged extravagantly, stepping back and forth, right-to-left, completely fused, as if we were dancing slightly. His breath was beery. His shirt smelled of detergent and limes and something unmistakably musky and Zack-ish. He was in astonishingly good shape: all muscle, his shoulders and back as hard and smooth as polished agate. He must have felt my surprise because he disengaged and stepped back and flexed both his biceps. "I know. Check out these guns, right? You like? I'm like fucking Rambo now. All day long, I'm hauling chain."

I made a big production out of squeezing his bicep like a caliper, quietly thrilled to have an excuse to keep touching him. "What're you? In a prison gang?"

"Ha! No. C'mon, I told you. I'm a rigger. The guy who does all the lighting and scaffolding and stuff at events. I'll take you by the site tomorrow. You can see for yourself."

"Hug me more first." He fit into me perfectly. As I smoothed my hands slowly over his back, it felt like matches over flint. He stroked my hair, one hand desperately gripping my waist. Neither of us seemed inclined to let go. I was too exhausted at that point, or too engaged, to care whether my belly and hips felt bigger or too soft to him now. He pulled me closer and closer, and nuzzled my neck. "Oh, Belladonna," he murmured.

"Welcome back," I said.

After more than a quarter of a century, there was so much to discuss, so many blanks to fill in. A library's worth of history.

But instead, we kissed. We kissed like two people about to burn at the stake. Zack's mouth and his tongue, they tasted of beer. It was a kiss that winded me like a tornado, that lit me up like a Roman candle, that almost made me fall to my knees. It consumed and liquefied me. It was a kiss you wait a quarter of a century for. All I knew then was that I wanted another. My drug of choice above all others. It was back.

"Wow." Zack stepped away and stared at me with unabashed hunger. "Jesus Christ. Do you know how badly I want to rip off all your clothes and carry you into the bedroom right now and fuck your brains out?"

Hearing this, I actually started to giggle like a sixteen-year-old. Who else in the world ever spoke like that to me?

Except we weren't sixteen anymore, of course. "The thing is, I've got to be on-site tomorrow first thing," he said. "They need the whole thing set up by, like, 3 p.m. for the sound checks."

"Yeah. I hear you. I've been driving since sunrise," I said. "I'm about ready to pass out."

"But damn." Looking me up and down, Zack wiggled his eyebrows in his old cartoonish fashion. He ran his finger teasingly down the front of my jeans. "Well then. I guess this is just one present I'll have to wait 'til tomorrow to unwrap. It'll be like Christmas fucking morning."

"Oh my God. You really haven't changed at all, have you."

"Yeah? You like that line? Pretty good, huh?"

"The East German judge gives it a solid seven."

"Boo-yah!" He leaned over and kissed me again. Long, tenderly. "Okay, if I don't leave now, I never will."

"Yeah, I need my beauty sleep."

"No. No you don't."

"Oh, that's even better. That's a solid eight."

"Hey, well. I checked you out in the parking lot, Ms. Cohen." He glanced at the food he had brought. "You want me to leave that for you?"

"No. Take it. Take it all. Please."

Rapidly, he wrapped it all back up in the bag. "When does your music stuff start?"

"Excuse me?"

"You said you had to come down here for some music business?"

"Oh. Right. Yeah."

"Because, if you're free tomorrow during the day, I can get us a tour of Fontanel. You will fucking love it. It's this estate that used to belong to Barbara Mandrell. Totally *sick*. It's got its own heliport and a gun range. And then, of course, I can give you an exclusive private behind-the-scenes look at Kid Rock."

Barbara Mandrell and Kid Rock? Club me over the head with a polo mallet and be done with it. But I said, "Sure. Sure. Absolutely. I'm all yours." I added pointedly, "Day and night, in fact."

"Well then." He gazed at me, seeming to decide something. "You know. And this is just a suggestion. If you want to save a little money on lodging, you could stay at my place tomorrow instead. You can see the Zack Shack."

"I thought you said you were based in LA."

"LA? Oh, yeah. And Miami. I've got a whole fucking empire. But just for right now, I happen to be based mostly here. Tomorrow, whenever you get up, check out, bring all your stuff with you, and come meet me at Fontanel. Afterwards, we'll head back to my place together. You can see where the magic really happens."

I looked at him. Something clicked suddenly. "Oh my God. You stinker. That's why you were spying on me from across the street. You wanted to make sure that I was still hot before you committed to anything else."

"Well, you were hedging your bets, too, weren't you? Asking me to book you a hotel?"

He leaned over and kissed me again, long and lingering. When we finally pulled apart, we stood with our foreheads pressed together, the way we always had in high school, blinking at each other so close our eyes nearly crossed, breathing in each other's breath. With my pupils fixed on his, I suddenly felt like I could see into his soul. I felt like I was stepping through doorway after doorway in his irises, going back in time to when we were eighteen, seventeen, sixteen, screaming in the parking lot, laughing together in the rain by a pay phone, Zack with his sax, me with my guitar, backward, backward, fucking in the grass by the train tracks after we'd nearly let ourselves get killed, him unscrewing the bottle of rum and handing it to me, me lying down alone on the rails, my mother dying, him sauntering toward Rooster's truck spinning the ignition key around on his finger, me spying Zack in the mudroom of Anne-Marie's, backward still, through time, rocketing through a thousand different lives together like a deck of flip cards, back, back, through a vortex of space and stars and nebula to the very birth of the universe itself.

Slowly, he brought my hand up to his mouth and kissed it. "See you tomorrow," he said.

Chapter 11

WHEN I AWOKE IN the purgatory of my hotel room, it was well past eleven. Sun sliced through a gap in the blackout curtains. All I could hear was a distant whoosh of cars from the highway. Snatching up my phone, I scrolled through dozens of alerts: messages from Joey and Joey again and the Privileged Kitchen and an events manager at the West Bloomfield Mall and Brenda (**You cleaned my house? You really did not have to do that. Thanx**—its tone indecipherable) and some kid on Facebook who'd invited Kayla McMullins to play Farmville—how the hell did I shut that fucking thing off already—until finally, to my relief, I came upon a text from Zack:

Hard at work @Fontanel. We still on for this afternoon? Txt me when u get this.

I'm awake! I typed back frantically. **Just got up!!!!**

My phone pinged. **Glad you got some rest. Save your nrg!!! U r gonna need it! LOL.**

Staring at this as I lay in bed, I began fantasizing about the sex that awaited. It didn't take much. For years, I'd imagined being in bed with Zack.

But. Does anyone ever have the discipline to rein in their daydreams once they take off? There is no modesty in fantasy. Surely, there's not an athlete in the world who spends time picturing herself coming in sixth at the Olympics or a musician who lies in bed at night dreaming about playing bar mitzvahs. Quickly I found myself fantasizing about not only the sex, but embroidering entire, elaborate scenarios in which I would join Zack on the road when he left for LA. How exciting and romantic would it be to jet-set around with him for a while? Where else did he say he had apartments? Miami? I pictured us having sex in hotel rooms in various cities with room service and panoramic views—him fucking me up against the enormous, plate-glass windows high above the sky- lines, in mirrored elevators—and also on the various concert stages he was assembling—while I would do what, I wondered? Okay, here I hit a snag—but I was determined to fit all the puzzle pieces into place— surely, with Zack and his work, I could figure out some way to get back into some aspect of the music business, reignite something I loved.

The more I let myself get lost in this alternative life—imagining the witty things we'd say to each other in airports, the endearing and wildly romantic gestures he'd make, until—*c'mon, okay*, I told myself, *earth to Donna!*—I saw how it could *actually* happen. Zack and I, we were great, eternal lovers. Who knew how many lifetimes we had known each other? Twenty-six years—and bam! Those first few kisses were all it took. We were both nomads at heart—we still made each other laugh—we knew where we came from, knew each other's fucked-up families.

Families. Okay. On that, I got stuck. In my fantasies, I could easily jettison Joey. (In the past, I'd sometimes dispatched him in daydreams by imagining he'd had a heart attack while heroically rescuing children and puppies from a burning building, thereby leaving me, the grieving widow, to be comforted by George Clooney. Now, just thinking about him with Mistress Tanya was enough.) But Ashley and Austin? How, exactly, would they fit into all this? I told myself that I'd spent all my life taking care of them—and they were almost all grown up anyway— couldn't I have just this one erotic adventure? Didn't I deserve at least *this*?

Besides, if I took off for a few months, would they even really notice? Or care? Neither of them needed me much anymore—beyond money and occasional rides, there was so little I could do for them—I was essentially obsolete. So?

My phone binged again. **Hey, you checked out yet? I should be done in another hour or so. xoxo**

Hurrying into the bathroom, I swallowed an Ativan and an Adderall—one to get me going, the other to calm me down—thank you, children—these were absolutely the very *last ones* I was borrowing from their stash—then showered, shaved, moisturized, plucked, deodorized, perfumed, and blow-dried. Standing before the mirror, I gently lifted my breasts and twisted my torso from side to side as I had when I was a teenager, assessing myself. Small love handles like fleshy commas flopped on either side of my waist now; my breasts were certainly more elongated. The beauty mark just to the right of my navel had grown darker with time. Yet I was still curvy in a compact, sturdy way. There was still a lusciousness to me. "Not bad for a middle-aged broad, right, Aggie?" I said.

As I wriggled into a leopard-print miniskirt and a clingy black pullover I'd found at Macy's in New Jersey, I remembered Ashley at age fifteen, sprawled across my bed, watching as I got dressed for a Privileged Kitchen sales luncheon. I'd chosen a chic little rose-colored dress with metallic ankle boots not unlike a pair she herself owned. "The problem, Mom," she'd said, "is that your face just doesn't match your clothing."

Well, fuck it, I thought now. From here on in, I was a rock star, and most rock stars' faces that I knew these days didn't match their clothing, either, thank you very much. Why was the world so hostile to older women trying to remain attractive? Did people subconsciously fear that we might actually trick all men into falling for us—diverting all the world's sperm away from the younger, more fertile women—until the entire human race died out? The vitriol and contempt and mockery directed at us was astonishing. Not that I was necessarily any better: How many hours had I spent clicking on websites showing "bad celebrity plastic surgery" photos and forwarding them to my book club? Well, that was over now.

"Oh. Aggie. Have I mentioned?" I tossed my head seductively toward my guitar. "I'm taking a lover." I delighted in the words, the anachronistic licentiousness of them. And Zack's kiss. *That kiss.*

As I rolled my new violet suitcase down the corridor, I passed the maids chatting by their towel trolley. I could see their eyes following me. They could tell instantly what I was up to; I was certain of it. Every smoke alarm in the hotel, I imagined, was starting to whoop as I sauntered past.

Having slept through breakfast, I was ravenous. Down the road, I found a country buffet restaurant, where I piled a plate with mac-and-cheese, hush puppies, fried chicken, creamed spinach, even a spoonful of blueberry cobbler—refusing to track the calories—certainly, I'd earned this, too—plus, it was likely I'd be unable to eat around Zack out of nerves and erotic propriety for days—so what was a little splurge—plus, this was the South—okay, yeah, there was also an Indian restaurant and a Thai place right nearby in the same strip mall—globalization had come to Goodlettsville, apparently—but it was only polite, of course, to eat the local cuisine, and I was nothing if not a gracious tourist. I poured myself a glass of sweet tea, which proved hard to balance on my tray. Then my phone started ringing in my bag.

"Fuck." I knocked over the glass. By the time I managed to set everything down and dig out my phone—I assumed it would be Zack, with his velvety, aphrodisiac voice—I saw that it was actually Joey calling. Yet it was too late; reflexively, I'd answered. I felt trapped. I said something that came out sounding like "Yuuuhhhh?"

"Donna?" he said in an oddly formal way.

"Joseph?"

There was a long silence.

"I've been trying to reach you for two days now."

"Well, I didn't feel like talking."

"Ever?"

I was quiet.

"Okay. Donna. Look. Please. Tell me. No judgment. But are you sober right now?" Perhaps because his nose was broken, "sober" came out sounding like "somber." "Can we at least have some sort of conversation?"

"Jesus, Joey. Yes, I'm sober." I jabbed a plastic fork into the mac-and-cheese and shook my head. An elderly couple in plaid shirts glanced over. "I've been sober for five years, six months, and eighteen days now."

"Donna, you went to a roadhouse. I saw on the internet."

"Yeah, well, if you'd bothered to really investigate, you'd have found out that I just ate chicken wings with the Knights of Kiwanis, Joey. For *charity*. For children in western Pennsylvania with hiatal hernias." I knew I was on thin ice here and laying it on thick, but I didn't care. I started to shovel up some of the spinach, then saw it was soaked with sweet tea and set my fork back down.

I heard him sigh. "Donna. C'mon. What about the meds?"

"I'm not a pill-head! Jesus Christ, who do you think I am?" More people at the buffet looked over at me, so I stood up and stalked outside and paced on the sidewalk where I could still keep an eye on my lunch.

"Yes. Okay. I filled Austin's and Ashley's prescriptions for them. *Like I always do.* Because I'm *a mom.* Because *I'm* always keeping a running list in my head of everything they need. I was *multitasking.* And I thought I'd be coming home. But then I changed my mind. So what?"

"So what are you saying?" His voice shrank. "You are coming back, Donna, aren't you. I mean, c'mon."

For the first time since our fight, my anger wavered and I felt a flicker of pity. Joey. Poor, fucked-up Joey, with his broken nose and his desperate, fetishy pinafores. He had no idea just how far gone I was now.

"Just write them another prescription, Joey. You're a dentist. You want to be subservient? So *you* be the *mom* for a while," I said. "*You* make time in *your* busy workday to go to Walmart or Walgreen's or wherever, and get Austin his Adderall and Ashley her Ativan, and then *you* go through the hassle of mailing it to her overseas. Just like I do. It's not rocket science." Though I couldn't help adding, "But use Express Mail instead of FedEx, because it's cheaper internationally. Oh, and make sure Ashley knows it's coming first, because she'll have to be there to sign for it. And use WhatsApp or email or Skype because, trust me, she never picks up her phone."

For a moment, there was more silence.

"Donna, where are you?"

I pulled open the door and wandered back toward my table. I needed to eat, I realized. I was light-headed. "I'm in Nashville. With my brand-new guitar." This was the truth, and it felt good to say something that would sting.

"Nashville?"

"Kid Rock's having a fish fry."

"Kid Rock?" Joey said with confusion. "Since when do you like Kid Rock?"

I shrugged—though, of course, he couldn't see this over the phone. "I have some secrets, too, you know, Joey. You like dressing up as a French Maid in a grotesque parody of a woman and destroying our marriage, and me, I like Kid Rock."

"Okay, now you're just being nasty."

"Why are you so surprised that I might want to take some time off to go to a music festival?" Without looking, I jabbed my fork at my plate and found a hush puppy impaled on it. I tried to take a bite without Joey hearing me chew. "Or, you know, maybe I'll even try playing some gigs myself? I used to have a music career, you know."

"A 'career,' Donna?"

I pulled the phone away and just stared at it for a moment.

"I'm sorry," he said quickly. "That came out wrong."

"You've always thought my music was a joke, Joey. My CDs were just some novelty to dig out and show our friends at Christmas."

"Donna, I didn't mean it that way," he said quietly. "I've always been proud of you, you know that."

"The only reason you liked my music was because it made *you* look cooler by association. You treated me like a punch line." I suspected this wasn't entirely accurate. But now that I'd found a vein of righteous indignation, I was determined to mine it.

"Look," Joey exhaled into the phone, "if you need to do this, Donna, if you feel there's some part of you that's dying to be expressed, or if you just really want to hear Kid Rock—or whatever—okay. Do what you need to. I get it. Believe me. *I* know better than anyone what it feels like to have some part of yourself—"

"Oh, don't you dare. This does not excuse your cheating, Joey. This is not equivalent."

I felt my anger flare again. I refused to cede the higher moral ground on this. Yes, okay, I myself had just driven over a thousand miles for the sole purpose of hooking up with an ex. But does anyone ever cheat in a vacuum—and without feeling some perverse self-justification while doing so? Joey had betrayed me first. And I'd been in love with Zack long before: Wasn't there some sort of grandfather clause for old flames? Maybe it wasn't even cheating so much as embarking on a crucial midcourse correction in my life; maybe Joey *himself* had been the detour, the decades-long mistake.

Again, he was quiet. "Listen, Donna," he said finally, "if I felt like I could control it—"

"How's Austin?" I said abruptly. "He said he had a math test?"

"He's okay, I guess. His friend Rodrigo stayed over last night. They're working on some rap song."

I blew my nose. "What about Ashley? Any word?"

"Not since a few days ago, when I got a couple of dozen links from her. Sanders for president. Dead babies from Syria. Some Indian burial ground coming under attack. The usual. Oh, yeah. And some vegan spaghetti recipe."

"Yeah. Here, too. Well." I shook my head. "No one can ever accuse her of being frivolous, I guess."

"Ha. No."

The moment hung heavily in the air between us. My phone pinged.

Zack: **Should be done soon! Meet me at Fontanel at parking lot by the distillery. Rt off route 65.**

Distillery?

"Look, I should get going," I said.

"Well, keep me posted, okay?" he said miserably.

"Okay." The breeziness of my own voice astonished me. I'd always imagined that if I committed adultery, the ground beneath my feet would actually quake and my skin break out in boils. Yet how effortlessly I lied! It was positively mundane, in fact, as easy as sliding into a pair of slippers. Unless you got caught, there really was nothing to it. So this was how people could become spies, I realized. Or white-collar criminals. Or adulterers like Joey and me. And I was surprised by how powerful this casual deception made me feel—*my husband had no clue!*

"And let me know if you hear anything from Ashley?" Joey said. "Oh, also. Some folks have been calling saying you were supposed to do cooking demos for them. They sounded pretty angry. And Colleen Lundstedt's been calling asking what's going on."

"Shit."

"What do you want me to do?"

I sighed. "Tell them the truth, Joey. Tell them there's a family crisis. And I'm temporarily indisposed."

"You don't think that sounds sort of fishy and vague?"

"So then make up some excuse. Or no. Wait. Don't. Good God. We both know your track record. Tell them it's none of their fucking business. I'll deal with Colleen myself."

When Joey hung up, I scrolled through my phone for her email address. I didn't have to look far, because it turned out she'd just written me.

Dear Donna, it began. **As you know, I've always liked to think of our Privileged Kitchen Culinary Ambassadors as family...**

Uh-oh. No email that started like this could ever be anything good.

Quickly, I scanned it. **As a working mother myself, I understand the challenges...however, as a Privileged Kitchen Culinary Ambassador...a modicum of decency and respect...at least 48 hours notice when canceling events...keep PK headquarters informed of any inability...our good name is something we lend to you in good faith...**

Blah, blah. I could just see her, tapping out the message on her phone with a silver stylus so she wouldn't chip her manicure.

She concluded by reminding me of Privileged Kitchen's policy of buying back all unsold inventory from any ambassador who "no longer wishes to remain in our family" for "30% of the original wholesale price should you wish to do so at this time."

"Oh, for fuck's sake," I said out loud. I scrolled through my calendar. At that very moment, I saw, I was supposed to be demonstrating how to bake "Healthy Pumpkin-Spice Halloween Treats your whole family will go wild for" using PK's "no fuss, no stick" silicone muffin molds at the home of one Teresa Wipnicki in Sterling Heights, Michigan. *Fuck.* When all was said and done, I saw, I'd been MIA from Privileged Kitchen appointments for exactly four days. Seven demos in total. Okay, that was something—but still. Every goddamn mile I'd driven over the years—how I'd thrown my heart and soul into selling colanders and egg-slicers—the best years of my life I had spent as a slavish and devoted sales rep for the Privileged Kitchen, talking it up at dinner parties and book clubs, always keeping some of my inventory in my car just in case I could make an unscheduled pitch or ran into some-one, somewhere, who might be in need of a kitchen timer or a meat thermometer as a last-minute present. And this was how I was being treated? Reprimanded like a child—or a robot—after a mere handful of missed demonstrations?

Dear Colleen, I began to type.

Please don't lecture me about "decency and respect." I've been busting my ass for your company for twelve years now. Until this month, I have had a PERFECT attendance record, including seven whole years when I often performed PK demonstrations stinking drunk. You didn't know that, however, BECAUSE I AM A CONSUMMATE PROFESSIONAL. Even blitzed out of my brain on Costco tequila, I was capable of turning out a perfectly golden chicken divan using a toaster oven

in the middle of a fucking shopping mall. I have consistently outsold every other PK sales rep for years, yet you just gave your biggest sales award to some insane CHILD with a Twitter feed. I have never, until now, had "unsold inventory," and if I continue to do so, I will sell it back to you if and when I damn well get around to it.

I thought about closing with some other line about where, exactly, Colleen Lundstedt could shove her unsold kitchenware, but I decided against it. I was, after all, a *consummate professional*. It did occur to me to pause for a second before hitting Send. But then I thought: *Fuck it*. I'd been on pause in my life long enough. Now, I was in Nashville. Now, I was just *done*. I hit the Send arrow, and, just for good measure, switched my phone to airplane mode. Then I headed off to meet my old high school sweetheart in front of a distillery.

Fontanel, nestled in the Tennessee hills in the little town of White Creek, was a recreational area boasting miles and miles of "Hiking trails! Zip lines! Fine dining! A boutique country inn! An outdoor amphitheater! Fun for the whole family!"

The entrance was flanked by Pritchard's Distillery on one side, and a place called the Natchez Hill Winery on the other. As I eased into the parking lot, I felt like a priest pulling up between two whorehouses. "Really?" I said. "First thing?"

I got out of the Subaru, righted my miniskirt, reapplied my lipstick. The air smelled peaty, of damp leaves and soil. The place was oddly empty. A mud-spattered ATV careened into the lot and jerked to a halt right beside me. "Hey, hey, gorgeous!"

Zack was wearing a construction worker's hard hat and a laminated ID card on a lanyard around his neck. In the daylight, I could see more flecks of silver in his razor stubble and ponytail. "Here I come to save the day," he sang grandly, rising up in his seat. "Welcome to Fontanel."

The ATV looked like a hybrid between a motorcycle and a Tonka truck.

"What. No monster wheels?" I deadpanned, though I could not conceal how thrilled I was to see him. In my heeled boots and miniskirt, it was a bit of a struggle to mount the vehicle gracefully. "Do I need a helmet?"

"Nah. Speed limit here's 15. Most people ride around on golf carts. I just wanted to make a grand entrance. You like?"

"Of course. You know me. I like anything fast and hard, baby."

"Ha-ha! Damn but I've missed you, Bella!"

The enormous machinery thrummed beneath us—every one of my vertebrae vibrated—it reminded me of those kiddie rides where you fed a quarter into a slot, then jiggled violently atop a metal hobbyhorse on the sidewalk outside Kroger's supermarket for three minutes. "It's fucking awesome, isn't it?" Zack shouted. "Even at fifteen miles an hour! You and me, baby, we're going to be riding around on these things when we're, like, eighty. No wheelchairs for us!"

I squeezed him tighter and grinned. *When we're eighty.*

"I got us some free tickets for a tour of the big house." He pulled into a visitors lot. "Wait'll you see this. There's a helipad. A glass-topped swimming pool. An indoor *gun range*."

The Mansion at Fontanel was described as country star Barbara Mandrell's former "log cabin–style home"—and it was, all right, in that it incorporated a whole lot of logs. Otherwise, it was a 30,000-square-foot estate that looked like what Versailles might've been like if it had been designed by the creators of *Hee Haw*.

I looked around dubiously. "Zack?" I took his hand. "I don't want to go on some cheesy house tour. I want to see *your* world."

"Oh? Do you now?" Teasingly, he dragged my hand down the front of his jeans. "Oh, I'll show you my world, all right." Then he slapped himself playfully on the cheek. "Zakkolator! Behave!"

Zack's worksite looked like a carnival being assembled. "Welcome to 'Redneck Woodstock'! And here, that ain't no insult, neither!"

He helped me down from the ATV and led me across the fairgrounds, sauntering ahead of me with his tool belt flopping around his hips, high-fiving the security guards and the carnie who'd trucked in the Ferris wheel and the crew who were setting up some marquee tents, looping garlands of wire between them. "Hey guys! This here is my gal Bella-donna! Numero Uno kickass guitar-player from Michigan!" Some of the staffers seemed caught off-guard. As he bounded toward them, they got a deer-in-the-headlights look.

On a little rise was an antique Chevy pickup with the Fish Fry logo painted on the side. "Check this out. Awesome, right? Let's get you up close to me." Angling his phone, Zack snapped the two of us beside the truck. It reminded me of when we'd gone to a county fair one weekend and taken photographs of each other in front of a giant tractor. Zack had won me a cheap, sawdust-filled purple monkey with a tinny jingle bell around its neck. "Hi, Bella!" he'd said in a terrible falsetto. I'd named it Thelonious Monkey.

Zack was moving so quickly across the grass now, it was hard to keep up. I wanted him just to stand still with me for a moment, for us to be *us* together, to breathe him in.

"Hey." I grabbed his arm. "Slow down." I drew up close. "Do you remember that time at the Oakland County Fair?" I said. Afterward, we'd parked behind a water tower. Zack had peeled off my panties with his teeth. "And in your van later? And Thelonious Monkey?"

"Who?"

Spotting a guy from his crew, Zack hollered across the field, "Yo, Hellboy. The Condor's free, yes? Here's what I do remember," he said, turning back to me finally. "That very first day we met. On those railroad tracks? When I rescued you? Oh, now *that* was hot."

"Ha!" I slapped him playfully on the shoulder. "The first time we met was at Ann-Marie Larkin's house. You were with Rooster, delivering weed. And it was *you* who crawled off those tracks first, not *me*, baby. I was down for the count."

"Yeah. Right." Rolling his eyes, he squeezed me affectionately around the waist. "You were like, lying there on the tracks, all ready to kill yourself. This damsel in distress. And I remember being like, what the fuck? And I pulled you off at the very last minute."

"What? Excuse me? Are you serious? No way. That's not how it happened at all."

"Yuh. I totally remember. I sat down beside you, and I was, like, 'Hey, you're not committing suicide, are you?' And you were, like, 'I dunno. Maybe.' And then we started joking how we should make a pact. Everyone in Dry Lake would think we were these tragic lovers, when actually, we barely knew each other. And we'd become, like, this legend."

I had absolutely no recollection of anything like this, though I had to admit, it sounded eerily like us. "I was not trying to commit suicide," I said.

"Hey. Com'ere. Check this out. Tah-dah."

We were at the amphitheater itself now. A tented roof was suspended high above an open-air stage by metal lattices. Risers had been set up. Dozens of road boxes and base bins sat waiting to be unloaded.

"Just for the record," I said, "you jumped off the tracks first."

"Now *this* is what I do." Zack waved from corner to corner. "Our rigging crew, we come into a venue—it could be a park or a field. Or a stadium. We assemble everything you see. Right here. The scaffolding. The screens, the lights. All of it."

He motioned to the fretwork overhead, though I wasn't really paying attention. I was overwhelmed by the scent of him again. The sensation of his hand in mine was like an electric current running straight up my arm, then down between my legs. But also, I was smarting a little.

"Now, here we do a load-in with a Condor. But in indoor arenas, when there are lights all the way up in the rafters? Hundreds of feet up? Well, baby. That's me. I crawl out on the grid and hang everything." He pointed to the rows of lights above the stage, aimed downward. "As soon as the concert's over, we take it all down again: every chain and screen, strike the scaffolds. Melt the steel."

As he pointed, I noticed a tattoo on his forearm. "Lexie" in extravagant script, a heart dotting the "i."

"Oh. Who's Lexie?" I tried to sound casual.

Zack looked down at it as if he'd only just realized the ink was there. "Ha! That, my dear, is the love of my life. Hang on."

Fumbling for his phone, he began scrolling through thousands of photos. I felt my stomach twist. "Donna Cohen, meet Lexie Amelia Phelps." I saw a blond, pubescent gap-toothed girl with Zack's eyes and impish smile staring directly into the camera, holding out a Denny's milk shake as if offering it to me. "Isn't she awesome?"

I thought of Ashley when she had been that age. Then of Austin again. **Mom, u can call me.**

I nodded. "She really is." My voice cracked. Zack tucked his phone back into his pocket.

"Sorry." I fanned the air around my face in little flutters, blinking. "Sorry, sorry. Whoa." I sniffled. "I did not expect *that*."

He kissed me lightly on the forehead. "You okay?"

"Mmhm."

He frowned, cocked his head.

"I just get really emotional sometimes. *You* know that."

I didn't want to explain any further. I didn't want to be Donna the alkie or Donna the mom or Donna the wife or Donna in perimenopause. I just wanted to be Donna Cohen at sixteen again. For just a few minutes. Donna of Zack-and-Donna.

He turned back to the scaffolding. "Every day, it's like I'm playing with a giant erector set." He pointed around his tool belt. "Every rigger, we've got our own equipment. I've got my own harnesses, scaff hammer, podger, c-wrench, knife—"

He unclipped a flat metal trapezoid that looked like a piece of mountaineering equipment. "This is a carabiner. You fall in a harness with a tether clipped to this thing, believe me, it'll hold you. I almost never use a harness, though. The other riggers, they call me 'Spider-Man.'"

"Spider-Man? Seriously?"

"Yeah. Welcome to my web, ha-ha." He walked me around to the back of the stage. A small construction trailer was set up behind it in the mud, as well as what looked like a folded-up cherry picker. Twilight was setting in, and most of the crew had left by now. "Wanna go up?"

"In a cherry picker?"

"Please, woman. That's not a cherry picker. It's called a '*Condor*.'"

Yeah, sure. Of course it was. But still—it was a cherry picker.

"Okay," I said nonchalantly, though a bubble began to rise in my stomach. Zack had forgotten, I realized, how much I hated heights.

He disappeared into the trailer and returned with two harnesses. They looked military. "You asked for it, baby! Here, put your hands through."

He held it open for me to step into like a jumpsuit, legs first. Was I really going to do this? Absolutely. I needed to disabuse Zack of the idea that I'd ever been some mere damsel in distress on those tracks. The whole point of us was how wild and daring and fierce I was.

Ironically, just three days before, I had grudgingly donned a bustier for my husband. Now, Zack was strapping me into a body holster, cinching the padded belt around my waist and yanking the strip that fastened across my chest. The straps dug into my inner thighs and my breasts jutted out. I felt sexy as hell—porn-starrish actually—but I also found myself starting to sweat. And—okay—chafe a little. I clutched his wrists.

He grinned. "You like, this, huh? I thought you might."

I swallowed. "Okay. Now I'm doing you." I held open his harness for him. He climbed into it obligingly. I yanked the straps as tight as I could, drawing his pelvis right up to mine.

"Oh," he said as I finished binding him in. "Oh, hello there." He wiggled his eyebrows. Were we eroticizing safety harnesses now? Seriously? Though as I'd learned, there seemed to be no shortage of things to fetishize in this world.

Ushering me to the little metal basket, he unlatched the gate and held it open for me like a gentleman. Our harnesses each had a tether on one end. He showed me how to clip the carabiner to a safety hook on the frame of the basket itself, which was not really a basket at all, but a small grate ringed with two sets of bars. It would be ridiculously easy to slip through the spaces between them. My hands were shaking, but I tried not to let him see.

"Okay. Hold on. Here goes." With the turn of a key, the motor growled to life and a loud warning *beep* bulleted the air. Slowly, the Condor's metal arm unfolded. The basket began to rise on its hinged neck, slicing upward with astonishing speed. "Woohoo! Yeah, baby!" Zack hollered. I felt the same burst of panic that I did on amusement park rides and airplanes when they first took off. I found myself gripping the railing so hard, my hands were cramping. "Is this totally fucking awesome or what?" Zack shouted. I nodded as best I could, trying to smile with intense bravery. On one side, we were hovering above the stage, and I could see clearly all the Day-Glo X's taped to the floor, and the piles of wires and extension cords coiled out of sight behind the platforms. On the other side, just muddy earth falling away.

We levitated higher, so that the layout of the entire stage was now visible below us, a puzzle of black and pine-colored pieces. "See that? Over there is 'guitar world.'" Zack pointed. "That's where you'd be, baby, hooked up to your pedals and amps." He began explaining all sorts of logistical and technical details. I tried just to focus on the horizon, not on the ground, which was getting farther and father away. So this was how I would die: plummeting to the earth in a Day-Glo safety harness above an amphitheater in White Creek, Tennessee. Was this how I wanted my family to find me?

I clung to Zack, his rough hand pressed against my hip as we slowly ascended above the tree line. "Are you okay? You look a little pale," he said.

My sixteen-year-old self wouldn't have balked for an instant. I saw Zack watching me, his eyes glittering. "Go higher," I ordered, though my queasiness grew. I wanted him to ravish me with his eyes, drop to his knees in awe. I was clipped in. It was only the illusion of danger, I reminded myself, just as it had been back on the railroad tracks in Dry Lake.

A wind was starting to blow now, ruffling our hair. My teeth began chattering.

"Are you sure? Baby, you're shivering."

"Higher," I barked.

Zack laughed his lunatic laugh. "Okay, woman. Your wish is my command."

From the other side of the basket, the soft hills of Tennessee were now visible, rolling off toward the horizon like an ocean, a few towns twinkling forlornly in the distance like tiny lanterns, the sky striated with deepening bands of lavender and peach and gold. The wind blew more fiercely now; we were beyond any talking. Or maybe Zack was talking to me, but all I could hear was my own breath, as loud as a heartbeat in a sonogram. We were high above the amphitheater, looking down at Zack's meticulous rigging, the rows of black stage lights like dark hydroponic orchids peaking out beneath the tented roof. Miles of trees spread below us, thrashing. The whole world as I knew it was being transformed; it was falling away completely, and it was only the two of us now, me and Zack, on this tiny platform thrusting upward in the Condor toward a darkening sky.

Finally, with a lurch, we stopped. The absence of motion made it no less terrifying. "One hundred and eighty feet," Zack announced. "Oh my God, Bella, look at this. *This* never gets old." He blinked out at the landscape, the slight curvature of the earth, the marvel it was in the sinking sun. I let my eyes run over it all rapidly—it was magnificent, dream-like—though the vertigo was almost unbearable. I returned my gaze to him and fixed it there on his face instead. "Zack Phelps," I said.

He gazed at me. "It's wild, isn't it? All the way here, from that shithole in Dry Lake?"

I snuggled in closer to him. "For the record, though," I said softly, "I was not trying to commit suicide that day."

"What? Oh, c'mon, Bella. Forget about it. I was just playing with you." He kissed me lightly on the forehead. "Jesus, you're still shivering.

Hang on. I got something for that." Reaching into one of his utility pockets, he pulled out what looked like a small plastic travel shampoo bottle. "Here. This'll warm us up."

As soon as he twisted off the cap, I could smell it. And I wanted it. At that particular moment, I wanted it more than I even wanted him. It would be so easy. It was right there. We were not even on the earth anymore; there were so many excuses, so many ways to make it never count.

I looked at him helplessly. "I won't be able to drive back," I said hoarsely.

My voice was thoroughly unconvincing. Yet to my great disappointment, he replaced the cap. "Well, I can't either. Not when I'm operating heavy machinery. Although..." He paused. "Ah, but there is one way around this." Winking, he took a quick swig, then pulled me up against him. Before I even knew what was happening, his warm tongue and the tequila were all mixing together in my mouth. When the kiss was finally over, he tucked the bottle back in his pocket as if he were putting away an instrument. He smiled. "There we go."

Every nerve in my body was now on alert. *More, please,* I was thinking. *I need. I want. Fill me.*

More, more, more.

Chapter 12

FOR SOME REASON, I'D imagined Zack living in an exposed brick loft in the heart of downtown Nashville, a wide-open industrial space tricked out with a black granite bar and a big neon guitar glowing on the wall. Yet his apartment turned out to be a unit in a housing complex outside of a town called Murfreesboro. Three long, low, identical buildings with stucco walls the color of old tube socks had dark timber nailed across their facades to give them a mock-Tudor look. A couple of pickup trucks and an old motorcycle sat parked outside. A sign wicketted into the lawn out front read MONTHLY RENTALS. NOW LEASING. When I climbed out of the Subaru, I could hear the roar of the interstate. Zack's building was the one farthest from the road, abutting a wheat field. A metal staircase zigzagged up the side to a small second-story landing with a door. "Right up there in the corner. That's my place." He insisted on carrying both my suitcase and my guitar. "We'll go through the lobby, though. Those stairs are sort of busted."

I was let down by the feel of the place, though it barely registered. As we made our way up to his apartment, we could barely dare to look at each other or speak, the private hurricane brewing between us was gathering such velocity.

He pushed his front door open with his knee and set down my belongings with a flourish. "Welcome to the Zack Shack!"

The door opened directly into a small living room. All I glimpsed was a fat leatherette sofa and a giant, flat-screen TV with a gaming station that took up an entire wall like the control panel of a spaceship. Immediately, Zack pushed me up against a closet door and I grabbed him by his collar and we started kissing wolfishly. When I released him, his eyes were glittering.

"Shirt off," I said. "Now."

"Oh?" He laughed. But he wriggled out of his jacket and shirt, leaving them in a puddle on the linoleum. As we continued kissing, he guided me backward toward the couch, sloppily, in a loose, easy dance, his hands clamped to my hips like starfish. His tool belt kept flopping between us and digging into my stomach. He paused to unbuckle it and flung it on the floor beside a milk crate, where it landed with a clank.

"I can't believe you're actually wearing a tool belt. You're, like, straight out of porn."

"Ha! I knew you'd get a kick out of it. Why do you think I kept it on after my shift? It's all for you, baby. Bow-chicka-bow-bow!" He pulled me toward him and yanked open the buttons of my blouse, exposing the lacy cups of my new blush-colored bra.

"Oh my God! Look at you, Bella. You are *still* a fucking goddess!" Lunging, he buried his head between my breasts. My eyes closed. I heard myself giggle.

"Carry me to the bed," I commanded. I knew it sounded ludicrous, but Zack scooped me up obligingly and carried me like a bride into an adjoining room where a king sized bed seemed to consume the space. He threw me down on it. Wrestling with my bra hooks, he unleashed me, flinging the bra like a broken balloon across the mattress, and I lay bared before him in the powdery light; he looked at me impishly, reverently, from beneath his corona of hair, then buried his head between my breasts again. I cupped his chin in my hands and yanked his face up and kissed him hard on the mouth. When I finally let him go, he was breathless. Hurriedly, he pulled off his pants, then my skirt, my black stockings, the lacy purple panties I'd selected especially for him, and he ran his hand up between my thighs lightly, teasingly. As he kissed my neck and stomach, I clutched the sheets, yanking them from the bedframe. This was the first time I had ever, ever been with Zack sober, and I was amazed how every single nerve in my body seemed to vibrate like a tuning fork. He still knew. He still knew.

He smiled. "You like that, huh?" I kissed his collarbone, his sweet, damp shoulders, the plates of his chest. He'd acquired a couple of new tattoos on his forearms and shoulders. I ran my tongue over them without seeing.

It had been so long since I'd abandoned myself to such a frenzy of want, been so wholly unbridled. I ran my hand down the length of his cock, which was hard as machinery and long and slender and, I'd forgotten, curved slightly to the left. So different from Joey's.

I felt positively drunk, high on my own hotness, high with an erotic desire I had not felt, frankly, for decades: wholly alive, resurrected, ignited with fury and love and desperation and hunger all at once. His head was between my legs now, his tongue making curlicues— My God, I had fantasized about this for so long, it was hard to believe it was actually happening again—I grabbed his hair and pushed him deeper. Then his pelvis was between my thighs, then his head again, then his pelvis. I wrapped my legs around his hips.

I was fucking Zack Phelps. I thought suddenly of Joey, then banished it. I gripped Zack's back. It was broader than I'd remembered, and I was surprised to feel a few wiry hairs and pimples between his shoulder blades, and also the bulk of him was heavier on me than I'd recalled. He thrust and thrust with a few loud, animal grunts. The angle wasn't quite right, for some reason—I felt a slight sear of pain—until we readjusted ourselves somehow. To come, I needed specific rhythms established with his hands, his tongue—I'd have to surrender myself entirely, greedily, and stop being sentient of anything around me—the unfamiliar bedroom in Murfreesboro, Tennessee, with its Scotchgard-ed carpet, the thrum of its ventilation system—having a different cock inside me for the first time in twenty-six years—and the astonishing agelessness of us, too. I couldn't disconnect from all this stimuli—nor did I *want* to— I wanted to look down on us and watch and look up at him and see and feel everything all at once and brand it in my memory and be totally *in* that very moment—until all of a sudden, as Zack's groans grew louder, I gave a start: "Wait. Do you have anything?"

It had been so long with anyone besides Joey, I'd nearly forgotten.

Groaning, he staggered up and pulled a foil packet out of his bedside table. Together, we watched him unroll it methodically like a doctor preparing for surgery, snapping it in place. "Ah. Just like old times, eh?" he teased. "You like? Here you go, babe. Eight inches of latex greatness."

Afterward, he lay beside me with one wrist pressed to his forehead, panting. "Jesus," he gasped after a minute. "Nuclear." He was glistening.

I smiled over at him. He still was so fucking beautiful. The only part of him that seemed discordant, as always, was the cock that he was still so ridiculously proud of—gizzardy in its gummy condom. (Penises: Why weren't there little accessories to make them more visually appealing? Maybe ribbons you could tie around them with applique flowers? What was that word? "Nosegay"?)

"You good?" Zack said dreamily, rolling onto his side toward me, his eyes at half-mast.

"Actually, nuh-uh. Your mission here, sir, is not fully accomplished." Now that I was fully relaxed, I was actually ready and edgy and primed. What's more, now that I was forty-five, I knew how to ask instead of just waiting and hoping that someone else would instinctively know how to bestow pleasure on me.

"Oh? No?" Zack laughed exhaustedly. "Oh, shit. Damn, I thought you— Okay. Gimme a moment. I've got to recharge." Then he squinted past me, "What the hell?" He reached over my shoulder and grabbed a clutch of $20 bills.

"Oh my God." I sat up. "I totally forgot."

"Whoa, they're all over the place. It's like a money bomb went off." He switched on the small lamp on his bedside table. "Wait. Turn around. I think there's one stuck to your back." He peeled off a bill and held it up to the light and stared at it. "Wow. Is this real? Jesus Christ. How much dough do you have here?"

As quickly as I could, I gathered it up. "I don't know," I lied. "Two hundred dollars?"

"It looks like a lot more than that to me." He picked up a clump, letting it fall around us like leaves.

I collected it as fast as I could, hurried back into his living room, and jammed it into my purse. In New Jersey, I'd gone to four different ATM machines, withdrawing the limit each time from my savings: I was determined not to let Joey track me anymore through my purchases on our Visa. But it had seemed risky to walk around with a thousand dollars in my wallet; that morning, I'd stuck most of the wad in my bra, then, of course, forgotten about it.

"Here's some more." Zack waved a couple of bills and squirreled them away in his nightstand. "I'll just hold on to those for safekeeping. For services rendered, ha-ha."

I stared at him.

He held up his hands. "Jesus, just kidding, Bella." Though it seemed to me he took his time returning it. "Tonight's drinks are on you, though." He cupped his hands over his crotch and looked around distractedly for some Kleenex.

I gathered the remaining bills. I tried not to, but I thought about the account they had come from, how painstakingly Joey and I had worked to re-amass some savings. Back in Michigan, it was an hour later than in Tennessee, about 7 p.m. I pictured Joey, alone in the kitchen, dialing for a pizza, white gauze taped across his nose like a hyphen. Austin, ensconced upstairs in his room, a cave of dirty laundry and posters, the screen saver of his computer tossing shards of pale blue light across it like a fistful of stars. Oh my God: I'd committed adultery. It was official. *Well*, I supposed, *Joey and I are even now*.

Wrapping the sheet around me like a toga, I padded into the living room and tucked the money back in my purse. Through an archway was a small but serviceable kitchen. A laminated breakfast bar separated it from a dining alcove, where a second door, limned with dead bolts, opened onto to the metal stairway outside. In place of a table, Zack had a weight-lifting bench and a rack of dumbbells. A couple of rolled-up yoga mats, navy blue and violet, sat propped in the corner by the door. Zack did yoga?

I strolled around the kitchen, opening drawers (one cluttered, the rest empty), cabinets (ditto), picking things up and setting them back down. Though I tried to imagine the ways I could spruce it all up, it was hard to imagine anyone spending lengthy amounts of time here. A roll-on bottle of Biofreeze gel and a jumbo canister of protein powder sat on the counter beside a half-full Melitta coffeepot. Tossed in a basket were receipts from a 7-Eleven. A card from a strip joint. A pile of scratch-off lottery tickets. Zack didn't seem to have won anything.

A schedule was stuck to the refrigerator door with a magnetized "Souvenir of Tijuana" bottle opener: Nashville was at the top of the list, then LA, Baltimore, Orlando, Seattle, LA again, and Houston. Travel times and flights were scribbled beside a few. It was exhausting just to read. Could I really follow an itinerary like that? I loved the idea of being a gypsy with a guitar and a leopard-print miniskirt, and the two of us on tour together—though I did hate airplanes. Would Zack ever be amenable to just driving?

"Hey gorgeous. You spying on me?" He padded into the kitchen stark naked and yanked open the refrigerator—all I could see inside was a six-pack, a Styrofoam carton of eggs, a half-empty jar of salsa —no surprises there —and grabbed a bottle of water from the inside door. "You want?" he swigged and handed it to me.

I looked at him. I wasn't sure if his erection was on the decline or the rebound. The grimness of his apartment saddened me, yet my physical arousal hadn't diminished: I was full of ideas. I slinked behind him, wrapped my arms around his waist.

"Historical reenactment," I announced. "Remember that time at the gas station? In your boss's chair in the back?" I looked toward his living room.

"Are you kidding?" He grinned. "Jesus, Bella. You know, I actually still jerk off to that sometimes."

He planted himself in an ugly recliner, his legs spread slightly, his face happy and expectant. Pushing him back farther into the cushions, I dropped to my knees and took him in my mouth. When he started to moan, though, I stopped. "Okay. That's just the opener. Remember that time at Ann-Marie's?"

Ann-Marie Larkin's house in Dry Lake had a paneled bar in the basement; one night, while everybody else in the band was upstairs doing shrooms and watching the play-offs, Zack and I had fucked on top of it. We'd thought we were being outrageously kinky.

Hurrying back to his kitchen now, we cleared off his breakfast counter. A jumbo bottle of ibuprofen rolled across the tiles, rattling like a maraca. Zack swept the protein powder and a stack of junk mail into a bin.

"Oh, wait, hang on!" I shouted. Retrieving my phone, I scrolled through my music and punched Play. The deliciously nasty, bump-and-grind riff of the Clash's "Should I Stay or Should I Go?" blasted tinnily through the kitchen. "Remember this? Wasn't this the exact song that was playing? I've made a whole playlist. INXS, New Order, Concrete Blonde."

"Wow," Zack said. "You've been busy." He started to kiss my nipples. I hoisted myself up onto the countertop, smiling with what I hoped was seductive savagery. He regarded me then with *that look*—that look I'd been craving all along—of astonishment and reverence with just a tiny sparkle of unease and began to mount me atop the counter.

Suddenly, he stopped. "Oh. Whoa, whoa, whoa! Hang on!" he shouted. "If we're doing historical reenactments here—Jesus fucking Christ, how could I forget?" Yanking open his freezer, he pulled out a bottle of tequila. "The 'Donnarita'!"

He stared at me, then at the tequila bottle, and started to laugh his low, crazy laugh.

"Oh. My. God." I had totally forgotten. Or had I? I clamped my hands over my mouth.

"Lie back, princess. You asked for it."

With exquisite care, he held the bottle aloft and slowly poured the tequila over me as if anointing me with oil, as if he were preparing to flambé me. Its coolness was a shock, and I heard myself squealing as it streamed between my breasts and pooled around my navel and ran down my thighs—just as it had back at the Larkins'—because when else do you pour liquor and foodstuffs all over your body during sex, except when you're young?—and back in Dry Lake, there had been salt and lime wedges involved, too, if I remembered correctly—and just as he had then, Zack was smiling down at me triumphantly. For one quick second, my older self kicked in. *Stop. You. Are. An alkie.* How on earth was this in any way a good idea? But as Zack began to lick the liquor teasingly off my neck, tracing the rivulets of it down over my skin as if it were a map, I asked myself, *I'm not actually drinking now, am I?* Being doused with alcohol didn't make you *drunk* any more than letting someone snort cocaine off your stomach made you high. Surely, I could pass any fucking Breathalyzer test in the nation. And as he began to part my thighs and lick off all the tequila—ow, okay, that burned a little— my entire body started to respond, and that pretty much settled it—and I found myself actually pouring more Patrón between my legs for Zack just to help things along. "Hey," he said resurfacing. He grabbed the bottle. "That's my job. I'm the bartender here."

"Then more, please. Everywhere but in my mouth."

His lips, his fingers, his shoulders: everything now reeked of tequila. Skin and sex and the sharp, scorching smell of alcohol. I could not absorb enough of it; I was so wildly turned on, I thought I would rocket right out of my skin. Zack licked all of me right up to the insides of my thighs. I could feel myself starting to writhe. Just before homing in, he attempted to shift me around on the counter slightly so my head didn't dangle over the edge.

"No. Let it go," I whispered. I was dizzy, and I wanted to be dizzier. I pushed his head back down and inhaled the scent of tequila as deeply as I could. "Obliterate me."

He released me and suddenly the entire world turned upside down. The kitchen appliances, his weight-lifting bench, and a cheap spotlight lamp in the corner now hung from ceiling. He nuzzled and buried his tongue deeper and I felt myself clench and scream—and when I came—volcanically—he moved up immediately and mounted me. I closed my eyes, and Zack began to pump away inside me as if he were performing CPR. There was nothing left of us but hot flesh and muscle and liquid and pulse, heaving like a singular organism, my arms locked around his damp back, his mouth fused to my neck—Echo and the Bunnymen were on rotation now—"Lips like sugar / Sugar kisses" wailing hauntingly through the room—each thrust pushing us back through time, all the way back to Dry Lake, Michigan, until we were still just two teenagers now in a friend's grungy basement fucking on top of a paneled bar with a novelty Schlitz lamp hanging over it garlanded with Mardi Gras beads. Soaked in tequila, but no alcoholism, no corrosion, no bills or debts or failure. It was just Donna and Zack in a singular, ecstatic moment, crazed with love, aware of nothing but our young bodies—and a little electric box full of music. Both of us full of desire. Full of nothing but hope. I heard myself scream. I heard myself cry.

Afterward, we somehow managed to stumble to his bed and flop down side by side. Zack reached over and squeezed my hand chummily.

"Better now?" He said this is an oddly paternal way, as if I were a patient.

"What do you mean?"

"I don't know." His eyes were closed. "You just seemed to be in some sort of state. Like, insanely horny."

I felt judged suddenly. *Horny?* I hated that word; it sounded reptilian. "Well. Weren't you?"

"Yeah. Obviously." Rolling over, he cracked his back and winced. "Fuck." He twisted until his spine cracked a second time, then turned on his side to face me. He ran his index finger over my hip. "So. Belladonna Cohen. Just how married are you, anyway?"

I felt stung. "I don't want to talk about it."

"O-kay? So you just want to show up after twenty-six years."

"I just want to be here with you, Zack. Right here, right now. *This life* we have. Ours. That nobody else has ever touched." Leaning over, I kissed him softly this time, lingeringly. "Can't you please do that? Just be here with me? In our own little bubble? Beyond all space and time?"

He nodded at me almost sadly. "Come here," he said quietly. He pulled me to him, and we spooned, his muscled chest pressed against my back. After a moment, he said, "Sometimes, I get so lonely, I feel like a piece of old film. When it melts in the projector."

Tightening his arm around me, I nodded. I listened to us breathe in unison.

"It's like, I'm just—I'm just struggling to keep my head above the water all the time, you know?"

He pressed his chin against my shoulder. Neither of us said anything. Bronski Beat was playing now, Jimmy Somerville's plaintive falsetto pleading, "Tell me why-hy-hy?"

"Fuck," Zack said into my neck. "Are we still listening to New Wave?"

"What?" I twisted around. "These are all our old songs, Zack. I thought you liked them."

He kissed me on the shoulder. "Nah. I only pretended to because you were so into it."

"What?"

"C'mon, Bella. I'm a redneck. I cashed in some serious chits to work the Fish Fry just so I could see Kid Rock."

My legs were so jellied, they felt like they would buckle, but I heaved myself up off the bed and went and got my phone from the kitchen and switched off the music. I felt strangely rebuffed. Back in the bedroom, I noticed the sliding, mirrored door to his closet.

"Hey stand up. Come here."

Positioning Zack behind me, I posed him like a mannequin, with one of his arms snaked down around my waist, his other hand lightly cupping my breast. I sucked in my cheeks and elevated my chin in a sultry, defiant way and motioned for him to kiss me on the neck. Together, we gazed at our reflection. We looked undeniably like grown-ups now, but still. There it was. Still erotic.

"Remember this? In my bedroom?"

Zack nodded—more wistfully than I'd expected. "Our cover. *Rolling Stone*. 1987."

We locked eyes in the mirror. "Zack. Are we just pathetic now?"

"Nuh-uh. Not at all. Look at us. We are fucking *on fire*. We are fucking *bringing it, man*." Grabbing his phone, he aimed it at the mirror. "Hotness for posterity."

"What? No. Stop! Don't!" I could only imagine how a nude photo could get away from him over the internet. I'd once even sat Austin and Ashley down and given them a lecture about posting pictures, though it hadn't gone at all well.

He snatched up my phone instead. "We'll use yours, then. Just take one look at how fucking hot we are. *You* are. Then you can delete it."

I stared down at the screen. Through the lens of his desire, I did look actually gorgeous, indomitable. I was a goddess rising from the sea-foam, one arm folded luxuriantly behind her head. "Wanna few more?"

I knew I shouldn't, but I found myself giggling and flouncing back down on the bare mattress and posing. "I'm going to delete these as soon as you take them."

"Whatever. Your prerogative. Okay, head back. I'm just going to focus on your neck and your tits," he directed. "Oh, fuck, that's good. Fuck, that's hot. Now arch your back. Okay, baby, I'm comin' in." He lay down naked beside me. "No, delete those! Delete those right away!" I shrieked, laughing.

"Okay, okay, I am." He pressed the button, tossed the phone back on the nightstand. Then he leaned down to kiss me. "Ow. Hang on. Be right back." I watched his beautiful shoulders in the gold half-light of the doorway as he disappeared into the kitchen. He returned with the tequila and a beveled shot glass. "You want?" he asked. I shook my head; as drained as I was now, it was easier to say no. He poured himself two fingers' worth of Patrón, tossed it back quickly, then shook his head like a wet dog shaking himself dry. Twisting again, he cracked his spine. It sounded like a tree branch breaking. He lay back down beside me. "Do you mind just kneading my lower back?" He guided my hands down to his lumbar area. "Oh, man, that's good. That's so good."

"You pulled your back out?"

"What? Of course not. Look at me. I'm in fucking great shape. I'm in better shape than I was when I was fucking sixteen. I've just been pulling chain and lifting shit all day like you wouldn't believe. I mean, half the guys on my crew are in way worse shape than I am."

He sat up, scratched his scalp vigorously with both hands, blinked around the room. "The doctors, you know, they prescribe us all these painkillers. Muscle relaxants and all sorts of shit. But I stay away from them. Big Pharma, man, they deliberately want to get us all hooked on opioids."

He looked at me darkly. "Big Pharma, you know, they paid Congress and the FDA to say all their shit is safe, then got all these doctors to prescribe it like candy—and then Phizer, the AMA, the politicians—all of them made a killing on the stock market." He snorted, grabbed a pillow, punched it into shape, and settled it under his head.

"They got half of America hooked on opioids, *then* stopped prescriptions. So now, of course, everyone's been switching to heroin. Which—guess what?—the American government just happens to be shipping in covertly from Afghanistan in its secret deals with the warlords—"

"Oh, Zack," I said softly, reaching for his hand.

"Hey, I read the fucking news, Donna—go on the alter-net—you'll see for yourself. Wall Street and Big Pharma and the White House, they're the real dealers, not all those poor dumb fucks in prison. It's one giant circle-jerk." Unable to get comfortable, he stood up and stretched. "They've created an entire nation of addicts so they'll have an endless profit machine." He picked up the bottle of tequila and waggled it at me for emphasis. "So I'll just stick with my old friends Jose Cuervo and Patrón here, thank you. Oh, and check this out." Proudly, he slid open the mirrored closet. Stacks of cartons were piled up inside to the ceiling.

"Ammo. Night-vision goggles. A .45, a Beretta, *and* an AR-15." He pointed to a box stamped MEALS-READY-TO-EAT, MENUS 13–24. "A solar-powered generator. A water purifier." He pointed at me. "Barbara Mandrell had the right fucking idea, man. When the time comes, you're gonna want plenty of guns and a private helicopter. You're going to be glad you know me, Bella. I'm telling you right now."

I stared at him. The sight of all these stockpiles in his closet was disturbing. Yet then, I saw in my mind the signal house by the tracks in Dry Lake again. Zack with his boom box and his sleeping bag and his hurricane lantern. He was still the same boy, trying to survive by himself in the woods. I knew where he came from.

"Oh, Zachary," I said softly.

"One day, Bella. Shit's going to go down. Shit's gonna get real." He announced almost happily, "And the Zakkolator's ready!"

He flexed his biceps. "Ha. Ha. Speaking of guns." He picked up my phone and aimed it at his muscle. "One more for the ladies!"

A series of loud musical, staccato bleats went off in his hand.

"Whoa, shit. You've got an incoming call." He squinted at the screen. "Someone named Austin is trying to Skype you?"

I ran down the steps to the apartment complex's small, grungy vestibule, my ballet slippers from Walmart flopping off my heels; I'd just grabbed random items to wear out of my suitcase. "Oh, Shit, shit, shit." I looked around frantically for a private place to call Austin back. Clearly, something bad had happened back in Michigan. Joey had been driving with his broken nose and skidded. He and Austin had been shot at by some lunatic with an AK-47 in a supermarket—these were the times we were living in now. Or Ashley: Had there been a terrorist attack in London?

It could only be something catastrophic because Austin had never once Skyped me before in his entire life and because—I realized now with horror—I deserved it. Look at me, running off, leaving my family to go buy a guitar and a miniskirt and cavort naked with my lover, dousing myself with tequila like Chanel No. 5. How dare I expect to get away with this? It was a Newtonian law: For every action there is an equal and opposite reaction.

There was an old love seat in the vestibule by the mailboxes. "Austin?" I shouted as my Skype call finally went through. "Austin, what's wrong?"

Austin's face appeared pixelated over the tiny screen—he looked more like an anime graphic than his real self—the Wi-Fi reception was patchy at best—and he said something, but it sounded like those recordings of whales they played at the aquarium.

"Hang on a sec," I shouted. "Shit, I can't get a good signal." I stepped outside into the parking lot, but it was dark now, and the sound of the nearby interstate was too loud. Finally, I walked around to the side of the building and sat down on the corroding metal steps beneath a sodium light.

My son's face came into focus, his hair scraggy and unwashed. I could see in the background his bulletin board covered with skateboarding posters and his graffiti art, his half-opened closet.

"Uh, hey Mom. Do you know your Apple password for the TV?"

"Excuse me?"

"I'm trying to reset the TV for Dad. So he can watch *Game of Thrones?* His password doesn't work anymore. I dunno. I think he changed it, then forgot."

"You want my password," I said slowly. "You're calling me all the way here in Nashville so you can program the television." Leaning back against the steps, I shut my eyes. *The glamour: It never ended in my life, because it had never, ever started.*

"Sorry. Dad said not to bother you. But Uncle Reggie and Stew and Marty are over to watch *Game of Thrones* and Dad logged out or something by accident."

Oh good God. I massaged the bridge of my nose and shut my eyes and looked up the code on my phone and gave it to him.

"Thanks, Mom."

"Is that it?"

"Um, well. I was also, sort of, wondering." He shifted around. I saw a flash of blond wood. The Traveler Guitar I'd bought him. "Would you maybe be able to help me with my homework? Like, could you teach me a few guitar chords?"

"You want to learn guitar?" I said dumbly. "From me?"

"Well, Rodrigo and I, you know, we have to do a project on *The Odyssey* for English class? And our teacher said that Homer was this famous poet, except that in ancient Greece, the poets sang their stuff instead of just reciting it? So, Rodrigo and I, we're thinking that Homer was, like, the equivalent of a rapper back then. So, instead of just doing some boring report, we figured we'd do a hip-hop version of *The Odyssey*."

"And you're using a guitar?"

"Well, Rodrigo's going to beatbox while I do the words, but we tried it out, and we thought maybe it would sound even cooler if I could play an actual, old-fashioned instrument, too. I mean, we could just use a music program on our phones, I guess. But we wanna try and make it sound like maybe, thousands of years ago, when there were no computers or electricity or anything."

"Wow," I said. *My kid.* I didn't have the heart to tell him that I didn't think there were guitars thousands of years ago back in ancient Greece, either.

"I mean, I don't know if you wanna hear any of it, if that would, like, help you figure out what I need to learn?"

"I would love to hear it, sweetie. Let me try to get a little more comfortable here." I didn't want to move and lose the signal, plus, my legs were still jellied. I hadn't put on any underwear beneath my yoga pants, and the cold from the metal steps was burning through the fabric.

Suddenly, Austin got sheepish. "I mean, it's, like, still a work in progress."

"Don't worry. I've written songs before myself. I know how it goes. No judgment."

"Okay." On the tiny screen of my phone, I saw him shrug his shoulders and roll his head like a prize fighter preparing to go into the ring, donning an attitude like a leather coat. Slicing a beat in the air with the sides of his hands, bobbing his head, he bleated:

I'm-a drop you an epic, by Homer (not Simpson)
About Odysseus leaving Troy
(That's Asia Minor, not Michigan)
Odysseus was a warrior; he designed the Trojan Horse
He found himself victorious, but soon shipwrecked into worse.

"Wait, hang on." He paused to cross something out on a notepad, then scribbled something else down.

He landed on an island where he was imprisoned by Calypso
She had it bad for Mr. O.; this goddess was a psycho
She kept him as her boy-toy, she was crazy-ass in love
But luckily for Odysseus he got a shout-out from above.

He looked at me uncertainly. "Is this totally lame, Mom? Should I stop?"

"No. No. Please." I nodded. He glanced down at his paper, cleared his throat, and continued:

Athena went to bat for him at Zeus's counsel of the gods
She said, "We gotta get our O home," and they gave her all the nod
She sent Hermes as a messenger (the god, not the scarf)
He told Calypso to release O, so she sadly saw him off
Odysseus sailed away, as soon as he had the tide in
And he might have kicked it back in Ithaca if he hadn't dissed
    Poseidon.

He stopped. "Mom? Mom, why are you crying?"

I shook my head and snuffled, hugely embarrassed.

"Is it bad? I mean, we haven't been working on it that long."

"No, no, no." I shook my head vehemently. "Let me go get my guitar. It'll be better if you can see what I'm doing. I'll Skype you back in five."

Back in the apartment, I grabbed Aggie. Zack was in the shower, but there was no way I wanted to risk Austin catching sight of him, so I headed back to the lobby and tried to get an okay signal. I propped the phone up on some cushions on the love seat and sat at the far end facing it so that Austin could see my frets. "Do you know the basic six strings?" When he shook his head, I said, "Okay, then repeat after me: Eddie Ate Dynamite. Good Bye Eddie."

This was the mnemonic device my own mother had taught me to help me remember E-A-D-G-B-E, the order of the strings. Once he had that, I showed Austin the finger positions for the A, D, and E chords. It was tricky, because I had to hold the positions with one hand while angling the phone with the other, and the visual kept breaking up because of the shitty Wi-Fi. I wondered, suddenly, why Austin hadn't simply called up a YouTube demo on his computer. Surely there were a zillion beginner tutorials online.

"Is that enough to start with?" I asked. "You want to practice those first, and then we can do C, G, and E-minor the next time?" As soon as I said this, I regretted it. I didn't want our session to end. When was the last time I'd had the pleasure of teaching my son anything? I wished I could beam through the phone right now into his bedroom.

He nodded. "Maybe this weekend?"

"Sure. Sure. Whenever you want." I looked at him over the tiny screen. "Are you sleeping okay, A?"

"Yuh-huh."

"What about food? You and your dad eating all right?"

He shrugged. "It's mostly, you know, pizza. Though, Dad, he's not really eating."

"At all?"

"Nuh-uh."

"Because of his nose?"

"Not sure."

"Is he sleeping?"

"Um, I think he's staying up playing lots of video games?"

"I see."

"Yeah. So, like, tonight, everyone's over and Uncle Reggie is doing tacos."

An SUV pulled into the parking lot of the complex, pulsing with music. It screeched into a parking space directly across from me. The driver kicked open his door and a mutt ran out yelping in frenzied circles and then a woman got out and began shouting at someone still inside the vehicle. Bumperstickers plastered across the back read "Put God Back in Schools" and "Keep Honking. I'm Reloading."

"Austin, sweetie. I should probably go," I said. "I think World War Three is about to break out here. When's your presentation due?"

"Uh, next Friday?"

"Okay, so we've got a week."

"Yeah, sure. But, hey, uh, Mom?" I watched him glance away, chew on the edge of his thumbnail. "You know when I texted you the other day, and said, like, 'Don't come home' and 'Go be with the other drunks.' You know, like, I didn't mean it, right?"

"Oh, honey," I said. "Oh, honey, I know."

"So, like, you are coming back, right?"

I smiled at him sadly. "Oh, sweetie."

"You don't know? Or you're just not saying?"

I swallowed, looked away.

"Really, you're not going to tell me?" His voice rose. "Or Dad?"

"Look, I'm taking some time, okay?"

"Seriously, Mom?"

As if reacting to my emotions, the screen began to pixelate and blur. "I love you, Austin," I called out. Though, already, the connection was gone.

Back at Zack's, our clothes lay strewn about exactly where we'd left them, like a crime scene. The bathroom door was flung wide open, releasing fumes of humidity from the shower. Wet towels lay clumped on the bedroom floor. The living room was empty though, and the lights were out in the rest of the apartment. "Zack?" I called plaintively.

I heard a faint, rubbery squeak. In the dining alcove, I found Zack lying naked on the blue mat on the floor in the dark. His right knee had been heaved across his body, and he was pressing it downward with his torso twisted violently in the opposite direction. As my eyes adjusted to the darkness, I noticed a white wire emerging from his ear, falling across his body, disappearing into his phone.

"Oh, hey." Uncurling, he made no move to get up, though he yanked out one earbud. "You're back." Returning his leg to its cross-body position, he stretched again, counting to eight, concentrating solely on his breath, seeming to ignore me. Only once he finished did he hoist himself up. He felt around for his phone and rolled up his mat indifferently. "So. You sticking around? Or did you get a better offer?"

"What? I thought we were going out tonight."

"Well then, you probably should shower first." Standing up abruptly, he threw his mat in the corner. "No offense, but you stink of tequila."

"Are you—is everything okay?"

He walked back into the bedroom and began rooting through a duffel bag without looking at me.

"Sure. Why wouldn't it be?" Pulling out a dark blue button-down, he punched one arm through the sleeve, then the other. With his back turned to me, he began buttoning it jerkily.

"So," he said to the wall. "How's your husband?"

I couldn't stop myself from smiling. When was the last time anyone had been the least bit jealous over me? Possibly never.

"That wasn't my husband, Zack," I said gently. "That was my kid." I plopped down on the edge of the mattress and lay back and gave a little laugh toward the ceiling. "That was my kid—who up until two days ago didn't even seem to own vocal cords—calling me up for emergency help with his homework."

Turning, Zack cleared his throat. He yanked on the hem of his shirt to smooth it out. "Austin's your son."

"Yep. And dig this. Apparently, he's doing a hip-hop version of *The Odyssey*."

"Wow." Zack gave a quick, happy little laugh. Noticing that he'd buttoned his shirt cockeyed, he began undoing it. "So he's musical. Just like his mother. That is so cool. How old is he?"

"Sixteen."

"Whoa. Just a little older than Lexie. Right. Okay," he said abruptly. "Here, you still want to shower?" He picked one of the damp towels off his floor. "Sorry. I forgot to do a laundry. It's not too used."

I went into the bathroom. The prospect of getting my hair wet, then drying everything off with a single dirty, soggy towel did not hold much appeal for me. Besides, the way I reeked of sex and tequila was thrilling—it was like a vapor of lust hovering around me—and as I inhaled deeply, I saw in the mirror that I looked unmistakably ravaged and sated and fucked. Oh, how I'd missed this state! Oh, how I loved it. A dry hand towel looked clean, so I just washed my face, armpits, and crotch in the sink with Zack's liquid soap and left it at that. I brushed my teeth with my finger and—why not?—sprayed on just a little of his cologne to add to the mix. It didn't smell quite as good as in the bottle or on me as it did directly on him, but just sniffing it got me mildly aroused again. I picked up his toothbrush—*his* toothbrush—frayed and still damp from his beautiful, oh-so talented mouth. His black plastic comb, with a strand of his hair that I plucked and held to the light. A cheap vinyl dopp kit held a razor, pill vials (Viagra? Really? Had he needed it with me? It hadn't seemed like it . . . plus a prescription I didn't recognize from 2013, unopened, untouched). Tiny snippets of hair freckled the sink, an electric razor recharging on the back of the toilet. A little tub of Vaseline. Unable to resist, I dabbed some on my mouth, then kissed his mirror several times, leaving lip marks.

When I came out, Zack was dressed and sitting on the couch, texting. "You know, I love that you're still a rocker chick, Bella, that you never gave up on that. That is just awesome."

I glanced at Aggie, propped in the entryway. Zack had no way of knowing how new it was. Guiltily, I thought of Austin. "Actually," I said. "Do you mind if I practice for a little while before we head out?"

"No, no. Please. Be my guest. Do what you gotta do. We're in 'Music City,' baby! I can keep myself entertained for a little while." Sauntering into the kitchen, he returned with another drink. "I figure, one more now is one less on our bar bill, right?" Almost as an afterthought, he said, "You want one? I've got some mix in the fridge. There might even be a lime."

"No, no, go ahead." I swung Aggie up onto my lap without looking at Zack. "I'll be the designated driver tonight." As I arranged my fingers on the frets, however, I leaned over and inhaled deeply, trying to get a quick whiff. *Just focus on the strings, Donna*, I told myself. Eddie Ate Dynamite. Good Bye Eddie. I shifted about uncomfortably on the couch, the guitar like a barricade. I hadn't played at all since Vegas, and just showing Austin the chords earlier had hurt my fingertips. I didn't know how I was going to manage to build up all the calluses I needed just to be an okay teacher.

Zack leaned over, kissed me lightly on the forehead. "You sure? We can Uber it instead if you want. Though it'll be about a zillion bucks from out here."

"No, no worries. I'll drive." I glanced at the bottle of Patrón. There didn't seem to be much left in it.

His gaze followed mine down to his grip. "Don't worry. I'll save you some for later, princess."

I stared back down at my guitar. I didn't even know where to begin, what to start with. So I just closed my eyes and began to strum, hoping beyond hope that a song would come to me and I would still sound halfway decent, that I would sound as though I actually knew what the fuck I was doing.

After a few minutes, Zack reappeared. He'd switched some lights on, and the apartment looked more inviting in the honeyed light, with the wheat fields and sky dark in the window. He leaned against the doorframe, waggling his drink around in its glass, listening. I tried not to look at him, tried not to focus on anything but the notes rising in the air. Slowly, I started to sing. No words, just a plaintive, mournful vocal.

"Oh, Bella," Zack said, shaking his head. And was I imagining it, or was he beginning to tear up? "Look at you."

And for that singular moment, with the guitar balanced on my lap and my fingers plucking at the chords and Zack gazing at me, I felt like finally, finally, I might be exactly where I was supposed to have been in my life all along.

Chapter 13

AND THEN WE WERE in public, with our hands jammed into each other's back pockets. When we'd fucked as teenagers, afterward I'd always felt as if pieces of my heart had broken off into his bloodstream. Now, I was surprised to feel this same sensation again, as if I'd fused with him on a molecular level. Giddy, free-floating, no longer rooted in myself.

Neon guitars and neon cowboys and neon marquees cascaded above us on Lower Broadway. The Tequila Cowboy. Paradise Park Trailer Resort. Layla's Bluegrass. Tootsie's Orchid Lounge. The bars' very names like song titles.

If making music in the twenty-first century had largely become a solo, digital enterprise, well, Nashville never got the memo. As Zack and I sauntered past the storefronts, it was like flipping the dial on the radio; one snippet of live music quickly gave way to another. A bluegrass jam was going full-throttle, followed by a Patsy Cline cover, followed by— was that a half-time country rendition of Michael Jackson's "The Way You Make Me Feel"? Yep.—followed by a goateed man in a butcher's apron going to town on an electric fiddle, lacquered in violet light. Cars and SUVs had their sound systems blasting, making the night air vibrate with the heavily synthesized songs my kids listened to: Fetty Wap and Justin Timberlake and Lana Del Rey. Horse-drawn carriages full of tourists clopped by. The warm air glistened with humidity, and as we made our way through the crowds, it smelled of barbecue char, cigarette smoke, and sweet, cloying, hay-ish manure.

"I can't believe you've never been here," Zack shouted. "Welcome to my stomping grounds."

"Kiss me," I commanded. And he did, right there in the middle of Lower Broadway.

"Woo-hoo! Get a room! Get a room!" A "Pedal Tavern" jerked to a stop in the street beside us, propelled by a group of giggling young women in matching BRIDE TRIBE T-shirts. One of them had a fountain of white tulle erupting from her head. Holding aloft a red Solo cup, she shouted, "Pay attention, motherfuckers! This bitch is gettin' hitched! Woohoo!" A friend sitting beside her aimed her drink at Zack and me, her voice slurry. "You folks married? Or just doin' the nasty?"

"We're high school sweethearts!" I hollered.

"Woohoo!" yelled all the girls in unison. "Woohoo!"

"So are these two!" one said, motioning to the bride-to-be. "To Cassie and Tyler!"

"To Cassie and Tyler!" All the girls raised their Solo cups.

"Hang on, hang on. Do you ladies know that you're in the presence of like, the world's greatest Instgrammer here? Allow me." Whipping out his phone, Zack made them pose, their cups held aloft like lanterns. "You gals are gorgeous. Oh, you're gonna love this. What's your Instagram?" he asked the bride. "I'll totally post these!"

"Oh my God!" the girls chorused. "You are soooo cute!"

"Here." One handed him a Solo Cup to consume on the spot.

"Chug, chug, chug!" the girls chanted. "Woohoo!"

As they pedaled off noisily, I squinted after them. "Wow," I said. "In another lifetime."

Zack punched the air. "Boo-yah!"

We stopped into one place where Zack seemed to know the bartender, then another. At each, he had a beer or a tequila shot. I tried not to keep count. I'd sworn to myself that I was done being the Enforcer, the killjoy, *Mo-o-om*. I was going to work with this, go with the flow. Everything with me and Zack was going to be the exact opposite of me with Joey. Besides, for the first time in years, for as long as I could remember, "*I need; I want; fill me*" had been stilled. With Zack, I could feel sated. I actually might not even *want* to drink.

He squeezed my shoulder. "Hey, do you have any of that cash on you? I'm running low." Digging around in my purse for my wallet, I handed him a twenty. "Great. Thanks. Don't worry, princess. After this, we'll go to a place that's a little more your style."

Yet when we got back into the car, the traffic was terrible and the street layout didn't make any sense to me. I felt myself starting to wilt. It had been a very long day already. I'd neglected to bring any Adderall. Zack kept pointing out all the places he'd worked as a rigger—this stadium, that auditorium, recounting how he'd once shown Steven Tyler how to use Spotify. How he'd had to hoist LeAnn Rimes up onto a stage himself after a hydraulic lift jammed. How he'd eaten vegan curry backstage with Maroon 5. Had he always been such a talker? I found myself starting to edit him in my head.

"Zack. Look," I said finally. "Are we actually going anywhere?"

"Whoa, whoa, whoa. Just one more detour, okay? I promise. You're going to fucking love this." Per his instructions, I drove through a park. Before us rose a colossal pillared temple straight out of antiquity. Amber lights angled up at it.

"What the hell?" I said. "That looks like the Parthenon."

"Exactly, exactly! It is the fucking Parthenon. Bella, am I good, or what?" Grinning, he held up his palm for me to high-five. "Nashville used to be called 'the Athens of the South.' So some guy decided to build an exact copy of it for the World's Fair or something. There's even this giant gold Athena inside."

"Jesus. Hang on." I unclicked my seat belt. "Let me get a picture for my son." You had to love the ancient Greeks. In the end, they decided to name their capital after the goddess of wisdom—not beauty, not hunting. In the end, they picked a female deity with brains to represent them.

"Here. Let me take it," Zack said. "One goddess in front of another."

"Oh, that's good. That might be your best line yet."

"I know, right? The East German judge gives it a solid nine."

A few blocks away, he led me down an alley to a graffitied courtyard. On a bulb-trimmed sign, in plastic marquee letters, were the words PUBIC LICE. At first, I thought "Pubic Lice" was the name of the bar—worst name in all of human history—until I realized: No, "Pubic Lice" was the name of a band.

"Tah-dah. Welcome to Nashville's premier punk-indie club," Zack announced. "The White Stripes have played here, REM. Pere Ubu. This is your tribe, woman."

But the bouncer barricaded the door with his arm. "Sorry." Though half of his head was shaved, he looked to me about twelve. "Tickets to this sold out three days ago."

"What? How?" said Zack.

"Online? We've got an app?"

"You have an app?" I heard myself say. "How is that in any way 'punk'? What the hell happened to paying at the door?"

"Yeah," said Zack. "And in cash, man. None of this credit-card or Bitcoin shit. Don't you know, that's how the government tracks you?"

"Sorry, ma'am, that's how it is," the bouncer said to me.

"'*Ma'am?*' Are you kidding?"

At that moment, the show started; the courtyard was assaulted with music. Pubic Lice was screech metal. It was juvenile and atonal and just, well, *loud*. All the bones in my face seemed to rattle; I felt myself recoil. Worse yet, I found myself thinking: *You're a bunch of white twenty-year-olds in America with high-end musical instruments. What the fuck do you have to be angry about?*

"Zack, forget it. Let's get the hell out of here." I nodded back toward the alley. "Thanks for a great tour, baby. It's been a terrific evening."

He threw his arms open. "Are you fucking kidding me? Woman, we are just getting started here. Woman, this is Nashville! This is *us!*"

He led me next to an overblown shack with a pool table. Then to a bluegrass club that felt like a cattle car. "Bella, you sure you don't want one drink? C'mon. One drink's not going to kill you. The cops won't give you a Breathalyzer if all you've had is a vodka."

Having to say no all the time was starting to needle me. "Really? You're going to keep making me drink alone here?" Zack kept saying. But before I had to resist again, he kissed me hungrily. "God, I can't wait to take you back to my place and fuck you again."

My feet began to throb. I told myself that I was still the wild girl, still up for anything. Zack was the great love of my life. Surely I could still keep up with him sober. Surely I could manage this.

He guided me toward another wobbly stool in another crowded bar. "Yo! Lee-Juan!" he called out.

A heavyset man with a Fu Manchu mustache and a red bandanna around his head waddled down the length of the bar. "Hey, hey, hey. It's the Zakkolator." He and Zack exchanged an intricate handshake, as if preparing to arm wrestle. Lee-Juan's chest, arms, and neck were inked with gargoyles and Komodo dragons. "Long time no see. How you been, Zakkolator? You here with your crew?" He eyed me casually.

"Lee-Juan, this is Belladonna. All the way from Michigan. We go back, like, forever, man. Like, three or four hundred lifetimes. Ha-ha."

Lee-Juan nodded. "Welcome to Nashville. Ain't nobody better to show you around than Spider-Man here." He tilted his head. "Just watch out for his webs, is all. This guy can spin 'em."

"Bwhahaha!" Zack slapped the side of the bar. "Bella, LJ here is the number one bartender in all of Tennessee. He is, like, the maestro of all margaritas. The lord of all liquor. Ain't that right, LJ? So." Zack leaned over the bar. "Set 'em up, my man."

Lee-Juan took down a beveled highball and made Zack a margarita with salt, no ice. He turned to me. "For you, ma'am?"

Ma'am? Again? "Just club soda and cranberry." I tried to look put-upon, though the truth was, I was getting increasingly irritable. "Designated driver."

Zack raised his glass. "To hot sex and cold tequila. Lee-Juan," he said, "you guys still host open jam sessions here?"

"Why? Did someone suddenly convince you that you can actually play the saxophone, Zack?" Lee-Juan scooped ice into a shaker and grinned. "'Cause I'm telling you right now, brother, that's only tequila talking."

"Oh my God." I turned to Zack. "Your sax! Do you still play? Not the one I got out of hock?"

Zack peered into his glass. "Wow. Now, *that* was a long time ago." Leaning forward, he seemed to consider whether to tell me something else. "Cindy actually pawned it for good, one night when she got pissed at me."

He braced for my reaction, as if awaiting the reading on a thermometer.

"Cindy?" I said after a moment. "Oh. My. God. That bitch?"

Senior year in high school, Zack had moved into a double-wide in Inkster Township owned by a woman named Cindy. She was a twenty-two-year-old chain smoker with fried blond hair and heavy eyeliner and a six-year-old kid. She worked the cash register at the gas station with Zack. After his stepdad kicked him out one time, she'd let Zack stay with her for free because, she claimed, she needed a guy around for "show" in case her ex came around hassling her again—and also to help with her kid. They were totally *just friends*, Zack insisted—she wasn't even his type—but I'd started hearing rumors at school. Sure enough, one Saturday afternoon when Zack didn't show up to rehearsal, Danny Thurman drove me over, and we found them both stoned out of their minds and her blowing him in the kitchen. Zack had insisted that it was no big deal—that he just had sex with her to placate her—she was totally in love with him—what could he do? She was crazy! If he didn't fuck her, he'd be out on the street.

It was our most epic breakup. Eventually, Zack moved back into Rooster's van and convinced me that he still loved me and only me. But after he and I had broken up for good, I'd heard he'd gone back to Cindy. To say that she'd been a point of contention between us was an understatement.

"Cindy, Jesus. Was that chick ever a nightmare. Wow. I haven't thought of her in years," he said now. "I think Rooster told me she OD'd." He shook his head quickly as if to disperse the memory. Reaching over, he squeezed my hand and pressed it to his heart. "Man, when your name popped up on my screen the other night, Bella? I almost fell off my fucking scaffold.

"Hey, Lee-Juan?" he called down the bar. He put his arm around me and squeezed. A little too hard. "Did you know that Belladonna over here is a total kick-ass guitar player? Back in the day, in Michigan? She used to stage-dive into the audience wearing nothing but a leather bra and a dog collar."

He was making me sound not like a guitarist so much as a stripper. I found myself saying with annoyance, "Actually, I was more like Sonic Youth or Iggy Pop musically."

"She was fucking huge. Locally. Like, a cult following."

"Really?" Lee-Juan said mildly. A waitress at the other end of the bar signaled to him and he slid her a mug of beer. "What were you called?" He took out his phone.

"Toxic Shock Syndrome," Zack informed him.

"It was a long time ago. It was no big deal," I said quickly.

Lee-Juan frowned at his screen. Our group, of course, had no digital footprint whatsoever. "So if you're from Michigan, did you ever know Kid Rock?"

"Totally," Zack said. "In fact, did I tell you, he's got us down on the VIP list for his show tomorrow? We're the Michigan contingent, man. Special guests. We'll probably even party with him afterwards."

Without being asked, Lee-Juan pulled the bottle of tequila out and poured Zack a shot. I had the impulse to stop him. "If you wanna play, come by any Tuesday or Sunday, two to six p.m.," Lee-Juan said to me. "Open mike. You sign up on the whiteboard in there, and the musicians rotate. It's real casual. No money. Just pass the hat."

"Boo-yah!" Zack pivoted around and high-fived me so hard, my palm smarted. "Did I tell you? When she's a big star here, LJ, you owe me, man!"

Throwing back his drink, he slammed the glass down on the bar.

"And now that my work here is done, people," he announced happily, "Spider-Man's gotta take a piss."

Lee-Juan and I both looked after him. As he made his way to the bathroom, he nearly collided with one of the waitresses; bowing, he pantomimed tipping a hat. Then he lurched into some pool players he knew and gave one a big, slappy bear hug. As he continued through the crowd, I saw him wince and press his palm to his spine. He looked suddenly abstracted and hobbled and lost, and I again saw his fundamental rootlessness in the world, just as I had seen it when we were sixteen, and again back in his bedroom that evening, when he'd shown off his case of army surplus meals.

"Hey," I said to Lee-Juan. "Should I be worried about him?"

"Ah. Zack's a wild man. But he's got a big heart." Lee-Juan aimed a soda spigot into a pitcher. "When I was first out on parole, he let me crash with him for almost two months. No rent, no questions asked. Not a lot of guys would do that." Lee-Juan motioned to my empty glass. "Refill? Sure you don't want anything stronger?"

I shook my head. "You were paroled?"

Clearing his throat, he poured me another cranberry and club and squinted across the room. "I haven't been nearly as lucky as the Zakkolator. The charges against me always seemed to stick."

I picked up my glass, then set it down. "Zack's been arrested?"

Lee-Juan fixed me in an unreadable gaze. "Ah," he said after a moment. "I'm just messing with you." A customer flagged him; he waddled back down the bar.

I shifted about uneasily on the stool. It seemed to me that important pieces of information were being withheld from me. What the hell did I *really* know about Zack now? Twenty-six years was more than half my lifetime. Okay, yeah, sure, Zack still felt like Zack. He still looked like Zack. He certainly kissed and fucked and enthused like Zack. But? I thought of him photographing me in front of Nashville's fake temple, calling me a goddess. He *was* my greatest love. I *knew* him, didn't I? I'd known him forever, in fact. He'd been in my cards.

I scrolled through my phone. I chose the best photo Zack had taken of me at the Parthenon to send to Austin as a peace offering of sorts. **In the spirit of your Odyssey rap,** I typed, squinting at my phone. **A piece of Greece from Tennessee.** Well, that rhymed. I was very careful, however, to make sure I was sending *only that*. I hadn't yet deleted all the photos from the bedroom. While I knew I should get rid of the evidence, it had been years since I'd seen myself look so unabashedly sexy. *That one* in the mirror: I would likely never, ever look so good again in my life. From here on in, it would be only gravity and erosion. Was it so terrible to want to hold on to some indisputable proof that I was once, in fact, beautiful? Desired? Loved? I could squirrel the picture away in some made-up file labeled "pap smears"; it would be like a modern-day digital locket.

Zack finally returned from the men's room, still tugging at his jeans, the phone in his hand vibrating with alerts. "LJ, my brother, we have an emergency. My glass is empty." Leaning into me, he clutched my chin in his hands and kissed me. He was drunker than I'd realized. I felt assaulted with slobber, wholly devoured. Perhaps because I was sober and it was late, his tongue now felt eel-like, thick, slightly repellent.

He wheezed into my face. "Hey, remember that time you gave me a blow job while I was driving Rooster's van? And I came so hard, we almost crashed into that dumpster? Oh, and that other, time, with the Reddi-wip I stole from the gas station?" His eyes were on me but heavy-lidded now; he seemed to have trouble focusing. His voice was getting increasingly loud. "Oh, man, and that other time, remember, when I fingered you in gym class, and you were all wet and—"

"Zack. Jesus Christ. Lower your voice!"

"Whoops. Sorry," he said in an exaggerated whisper. "My bad. Indoor voice only. But oh my God, Bella. Feel how hard I'm getting."

Lurching, he grabbed my wrist and pulled it toward him. I yanked it away. "Will you stop?"

Leaning in toward Zack, his eyes glossing over me, Lee-Juan said in a low voice, "Listen, brother, I don't wanna ruin your party here, but I think I better warn you. Anita was in earlier, asking about you."

Zack jerked violently. "You're kidding. Here?"

"She's been coming around all week." Lee-Juan looked at us both haplessly.

"Fuck." Zack raked his hands through his hair. "What did you tell her?"

"Who's Anita?" I said.

Lee-Juan held up both his hands as if in surrender. "I told her I hadn't seen you for months. I said, last I'd heard, you were on the road indefinitely."

Zack leaned against the bar and let his head drop, mop-like. "Oh, fuck."

"Who's Anita?" I said again. Though I was only too aware of my own foolishness. If you have to ask a man twice, you probably already know the answer. A queasiness rose in me.

Lee-Juan said, "She was asking if I thought you might be working the fish fry or over at the stadium."

Hooking his hands around the back of his neck, Zack stared up at the ceiling. "Okay," he exhaled. "Bella, mind paying up?" He turned to Lee-Juan. "Thanks for the heads-up, man. Look. If she comes back here tonight?"

"I know nut-tink, I see nut-tink. You vere not here," Lee-Juan said in a German accent, shaking his head vehemently. "Two margaritas, comes to $12," he said to me. "The cranberries are on the house. Welcome to Nashville."

Miserably, I dug out a twenty and told him to keep the change.

Zack was already halfway down the steps when I caught up to him.

"Crazy, fucking bitch." He glanced distractedly around at the street, the cars, scanning the distance. "Claims I owe her money, when I totally fucking don't."

In the Subaru, he turned on the radio full volume to some sort of thrash-metal station until I had to yell, "Zack!" He snapped it off and sat slumped against the window in silence, glaring at the dark streets sliding by. When I made a wrong turn, he said, "Jesus Christ, Donna, don't you have a fucking GPS?"

I glanced at him and said, my voice hard, "Zack, do you really have apartments in Miami and LA?"

"Huh? What are you talking about?"

"Tell me, truthfully. Have you ever been arrested?"

"Excuse me. What the hell? What is this, the Jewish gestapo?"

I pulled the car to a screeching halt. "Oh. Don't you dare."

He threw up his hands. "Hey, hey, I'm sorry. I'm sorry. Okay? Just trying to make a joke. I'm a little drunk, okay?"

"More than a little," I said bitterly.

He stared at me. "Is that what this is about?"

"Is that what what's about?"

"C'mon. Oh, please. You think I haven't noticed? 'No thanks, I really can't.' 'Oh, I'll be the designated driver tonight.' C'mon, Donna. I'm not an idiot."

"That's not what this is about, Zack."

"Oh no? 'Cause that seems like it to me. You're all pissy because you're the one not drinking. I told you that one drink was not going to get you pulled over. But instead, you've decided to be all Miss High-and-Righteous."

"Excuse me? Excuse me? I paid for every one of your drinks tonight, Zack, in case you didn't notice." I put the car firmly into park, yanked off the ignition. I had no idea where we were. Someplace on the outskirts of southern Nashville, past a river.

"Who's Anita?"

"Ah. Of course. There we are. 'Who's Anita.' So that's it. You fucking women. You're all alike." He threw up his hands. "I told you already. Anita's this insane chick who keeps claiming I owe her money. When I totally don't." He looked at me reproachfully. "She's like this weird, psycho stalker. For the past year and a half or so, she's been, like, obsessed with me."

"Oh, right. Sure. She's totally in love with you for no reason at all. Just like Cindy was."

"Cindy? Cindy? Are you fucking kidding me? Are we still stuck on that?"

I glanced away. "I know when you're sleeping with somebody, Zack.

Believe me." I knew it was ridiculous to feel proprietary after twenty-six years, but I did. We were lovers again; it changed everything for me.

"Oh for Christ's sake, Donna. Anita's a fucking lesbian. She's another rigger and, like, a total bull dyke." He fixed his eyes on mine as if he were attempting to drill his words into the back of my head and affix them there. "She's this Russian immigrant who grew up in, like, Siberia, and she just latches onto people and gets all paranoid and KGB on them. I don't know, her childhood was bad or something. But we're both in the union here. There's no getting away from her."

We sat there for a few minutes, breathing loudly, looking at each other in a face-off. The outlandishness of his explanation was an affront to my basic intelligence. He must have sensed this, too. But this was Zack. This was how he lied. This was how he'd always lied many, many times before, I realized. It was like a song I knew from high school. I knew it as intimately as the scent of his skin, and the curve of his penis, and his sneezy, lunatic laugh. Somehow, though, I'd completely forgotten it.

"A Russian lesbian stalker, Zack? Really. That's the best you can do? Are you sure she's not an amputee as well?"

Zack's face softened. Slowly, gently, he began to laugh. "Oh my God. You're jealous. You're still jealous. That is so sweet. That is, like, the nicest compliment anyone's ever given me." He reached for my hand and kissed it before I could jerk it away. "Oh, Belladonna."

He gave me an adoring, puppyish look. "Wow. You really think I'm that much of a player now? Look at me, Bella. I'm forty-fucking-five."

"Well so am I. And I'm too old for this shit anymore. For these games."

"What games, Bella? What games?"

I unclicked my seat belt and turned to face him. "I don't know the first thing about your life now, Zack. You're here, you're there. You tell all these stories. I'm sick of not knowing what the fuck is going on, of having people lie to me, of having men pull all this shit on me behind my back."

I felt like someone was pressing down on my thorax. Kicking open the door, I climbed out into the street, gulping in air so quickly, it sounded as though I was dry-heaving.

"Jesus Christ, Donna." Zack was out on the street now, too, coming around the front of the Subaru, his arms outstretched as if to demonstrate that he wasn't carrying any weapons. "What the fuck do you want from me? The whole reason you don't know anything about my life now is because *you* said you didn't want us to talk. You said flat-out, 'Zack, I just want to be in the moment. Zack, I just want us to be in our bubble. Our life beyond space and time.'"

I looked down. He was right, of course. He was right, and I hated it. There was nothing at all I could say.

"I could grill you, too, you know," he said. "I could press you about your husband. About why you're not with your kids. And about why the hell you've just shown up here out of the blue with like, a thousand bucks in cash rolled up in your bra, and about what the hell you've been doing for these past twenty-six years. But I haven't. Because *you've asked me not to.*"

I stood there in the street with my arms wrapped around myself, staring at him. It was warm and humid, yet for some reason I was shivering. I shook my head and leaned into him. Suddenly, I started to cry. Everything was just such a mess now. He put his arm around me and propped his chin on the top of my head. His chest shuddered. I heard him sniffle, too.

"I mean, fuck, Donna. You saw the guys I work with. Most them are, like, half my age. I figure, if I'm lucky, I've got five, six years left. Then what? I'm the Zakkolator. I'm Spider-Man. Since when does Spider-Man need fucking yoga?"

He bit his lip. "Sometimes, I think all I have to show for myself in the end is just a big-ass, flat-screen TV with surround sound."

I sniffled. "Zack, my husband cheated on me," I said quietly. "And my kids both think I'm the world's biggest embarrassment, this pathetic bad joke. My only so-called 'personal achievement' in twenty-six years? It was to 'just say no' to drinking. I'm an alcoholic, Zack. I've been in recovery exactly five years, six months, and eighteen days now. And it almost never, ever seems to get any easier."

He closed his eyes as if in physical pain. "Damn," he whispered. "Donna, I'm so sorry."

We stood there for a while, just holding each other tightly, tighter than I could ever remember, staring out into the night. Our breathing synced.

"I just kept thinking, okay, maybe my husband cheating on me was actually for some higher purpose, you know, like to get me back to you." I shook my head. "Is that insane? But I kept thinking, could you and I maybe do better for ourselves together than apart? Now that we're adults? You know, when we were back in Michigan, we were, like, amazing together. Telepathically connected. And in love. And the sex."

I turned and looked at him. Wiping his eyes with the base of his palms, he gazed at me, the muscle in his jaw twitching. Cupping my face in his palm, he gently brushed the corner of my mouth with his thumb. "You are still so beautiful, Donna," he said hoarsely. "You were my first great love." Leaning forward, he let his luxuriant mane of thinning hair fall forward into his face. "But what I really need to do right now is lie down. I have had way, way too much to drink."

Gingerly, I maneuvered him back into the Subaru. Immediately, he pushed the seat as far back as it would go and shut his eyes. I found his address in my phone and drove us slowly back toward Murfreesboro. I was surprised by how quickly Nashville dropped away into rural darkness. The car was quiet now, except for Zack's strangled snoring. I kept glancing over, making sure he was okay as the lights from the highway slid across his supine form like inverse shadows. When we reached his apartment complex, I parked as close as I could to the entrance, went around to the passenger side, and gently woke him.

"Ah, Bella. Belladonna," he smiled, holding open his arms magnanimously. "Let's dance. Let's dance me into the shower, then dance me into bed." Using me to support himself, he struggled out of the car and stood wavering in the parking lot. He shook his legs out, one then the other, as if doing the hokey-pokey, then twisted from side to side until his back cracked.

"There we go. There we go, baby. Okay. I'm okay now. Just needed a little shut-eye. Fuck, Bella. I usually don't drink this much. I was just nervous. Seeing you again. You are totally, totally right. We *are* soul mates, baby. And we can totally do this, now. Just start over. Or pick up right where we left off. I mean, fuck the rest of the world, right? Fuck it, man." He put his arm around me and we walked to the lobby, zigzagging slightly. This was why I'd given up drinking; this had been me, too many nights to count. I didn't miss any of this part at all. It was a critical reminder. Maybe—I didn't know—could I drag him along to a meeting with me tomorrow, under the guise of moral support? Suddenly, I was just so tired.

"What do you say we have a ménage à trois?" Zack pointed to himself, then jabbed his finger twice in my approximate direction. "The one of me with the two of you?" He started to laugh.

"Oh, Zachary." I shook my head.

A man in an undershirt sat out on the stoop smoking. Inside the vestibule, two blond girls were slumped on the grimy love seat, staring sullenly into their phones. No one made a move to help me with the door. After I struggled to heave it open, however, one of the blonds leapt up.

"Where the fuck have you been? I've been calling and texting you all fucking night, you drunk-ass piece of shit." She waved her phone. Zack jumped back with his hands up as if he were being robbed at gunpoint. "Whoa, whoa, Janine. What the hell?"

"Don't fucking 'Janine, what the hell' me. I drove almost three fucking hours and you couldn't once pick up your fucking phone?"

My hands went up to my mouth. *Oh no*, I thought. *Oh, Donna, you idiot.*

She was clad in capris and a filmy white camisole that clung to her nipples and showed off the orangey sheen of her skin. Her blond hair was tousled. She was attractive in a junk-foody sort of way, shiny and sugary-looking and artificially colored. "Look who got suspended, Zachary. Look who's been lying to me and cutting class for the past two weeks and shoplifting and selling pot to the ninth graders."

Curled shrimp-like and sullen on the love seat was a red-eyed blond girl in a peach hoodie and mauve short-shorts, her legs scabby with mosquito bites. She was fiddling with a pair of plastic headphones. She had a wounded look. An overstuffed pink backpack sat at her feet with a tiny gingham teddy bear hanging from its zipper. Beside it: a small, cheap suitcase. I recognized her instantly from the photo. "Hey, Dad," she said almost inaudibly. "Janine, like, kidnapped me here. She's in total psycho mode."

"You can't fucking kidnap your own kid!" Janine shouted. "I told her, Zack, just like I'm telling you. I am fucking done. Do you hear me? D-U-N. I am not running a hotel or a juvie center, and I am not a fucking ATM. She can live down here with you now, for all I care."

"Nice spelling, Janine. It's D-O-N-E, brainiac," said Lexie.

"You hear that? She calls me 'Janine'!" She whirled around to Lexie. "I am your *mother*. I deserve a little fucking respect."

"Then Jesus. Stop being such a total bitch all the time. So what if I sold some brownies? You're just pissed 'cause it was *your* pot. *Jah-nine*."

Wow. I looked from Lexie to Janine to Zack, the three of them, knotted in a cat's cradle of history and genetics. So this was Zack's ex. I tried to imagine him with her; them meeting, fucking passionately, having a kid together. Did he go with her for her sonograms, brush her hair back from her face as she sweated and heaved with morning sickness? Did they take out the garbage, pay the cable bill, order pizza together? Hamstrung between his ex-wife and his daughter, Zack looked suddenly trapped and ashen, slightly concave.

He hiccuped. "Uh, Lexie. Try calling your mom, 'Mom,' okay?"

Three hours' worth of accumulated fury and recrimination from their drive down to Nashville was now being unleashed. Lexie and Janine both began yelling their case at once.

"I wouldn't even have to sell brownies if you paid me a fucking allowance like a normal person!"

"I'd pay you a 'fucking allowance' if you'd put down your goddamn phone for five minutes and lift a finger around the house from time to time! I am a single parent, Lexie, and I am working three jobs—"

"Oh my God, Mom! Why did you even bother to have kids, then? I didn't ask to be born. I didn't ask to come into this world."

"Listen, you lazy, ungrateful little piece of shit—"

Zack waved his arms emphatically. "Hey, can everybody just chill for a minute?"

"Oh, suddenly you're the big peacemaker? Fucking Gandhi here. The guy who won't even pay child support."

I hung back, hugely embarrassed. It was one thing to watch reality shows or *Jerry Springer*. But to bear witness to a family combusting in person? Unfortunately, there was simply no room for me to maneuver around them.

"How many fucking times do I have to tell you, Janine?" Zack shouted. "The feds are garnishing my wages."

"Yeah, and whose fault is that, asshole? That's what happens when you don't pay your taxes for ten fucking years."

"Oh, like *I* should be subsidizing the fucking government? Is that what you want?"

"Dad," Lexie interrupted. "I *want* to live with you, okay. Evansville is, like postapocalyptic zombieland. We don't even get Netflix."

"Oh? Now, you *want* to live with your father, Lexie?" Janine looked newly injured. "Well that's just great, that's just fucking great because we are finally in agreement here on something."

Picking up Lexie's suitcase, she hurled it across the lobby. It hit the wall behind Zack and landed at my feet.

"C'mon, Janine," Zack said. "Seriously?"

"Hey look," I said finally. "I think I should maybe wait outside?" No one paid me the least bit of attention.

"Here you go, precious. Go live with your father, then! You've got a whole new life ahead of you now—with his lies and his bullshit and his skanky girlfriends—why look, there's even one right here. Look, Lexie, you've probably got yourself a brand-new fucking stepmother right here in the lobby. Me? I am just washing my hands of you." Janine held up her hands and brushed them together exaggeratedly. "Washing. My. Hands."

Lexie looked alarmed.

"Whoa. No. Hey." I put up my palms like a traffic cop. "I'm just an innocent bystander here. If anything, Janine, I, of all people, think I understand what you're—"

Suddenly Janine pivoted around. Only then did my presence fully register with her. And too late, I realized my mistake. She was like a drunk at a bar, itching to pick a fight. If her initial target didn't pan out, she'd just fix on the next one. In a flash, she was yelling, hot-breathed, in my face.

"Oh. *You* understand *me*? *You* understand *me*? Who the *fuck* are *you*?"

"Janine!" I heard Zack plead.

Like an expert pitcher preparing a windup, she drew back her fist and slugged me.

Chapter 14

AT TWO O'CLOCK in the morning, the highway out of Nashville was a furrow of darkness glistening with fog. With almost no one else on the road, it felt quietly treacherous. I suspected I had no business driving, but thanks to Kid Rock's fish fry, there wasn't a motel room to be had in a forty-mile radius.

"Well, according to these signs, I guess we're heading to Memphis," I said to Aggie. I'd belted the Rogue Dreadnought into the seat beside me like a passenger. I tried to concentrate on the white lines glowing beneath my headlights, but the Subaru kept seeming to fishtail. Furious whirlybirds of light bounced off my rearview mirror, redblueredblueredblue, growing closer and closer, until the interior of the car itself seemed to blaze with them. Only then did I hear the sirens.

I jerked over onto the shoulder and switched off the ignition. A chorus of doors slammed; there appeared to be not one, but two—or was that three?—white SUVs pulling up behind me. Policemen in navy uniforms emerged quickly from the darkness on either side of my car. One of them held a long flashlight above his shoulder like a javelin, the other restrained a German shepherd on a leash. Clearly, I was being caught up in some sort of manhunt along Interstate 40; this was far too big a force for a simple traffic patrol. It was my second run-in with the police in three days, I realized. Even when I was drinking, I hadn't had so many regular encounters with the law. It was a personal record.

My heart grew almost arrhythmic as they approached. I had the general

idea that Southern police forces didn't take kindly to us Northerners—
certainly, I'd seen news clips and documentary footage—not to mention
the movie *Mississippi Burning*—and, okay, *Deliverance*—yes, I know,
that was hardly the same as being stopped on I-40 in Tennessee, but
somehow, my Michigander-Jewish brain lumped it together. I sat there
gripping my steering wheel at ten-and-two, telling myself *Yeah, okay,
technically, you're a Yankee and a Jew, but c'mon, you're a middle-aged,
suburban white woman in a Subaru—you are not who they're looking
for*—and for the first time, I realized, shamefully, what my daughter
had meant all those times about our "white privilege"—but still, overall,
I hoped and assumed that being polite and charming and deferential
would smooth over any cultural breaches long enough to win them over
and they'd just wave me on. Besides, I had nothing to hide, I reminded
myself proudly: I was not drunk.

"Ma'am, you've been driving erratically, and we clocked you going
thirteen miles above the speed limit." An officer shined the flashlight
directly into my face, then squinted at the paperwork I handed over.
"Michigan, hmm? You're pretty far from home to be driving around here
so late at night."

I blinked up at him. He was a florid man with tiny features smushed
together beneath a wide brow, a miniature face adrift in a fleshy
pancake. His voice, with its Smokey Mountain twang, was as languid
and sweet as syrup, and his nametag read "M. Petty." Officer Petty? I
suppressed the nervous urge to make some sort of quip.

Officer Petty aimed his flashlight in my face again. I expected him to
start writing me a ticket, but his expression changed suddenly. "Ma'am.
Are you all right?"

Reflexively, I touched my fingertips lightly to the left side of my face.
I could feel the swelling, a dull, steady throb beneath the skin. The
corner of my eye had already been turning purplish as I'd left the hotel.
Janine could've been a welterweight. "Ma'am, have you been in a fight
or an accident?"

I shook my head, then nodded, then shook my head again. I was so relieved to hear concern in his voice. The only sound that came out was "Yuuuuhhhhhuuuunn."

"Is that a yes or a no, ma'am?"

The officer cocked his head. "Did a stranger assault you, ma'am, or was it someone you know? Your husband or your boyfriend, ma'am? Because if this is a case of domestic violence—"

I shook my head miserably. "My boyfriend's wife punched me." The instant I said this, I wished I hadn't, because I realized just how trashy it sounded. Those six words suggested an entire trailer park's worth of melodrama and bad judgment—and over the hood of my Subaru, the two officers exchanged a look, and the mood instantly switched back to one less generous.

"I'm such a fool. I'm such a total moron," I tried to explain, smiling ingratiatingly despite my tears. "I mean, good God, Officer. Who decides to meet their high school sweetheart over Facebook, right? It's just that I loved him so much. I really did. He was my great— Since we were sixteen years old, but then he—"

"Ma'am," the officer said impatiently, "are you by any chance intoxicated?"

I shook my head violently. "Oh, no. No sir, Officer. No, no. In fact, I haven't had a drink in exactly five years, six months, and eighteen— whoops, no—it's after midnight—*nineteen* days now."

Somehow, this answer only made me sound less sober, not more. Plus, I realized, my Subaru had a faint whiff of tequila left in it from Zack.

Officer Petty presented me with a Breathalyzer. I took it willingly, and it revealed that there was absolutely no alcohol in my bloodstream.

Just for good measure, Officer Petty ordered me to walk a straight line, follow his pen tip, touch my nose while balancing on one leg. I had done these tests before. I knew them like a dance; they were the drunkard's version of the Macarena, the YMCA. When I mastered them, I had to contain my glee. But shivering there on the side of Interstate 40 at 2 a.m., clad in my leopard-print miniskirt and my Anthrax hoodie, with my eyeliner smudged and a plummy bruise rising on my cheek—

and a guitar case strapped into the passenger seat beside me like one of those inflatable dolls commuters used sometimes to cheat their way into the HOV lanes during rush hour—and my very Yankee license plates (MICHIGAN Great Lakes Splendor! Circa 2007)—I began to understand how maybe I looked like someone who should, in fact, be pulled over at 2 a.m.

On the pebbled shoulder of the highway, the moist air smelled of wet soil and gasoline. I glanced back at the patrol SUVs. Dark letters set off against the white read 23RD JUDICIAL DISTRICT DRUG TASK FORCE. From the other side of my Subaru, I heard a dog yelp.

"Ma'am," Officer Petty addressed me, clearing his throat, "we have 'probable cause' to search your vehicle. Would you be so kind as to pop the trunk for us?"

Nine boxes of shoes from the Designer Outlet tumbled out onto the roadside. With some effort, Officer Petty knelt on the ground behind the Subaru and carefully opened each one, probing them with his flashlight, unwrapping each shoe from its tissue nest, removing the clots of cardboard stuffed inside, his thick hands jamming deep into the toes of the metallic pumps and rhinestone kitten heels, feeling around. I felt myself sweating, my heart palpitating frantically.

Officer Petty fixed his eyes on mine. "Nine pairs of new shoes? Any particular reason, ma'am?"

"Um, I'm a woman?" I heard myself say. "And they were on sale?"

I'd hoped this would reassure him, disarm him, help him pigeonhole me as nothing more than a ditsy shopaholic with a shoe fetish like a zillion other women he probably knew. But his attentions had already moved to my new purple suitcase. Dumping out the contents, he sifted through my sexy, unworn underwear and clothing I'd purchased so hopefully just two days before (some with the tags still on). He tapped the sides of the suitcase and ran his fingers along the zippers and seams, feeling for a false bottom or something stashed between the lining and the outer canvas. Then he spied the large carton shoved toward the back of the trunk. He pulled it forward and pushed open the cardboard flaps. I heard a clatter of metal. He glanced back at me. "Is there any particular reason, ma'am, why you're traveling with a box full of tongs, strainers, knives, measuring spoons—and, what are these, ma'am? Are these meat thermometers? And kitchen scales?"

"Oh, those are my samples," I said. "Part of my inventory. I'm in sales."

"You're in *sales*?" he enunciated.

I started to panic. Somehow, everything suddenly sounded damning. Strainers, meat thermometers, scales: Could those in any way be used for illegal activity?

"They call us 'culinary ambassadors'? I do cooking demonstrations," I said quickly. "For a company called the Privileged Kitchen. 'High-end cookware at bargain-basement prices.' Everything from spatulas to non-stick casserole pans to lemon zesters—and not just any lemon zesters. They have little patented 'catch-sleeves.'" Good God: Why was I prattling on like this? Who talks about lemon zesters to a drug enforcement agent? But already, Officer Petty had stopped listening. His colleague was waving him over to the front of the Subaru.

"I found something here, Matt. Stashed in the guitar case." He held up the Walmart pharmacy bag. "There's a whole bunch of pills, and none of the names on the prescription bottles match the one on her license."

"Look," I said pleadingly, "you can see right there on the vials. Austin and Ashley *Koczynski*—it's the same last name as mine. Their dates of birth are printed right there on the labels, too, see? Do the math. They're sixteen and nineteen years old. They're my children, Officers— and these are my children's prescriptions. I'd filled them just a few days ago, but then, well, I got diverted and I didn't drive home right away. Here, see?" I said. "I've got the original prescriptions right here." Pulling out my wallet, I sorted through the billfold and located scripts with the receipts stapled to them from the Walmart in Ohio to submit to our insurance company.

"Well, here's the problem," Officer Petty sighed, holding the bottles up to the light and shaking them. "These were filled three days ago. Two of them have been opened. And the labels are smudged. And are any of these children right here with you in this car right now?"

His question was obviously rhetorical.

"Unless and until you can get a confirmation from your children's pediatrician that these prescriptions did, in fact, come from her, and that they are in fact legitimate, we have to assume, ma'am, that you are not in lawful possession of them."

"Excuse me? Officer, I'm their *mother*. Plus, it's Adderall. That's like, Tylenol practically. Half the kids I know in Michigan are on it."

"Adderall is not at all like Tylenol, ma'am. Adderall is a form of amphetamine. It's a Schedule II controlled substance with a molecular structure similar to methamphetamine."

"Crystal meth? Are you kidding me?"

"What's more, ma'am"—his colleague was speaking now, a young, heavy-footed man with a blond caterpillar of a mustache and a name-tag reading T. DEVEREAUX—"the volume of pills you have here well exceeds the limit for personal use. You've got how many here?" He rifled through the Walmart bag. "One vial of sixty Adderall and, gosh almighty. Three vials of Ativan, sixty count apiece. That's 240 pills total. That amount suggests intent to resell or distribute. That's a felony offense, ma'am."

"A felony?" I cried. "Oh good God. I'm not selling my children's meds. Please, Officers. I mean, why would I do such a thing?" Yet as soon as I said this, I knew: People everywhere were selling off bottles of medication, pill by pill. In locker rooms, PTA meetings, church parking lots. AA was full of prescription drug addicts now; the opioid epidemic was all over the news. Just a week earlier, in fact, a woman had been busted in Sterling Heights for selling Vicodin at a hair salon not far from Austin's school.

"My daughter, she's studying in London. I was just sending her a supply for the semester," I said faintly. "She forgot to pack it, and the cost of shipping one vial overseas every month—"

"Well," said Officer Devereaux, "unless her doctor can confirm it—"

"Absolutely, of course," I said. "But it's two o'clock in the morning—"

"And if you don't mind my saying, ma'am," Officer Petty interrupted, motioning to my wallet, "that seems to be an awful lot of cash you have in your possession. May I?" With a rising feeling of nausea, I surrendered it. What else could I do? I wished I'd kept it rolled up in my bra, as I had earlier—though I suspected that if they decided to search my person in detail, well, that would only look worse.

Officer Petty leafed through my billfold, counting quickly to himself. There *were* an awful lot of twenties. "Eight hundred and twenty-four dollars. That's an awful lot of money to be driving around with, don't you think, ma'am?"

He nodded at me so vigorously I found myself nodding, even as I managed to concoct what I hoped was a plausible explanation. "The thing is, I just prefer to pay for things in cash. That's not a crime, is it? You see, well, I already maxed out my credit cards for this month." I decided to add, "On shoes?"

"So, you're selling pills and kitchen utensils to finance a shoe addiction. Is that really what you're telling us?" Officer Petty crossed his arms irritably.

"No, I, what I am saying is that—" But before I could elaborate, Officer Devereaux called from the passenger side, "I found another vial here, Matt. In the glove compartment."

Sauntering back around toward us, he held out another bottle of pills. Borrowing Officer Petty's flashlight, he squinted at it. "Who is Alonso Jimenez?"

For a moment, I had absolutely no idea. I felt a bolt of horror: I was being set up. I was being framed.

Officer Devereaux handed the vial over to Officer Petty. "Well, this bottle here, ma'am, says it comes from a Mount Sinai Hospital in New York City."

Brenda's medicine cabinet. The bottle I'd filched impulsively.

"It says here that it's a prescription for—*Propecia*?" Officer Petty looked first at Officer Devereaux, then at me. He shook his head, took off his hat, and ran his hand over his scalp, as smooth and shiny as oiled leather. "Well, now I've seen it all. Ma'am, would you like to tell us why you're driving around with someone else's prescription for male-pattern baldness drugs?"

I stared at him. I felt myself short-circuit. Somewhere deep in my brain, I felt a pop of relief that I'd just happened to grab something so innocuous—I could even picture one of Brenda's fellow interns, Alonso, worriedly studying his hairline in her bathroom mirror—but then, I realized I had to come up with some plausible explanation. Suddenly, all I could think to say was:

"Um, vaginal dryness?"

"Excuse me?"

"Uh, I read on the internet somewhere that for women, if you take male-pattern baldness medication, it can help you, you know, with the symptoms of menopause? Hot flashes and dryness and so on? And so I borrowed some from my friend."

Back when I was a drunk, I'd once told the cops that the reason I was speeding was because I was bleeding through my tampon and staining my car upholstery. They could not get rid of me fast enough. They didn't even make me get out of the car; I was waved on without so much as a warning. The last thing any traffic cops ever wanted to hear about was a woman's vagina. It was like kryptonite. It had become my foolproof way for wriggling out of speeding tickets and Breathalyzers.

Now, Officers Petty and Devereaux glanced at each other. "Ma'am," Officer Petty said, "I'd strongly advise you to watch your language here. Maybe you can talk like that up in Michigan, but down here in Tennessee, we're Christians. If you've got problems with your lady parts, frankly, that's your own business, and we'd prefer that you keep them to yourself. We don't want to hear about that sort of stuff, you understand? And nor, I suspect, will the judge."

He instructed me to hold out my wrists. "Under the laws of the state of Tennessee, you are hereby charged with 'possession with intent.' You have the right to remain silent," he began.

*   *   *

Charlotte, Tennessee, might be a tiny, sleepy town nestled in the wood-
lands, but its Dickson County Jail remained open 24/7. A concrete,
slit-windowed bunker, it gave every appearance of being the sort of detention center that, if it were in, say, Guantanamo Bay or Argentina in the
1970s, no one would ever emerge from it once they set foot inside.

A weary, sallow-faced deputy processed me quickly. He was polite
enough to pretend not to notice how badly I was shaking, how palsied
with fear I was as the forms to book me were filled out and my finger-
prints taken. Possession with intent was a "Class E felony" that carried
with it fines of up to $3,000 and sentences of between one and six
years in prison. "Is this a dream? Please, tell me, is this just a bad
dream?" I heard myself ask the air. My teeth were chattering so hard, in
fact, that they had trouble getting my mug shot. "Ma'am, please. Take
a deep breath. A deep breath, ma'am. There you go. It's just a camera,
ma'am."

As they had me remove my jewelry and my pantyhose (as if I could
hang myself with them? Did they understand how easily those things
ripped and stretched out?), I heard myself insisting, "I'm just a mother of
two. A forty-five-year-old kitchenware saleswoman from Troy, Michigan,
nothing more. Nothing more. I promise you," over and over. I kept waiting for someone to recognize what a hideous mistake had been made.
Hell, practically everyone I knew back in Michigan was taking Ativan or
Adderall or Ritalin or Zoloft or Paxil or Xanax or all of the above. Surely,
someone could see that the prescriptions were for my children—and
okay, yes, I was a mess, yes, absolutely, perhaps even in the throes of
a nervous breakdown; fine, I'd happily sign a written confession to that
in a heartbeat—and to being a shitty mother and to not being anywhere
that a good Jewish girl should ever be at two o'clock in the morning—I
was a bad wife and a bad friend and a lousy person overall—fine, yes—
I'd swear to all of this in an affidavit. But a drug dealer?

But when the magistrate set my bail after I was processed, it became all too clear exactly how the Tennessee judicial system regarded me. Because I lived in Michigan, I was informed, the court considered me a likely flight risk who'd inevitably skip town the minute I was released. And so, my bail was set at $100,000; in a small town like Charlotte, there was not a single bondsman who'd insure me for such a sum.

If I couldn't make bail myself, I would have to remain in jail until appearing before the DA—perhaps sometime the next day, but also, perhaps, not until the following Tuesday, given that we were approaching the Columbus Day weekend. (I might have to spend four whole nights in jail?) I was told I'd be assigned a court-appointed attorney the next morning if I couldn't afford one on my own. I was asked if I understood, but although I nodded, by then my eye was nearly swollen shut, and I was shivering uncontrollably, and all the events from the past four days seemed to tornado around me in a furious vortex lifting me into a whirl of debris, the great, jagged wreckage of my life spinning around me in a great whoosh of misery—and I began having an out-of-body experience, in which I was seated at a metal desk in a dreary DA's office with dropped ceilings and jaundiced fluorescent light but also watching myself from above, hovering somewhere amid the pitted ceiling tiles by the air duct.

Just like in the movies, I was told that I could make a phone call. It was 3 a.m. now, which meant 4 a.m. in Michigan. On a cinder-block wall in the corner was a pay phone. Dialing our landline, I began to hyperventilate.

As the phone rang on the other end, I imagined the electronic bleat of it echoing through our house. Our house! I saw the carriage light above the garage emitting its weak halo of warm coppery light over the driveway. I pictured Mr. Noodles twisted like a cruller on the linoleum beneath the computer nook in the kitchen, snoring and farting and slobbering fitfully. The refrigerator humming, full of discount half-gallons of skim milk and Mountain Dew, the magnets holding 2-for-1 coupons and school printouts. I saw our bathroom upstairs with its outdated vanity covered with kisses of goo from melty, fruity glycerin soaps and Barbasol shaving cream and dabs of toothpaste stuck to the side of the sink like paint on a palette. I saw Austin in his bed, the great, beautiful lump of him, and then Joey asleep across the hallway from him in our bedroom. He'd be curled on his right side, facing my empty space in the bed, perhaps gripping one of my pillows as a substitute for spooning me— and the love and the longing I felt at that moment was so fierce, it felt like a sharp blow to my chest.

Our phone back in Michigan continued to ring.

"C'mon, pick up, Joey," I whispered.

In a few minutes, it would be better. Amid the insanity of the world, I did have someplace. I belonged somewhere, imperfect as it was. Joey and I, we were not rich, but we had some resources—something that could serve as collateral, no? I was middle-aged, white, female without so much as an outstanding parking ticket or an overdue library book (okay, not that I read anymore). It had been a terrible mix-up, was all. Certainly, I could not be locked up in a Tennessee jail as a flight risk and a felon.

On the seventh ring, Joey finally answered and accepted the reverse charges. "Yuuuh, hello? Hello? Ashley, is that you? Ashley, are you okay?"

"No, Joey. Joey, it's me. Donna. Sweetie, I'm in Tennessee. I'm in a little bit of trouble."

On the other end, there was a crackle of silence. "Fuck," he said after a moment. "Well, can we please talk later, Donna? I'm waiting on a call from our daughter."

"No, Joey. No, I can't. You see," I said carefully, my heart pounding, "this is my one phone call. The one phone call they're allowing me. As in 'from jail'?"

Again, silence.

"You're in jail, Donna?"

"In Charlotte, Tennessee, Joey. There's been a mistake." As quickly as I could, I sketched out the broad circumstances of my arrest. "So, I need your help, Joey. I need you to contact our lawyer and also Dr.

Seidel to confirm the kids' prescriptions. And is there any way, I don't know, we can come up with $100,000?" It seemed like a long shot, but there were second mortgages, our 401(k) accounts, maybe Joey's practice as collateral.

Before I could continue, he cut me off. "Why are you calling *me*, Donna? Why not go ask your boyfriend to rescue you?"

"Excuse me?"

"He seems to have plenty of talent. Plenty of skill."

"What are you talking about?"

"Certainly, he's a great photographer."

"What?"

On the end of the line, I heard a great intake of breath. "Imagine my surprise tonight, Donna. Me and Stewie and Reggie, all the guys, we're sitting down to watch *Game of Thrones* here in the den. And it's all cued up for us on the Apple TV. All set up for us by Austin, so I won't have to do anything. Because as we both know, Donna, me? I'm not so hot with the electronics. And so me and the guys, we're all watching, and in between one of the episodes, we all get up, go to the kitchen to get ourselves some of Reggie's tacos, and some beers, and when we come back, we've been gone long enough that the screen saver has come on, I guess. And first, all we see on the TV screen are photos of kitchenware, all your Privileged Kitchen shit—close-ups of bar codes on cheese graters and fancy bread slicers. A few from Vegas, of some sort of ceremony—pictures you've taken with your phone, apparently, for work. In fact, one of the guys, Stewie, I think, he goes something like 'Wow. That Donna certainly knows how to have a wild time out there, doesn't she?' And we all laugh. But just as he says this, this nude close-up of a woman, Donna, pops up on the television. Full frontal. Squeezing her tits together, arching her back, like some porn star."

"What?" My breath suddenly felt like broken glass.

"And it takes me a minute, Donna. It's just from the neck down. So the guys, they don't realize. But me? I know that beauty mark on your belly. I know that scar—"

"No," I said.

"And at first, we can't believe it, and the guys start hooting, 'Is that on Donna's phone?' And me, I'm like an idiot. I'm going, 'How is that on Donna's phone?' And Reggie has to explain to me that whoever's account is used to log on to Apple TV, their photos are streamed directly from their iPhone onto the television as a screen saver."

"Oh no! Oh no no no no." I actually slid down the cinder-block wall to the floor.

"And I'm thinking, maybe you did it as a joke or something, or I don't know? But then, another photo pops up, Donna, and this time, it's you and some long-haired guy with tattoos, posing in a mirror, head-on, buck naked, and he's holding your tits and kissing your neck, and you are staring directly at the camera. And there is no mistaking it now, Donna. It is definitely you. And then, our TV screen is suddenly full of you and that guy with his dick out. Full-on, one hundred percent porn. So congratu-fucking-lations, Donna. You wanted me to see, and I did. In fact, the whole fucking neighborhood did. My brother saw it, Donna. And Stewie."

I looked wildly around the corridor for a garbage can.

"Oh no. I didn't want that, Joey. Not at all," I choked. "I swear."

"Sure. Right. Of course you didn't. Abso-fucking-lutely. That's why you gave our son *your* password, and had him set up the TV with your account—"

"Are you crazy? Do you think I know how Apple TV works either?"

"Wow. The funny thing is, Donna, revenge-porn? It's usually supposed to be when someone posts nude photos of their ex-girlfriend or boyfriend to get back at them. They don't take photos of *themselves* and use *these* to humiliate the person *they've just left*. I've gotta hand it to you, Donna, oh, you're good. You are really fucking good."

His voice cracked then. He was weeping, I could tell. Blubbering outright. "Well, we are certainly even, Donna. Just like you wanted. In fact, we're more than even now. You've won. You have broken me, and us, and the whole damn enterprise. I'm done. I surrender. I am fucking shattered. Are you happy? Are you fucking happy now?" I heard a whoosh of air. "Good luck making your goddamn bail." With a *click!* the call ended.

The young policeman who'd processed me had been hovering nearby, trying respectfully not to listen. "Ma'am?" he said as I hung up the phone. He reached for my elbow to guide me down the corridor, but I shook him off and grabbed the garbage can by his desk and bent over it, heaving.

The jail was meat-locker cold. A few caged bulbs high overhead on the cinder blocks fluttered spastically like strobe lights. A stainless-steel cervix of a toilet was bolted to the wall in the corner; the concrete floors appeared soiled and stained. The air smelled of urine, of course, and whiskey and the scallion-y scent of body odor. But I was the only woman there reeking of vomit, and I supposed, in a perverse way, that was not entirely a bad thing. Because along with the bruise beneath my eye, it helped me blend in with the other women in my cell.

Chapter 15

SINCE I WAS THE last one to be incarcerated that night, the pair of bunks had already been claimed. A morbidly obese woman lay snoring in a fetal position on the top one; her orange uniform had ridden up high above her waistband, exposing flesh like raw cookie dough. On the bottom bunk, a pair of desiccated young women huddled, trembling, as if they were on the deck of a ship pitching in a storm. One of them kept mumbling, '*I told him Brandon had the ice, Brandon had the fucking ice, dude...*' She was scratching frantically; though her fingernails were bitten to the quick, they left little trails of blood across her forearms, which were covered with the same sores as her face. She fixed me in an annihilating stare: "What the fuck are you looking at, bitch? What the fuck are you looking at?" The woman beside her grinned malevolently from behind her tumbleweed of dirty blond hair, exposing a mouthful of broken teeth, a chin blotchy with scabs. She was tapping the frame of the bunk relentlessly. *T-heet t-heet-t-heet*.

I bent over the steel cone of the toilet and vomited again.

Joey.

"Oh, fuck man, fuckman, fuckfuckfuck," the first one shouted. "I can't believe you just puked in here. The devil sent you. I know the devil sent you. You're Satan's bitch, Grandma."

I'd been handed a thin foam mat to sleep on—practically a nap rug like Austin and Ashley had in kindergarten. Shivering, I unfurled it in the farthest corner. I drew my knees up to my chest and hugged them. My uniform reminded me of the hospital scrubs Brenda had lent me, except these were a scratchy, retina-frying orange and stank of insecticide.

Oh, Joey.

What have I done?

Please, God.

Don't leave me here.

A fourth woman was slumped against the wall adjacent to me. She was even paler than the rest of us and skinny, with a grim, hangdog face and hair dyed in an ombre effect, graduating from midnight blue at her scalp to washed-out teal at the ends. Her tattooed arms were crossed, her eyes closed. Her head kept lolling to one side, snapping her awake. She was where the whiskey smell was emanating from, I realized; she was like a human room deodorizer in reverse. As I settled in, she opened one eye and regarded me blearily.

"Thank God," she murmured in a heavy Southern drawl. "Last thing we need in this box is another whacked-out meth-head. What they got you for?" She nodded at my swollen cheek. "Barroom brawl? DUI?"

I shook my head. I didn't even have the will to lie. "Pills."

"Yeah?" She suddenly perked up, unfolded herself from the wall. "Oxy?"

I had the urge to slam my head against the cinder blocks until I cracked my own skull.

To make things worse, my internal heat lamp chose this moment to blaze on. Excruciating pain was radiating from my lower back down along my sciatic nerve. Stiffly, I spread out on my filthy mat on the filthy concrete floor and tried to stretch before my entire leg seized up. I felt wretched and self-conscious and ridiculous: Who the hell does yoga in a jail cell? I flashed upon Ashley telling me how bourgeois and privileged I was.

But then I thought: *Fuck it.* What did I care what the other inmates thought? I was just another addict. My name is Donna Koczynski, and I'm an alcoholic. I'd beaten my own husband with a fish spatula. I'd abandoned my family, stolen pills from my best friend's house, and committed adultery. I'd made homemade pornography and ripped my husband's fucking heart out and driven a stake through everything lovely we'd built together. The meth-head on the lower bunk was exactly right: I *was* Satan's bitch. And now I was going to do fucking yoga in my fucking jail cell because it was the only thing I could think of to do in place of killing myself.

Lunging forward in what little space I had, I did a downward dog. The lumbar relief was immense. Slowly, I maneuvered into an awkward cobra. I heard a *thunk*. The smelly, blue-haired woman was right down on the concrete beside me stretching gracefully.

"Yeah, no way in hell I'm supposed to be doing this. But I'm still too drunk to feel it. Or care," she announced to no one in particular.

I glanced at her.

"I used to be a big-time kundalini instructor down in Pensacola," she volunteered. "'Til I herniated one of my disks. See? See the scar? Woo, boy. That's when shit really got real. I'm telling you."

Rolling over, she scooted across the concrete, leaned against the wall to where I'd been sitting, and closed her eyes. "Yeah, okay. That's enough for Kimmie now," she said. Then passed out.

Watching her chest heave up and down in its bright orange polyblend, I thought of Zack, and all he'd been trying to avoid. Then I thought again of Joey in our family room, his mouth dropping as the images of me began to slide before him and his friends on our television screen.

All this love, all this betrayal. Everybody: We were all so utterly broken. I curled up in the corner and pressed my fists to my eyes.

"Oh, lookie, lookie," one of the girls on the lower bunk taunted. "Grandma over there's crying."

I stood up and walked over. "Shut the fuck up. Or this perimenopausal bitch of Satan will beat you to a bloody pulp and break your fucking nose," I said. "Just like I did to my husband."

And I must have sounded genuinely psychotic, too, because after that, even though I was shaking, the entire cell went quiet.

"I've got to say, Mrs. Koczynski, we have some luck here," the public defender announced the next morning as he lowered himself into the small plastic chair across from me in the holding room. Like everyone else, he'd mispronounced my last name. *Coka-zeye-en-skee*. Whatever. I was so happy to see him, I was dizzy. Isaiah Nickels was a young, light-skinned black man with an angular, solemn face and big ears and neatly shorn hair that adhered exactly to the curvature of his skull. He was wearing small wire-rimmed spectacles and a stiff, brand-new powder-blue suit jacket and a plaid tie that looked like they had been purchased off the rack somewhere and not yet taken in. On his wrist I noticed the glint of an antique rose-gold watch older and grander than anything else in the jail. I somehow imagined it was a family heirloom. I could picture it being given to him by his own father on the day he'd graduated from law school. It comforted me to see it, somehow.

Isaiah Nickels leafed through my file quickly. "Because Columbus Day weekend is starting, Judge Bullard wants us to be out of here no later than 2 p.m." His Southern voice was soft as peaches. "Your case is fairly straightforward. It says here that the majority of the pills in your possession were prescribed to your children. So, ma'am, as I see it, you were just being a responsible mother, picking up your family's medications at Walmart. Now, all right. I do see that this Walmart was, in fact, in Ohio. But going for a long drive by yourself should not in any way be a crime, now, should it?" He gave me a long, embittered stare and I nodded.

"I just got distracted," I agreed.

Sighing, Isaiah Nickels looked down at the file. He had a habit, I noticed, of nodding to himself slightly as he thought. "Now, it says here that a few of the pills are, in fact, unaccounted for. But certainly, this amount is not enough to classify you as a drug trafficker. What we will have to do is contact your children's doctor and have her send Judge Bullard a written confirmation that she did, in fact, prescribe them. Now, as for the Propecia?" Isaiah Nickels shifted slightly and swallowed and kept his eyes fixed on my file. "It says here you borrowed these pills from a 'friend' for, 'lady problems'?"

I nodded. "It was so, so stupid, I know." I felt my eyes well up. "It's just that I'm feeling, well, a little desperate these days."

Isaiah Nickels balanced his pen between his fingers like a tiny baton, flicking it back and forth. "Well, I do think we want to keep the word 'desperate' as far away from these proceedings as possible, ma'am. The words 'desperate' and 'innocent' tend not to marry so well together in a courtroom, do you understand?"

I nodded again. From down the corridor I could hear a door slamming.

"Now, the good news here is that the prescription for the Propecia itself was for only thirty pills, which is within the defined limits for 'personal use.' Also, trying out someone else's male-pattern baldness drugs is not, in any jurisdiction, from what I understand, a felony." He leaned in toward me. "Look, Judge Bullard, he's conservative, but he can be fair-minded. One of his most frequent courtroom mottoes is, 'If stupidity alone was a punishable offense, the whole damn world would be in prison.'"

Isaiah Nickels took out his cell phone to google my kids' pediatrician. "Plus, more than anything else, he hates when the Twenty-Third Task Force arrests people just before a long weekend."

The Dickson County Courthouse looked like an old redbrick schoolhouse with a prim little white belfry: a Grandma Moses painting come to life. Yet the proceedings moved with astonishing speed. Judge Bullard banged his gavel and moved through the cases as if he were an auctioneer. It made me nervous, but Isaiah Nickels touched me lightly on the elbow and gave me a reassuring nod. When I was ordered to rise, the judge barely glanced at me. Up to six years in prison, I could get. My mind reeled. I'd miss Austin's graduation from high school *and* college, Ashley's from Michigan—maybe even her wedding, if she married young, like I did—all the fruits of my labors as a parent snatched away from me forever by a single roadside incident.

I was so anxious, my vision blurred. I was cognizant of neither the judge's face nor the bailiff's, nor of anyone else in the courtroom—were the arresting officers even there? Was there a stenographer like they always had on TV? All I could focus on was the deafening backbeat of my pulse and the giant sweat stains forming in the armpits of my orange prison shirt. My face was on fire, my skin glistening and releasing little droplets right onto the polished hardwood floor of the historic courtroom. I began fanning myself with my hand. I thought I was literally going to explode.

Isaiah Nickels approached the bench and handed the judge a piece of paper. The judge scanned it and shook his head and murmured something and looked back down at my file and glanced at me and shook his head again. A hurried exchange followed. Straining, I thought I heard the judge say something that sounded like "overzealous" and "*lady problems?* Are you pulling my leg, Counselor?" and "My time, it doesn't grow on trees, folks." As he banged his gavel and barked his decision, he refused to even glance at me. I felt my knees buckle.

But suddenly, Isaiah Nickels was shaking my hand vigorously. "Ah. I told you, ma'am." He beamed. It was the first time all day I'd seen him smile.

The bailiff was now beside me in her uniform, ushering me toward the front door of the courtroom.

"Wait a minute. I'm free?" I heard myself saying. "I'm free to go?"

"Yes, ma'am. Your case was dismissed."

"I don't have to go back to jail or post bail or anything?"

"No, ma'am."

"Will I have a record?"

"No, ma'am. Mr. Nickels has already filed to have it expunged."

"Oh my God. Oh my God. Can I give you a hug?"

"No, ma'am."

"Thank you anyway," I said to her. "I'm sorry. That was inappropriate. I'm just so emotional."

"I can see that, ma'am," the bailiff said stiffly. She started to retreat back toward the bench, then paused and pivoted around, her utility belt flopping around her hips. "Black cohosh, ma'am," she murmured. "And plenty of yams."

"Excuse me?"

"To help with the hot flashes, ma'am. Don't you be messing around with that Propecia."

My necklace, pantyhose, and keys were returned to me. My purple suitcase, handbag, and guitar materialized. Somehow, I was back to wearing my ridiculous leopard-print miniskirt and ANTHRAX hoodie. Yet the $840 dollars in my wallet was gone. More alarmingly, my Subaru had been impounded.

It was only at that moment that I learned about something I'd been utterly ignorant of for the first forty-five years of my life: forfeiture laws.

Under Tennessee's legal code, it turned out, police could seize cash, personal property, and vehicles from people merely *suspected* of drug-related activity—without getting a criminal conviction first. This meant—I saw very quickly—that officers had financial incentives to arrest people—the unknowing, the disadvantaged, the out-of-staters, the minorities—any schmuck like me who happened to be driving along I-40 (considered—who knew?—a major drug-trafficking thoroughfare)— anyone who happened to be driving a little too quickly at two o'clock in the morning with, perhaps, a little more cash than usual or a broken taillight or their kids' antianxiety meds or anything, really, that might possibly bring a few more dollars into the coffers of the police force.

"Wait a minute," I said, trying to keep the panic out of my voice, "so the officers who arrested me last night can keep my car just because they suspected I was drug trafficking?"

The clerk nodded. "'Fraid so, ma'am."

"But my case was just dismissed. All the charges against me were dropped. I did nothing wrong."

"Yes, ma'am. So you can get your car back. You'll just have to file a petition for it."

"Okay. Can I do it right now, then?"

"Well, you'll have to get the forfeiture reversed by the state attorney general, ma'am. The case against you here was criminal. But the one for your car, that's a civil proceeding. We can't handle that here in Charlotte."

"Are you kidding me? But how long will that take?"

"On average, I'd say about three months. You'll probably want to get yourself a lawyer, ma'am."

"Hold on. You're saying I need to hire a lawyer just to get my own car back? My car that was wrongfully confiscated in the first place?"

"It wasn't wrongfully confiscated under the law, ma'am."

"But there's no case against me! They stop me for speeding, they happen to find my children's legal prescriptions, and boom? They can take away my Subaru? Are you kidding me? How is that not literal highway robbery?" My voice was rising. The clerk was a middle-aged, churchy-looking woman with thick glasses and carefully crafted hair. Me, I was still in my ANTHRAX hoodie surrounded by local law enforcement and the full trappings of the Tennessee judicial system. I knew I had to rein myself in—and fast. But back in Michigan, I'd once had my car impounded for drunk driving, and getting it back then *with* a serious traffic violation hadn't been this elaborate.

"Please, ma'am," I pleaded, affecting as genteel a tone as I could manage. "I don't live anywhere near Tennessee. I was just driving through. And now my car has been seized, and you're telling me there's no way to get it back?"

"I didn't say that, ma'am. Like I've explained to you, you've simply got to file a petition with the state."

"But that could take months?"

"Well, yes, ma'am. Providing you expedite it."

I couldn't help it. I glared at her. "Are you sure this isn't just happening to me because I had out-of-state plates?"

She gave me a pursed, unreadable look. "We're all God's children, ma'am," she said curtly.

"But. Well? Then how am I supposed to even leave town?"

She shook her head. "I believe, ma'am, there might be a taxi service."

I frantically dug through my purse for my cell phone. It was nowhere to be found. Then it dawned on me with a sliver of horror: When the officers had ordered me to step out of my vehicle, my phone was sitting beside me in the Subaru in the cup holder. "I don't suppose you could call it for me?"

She looked at me. "I don't suppose I could," she said with asperity. "That would go against regulations. And be a misuse of county resources, ma'am." She turned back to her paperwork. But after a moment, without looking up at me, she said, "Just to the left across the street, you'll find a bank machine. And then, over there"—she pointed—"you should find a pay phone."

In the daylight, Charlotte revealed itself to be a single church spire, a garage, and two or three forlorn streets. I found its ATM easily enough, though the most it would dispatch was $80, as if the machine itself did not trust outsiders and wanted to punish us. I could only imagine the conversation that would ensue when I asked the court clerk if she could break a twenty so I could use the pay phone.

Isaiah Nickels was just heading out as I was wrangling my suitcase and guitar back up the steps of the courthouse. "Uh-oh. They got your car, didn't they?" In the pale late-morning sun, he appeared taller, yet wearier. "This whole damn thing is a racket." He motioned to a forest-green Toyota Camry parked at the foot of the stairs. "If you don't want to wait for a taxi, I can drop you off in Dickson. You can rent a car there to drive to Memphis."

Memphis. That was where I'd been headed before my arrest, wasn't it? City of Elvis, of B. B. King. Yet all I wanted to do now was get the hell out of Tennessee. Certainly, the last thing I wanted to do was drive in it anymore.

Isaiah seemed to intuit this; squinting off in the distance, he scratched the back of his neck. "Or, I'm on my way to my mother-in-law's. If you want to ride all the way with me to Jackson, it has a direct bus."

A bus. A bus sounded infinitely better. Safety in numbers. But Jackson was so far.

"Mississippi? You'd take me all the way there?"

"Oh, nah. Nah. I meant Jackson, Tennessee. 'The other Jackson,' as we like to say. It's a couple of hours west. As long as you don't mind books on tape." Isaiah aimed his key at his car. It clicked open with a hiccupy beep.

"You don't mind riding with a hardened criminal?" I was attempting levity—some little joke to mask my desperation—though my voice came out sounding broken and sad.

"Heh. Listen. You're not the first defendant I've given a ride to. Out-of-state plates get pulled over all the time here."

He heaved open the trunk, and we loaded in my belongings. All my Privileged Kitchen inventory and boxes of shoes had been impounded inside the Subaru; I knew I should be outraged, though I was secretly relieved not to have to deal with them anymore. What got me, though, was my iPhone. I kept thinking about it sitting in the cup holder by the emergency brake. It would be a miracle if it was still there in three months. I suspected it was already tucked into some officer's pocket. They'd returned to me only the things that were essentially worthless.

"Yes, ma'am. We do have problems here with opioids and meth," Isaiah was saying. "No doubt about that. Some members of our Twenty-Third Judicial Task Force, I know for a fact, they have family members themselves who are addicts. So they really want to stop traffickers. But others?" He shook his head bitterly.

As he shut the trunk, I noticed a teddy bear with a plaid bow tie and a pale blue bunny smiling goofily out the Camry's back window. A yellow BABY ON BOARD sign was suction-cupped to the glass; on the passenger's side, a car seat for a toddler was strapped into the back.

"Oooh. You have children?"

"Nah." He laughed. "My wife and I, we only got married in June. She's still finishing up her nursing degree." He noticed me still eyeing the kiddie seat. "Oh. Those are just helpful," he said, "for whenever I get pulled over."

Swinging down behind the wheel, he hummed lightly to himself as he fiddled with the ignition key, his countenance relaxing into that of a man now off duty, with a win under his belt and the prospect of a long weekend ahead of him with his new bride and her family. I could picture, suddenly, a barbecue grill and a ball game and friends in a backyard—all the good things now gone from my own life.

Clearing his throat, he started the Camry. "Your children, they're in Michigan?"

"One is. The other's abroad." I kept glancing back; seeing the little bear and plushy bunny. All those *children*, I realized, just stopped in the street. Trayvon Martin. That kid in Ferguson. I didn't even know all their names. "Well, the cops are in a really vulnerable position," Heather Mickleberg had said at book club. "I mean, how do they know if those people have guns or not?"

I'd just spent eight hours in a rural county jail. That alone almost undid me. I couldn't imagine being a teenager—or getting stuck behind bars for years. Whole communities swept up, hauled in for nothing—or for piddly shit, like I was. I thought about Ashley's outrage and tweets, #BlackLivesMatter. Brenda, raising her son. All the headlines I'd just sort of let slide by me.

My own foolishness was astounding.

"My daughter's studying in London right now, as part of her college," I told Isaiah, shaking my head. "She's so much more worldly than I was at her age."

"Heh." He turned his steering wheel sharply. "Well, let's hope so. Brianna and I, when we have kids, I've already told her, they *better* be smarter than I am. When I was a teenager?" He searched for the appropriate words. "I was a real knucklehead."

I gave a weak smile. "I had pink hair and a fake ID so I could sing in a punk band in scuzzy bars in Michigan."

Isaiah Nickels glanced at me. "Yeah? You had pink hair? Well, that makes sense, I guess. Since you're a musician."

I looked at him with confusion.

"Oh." I nodded back toward the trunk. "That. Yeah. Well."

I was so drained suddenly. Isaiah Nickels cleared his throat. He reached over and turned on the car stereo. A narrator's voice came on in bright, declarative waves describing an unmanned expedition on a planet. "You ever read *The Martian*?"

I shook my head.

"Brianna, she thinks I should read more."

Reaching over, he turned up the volume. "Naturally, they didn't send us to Mars until they'd confirmed that all their supplies had hit the surface," said the voice. Isaiah Nickels drove on, nodding slightly as he listened, while I stared out the window and watched as the world slid away from me.

My father had always wanted to see Memphis; *next summer, next summer.* "We'll pack up the car and go," he'd kept saying to Toby and me, though, like so many promises, this never came to fruition. Specifically, he'd wanted to visit Graceland—not only because he was a huge Elvis fan, but also "to investigate." For my father was secretly convinced that Elvis Presley was Jewish. In one of the alternative periodicals that he kept stacked in our basement, my father had read an article claiming that Elvis's maternal great-great-grandmother had been a Jew.

How anyone had divined this was beyond me—we couldn't even locate the whereabouts of my great-aunt Bessie, born in 1923—but if it was indeed true, it meant that by matrilineal bloodline and thus by Jewish law—if not in actual practice—Elvis Presley was Jewish as well. "And his middle name was Aaron!" my father said with the same insistent fervor he usually reserved for his theories about JFK and the Trilateral Commission. "You can't get more Jewie than that!"

One spring evening, while I was doing my math homework, my father came into the kitchen and slapped a magazine down on the table. "Tah-dah. Told you." It was a photograph of Elvis in his infamous white satin jumpsuit with the deep, rhinestone-encrusted V-neck. There, nestled unmistakably in the dark slice of the King's chest hair, was a gold necklace with a big Star of David on it. "Plain as day, man. And, Donna, you see this?" Excitedly, he showed me another photo of a low, wide gravestone. The words "Sunshine of Our Home" were flanked by a Jewish star on one side and a Christian cross on the right. Beneath it, the name GLADYS LOVE PRESLEY. "That's Elvis's mother's original headstone that the King designed *himself*. Look at it! It was only after Elvis died, and they reinterred her at Graceland, that they removed all the evidence! But c'mon, man, who puts a Star of David on a headstone for someone who *isn't* Jewish?"

My long-haired Leftie father had only contempt for organized religion. As a teenager, he'd read Marx and Saul Alinsky on the sly and become besotted with the idea of himself as a revolutionary. Eager to piss off his dutiful, synagogue-going parents—and contemptuous of the sit-ins staged by middle-class college students—he concluded that the only bona fide way to unite the world's proletariat class was to become a proletarian himself. And so, instead of college, he'd headed off to the Dodge plant. I can only imagine his shock when he arrived on the assembly line—a nice Jewish boy of eighteen—and found that his comrades in the United Auto Workers union were far more interested in duck hunting and ogling Ann-Margret than they were in Howard Zinn.

Adding injury to insult, he was soon classified 1-A. Without any student deferment or bourgeois loopholes to save him, he landed in Saigon on the morning of his nineteenth birthday—catapulted into battle against the very Communists he'd once lionized.

This made it even odder to me that he was obsessed with Elvis's potential roots. (He was almost equally fixated on the fact that both Marilyn Monroe and Elizabeth Taylor had converted to Judaism. "See, see?" he would say, as if some great hypothesis were being proved.)

Now, as I climbed off the bus in Memphis, I thought about my father as I hadn't in years. Elvis's picture was right there in the Greyhound Station on a big welcome banner amid a montage of tourist highlights. (No Star of David, however, was visible in the King's chest hair.) Staring at the photo, I felt an unexpected shudder of wonder, of grief.

I alone had made it to Memphis, my father's reluctant emissary. And it occurred to me, suddenly, that I was actually older than Elvis now. He'd only lived to forty-two. How was that possible? He'd always been so monumental, so larger-than-life and grown-up. Yet I'd already outlived him by three years.

And when my father wandered off into madness, he'd been younger than I was now, too. Had he ever thought of me over the years, missed me in his fugues? I missed my own children now with a deep, primordial ache. I'd have to reach them. And I knew I'd have to figure out some way to deal with Joey, too—though I couldn't for the life of me fathom how. How had everything accelerated into this? Spinning so far out of control? I elbowed my way among the bank of pay phones and grabbed a receiver and placed a collect call to Michigan. But there was no answer. Austin was still at school.

My plan was to book the first possible flight back to Detroit. But first I had to get cleaned up somehow. What's more, I needed to sleep, if only for a few hours. I got light-headed just sitting down to pee in the restroom. I fell back onto the toilet seat with my panties looped in a crazy-eight around my ankles, and I had to press my cheek against the cold metal of the stall for a few minutes. When I finally stepped out into the fluorescent scrutiny of the bathroom again, I saw in the mirror that I seemed to have developed a hunchback.

It was actually just the hood of my ANTHRAX sweatshirt stuck inside the collar between my shoulder blades. But oh. As I confronted my image in the mirror, I saw that the wreckage was even worse than I'd thought. My hair was partially matted on one side of my head, the other spiky and stiff with day-old hairspray like one of Tina Turner's late-career wigs. Since I hadn't put any ice on it, my cheek where Janine had punched me was now the size of a robin's egg, its bruise a rainbow of chartreuse and violet. My upper lip was cracked and swollen, too. My eyes were ringed with exhaustion. Beneath my leopard-print miniskirt, runs zippered my pantyhose.

Most appalling, however, was that an unmistakable whiff of tequila and Zack's cologne and vomit and industrial ammonia from the Dickson County Jail still clung to me, overlaid by the tweedy, chemical mustiness of the Greyhound bus. It was a wonder—and a true testament to his charity—that Isaiah Nickels had permitted me to ride inside his car with him at all (though a flacon of air freshener snapped into the air vent had continually fumigated the interior of his Camry with artificial vanilla. Now I knew why. Clearly, he had experience in giving rides to his clients).

Quickly, I washed my face and armpits as best I could in the sink, combed out my hair, dabbed off my flaked mascara with toilet paper. I would find a room, then a phone, then a flight.

Outside the bus terminal were taxis.

"Ma'am, you have an address? A particular hotel that you're going to?"

I drew a blank. Finally, I said the only street name in Memphis I knew. "Beale Street. Hotel."

"I'm sorry. The Westin on Beale Street, ma'am?" The driver glanced skeptically in his rearview.

"Yuh. Sure. The Westin."

"Usually, we're all sold out on Columbus Day weekend. But you're lucky. We just had a last-minute cancellation," the clerk said, staring at his computer screen, "provided you don't mind a room that's wheelchair accessible?"

The rate of $359 sounded obscene, but I'd just spent a night in a jail, so: Fuck it.

A moment later, however, the clerk frowned. My Visa card had been declined. Either I'd already maxed it out—or, possibly, Joey had put a block on it.

My "emergencies only" Mastercard was declined too. "But how? Why?" I barked over its 1-800 security number. "I haven't even touched it."

"Well, there appears to have been a flurry of recent activity on foreign websites—one in Denmark? Another in Croatia. Something called Easyjet.com? And we've just flagged a whole bunch of charges coming out of Greece. Do you have any idea what these might be?"

I didn't. "My daughter's studying in London. We put one card in her name, but she's in England. We don't know anyone in those places you've mentioned."

"Well, that's probably why it's blocked. It's been flagged as either lost or stolen."

"Shit," I said. "Shit, shit, shit." I was making the call from the landline at the reception desk, and the hotel clerk was getting impatient. I knew there was no way he'd let me telephone Ashley overseas to find out what had happened. All sorts of scenarios unspooled in my head, but the most likely one, I tried to reason, was that she'd left the card in a pub or a restaurant somewhere and hadn't even realized it was missing.

"I'll have to pay cash," I told the clerk. "I just need a bank machine." He directed me to one just around the corner.

When I tried to withdraw money, though, the only thing the ATM spit out was a paper tongue reading "Insufficent Funds." At first I thought it was a mistake or a joke—or Joey, being vindictive again. But as I dug through my purse for my bank receipts, it became clear that over the past few days, I'd unwittingly depleted the rest of my account. The $80 back in Charlotte had actually been the very last of my money.

Good God. Before I even dared to look at the contents of my wallet, I quickly did the math. The bus from Jackson had cost $29. Before boarding, I'd purchased a turkey sandwich, a Snickers bar, and a bottle of water from the vending machines: another $8.95. The taxi to Beale Street had been $28 and generously, stupidly, unthinkingly, I'd given the driver a $5 tip.

Frantically, I rummaged around my pockets for spare change, for any bit of cash the cops might have overlooked. But as I stood there alone on the sidewalk in the approaching autumnal twilight of Memphis, it was obvious. All I had left to my name now was $9.05. Nothing more.

Chapter 16

BEALE STREET LOOKED LIKE an aging, ravaged party girl without her makeup. The neon signs for juke joints and blues bars burned anemically, leached of color in the ebbing light. Without the night's electric glamour, you could see just how low some of the pressed-tin ceilings were and all the extension cords that had been jury-rigged to the speakers and secured haphazardly with duct tape. You could see lusterless floorboards and the patched, beat-up banquettes. On a single table by the service station, arrays of ketchup bottles were turned upside down to drain into other ketchup bottles, weeping tomatoey tears. The sadness of it all made me ache.

A few places had a happy hour going, with music blasting and an insistent, touristic joviality. Outside on the sidewalk, some buskers were playing professional-grade blues with full-piece bands and amplifiers to a small, appreciative crowd: the Beale Street equivalent of an early bird special.

The strip only extended a couple of blocks—I'd expected it to be bigger, somehow.

An older couple strolled, blinking dumbly at the street signs. A bicyclist maneuvered around me over the brick paving. I stood there with my suitcase and Aggie, not knowing what the hell to do. Nine dollars and five cents. Nine dollars and five cents. I kept halting every few steps and double-checking to make sure this was really true, that I'd counted right, my stomach twisting, hoping against hope that somehow, the dollar bills in my wallet would've taken it upon themselves to begin spontaneously reproducing like—what were those single-celled organisms that cleaved themselves into two—amoebas? Paramecia?

Then it came to me. I was in Memphis. With no money. Schlepping around a Rogue Dreadnought acoustic guitar. I could pawn it, couldn't I? If I could find someplace—though I'd likely only get twenty-five bucks for it—I knew how these things worked—at least back in Dry Lake with Zack's saxophone they paid a quarter of what anything was worth—I doubt that the business of hocking things had changed much—unless with eBay—but that, of course, was not an option... I looked down at Aggie. My last fucking friend in the world, really. Then I remembered what Brenda had said, seemingly so offhandedly: *You weren't thinking of getting back into music by any chance, were you?*

Of course. It was so obvious, it was absurd. The answer was literally right there in my hand. Could this have been what she'd meant all along by "an old love in a new face"?

Quickly, I staked out a corner across the street from an Irish pub that seemed to have a fair amount of foot traffic. Opening my guitar case like a clamshell by my feet, I looped Aggie's strap over my head. The weight of it suspended from my shoulders was surprising—a boxy albatross—it had been so long—it took a few minutes to adjust it and tune it after everything we'd been through in just the last day and a half. My fingers were still tender.

My mother had taught me the very first song I'd ever learned to play: "Leaving on a Jet Plane." A simple Peter, Paul and Mary folk tune I'd quickly come to despise for its sentimentality and echo of abandonment. But now, that's where my fingers went. As I began, I thought of her, sitting behind me on a rubber stepladder in our kitchen back in Dry Lake, her arms looped under mine, arranging my tiny fingers into position on the fretboard. The lemony tang of her Jean Naté cologne filled my nostrils; her dark hair tickled my cheek as she leaned over.

"Jet Plane" was good because it required so little concentration, and as my voice rose an octave into the refrain, "I'm leavin', on a jet plane/Don't know when I'll be back again," I was taken aback by how emotional I felt.

A middle-aged man in shorts and a baseball cap strolled past and tossed a handful of coins as if they were bread crumbs. A quarter and three dimes glinted. A mother walking with her toddler handed him a dollar; he trundled over to the case and dropped it in, delighted.

$1.55. I could tally it in my head like calories.

Toxic Shock Syndrome always got more tips if there was already money in the hat, so I took five of the dollar bills from my own wallet and sprinkled them lavishly around the guitar case, then launched into another song from my mother's repertoire, "You've Got to Hide Your Love Away." From what I could calculate, this brought in two dollars and twenty-eight more cents from passersby. I segued into my own favorites now, *my* music: "Bigmouth Strikes Again" by the Smiths.

"Sweetness," I sang, "I was only joking when I said by rights you should be bludgeoned in your bed." I found myself attacking the song gustily with only one or two mistakes, though my voice strained; it had grown husky with age and disuse. I sang Patti Smith's "We Three" next. Yet even though I tried to make it sound Elvis-y, no one paid attention.

An ambulance whooped, then a crew of motorcycles. Laughter pealed across the pavement. A group of college students blew through, shrieking "Whoa, that is so sick!" and "Dude! Shut up!" swatting each other and playing keep-away with someone's baseball cap. A few beefy, red-faced guys began congregating outside the Irish pub, carrying on as if it were their living room, talking loudly, telling stupid jokes, waving around their smartphones. A bottle smashed, then another; a cheer rose. An R & B band came on live in a nearby bar, the bass line pulsating sonically. I tried to sing over it: Siouxsie and the Banshees' "Christine." Yet I hadn't played it in twenty-five years. Without a synthesizer or any other instruments, it sounded surprisingly insipid. A young guy in a porkpie hat and leather vest wandered past gripping a 20-ounce can of malt liquor. "Jesus. Play some real music, will you?"

A corn nut hit the back of my shin. Another bounced off my right shoulder.

Back when the punk craze was big in Britain, enterprising fans had decided that the best way to show their appreciation was to spit at the bands instead of applauding. Like most cutting-edge trends, this one had taken more than a decade to find its way to suburban Michigan— which meant that after every gig Toxic Shock Syndrome played at the hard-core clubs, we were rewarded with a rain of phlegm. Then, some genius took our name to heart and decided to express his fandom by flinging tampons at the stage instead. People flung them at us by their strings, like little white mice. One night, one of them landed on Alfie Montana's foot. It appeared to be used. Even though it turned out to have been soaked only in ketchup, that was pretty much it for him. "This is bullshit. Nobody throws used tampons at Joe Strummer or David Bowie!" he'd said, storming off.

There was a reason, I realized now, why I had never, ever once performed sober.

Halfway through the Clash's "Spanish Bombs," I stopped. No one in Memphis, it seemed, cared to listen to a punk song about the Spanish Civil War. I tried the Pretenders' "Brass in Pocket." Each note I sang was like a soap bubble popping as soon as it was formed.

A bearded guy sauntered over and knelt down before my guitar case. He tossed in a five-dollar bill. My heart leapt. He smiled up at me, a big, edifying smile, bright as a comet. "Great song," he said, nodding. "Total classic."

"Thank you. Thank you so much." I actually felt myself tear up.

Still kneeling, he swiftly gathered up the five single dollar bills I'd scattered about the guitar case and jammed them into his pocket. "Sorry," he said. "But I really needed to break a five for my laundry."

The crowds on Beale Street became a steady stream, all these excited, eager tourists flooding past me, bedazzled and pointing up at the neon signs as if they were constellations. I stood like a ghost among them, strumming unnoticed until—it seemed inevitable—I was basically a goddamn cop magnet now—a couple of police officers materialized. "I'm sorry, ma'am," one of them said, not unkindly. "But you're not allowed to busk in the Beale Street area unless you have a permit. Otherwise, you have to play at least three blocks thataway."

Snapping shut my guitar case, I wiped my nose on the back of my wrist. Even with my ANTHRAX sweatshirt on, I was shivering. "Keep it together, Donna," I said aloud. I could talk to myself all I wanted: No one was listening.

The sun was low on the horizon now. A metallic, fall chill began settling over the city. Not knowing what else to do, I began walking toward the sinking sun. Block after block. I crossed a wide boulevard and found myself in a little sliver of a park right on the edge of the water.

The Mississippi. River of dreams, river of all-American mythologies. I had never actually seen it before. I had somehow imagined the river would shine as bright as mercury, like some liquid religious object, that it might speak to me in whispers. The promenade had been carefully sculpted, with railings and concrete terraces jutting out toward the water. I found a round bench amid the sea grass and set down my suitcase and guitar and stared out across the opaque, slow-moving river sliding past me like plates of mica. I was so tired. *Please, please,* I murmured.

Yet, in the dying light, I was offered no insights, no comfort. I could smell only the mud, its faintly vegetal brackishness. A scrape of traffic echoed off a distant bridge, amplified by the unbroken flatness.

My neck snapped. I'd started to nod off right there in the park. *Aggie. We have to keep moving.* Stiffly, I got back up and trudged toward Beale Street again, inland, then north, following the streets. I had to do something. But what? It amazed me how much of the world was barred to me without internet access, how much of my lifeblood remained locked away inside my confiscated iPhone back in Charlotte's impound lot. After this, I swore, I'd travel with one of those little paper pocket address books I used to keep tucked in my purse. If I could ever find another working pay phone, I'd try to call our landline at home again.

It was dinnertime. But already, I could hear it: Joey angrily refusing the charges, hanging up on me a second time, my heart shattering like an egg. And the only other number I knew was Brenda's, of course. But that was unfathomable. What, exactly, could I say? *Hi, I know I showed up on your doorstep after ten years begging for your advice, which I then refused to take. But now I'm in REAL trouble?*

Perhaps I could walk back to Michigan. Hundreds of thousands of Americans had once done that, hadn't they? Just headed north on foot. Well. I covered one block, then another. I passed an office building, a square.

Voices floated down the sidewalk. A group congregated outside a side door. A professorial, white-haired man with liver spots dotting his forehead stood talking to a plump young woman in a yellow-and-red fast-food uniform, her eyes spidery with mascara. A few skinny, long-haired guys with bug-eyes hugged each other like war veterans. A prim, middle-aged matron with a powder-blue shawl and pearl earrings shared a cigarette with a black woman in a beaded tunic and plastic sandals. Lots of people were smoking, in fact, and clutching coffee cups, their legs jiggling, their eyes darting about restlessly.

Instantly, I knew. I knew this place already, and I knew these people. You could always tell: a group that made no sense visually, congregating impatiently by the side entrance of a church or a community center.

Swallowing with relief, smoothing out my hair, I hurried over to one of the scruffier-looking men. "What time's the next meeting?" I asked.

He pressed on his phone and squinted. "Six minutes and counting."

"Hi. I'm Donna. And I'm an alcoholic."

"HI, DONNA."

"It's been five years, six months, and—oh my God, what day is it now? It's still Friday? Okay, so it's"—I counted on my fingers—"five years, six months, and nineteen days since my last drink. And I have got to tell you, I have never been so happy in my life to be here."

There was no podium for me to speak from. Just rows of folding chairs. A refreshment table was set up in the outer corridor offering coffee and bakery goods in exchange for donations. And I was so hungry, I'd splurged. Before getting up to speak, I'd tossed a dollar into the box and eaten two chocolate chip muffins and a raspberry jelly donut in rapid succession. The front of my sweatshirt was now dusted with confectioners' sugar.

But for the first time in years, as I stood before my fellow alkies, I did not perform my set piece about my father getting me drunk when I was eight years old. Instead, I stood before this group of strangers and told them my truth.

From start to finish.

I told them about catching my husband dressed as a French Maid with a dominatrix, then beating him by accident with a fish spatula, then taking my kids' prescription meds and running away to Rockaway Beach to find Patti Smith, then calling my friend the ex-psychic ("who shall remain nameless"), then—based partially on her predictions, but mostly on my own deluded wishful thinking—how I'd driven all the way to Nashville to reunite with my high school sweetheart, only to get punched in the face by his quasi-ex-wife, then arrested, then thrown in jail with my car impounded—blah, blah—I recounted it all unflinchingly right up to that very moment, where I had only $9 left and had just been busking on Beale Street and pelted with corn nuts.

I don't know how long I spoke—I had the idea that I needed to move it along, so I'd been sort of "speed talking"—losing my place from time to time, and my story came out in a jumble—plus, perhaps from the stress, I began having a hot flash right in the middle of speaking, then a cold flash, so I took off my ANTHRAX hoodie, then put it back on, then started fanning myself with the paper plate my donut had been on, the remnants of my mascara streaking my face with inky rivulets.

But I told them. That I was ashamed. That I was frightened. That I was lost and I didn't know what the fuck to do next. But that now, at least, I was here.

I might as well have ripped open my shirt, letting the buttons pop off and fly across the carpet, and just stood there with my breasts bared and my head flung back and my throat exposed.

As I stood there panting and spent, all I could hear was the faint *cluck* of a wall clock ticking and the electronic *blurp* of someone's mobile phone alerting them to an incoming text. From the back of the room, a cough; a plastic bag crackling. A few people glanced at each other, as if conferring. An older man in a tweed blazer hummed almost imperceptibly. I heard a woman murmur, "That is some bullshit," and somebody else shush her. Mostly, though, the audience just nodded at me sadly, dumbly.

"Thank you, Donna," the voices came finally, in a feeble chorus. "Thank you for sharing."

Somebody else got up. "Well, okay now. Wow." He sounded like an emcee deployed to rescue a variety show after a particularly bad comic. "Um. Hi, everybody. My name's Bradley. And I'm an alcoholic and a drug addict."

"HI, BRADLEY."

And that was it. Like a curtain had fallen and I was now absorbed back into darkness. Out by the refreshments table, my hands shook as I tried to hold the Styrofoam cup steady under the spigot of the coffee urn. The white-haired, blotchy-faced professor appeared at my elbow.

"Look, we all fall off the wagon sometimes," he said gently. "Twice this year alone, I've come to a meeting drunk myself." He gave me a look of indulgent sympathy. "The point is, you came anyway. You did the right thing. Never mind 'one day' at a time. Just take it *one hour* at a time. You'll get there."

"Excuse me, but I'm not drunk." My voice must've been far louder than I'd intended, because people inside the meeting turned and glanced in my direction.

"I'm not drunk," I heard myself insisting. My voice rose. "I TOLD YOU, I'VE BEEN SOBER FIVE FUCKING YEARS. WHY DOESN'T ANYONE FUCKING BELIEVE ME? DID YOU NOT HEAR EVERY-THING I JUST SAID?"

After the meeting concluded and everyone joined hands and recited the aphorisms and the Serenity Prayer, the others emerged from the inner sanctum looking renewed and anxious and exchanging soulful, weighted glances and slapping each other reassuringly on the back:

"So Allie, does eight-thirty work for you, then? It's not too late?"

"Dude, you coming?"

"I've got Bible study. Then the late shift."

"Dil says he picked up a cheesecake."

Nobody can linger the way a bunch of former druggies and alkies can—believe me, we can't bear to disengage from *anything*—but eventually, people drifted back out into the night, while I remained on the peripheries of the dwindling crowd—my desperation and muteness growing—hoping against hope that someone might take pity on me and invite me along with them or offer me what—a loan? A meal?

I was a stranger with a punched-up face and noticeable body odor. I looked like a catastrophe; hell, I wouldn't have invited myself anywhere, either. Had I in fact *been drunk*, I realized, my compatriots in AA would actually have been more willing to help. But I was sober. I was sober, yet still, somehow, on an epic bender. For anyone struggling just to keep themselves together—for anyone hoping and praying that getting clean would improve them—I was nothing but bad news and quicksand.

A chubby woman who had seemed to be overseeing the meeting began switching off the lights. She was dressed in a sea-foam-green sweatshirt and marshmallowy shoes. Her molasses-dark hair was growing out at the roots, so her scalp appeared cleaved by a seam. "Honey, you got anywhere to go?" She wheeled a plastic garbage container out into the corridor.

"No, but it's okay. I'm fine." Though I heard my voice quiver.

"Look," she sighed, throwing up her hands. Her face was pillowy and sweet and dark-eyed: an underbaked cookie with two raisins poked in it. "I'd take you in myself, but my husband and I, we got all seven grandkids down with us for Columbus Day, plus my husband's son Tyrone, and

Tyrone's girlfriend. Plus my dumb-ass brother Leo is driving over from Nashville tonight whenever he gets done with some Kid Rock fish fry. So we've got a full house already as well as a full RV parked in the driveway—"

"No, no, it's okay, really," I said.

"The most I have on me is a twenty." She reached for her handbag. "Any place that'd be safe for a woman alone around here—that's gonna cost you at least eighty, I reckon—"

"No, no. Please, I can't take your money."

She eyed me skeptically, but quickly dropped her wallet back in her purse. "You said you don't have a car?"

I shook my head.

Sighing again, she finished folding up the last of the forgotten metal chairs and glanced around the church basement as if hoping a solution would present itself. "Timothy," she called to a custodian sweeping up the corridor, "can I borrow your phone, please? Mine's not getting any service down here."

A moment later, she was googling something. "Okay, honey, I'm looking for shelters for the night. We've got a notorious shortage here in Tennessee. There's one over in West Memphis in Arkansas, near where I live. But trust me, it's no place you wanna be. The problem is, most of the women's shelters here are for families. Women with kids. And long-term. You here alone?"

I nodded. Thinking of Austin and Ashley, though, I started to weep. My children. My beautiful children. "Is there any place just for me?"

The round-faced woman frowned and shook her head. "Lemme ask you. With your face—well, we might be able to get you into a battered women's shelter, depending on, you know, your *story*."

Miserably, I shook my head. As badly as I needed a place to sleep, the idea of lying about my injuries and taking a bed away from a more deserving family in danger was too terrible to contemplate.

"Okay. Well? Hang on." Wearily, she punched a few numbers into the phone and waited. "Hey Danette, it's Celia...yeah...yeah...No, he's fine now, thank you. We really appreciated all the prayers...yeah, we got that, too. Dale's planning to share it with the grandkids this weekend, in fact. Julian, he loves those pears...Listen...Well, the doctor put him on something called an 'ACE inhibitor'? Yeah...that's right...yeah, and a beta-blocker...I don't know. 'Levatol'? 'Levatel'? Something like that?"

Celia shot me an apologetic look. With her free hand, she pantomimed a yapping motion.

"No...no...," she said distractedly to her phone. "Listen, Danette, the reason I'm calling is, well, my meeting just ended, and we've got a gal here from out of town. Sort of a 'book of Job' situation. And I was wondering. At your church, you volunteer for a homeless shelter down here, don't you?"

As I watched Celia's face for some indication of the response, I was astonished how hard my heart was beating.

"Okay, well. Thank you kindly, Danette..." Celia said after some time. "Yes, I'll see that she understands...and yes, absolutely."

She handed the phone back to the custodian and shook her head. "Well, Danette thinks the shelter takes women sometimes," she said. "Though she can't guarantee it. Check-in is at 7:30 p.m, though, so you'd have to be there in fifteen minutes if you even want a shot at a bed."

"Oh," I said, crestfallen.

"Though it's not far from here at all, honey. I'll draw you out a map on a napkin. Run like the wind. You can make it if you hustle."

A line of disheveled men clutching bundles and shopping bags and knapsacks snaked in a long line across the parking lot. I counted only one other woman, short and grizzled, with a cloud of crazed, gray hair obscuring her face, and layer upon layer of sweaters, making her appear rotund. A few of the men were in cheap suits and ties or shirts with designer logos; only when I looked at their shoes, with their worn, flapping soles, was it obvious how down-and-out they were. Otherwise, they were clearly trying to present their best faces to the world, still hoping to claim some dignity. One man, however, was fetid and clad in rags and swiping at the air around him.

Oh, God, Aggie. A homeless shelter? I dropped my guitar at my feet. It had been banging against my right hip as I ran, bruising it, and I was now drenched in sweat and panting so hard, I sounded asthmatic. But I was here in line—wherever "here" was. Floaters appeared before my eyes, clumps of molecules and protozoa rising and falling. My brain felt like a bottle of salad dressing that had been shaken and was now starting to separate. I was out of ideas. *I don't have to stay*, I told myself. And: *It's just for one night, right?*

My head throbbed. A dangerous sort of tunnel vision was setting in, all sense of time and space collapsing. It was the way I'd felt in those first fragile weeks when my children were newborns, hot and oceanic in their wailing, and I stumbled around the kitchen seeing only what was directly in front of me, thinking in monotone: *Put milk in pan. Put pan on stove.*

A shower. A meal. A bed. That's what Celia said I could expect. A shower. A meal. A bed. If I could only just sleep...

A young man at a table in the vestibule—who didn't look any older than Austin—did they let teenagers work in homeless shelters?—sat taking down names in a ledger. I watched as each person stepped forward. Another worker took their belongings and handed them a numbered tag in return as if for a coat-check. "Gentlemen, you know the rules," she announced. "If you don't want to check your belongings, you cannot stay. It's as simple as that. Safety and security first."

I could not believe I was going to stay here—that it had come to this—and when I reached the check-in table, I found myself glancing around wildly and waiting for some MTV game-show host to announce, "You've been punked!" Then, perhaps even more insanely, I found myself growing panicked that someone would see me here—someone I knew from back home—my friend Ann-Marie from high school—or the women in my book club. Heather Mickleberg. Or Colleen Lundstedt. Or my children! I felt paralyzed with shame.

"This isn't really me here at all. You know, I'm actually the mother of two teenagers," I heard myself announcing. "And a kitchenware saleswoman! I actually live in a nice Michigan suburb. I even have a dog—a Labradoodle! Who doesn't even shed! I'm in a book club, for fuck's sake!"

The staffer regarded me as if I were a package of explosives that needed to be handled with extreme delicacy. "O-kay, ma'am," he said. "But you're still not allowed to bring reading materials inside here. Everything except your wallet, you have to check."

In a large, high-ceilinged dormitory, metal beds were lined up as if it were an army hospital. The gray-haired woman and I appeared to be the only women; we were shown to two beds at the very end of the hall that the staffers hastily sectioned off with two movable partitions. The makeshift walls would do nothing to keep out the smell or the noise from the larger room—or, for that matter, the other "inmates," as I began to think of us all almost immediately—but I supposed I should be grateful for even a small modicum of privacy. My roommate and I were each handed a blanket, a fresh set of bed linens, a towel, and a tiny toothbrush and toothpaste travel kit sealed in a plastic wrapper reading *ADA of Greater Memphis 2007. Keep smiling!* Which reminded me of Joey, of course, and made me burn again with shame.

Each bed had a bare mattress and a pillow. "They call this place 'the homeless Hilton,'" my roommate announced in a voice like a coffee grinder. "Glad you're here with me, sister. They won't let women stay unless there're at least two of us." As she set about making her bed, she kept mumbling to herself. Even though our cubicle was not fully enclosed, it quickly filled with the stench of her, a sour gaminess mingled with rotting fruit. Then I saw why. As she began removing layer upon layer of sweaters, bits of horded food wrapped in Saran wrap fell out onto the floor. "Let me know if you need extra provisions," she said from beneath her tangle of hair. "They like to starve you in these places. Keep you docile."

After that, we tacitly ignored each other as we busied ourselves preparing our beds until it was time to shower. We were led down a hallway to an industrial bathroom with a big, communal concrete-block shower area. Shampoo/body wash was provided in dispensers bolted to the wall, one of which had been ripped nearly completely from its rivets and now dangled like a large, grubby white tooth on the last thread of its root.

"You ladies have ten minutes to wash up and do your business," the staffer announced without quite making eye contact with us.

The shower was large enough that the other woman and I could each claim our own corners and pretend to ignore the other's naked, filthy, collapsing flesh. But the concrete floor stank faintly of urine and chlorine—and the water—which I was hoping would come as a relief, a salve—was tepid at first and quickly graduated to cold. We'd each been instructed to keep our clothes where we could see them, and as soon as we were "clean," we yanked the thin towels around us and bolted back out to the dressing area clutching our stuff, our belongings wettening against our arms.

"In the other shelter I usually go to," my roommate grunted, scratching her wet scalp, yanking on her pants, "some of the workers there pay the supervisor to watch us ladies in the shower. Then, they film us," she said, nodding, her eyes growing wide and frantic. "For the government. And the New World Order."

After showering, we were led to the cafeteria. I was so hungry at that point, it felt as if my body itself were dissolving. We squeezed in beside each other on benches at low wooden tables like children at summer camp. We were a noisy, smelly bunch with wet hair and ramshackle teeth and pitted skin and sunken eyes, faces laden with resignation and bitter humor. As I looked around, the wind went out of me. So this was where I had landed. Just the night before, I'd been having sex with Zack; the night before that, I'd been eating noodles with Brenda and Eli; a week before that, I'd been a housewife and sales rep in Troy, Michigan, with a doofus-y dentist husband. There was such a thin, fragile membrane between worlds. I suddenly thought of my daughter at four. *What happens to the soap bubbles, Mom, when they go down the drain?* Her tearfulness had been wiser than I could know. Yet, mostly, all I could focus on were hot dogs. I could smell them boiling in the cafeteria, along with tomato soup.

Before we were allowed to line up for dinner, however, a man stood up on a chair and raised his hands in a "V" to silence us. "My friends, my friends," he bellowed.

A great, collective groan rippled across the dining room.

"My friends, before you partake, I want you to take a minute—take a minute, if you will—to reflect upon our God, our one and only true Lord and Savior Jesus Christ, who has made possible not only this meal you are about to receive, but the spiritual substance being offered to your soul—"

Somewhere to my right, I heard somebody whisper, "Man, just give us the fuckin' food, will you?" And another: "Fool. Sit down. Fool, why you be preachin' to a bunch of empty stomachs?" And another: "Blasphemers. Children of Satan. Can't say a prayer before your goddamn hot dogs?"

The man on the chair continued, "For you are all being given *good news* here tonight, my friends. Now, I know you are downtrodden. I, too, have had a hard life. Abuse. Addiction. I, too, have sinned. I, too, was once homeless. I, too, was once plagued by the drugs and the alcohol, and the sexual perversities that dominate the lives of people on the streets—"

On the streets? I thought. *Hell. Come check out suburban Michigan.*

"I, too, once, did not feel the full, awesome light of Christ's love. But the book of Luke, 4:18, says, 'The spirit of the Lord is upon me, because he has anointed me to bring good news to the poor—'"

I dropped my head in my hands. I'd been secular to the core— married a Catholic, even—but never, in my life, had I felt like such a *Jew.* At that moment, I longed to talk to my father so badly, it winded me. His Elvis obsession: It was not some fugue of mental illness, I realized. Rather, it was born from a feeling of intense aloneness and vulnerability. For if Elvis Presley actually had some connection to Judaism, it meant that we Jews were included in the bigger heart of America. We were not aberrations or outsiders or as wholly forsaken by the world as I felt now.

As the group prayer went on, I sat at the table alone with my God, my gratitude, and my shame. Only after the weak chorus of "Praise Jesus" and "amen" were we allowed to proceed to the serving line for tomato soup. And white bread. And hot dogs.

Per regulation, the dormitory went dark at 9 p.m. Yet the air crackled with grunts, cries, sniffles, coughs, snorts, farts, murmurs, whispers, belches, rantings, squeals, wheezes, grumbles, snores. Each time I rolled over and flipped my thin pillow to the other side in the hope of finding that one elusive patch of cool, the bed frame squeaked; I could feel the corsetry of wires and springs through the mattress. Steeped in misery and a wild, animal panic (that must be triggered by finding oneself in a strange bed in a strange setting and surrounded by actual strangers) I blinked at the partition and began to shiver.

Eventually I did fall into an obliterating sleep, my body contorted and leaden, emitting a yeastiness, my mouth leaking spindles of drool on the sawdusty pillow. A ribbon was being sewn up my right leg slowly, lingeringly, a thick, wet line, satiny and warm. Just as it was registering, I heard a vicious, animal hiss. A thud. "Don't you dare do that!" a woman shrieked. "You get the hell away." Jerking upright, I saw a form hunched near the foot of my bed, hands splayed to the sky, a figure clobbering him repeatedly, her hand rising and hammering. I could not shout. Could not move.

When the alarms rang in the dormitory in the morning, I awoke encrusted. Slowly, I came to. I had survived a night in a homeless shelter. My roommate, though, had vanished, her bed denuded. Blinking groggily around the dormitory, I couldn't be sure if what I had experienced in the middle of the night was real or a hallucination.

Sleep had restored me somewhat. Finally, I could think. As soon as

Aggie and my suitcase were returned to me, I asked directions to the nearest public library.

I was already waiting when its doors opened; I was the first person that morning to sign up for one of the free half-hour sessions on the computer. Skype would be infinitely better than calling collect on a pay phone. I'd keep Skyping our landline in Michigan as many times as I needed until Joey answered—I'd leave lengthy messages—I'd batter him verbally into responding. As I clicked onto the turquoise bubble icon, I realized I might even be able to reach Austin, if he ever checked his account. And Ashley. Six hours ahead. I was surprised by how much I sweated as I typed in my password: 5692AAJ. My wedding anniversary and my family's initials. Same as it ever was.

As soon as I was logged on, a series of alerts burst up on the screen. Eight, nine, ten of them, pinging so loudly, I got a savage look from the librarian.

Missed Skype call from Ashley Koczynski.

Missed Skype call from Ashley Koczynski.

Missed Skype call from Ashley Koczynski.

Missed Skype call from Ashley Koczynski.

Mom, r u there?

Mom, I need to talk to u.

Mom, pleez call me ASAP.

Mom where r u????

Mom, I need help.

Mom, Pleez. I'm in SERIOUS trouble.

And then, one from Austin, posted only nineteen minutes before:

Mom. R u still in jail?

The moment I Skyped Austin back, he picked up. My son. Right there on screen, bed-headed and wearing an old phys-ed T-shirt with a chewed-up looking collar. I felt my eyes well up. I kept my video off, however, so he wouldn't see my bruised face. Or my alarm. "Sweetie. What happened? What's wrong?"

"Hey Mom. Yeah. Uh. I just got this message from Ashley. It was kinda scary. It said that she was in trouble. But it also said 'Don't tell Dad, only Mom,' so, like, I'm telling you first," he said anxiously. "Plus, it was a Skype text, not a regular one, which I thought was weird because, we usually just WhatsApp or text. I almost thought it was a joke, but she called me 'Houston' which only Ashley ever does."

I felt a growing sense of dread. "Can you read it to me?"

"Okay. Um. Here. She wrote, **Houston, I need to reach Mom. ASAP. Am in big trouble. Am not at apt & don't have my phone & I keep trying to call her & she doesn't answer. WTF.** That's short for—"

"I know what that means, Austin."

"Then she wrote, **Will keep trying to reach mom & you later. BUT DON'T TELL DAD. ONLY MOM.** This is in all caps. Then, **This is serious. Tell Mom to go on Skype & don't log off!** And then there are some emojis with green faces like she's sick and like she's scared and like she's crying and one of a bed."

"Emojis?"

"So, then I wrote stuff like, **Are you okay, are you in the hospital, are you on drugs**, etc. But she hasn't answered."

"Austin, where's your dad? Put your father on."

"He's not here. He had to go in at, like, 8 a.m. today because he has all these root canals."

The timer on the public computer said I only had seventeen minutes left. "Okay, sweetie. Here's the thing. They confiscated my phone. I'm okay, but—"

"Your phone? Seriously? Who?"

"It doesn't matter. The cops. Outside of Nashville. I'm in Memphis now. But I'm on a public computer. So I've only got a few minutes. I need you to be my intermediary, Austin, while I sort out some stuff on this end, okay? I'll get back online as soon as I can again, but in the meantime, can you keep trying to reach Ashley? Try to find out exactly what's wrong, what happened, and where she is now. Ask her if there's a landline where I can maybe call her collect later."

"Wait. Hang on. I'm writing this down: *in-ter-me-di-ary*."

"Next, can you give me Dad's office number? As soon as we log off, I want you to contact him yourself and tell him there's an emergency, and not to hang up on me whenever I call, okay?"

"Okay. But I don't think he will, Mom. I mean, he's pretty freaked out already."

"Wait. So he *does* know about Ashley?"

"No. About you being in prison. The only thing he knows about Ashley is that, like, she hasn't been around school or her apartment. He keeps calling London, but everyone's saying they haven't seen her."

I felt sicker by the minute. It sounded like my daughter was in an infirmary somewhere. Though I didn't want my mind to go there, it did: *Has she been sexually assaulted? Had an abortion? Why else would she want only me to know, and not her father?*

I hated to get off the line with my son—to see his face freeze then snap into a void when I signed off. But I had to. My mind was reeling. The blaze of adrenaline I felt was a clarifying flame, precise as a laser beam. Joey could be performing oral surgery all day, but I called his office anyway and left a detailed message on his voice mail. Then, I got another idea. I called back and pressed "2" for Arjul's extension. His calls were always forwarded. He picked up instantly.

"Dr. Banerjee," he said in a singsong voice.

"Arjul, it's Donna." He could barely say hello before I launched into explaining the general gist of the situation, that Ashley needed me in London, that I needed to borrow money from him immediately—wired to Memphis—how it would be a personal loan, nothing to do with his business with Joey. He sounded stunned and more than a little dubious. "Donna, you are a good friend. But this is very out of the blue. And you are sounding like you are not quite stable now."

"I'm not stable, Arjul. Stable people do not need emergency loans wired to them across the country. You know I'm estranged from Joey at the moment. But you also know me. And our family. And we're in trouble right now—I can't fully explain—and I'm running out of options. So you're the person I thought of."

"Yes, it's just, this is a lot for me to take in so quickly."

Suddenly, I saw another call coming in for me over Skype. *Ashley.*

"Calling you back, Arjul!" Hanging up, I clicked the "answer" icon for my daughter. A blank screen appeared: no visual.

"Mom? Mom, are you there?" Her voice was distant and echo-y, as though she were calling from the bottom of a well.

"Ash? Are you okay? Ashley?"

The call cut out abruptly with a *ping!* An icon appeared with the message "Trying to reestablish the connection." A little circle of digital ball bearings spun around and around. I tried calling back. "C'mon, dammit!"

A line was forming by the computers. The librarian glanced at me.

Finally, the call reconnected.

"Ashley?"

"No. I'm sorry. The service is not good here, so I had to walk up to get a signal on my handy," said a woman with a heavy German accent. "You are Ashley's mother, yes? Ashley, she cannot get up. She is very sick."

"Sick? What's wrong with her?"

"She is very weak. She has a very high fever. She is not making much sense."

"You mean she's hallucinating? Oh God. Is she at health services? Has anyone contacted the administration? Her university health plan covers hospitals. Does she need to go to the hospital?"

"Oh, I am sorry. There are no hospitals here," said the voice.

"What? But the school sent us a list of them in London."

"Oh, but we are not in England."

"What? Where are you? Who are you? Where's my daughter?"

"She is with us here. In Greece. We are an anarchist collective."

The German woman tried to explain, though it was noisy on both ends and almost impossible to hear. By the time I managed to wrap my head around the basic details, our connection cut out, and I had only twelve minutes left on the computer, $3.68 cents in my Skype account. I called Arjul again, but this time, oddly, he didn't pick up. Perhaps he was talking to Joey? I needed a plan B, fast. Logging on to my Gmail, I told myself: *Don't think, Donna. Just type. If you do it quickly, it won't sting as much.*

Dear Colleen, I began, **you said that Privileged Kitchen was a family. Well, if that holds true, I hope you'll regard me as the Prodigal Daughter.** As fast as I could, I composed the most abject, groveling, apologetic missive I could think of. As soon as I hit Send, I scrolled through her emails, found her private cell number in one of them, and copied it down. I figured I'd let the apology stand on its own for a little while, then call her personally to "follow up." Colleen was a smart woman—she was ten years older than I was, a breast-cancer survivor with grown kids and two ex-husbands—and I half expected/hoped that once she heard a truncated version of my story, she'd connect the dots herself and volunteer assistance without my having to explain further or prod. But if not, I'd do what I had to. I would beg outright. Something you always learn in sales: The worst anyone can say is no.

With four minutes left before my session timed out, I looked up local addresses for Western Union, mobile phone stores, pay phones, bus ticket prices, airfares, a Walgreen's close to the library. Though Ashley's Skype account was no longer online, I typed out anyway: **Ash. I love you. Hang in there.**

Come hell or high water, I was not going to remain stuck in fucking Memphis.

Part Three

Chapter 17

THE PLANE CIRCLED MYTILENE for twenty agonizing minutes suspended above the sea. No announcement was forthcoming from the pilot. I'd managed to commandeer the armrest, and now I was clutching it in a death grip. The sun was just rising, the sky aflame. These small planes, these were the killers. Buddy Holly, Otis Redding, Patsy Cline, Aaliyah— you could make a list of musicians who died in small aircraft—and right now, that's exactly what I was doing. The plane banked sharply left. In the little oval window, I saw jagged mountains tilt, a lone road snaking along the coast. Rows of beach villas came into view on the bluffs. Yet as we descended, I saw they'd been abandoned, unfinished: Ghostly concrete boxes sprouted tentacles of rebar, home to no one. A cement mixer rusted beside them. Modern-day ruins: a tiny Detroit on the Aegean. This was the mythical island? Somewhere, somewhere down there beyond the wreckage, lying delirious in some camp, was my daughter.

When we landed, passengers applauded. Was this a European thing? As I wobbled down onto the tarmac, I was hit by the stench of jet fuel and sea wind mixed with eucalyptus. I was surprised how the air itself felt strange and unstable. The terminal was like an attenuated garden shed. Inside, nobody was speaking English, though I heard groups of passengers talking excitedly in French, Spanish, and German as they hoisted duffel bags, backpacks, and camera equipment off the conveyor belt and loaded their items quickly onto trolleys. Everybody seemed to be on a mission.

I looked around anxiously for the driver holding a sign with my name on it. Back in Athens during my layover, I'd arranged for an airport pickup online. It was insanely expensive—plus, who the hell rescues their kid from a bunch of anarchists in a *taxi?*—but there simply wasn't another option. Rental cars, it turned out, were in impossibly short supply. Besides, in my state, I knew I had no business driving. The last thing I wanted was to get pulled over by the police again. In *Greece*.

One by one, I watched the other arrivals disappear through the glass doors and duck into awaiting vehicles. I was seized with the urge to run after them, flag them down, beg them to help me find a map, find a guide, find Ashley herself, a translator, an ambulance: *something*.

Soon, the only person left in the terminal was a Greek baggage handler who spoke no English. None of the other facilities in the small airport were even open; it was far too early in the morning. I checked the new phone I'd bought back at Walgreen's in Memphis. Still no service. When I'd called Brenda before my flight out of the US, she'd warned me that an American cell might not work in Europe at all. She'd been right. My new smartphone lay useless and dumb in my palm—$99 of borrowed money: *poof!*

Not knowing what the hell else to do, I lugged Aggie and my purple suitcase outside. A narrow, two-lane highway ran past the airport and disappeared into oblivion. On the other side of the road, a line of low, feathery trees gave way abruptly to the sea. That was it. Right there in front of me. The very edge of Lesvos.

Oh, Ashley, I thought. *Couldn't you have had a garden-variety nervous breakdown in your dorm room? Or gotten your stomach pumped in the local ER after a frat party?* As soon as I thought these things, I felt terribly guilty. *Bad mother, bad mother!* But those crises, I could deal with. Here, I was halfway around the globe. Until this moment, the farthest I'd ever been from the USA was Cancún, Mexico, for my honeymoon.

A tiny white church stood across the road as if inviting me to pray. Were these my only options now: God or the cops?

Me and the cops: Oh, we were just *done* now. Ashley herself had warned me about the Greek ones, too. Before I'd left Memphis, I'd managed to speak with her one more time over Skype. Her teeth were chattering. I couldn't see her, but I could hear her feverishness across the ether. She did not entirely make sense. Between her and the German woman, Dagmar, I was able to glean that she was being held in quarantine in a camp someplace with an unpronounceable name on the north of the island. When I told her, "Ashley, I've got to let your dad know. I can't help you alone," she'd seemed to understand, but then she'd implored, "Mom, whatever you do, don't contact the police here, okay? They hate the anarchists. And don't say anything to any locals, either." She'd started sniffling. "Some of them are neo-Nazi sympathizers. We don't know who's who."

Yet now, alone in this strange, deserted pocket of the world, contacting the local authorities seemed like the one realistic course of action left. Though how would I even do this, since I didn't speak Greek? I took swift stock of the words I knew. Beyond names from mythology and letters on fraternity houses, there were exactly three: "spanakopita," "acropolis," and "souvlaki." I could only imagine how far those would get me.

I sat down on the curb with my suitcase and guitar and buried my face in my hands.

A growl came. A small orange car with "Apollo Taxi" on the side jerked to a halt. A young driver jumped out. "Excuse me, are you Donna Kay?" he panted, holding a printout.

Immediately, he grabbed my suitcase and my guitar. "I am sorry. It is so early in the morning. You think there is no traffic. But first, there are goats. And then, there is traffic. Come. I am Thodoris. But in English, you can call me 'Teddy.' This is easier, yes?"

He ushered me into the backseat, loaded my things in the trunk. The interior of his cab was clean and citrusy with a bottle of water sweating in a cup holder in the armrest. Looking at it, I almost cried.

"Welcome to Lesvos." He swung the car into gear. "This is your first time here?"

Lesvos. In the United States, it was still known as "Lesbos." In fact, when I'd first heard Ashley rasp, "Mom, I'm in Lesbos," I'd actually thought she was being euphemistic, that it was her way of coming out to me. Good God: the Greeks could build a monument to my ignorance.

"Yes, it's my first time in Lesvos," I heard myself tell Thodoris. There was, of course, a whole bunch of wisecracks to be made, but I suspected the people on this island were already sick of them. *Ashley*. Every time I thought of her, I swallowed.

Thodoris glanced at me in his rearview mirror. A small bracelet of worry beads dangled from it. On the dashboard was a photograph of a smiling baby. I wondered if it was a prop, like Isaiah's.

"You are journalist? A volunteer?" he asked.

When Ashley was an infant, she'd only go to sleep if I set our washing machine on "spin" and set her on top of it in her baby seat.

He followed my gaze and tapped his dashboard proudly. "That is my son, Dimitri! He will be one years old next weekend." Thodoris had a sweetly handsome face, with woeful eyes and an insipient double chin and goatee the color of butterscotch. A single small gold hoop glinted in his right ear. I was impressed by how well he spoke English—and hugely relieved. If I looked desperate and deranged to him, he did not let on.

"Next weekend is his christening. My wife, Stavroula. She is inviting forty people!" He turned the taxi left onto the long road. I felt glazed over. The entire way from Memphis to Charlotte, Charlotte to London, London to Athens, I'd tried to sleep. The airplane seats were only a slight improvement over the floor of the Dickson County Jail—and, come to think about it—over the cot at the homeless shelter in Memphis—and I'd dozed only fitfully, dreaming about searching for Ashley in a maze of corridors. And during my ten-hour layover in Athens, I hadn't slept at the airport hotel at all. I was too worried I'd miss my 5 a.m. connection. Where the hell was all that Ativan now?

"Do you have children?" Thodoris asked.

"Two," I said quietly. "A boy and a girl."

"Ah. A matching set. Like salt and pepper. So. Where are you from, Donna Kay?"

"America." Beyond the windows, the peacock-blue sea glistened. Lavender mountains rose up the other side of it. The Greek mainland was a lot closer than I'd thought; I was all turned around. "Wait, is that where Athens is?" I pointed.

"Oh, no. That is Turkey. So, you are from America. Where in America?"

We were that close to Turkey? How far across the water was that coast? It couldn't be more than a couple of miles.

"Someplace called Michigan," I said distractedly. I didn't want to make small talk.

"Michigan? Oh, I know Michigan! That is Detroit, yes?" Thodoris said happily.

"You know it?"

"Stavroula's uncle, he lives someplace called Royal Oak. He is chiropractor."

We came to a traffic light. Thodoris pulled over suddenly, put on his hazards. "Excuse me. But my brother, Yannis, he was supposed to drive you in *his* taxi this morning. But with everyone on the roads now, he had an accident last night. So I need for one minute to see where we are going. It says on the email you want to go to Sikamineas? Now, is this the town of Sikamineas or the beach, Skala Sikamineas?"

I looked at him blankly. I had absolutely no idea. All I had was the link that Dagmar had messaged me over Skype. When I'd opened it in the browser at the airport hotel, the names popped up only in Greek. I could recognize individual letters—alpha, delta, epsilon—but that was about it.

Thodoris studied the printout. "Okay. Yes. Skala Sikamineas. That is on the coast. Other side of the island. More than an hour. Maybe two if there is traffic. So you and me, we are going to be together for a while. Do you need a toilet, some coffee maybe?"

I shook my head, though I felt my eyes well up.

"Okay. Me, I will need some coffee. We Greeks. We run on coffee.

People think it is the Italians who are about coffee. But no. It is us," he shouted back to me over the noise of the engine as he started up the car again. "Also, we Greeks love to talk. Same as thousands of years ago. All those philosophers in the Parthenon. They never shut up. So we Greeks today, we never need therapy. Why? Because as soon as one Greek person meets another Greek person and says 'How are you?' we tell them everything. You go to café, you go shopping, everywhere you go, you are talking about your problems. By the end of the day, you come home, you are in wonderful mood. You have whole country of psychiatrists. Though right now?" He shook his head. "Right now, too much is happening. Too many problems."

A dog wandered out on the dirt road in front of us. Thodoris leaned on his horn.

"You see the news, yes?" he said.

I nodded. Up until two days ago, though, I hadn't even known where Lesvos was. In the USA, televisions at the airports had been focused on the Republican presidential primaries, Hillary Clinton, speculations about the World Series. In London, waiting to change planes at Heathrow Airport, I'd caught a debate on-screen about whether Britain should stay in the EU. ("They're all a bunch of bastards," the man next to me announced to no one in particular.) As for Greece? I'd heard a few snippets here and there, though most of what I knew, I'd glimpsed on Facebook, through Ashley's Twitter account. "I understand you guys are getting some Syrian refugees here," I said.

"Yes. Okay. That is one way to say it." Thodoris glanced at me in his rearview mirror.

He steered the taxi down a rutted little commercial strip with a news-stand, a couple of tacky-looking snack bars. I was surprised. The only images I'd ever seen of Greek islands showed yachts in turquoise lagoons and white stucco churches. We stopped in front of a gas station. An electric sign saying LOTTO—the same in Greek as in English, apparently—sputtered in the window. I thought of Zack's scratch-off lottery tickets. People everywhere, it seemed, were vying for better luck.

"Sorry. But since I get taxi booking last minute, I need to fill up gas now, when there are no lines. I will only be five minutes."

As he climbed out of the taxi, something occurred to me. "Thodoris?" Rifling through my purse, I found my precious clutch of Euros. "Is there any chance they might sell a burner phone in there? And a map?"

He looked confused. "What is a 'burner phone'?"

I glanced inside the gas station; a small refrigerator for drinks sat empty and unplugged. Behind the counter, a woman fanned away flies with her hand. "Never mind."

"You need breakfast?"

"No, no thank you." Just the thought of eating made my stomach seize. Thodoris disappeared and I sat there in the back of the taxi jiggling my leg and checking my watch, hoping that "five minutes" was only, in fact, going to be five minutes. Lowering the window, I looked around and wondered how Ashley was now, this very minute, in that camp somewhere near this Skala Sikamineas.

I could only hope my daughter sensed that I was on my way—that I was almost there, in fact. I hoped, too, that Austin had been tracking my flights so that he and Joey knew I'd landed okay. Joey and I were in communication now—my God, how could we not be—we'd had volleys of Skype calls back and forth from the library, Walgreen's, airports— we were as wired together in communication as two Secret Service agents—discussing the fastest way to reach Ashley—how quickly could he pay off the Visa bill so it was usable again—and could Arjul book international flights for me himself, even though we were not related? We even wondered aloud, in a vein of our shared, grim humor, why our daughter had chosen to suffer a major crisis on Columbus Day weekend—couldn't she at least have waited a week until the last-minute, economy-class flights to Europe out of Memphis weren't four thousand fucking dollars a ticket? All of these bureaucratic and logistical details masked, of course, the bottomless throb of misery between us—and, okay, residual love—and copious despair. All that would have to be dealt with later. For now, all either of us could focus on was our daughter in distress, and the handful of details we knew: Ashley was seriously ill, trapped in a camp somewhere with a bunch of anarchists on Lesvos. She had no money, no phone, no passport. But how this had happened—and where, exactly, she was, beyond some red teardrop on a Google map—was still a mystery. Given that Ashley initially hadn't wanted Joey to know about her predicament—well, I could only imagine what had *really* happened to her. In the bundle of first-aid supplies I'd purchased in Memphis, I had, among other things, a morning-after pill, along with all sorts of remedies Brenda said were good for treating trauma if we couldn't get medical attention right away.

My daughter. My kid. My baby.

Thodoris emerged from the café holding two cups of coffee. A large triangle of filo dough, like a three-cornered hat, was balanced atop each one in a slip of waxed paper. He set the cups down on the roof of the taxi, then leaned in toward the back seat. "I buy cheese pie. I have to buy two. There were only two in the case, and if I only buy one, the other, it will be so lonely. It makes me too sad for the one lonely cheese pie." He made a woeful face. "So if you want, you can have a cheese pie. If not, I will eat both, but we do not tell my wife, okay?"

Without waiting for my answer, he retrieved one of the coffees and cheese pies from the roof of the taxi and handed them to me. The coffee was small and dark and sludgy. "Greek coffee, you try it. If you don't like it, I will drink it, too." He winked.

"Also, you are in luck." From his back pocket, he pulled out a faded tourist brochure with a crude map of Lesvos on it, the names of major towns and attractions printed in Greek and English and cartoon illustrations of landmarks. A lighthouse. A smiling mermaid.

He started up the taxi again with his own cheese pie clamped in his mouth, his coffee cup balanced on the seat between his legs. I didn't think I could possibly chew or swallow anything, but once I started, I found I was ravenous. Whether this was breakfast, lunch, or dinner for me now, I didn't know. But I needed to eat; I should, I realized. I needed fuel and strength. The filo dough was wonderfully greasy and airy at the same time, and the cheese inside was creamy and salty, and suddenly, in spite of myself, I was covered with little dandruffy gold flakes and wiping my fingers off on the thin paper.

"Ah, you see. Sometimes, we do not know when we are hungry," Thodoris said.

The taxi ascended a winding road in the rising light, rays glinting through silvery-green rows of olive trees. As forewarned, Thodoris chatted nonstop, briefing me in great detail about Dimitri's upcoming christening—and the hideous state of the Greek economy in general— how the EU was punishing Greece with a bailout package that wasn't bailing out the country at all so much as "making us, how you say? In servitude?"

From there, somehow, he went on to contemplate the merits of the television show *Mad Men*, which he and Stavroula had been streaming over their computer to improve their English. "It is good show. Very easy to follow. I think Americans, you like the nostalgia, yes? You are watching people smoking cigarettes and drinking whiskey in the office on the TV show, and you say, 'Oh, look at those stupid people smoking and drinking in the office,' but really, you are also thinking secretly, 'Oh, I wish I could still be smoking and drinking in the office.'" He glanced back at me. "I think all of us like looking to the past when we are frightened. Times here are very bad. Maybe that is why Greeks like this show now, too."

At first, I found myself wishing Thodoris would just be quiet. I so desperately needed to get ahold of myself and think clearly and figure out a plan! I spoke no Greek, was living on borrowed money, and didn't even know what fucking time zone I was in. Yet I would have to find— and likely confront—an anarchist collective somewhere in a remote corner of a Greek island. The irony of this was not lost on me. I'd spent my youth, of course, stomping around in a clawed ANARCHY IN THE U.K. T-shirt, performing a cover version of the Sex Pistols' most famous hit in grunge bars in southeast Michigan. Toxic Shock Syndrome had even attempted to compose our own version, "Khaos in Amerika"—okay, originality was not exactly our strong suit—and half the time it ended with our guitar strings breaking and a bunch of disgruntled drunks pulling the plug on our amp because the song was so bad—but that was *true anarchy*, we'd insisted. Now, clearly, all the punk-rock pretentions of my youth had come back to bite me in the ass.

What the hell was I going to do: Just look around for a bunch of people with safety-pinned nostrils and pink hair? Pretend to be "down" with a bunch of twenty-year-old Greek rebels in riot gear? (Was that even what they wore? Where was I getting my ideas from now? I hadn't a clue. A YouTube video somewhere...?)

Through all of the noise in my head, Thodoris's voice actually became like a salve. It was the equivalent of setting me on top of a washing machine. I noticed he kept checking on me in his rearview mirror.

Maybe I can trust him, I thought. *I need somebody who can help me in this alien place.*

The taxi screeched violently. A bus careened around the corner. Thodoris leaned on his horn, swerved off the road. The bus was so crammed full of passengers, they were smushed up against the glass like laundry in a dryer; I could see the blur of their eyes as they barreled past. In a spray of mud and exhaust, the bus vanished around a curve just as quickly as it had appeared.

"Are you okay? I am sorry. These crazy drivers," Thodoris panted. "They are maniacs."

Slowly, he pulled the taxi onto the road again. "The problem we have here," he said, frowning, "is with all the refugees coming."

My heart snagged. Never mind. Ashley was right: Don't trust the locals.

"First the government says that any Greeks who help the refugees travel on boats or buses or taxis will be charged as 'human traffickers,'" Thodoris said. "They think that if Greeks do not help the refugees, they will stop coming." I watched his face in the rearview mirror; he shook his head again. "But that is crazy in the head, yes? Because the refugees, they are coming from war. They are running for their lives. They will not say, 'Oh, there is no bus service on Lesvos. So I will stay home.' In one month, fifteen thousand people arrive here on the beach."

"Here?" I said, my voice betraying my incredulity. Lesvos didn't seem to be much more developed than I imagined the Middle East to be.

"We are just five kilometers across water from Turkey. We are just gateway. The refugees, if they get here alive, they maybe go on to better places in EU, get citizenship, have a new chance. But first," he said, "they must go to one office here to register. In Moria, fifty kilometers away. And because we Greeks are not allowed to drive refugees, everyone, they must walk to Moria. Little children. Old people. Some are sick. But they have to walk. No shade. No toilets. No water."

"Could they set up porta-potties?" As soon as I said this, though, I sensed the folly of it.

He made a hairpin turn. "My family, we do not live far from this road. My ya-ya, she picks figs from her garden. Hands them to refugees. Some families from Syria, they are lawyers, businessmen, teachers. They have life savings sewn in their jackets. They take out one hundred euro bills and wave them at my taxi. 'Please drive my wife; she is pregnant.'"

He shook his head bitterly. "I do not take a hundred euros. Who does that to a family who has lost everything? But I cannot drive them all the way, either. I tell them, I am sorry, I drop you outside. I have a baby at home. What if I lose my taxi?

"Now, finally, the government sees the refugees are still coming. So they have changed the law again. Now, it is legal to drive refugees. Buses take refugees to Moria. But they compete for business with taxis. So they drive like race-car drivers."

He frowned, shifted gears again. He glanced back at me. He suddenly looked older than I'd first thought, his eyes sad and wet.

Slowly, I exhaled. I looked at him, hard. "Thodoris," I said carefully. "Do you know if there is a refugee camp in the place we're going to?"

"In Skala Sikamineas?" He executed another sharp turn. "There is a small camp by the water. But it is 'unofficial.' We are not supposed to know about it. So of course, everybody knows about it. It is a camp for refugees when they first arrive. For maybe a few nights. Too many people, though, I hear; not enough room. You will see. People, they sleep everywhere. No beds, no blankets. Not enough food, not enough water."

Was this where my daughter was—sleeping on the ground somewhere? Was she starving? Maybe I had gotten something wrong. "This camp. Do you know if it is maybe run by a bunch of—" I searched my brain for a euphemism, but I couldn't find one. "A bunch of anarchists?"

As I said this, I watched for a reaction. But he just shrugged. "If it is run by anarchists, they are very well organized."

"The anarchists here, are they dangerous?"

Glancing back at me, he gave a laugh. "Ha. In Greece, everybody is anarchist. We don't want to pay taxes; we always go on strike. Nobody trusts the government. Even our government, *they* quit the government. Our prime minister—you see on the news? He resigned. Then, a few months later, he gets reelected *because* he resigns! We think, Oh, he is one of us. He has no faith in government either."

Ha. Sounded like Zack. "Thodoris, listen," I said abruptly. "I need to find this group, and this camp. My daughter is in it, and I need to get her out."

His eyes widened. "Your daughter is refugee?"

"No, no. Just an idealist. And an idiot." I exhaled wearily. "You know. A *teenager*."

We were high in the mountains now. Undulant green peaks lifted us up, up, until I started to catch glimpses of a cobalt-blue sea far below.

The taxi zigzagged down a steep hill. I found my heart beating faster and faster—with anticipation that I would finally reach Ashley, but also with a backbeat of panic. Because once I found her, how would I help her? I had no idea what awaited me, what kind of shape she would be in, what the hell to do next. The situation on the island was clearly so much worse than I'd thought—though, to be fair, I hadn't thought much about it at all.

Yet Skala Sikamineas, it turned out, was only a tiny fishing village. The steep main street had a few terra-cotta-roofed houses on either side of it. At the bottom was a small two-story hotel, a one-room mini-market, and a tavern. That was it.

The road ended abruptly at the seafront. We lurched onto a small flagstone cul-de-sac in what passed for a town square—though it was barely enough space to turn the car around in. A few scrawny trees shaded it; two benches sat pressed against a small yard on our left. People were sleeping on the benches, I noticed, under what appeared to be airplane blankets, and others were camped in the yard itself, barricaded around their piles of belongings.

I had made a terrible mistake. This hamlet was far too small— too quaint and picturesque—for anything other than fishing. When Ashley had said she was at a camp, perhaps she had meant one farther inland—on our way down the mountainside, we'd passed a clearing full of tents. Or, could she have in fact meant someplace else entirely— perhaps that place Thodoris had mentioned, Moria or wherever? Good God: It was literally *all Greek* to me. How the hell was I going to find my kid?

Thodoris maneuvered the taxi around in the little public square, then pulled up beside the little white stucco hotel.

"Are you staying here? Or over in Pension Nikki?" He pointed directly across the street. Flustered, I looked from one to the other, then back again. I realized with shock—and a sliver of horror—that he was actually expecting me to disembark. This was it. Our lovely, comforting taxi ride was over. In another minute, I'd be wholly on my own again.

The pension had a blue doorway with a friendly, hand-painted sign. The other had small balconies facing the sea and actually said HOTEL. But where was the refugee camp?

Thodoris turned around to face me, concerned. "You do have a reservation here, yes?"

The tone in his voice had shifted.

"Of course, of course," I lied. "Either place is fine. I'll just—" I dug through my purse for my wallet. "Whichever hotel, it doesn't matter really. I'm not planning to stay long at all—I'll just—"

He sighed. "If you do not have room reservation already, that is a big problem," he said, not unkindly. "With all the journalists and volunteers and refugees coming, everything is full. Whole island, not just Sikamineas. And if there is room, they charge you hundreds of euros. Look, you see?" He motioned to the postage stamp of a park by the waterfront. "People are sleeping outside on the benches."

I blinked at him. If I had him leave me here as planned, I could wind up stranded with my stuff, effectively homeless yet again. Whatever remained of Arjul's loan would likely dissipate even faster, too. Suddenly, though, I was so tired, my thoughts simply evaporated. All I could think to do now was just run up and down the street screaming, "Ashley, Ashley," like some madwoman from Detroit. Watch me. I'd wind up back in a jail. And my daughter. *My daughter.*

"I'm sorry. I have no idea what to do next." My voice broke. I pointed to the building with the HOTEL sign on it. Perhaps they would take pity on me. "Just leave me here, I guess."

Thodoris switched off the ignition. I started to take out my wallet, but he held up his hand to silence me, then picked up his phone and dialed someone quickly. He spoke rapidly in Greek. When the call was finished, he tossed his phone aside, twisted around, and looked at me. "Okay. I cancel next pickup. You are a parent. Your child, she is lost. So. We will find her."

Before I could protest, he pointed down a narrow road along the water's edge, leading away from Skala Sikamineas. A stone wall ran along one side of it; the tide scraped up to it on the other. Scores of people were shuffling along. "This road, she is too difficult to drive on. But the camp, I think it is maybe five hundred meters. While you go, I stay here. I keep your bags locked safe in trunk." He picked up his phone again. He nodded toward the café by the water. "I will wait over there. I will have coffee. It will not be too terrible. When you come back, if your daughter is not here, we go look in another camp.

In meantime, I will call my brother, Yannis. We will find place for you to stay."

I looked at Thodoris, then at the narrow path with waves lapping against it, then the car key in his fist. Did I dare trust him? I supposed I would have to. He seemed a far better bet than lugging my suitcase and guitar by myself into the heart of an anarchist camp. Besides, I'd seen for myself: He couldn't even abandon a cheese pie.

How the hell did you say "thank you" in Greek? I had absolutely no idea, of course. Instead, I found myself bursting into tears. "I'm sorry, I'm sorry," I heard myself sniffle. *Thankyouthankyouthankyou.*

Thodoris waved his hands sheepishly. "No, no, no," he said. "It is no problem for me at all. When Stavroula's uncle move to America, all his new neighbors in Michigan, they help him. So now, we help you." He made a shifting motion back and forth with his hands. "So we balance."

How was it that the people you knew and loved most deeply in this world could hurt and betray you so profoundly, yet strangers could show you so much offhanded compassion, it made your heart break? As I stumbled down the road, wiping my eyes on the back of my wrist, I blinked out at the sea. The sun scattered nets of diamonds across the water. In another time, the road leading out of Skala Sikamineas would have been enchanting.

But now, I saw people were sleeping on the rugged shore, hunkered down beneath pieces of cardboard and tarps and even yoga mats. (*Yoga mats?*) I saw families in blankets along the roadside, huddling with their belongings, smoking cigarettes, standing by the sea talking on cell phones in languages I could not recognize.

About a quarter of a mile down, I came to an iron gate across from the beach. Hand-painted signs were posted in what appeared to be both Arabic and Greek, as well as—to my relief again—English: WELCOME and NO PHOTOS PLEASE. Down a wooded pathway, large tents were set up among tall trees, identified with various signs and arrows pounded into the muddy ground: *Food, Clothing, Women, Toilets, Medical*. With the sun glinting through the greenery, it almost felt idyllic—like a tree house or a children's summer camp—except that there were lines and crowds everywhere, and the noise was as loud as any airport or open-air sporting event—and occasionally great waves of stench came over the breeze: urine and sour milk and cigarettes and wet wool and rotting fruit.

For a split second—just a split second—I felt myself cower, physically recoil. But my daughter—with any luck—was actually somewhere in this mess.

I threaded my way past women in headscarves jiggling babies, young barefoot men shivering on the ground wrapped in metallic thermal blankets, families with vacant eyes standing stonily, dutifully, waiting in a line for porridge (Good God, I knew what *that* was like now). A young man with a chemical burn running from his calf to his thigh rocked in quiet agony by the medical tent.

After a night in jail, after a night in a homeless shelter—and as a daughter of Detroit itself—I thought I'd at least be somewhat prepared for crowds, for squalor. But this was of another magnitude. I was instantly overwhelmed by the sights and noises and crowds and palpable desperation and the struggle for dignity. I was surprised at how claustrophobic I felt, even outdoors, with the impossibly blue Greek sky arcing above us.

Was anyone in charge? A few people with nametags circulated around. Most were young men and women in their twenties, most of them fair-skinned, with an impressive assortment of tattoos and piercings and—what seemed to be a particularly twenty-first-century anarchist predilection—blond dreadlocks. But others looked like fitness instructors. Still a few others were much older, in drawstring cotton pants and gauzy scarves and wild gray hair, looking like the aged hippies they probably were. They tried to corral people into lines and hand out bottles of water and escort the injured. Several had teenagers by their side, interpreting.

Pushing my way toward the medical tent, I saw a freckled woman with a whistle hanging from a fluorescent green cord around her neck. She was trying to manage all the patients jockeying for attention while answering questions from a woman in a flowered hijab holding a crying toddler.

"People, please, please, everyone quiet down," the freckled woman shouted in English. "We only have one doctor this morning. One doctor." She held up one finger for emphasis. "We will try to get to all of you." She had a British accent, and something about its musicality seemed to calm people for a moment. (Or, well, it calmed *me*.) But glancing over, she gave me a drowning look. "Are you Anna? Did Gunter send you over?"

I shook my head. I felt terrible. "I'm so sorry. I'm looking for my daughter, one of the volunteers? A nineteen-year-old American named Ashley Koczynski? Five foot four with long, light brown hair, green eyes, very thin?" Yet the woman shook her head, her attention diverted by a small girl pointing to a bloodied knee. "I'm sorry. I just arrived yesterday. Try the main tent."

I pushed my way into another clearing, my boots sinking into the mud. These were the same cool leather boots I'd worn to meet Zack at Fontanel, that I'd been arrested in, that had been on my feet at the homeless shelter in Memphis. *Good God*, had I really purchased them only a week ago—on sale at a Macy's off the New Jersey Turnpike? It now felt like an entirely different universe. And just a week before that, I'd been in Vegas, smiling insipidly on a stage with Colleen Lundstedt beneath a battery of colored lights. It was absurd. How the hell had all of this happened to me so quickly? To *my family*? My insides grew hot; I felt a swell of vertigo.

The main tent was not nearly large enough to accommodate all the arrivals. I was stunned. So many women and children. Frantically, I stepped over clusters of people sitting on the ground drinking tea. Excuse me, excuse me. I found a young, clean-cut college student in a red polo shirt. "Oh, yes. Please, hello?" I said. Only when he gave me a helpless smile did I realize with embarrassment that he was refugee, too.

Finally, someone pointed me to a shaggy-haired, bearded man with a clipboard.

"Oh, wait. Yeah. The American girl." He pointed in the direction of a crude path leading farther into the woods. "Check in the quarantine tent, down past the latrines."

My heart beat faster and faster as I made my way through the shrubbery, almost bumping into a group of dark-haired children running back and forth between the trees giggling. Would Ashley be there? *Please, let her be there.* But would she be delirious? Still vomiting? What disease did she even have? All my years of hypochondriacal googling ("Do I have Ebola?"; "Avian Bird Flu: The First Seven Symptoms"; "How to tell if you may have been infected by Mad Cow Disease") came back to haunt me. Such folly, such indulgence. The Jew in me, too, wondered if my worry hadn't been a lightning rod drawing the evil spirits down— and these, being Jewish evil spirits, would be ironic—sparing me, but infecting my child. And yet where the fuck was WebMD now that I was really going to need it? I shouldn't have left my first-aid supplies back in my suitcase with Thodoris. Dammit, I wasn't thinking.

The tent was an older army-surplus type suspended from jute ropes like my father used to set up for Toby and me when we'd gone camping as kids. Its thick canvas had the same damp throw-pillow smell, too. For a moment, I was back in Michigan, 1975. Pulling back the heavy flap, I stepped into darkness.

The tarp underfoot was bunched and muddy; in the dim light, I slowly made out several wooden shipping pallets with bedrolls unfurled on them, some with ratty cushions or inflatable pillows. A cluster of backpacks sat piled in one corner, chained together with a bicycle lock. I nearly tripped over two young, heavily tattooed people sitting on a bedroll on the floor. They both had shaved heads and were dressed in identical sweatshirts with the sleeves and collars torn off and combat pants with Velcro pockets bulging on the hips; one (a girl, I saw, from the small breasts pressing through the fabric) was lying with her head in the other's lap, scrolling through something on her phone.

They glanced up indifferently. I started to apologize for disturbing them when I spied a figure curled on the pallet farthest away from the entrance. She was on her side in a snail-shell position facing away from me, only partially covered by a flimsy blanket—in fact, as I drew closer, I saw it was a beach towel. Her damp T-shirt had bunched up high above her waist, exposing her pale back and the shiny beige elastic of her bra. I could see the delicate keys of her spine and her ribs pressing through her skin and the downy triangular indentation of her coccyx peeking above the loose waistband of her jeans. Her chestnut hair streamed down over the side of the pallet, damp and tangled as seaweed as she heaved and shuddered. I had seen her lying in this position a thousand times before.

"Ashley?" I stepped quickly over the girls—they were both girls, I saw now. "Ashley, honey?"

The girl staring at her phone glanced up at me. "Oh, you are her mother?" She waggled her screen at me. "I am Dagmar. We spoke on my phone. I let her use it to Skype you."

I looked worriedly from Dagmar over to Ashley. "How high has her fever been?"

She shrugged. "We only got to use the thermometer once. So I think it was"—she looked to the other girl for confirmation—"38.8?"

I squinted at her in the dark. Nothing anyone was saying made any sense. 38.8? Was she frozen? I stepped over them and sat down on the pallet beside Ashley, watching her body heave. "Ashley, sweetie, it's Mom," I said softly, touching her cheek, then her forehead. It was burning.

"Yes, I am looking for it on my phone," interrupted Dagmar helpfully. For an anarchist, she was awfully solicitous. "38.8 is 101.84 degrees in Fahrenheit."

"Okay. That's high."

"A few other people here have had this sickness. The intestinal problems can last many days. But the fever is not usually so long. For that, we are worried. Our medications, they are all finished. Our friends are bringing more from Athens tomorrow."

"Ashley." I jostled her again, more forcefully this time. "Ash, wake up, honey."

Her eyes fluttered. She rolled fitfully for a moment. Then she jolted awake. "Mom, you came! You came! Oh, Mom." She sat up weakly, pulling me toward her, gasping, "Oh Mom. Oh my God, I am so happy to see you. I am so sick. And I feel so awful. I am so sorry. I am so sorry, Mom."

Holding her, I was shocked by how thin she had become; she was not that much more substantial than the anatomical skeleton in Brenda's living room. Letting out a sob, she wiped her nose on the back of her hand. "They took everything, Mom. Every single thing." Clinging to me again, she sniffled into my neck, "It's a total nightmare. There are children. And they gave this man mouth-to-mouth. And all these people just keep coming and coming in waves, and it doesn't stop, and the screams and the smells, oh my God." She doubled over. "I think I'm going to be sick again."

"Okay," I said with alarm. I didn't know if she was still hallucinating, or what part of what she was saying was real. By my count, she'd had a fever four days. That was a very long time. "Hang on, just hang on there, Ashley. Take a deep breath. That's it. And another. Now. Can you stand up?"

Tearily, she gulped and nodded. Gingerly, I helped her up from the pallet. Her thin shirt was stuck to her back with sweat. Now I could see her fully. Her hair wild and knotty. Her skin angry pink with not just fever, but blistery sunburn. Besides a dirty, lemon-yellow T-shirt that I did not recognize, she had on her favorite pair of low-slung jeans, now stained with mud to the knee, so that the legs looked as if they'd been dipped into brown dye. Otherwise, she was barefoot. A pungent odor emanated from her, acidic and grimy, of vomit and perspiration and musk. Oddly, it was like the whiff I'd caught of myself in the bus station after my night in jail.

"Do you have any shoes?"

She shook her head.

"You can take my flip-flops," Dagmar called over, nodding to a pair by the tent flap.

"You sure?" Ashley said uncertainly.

"Just pass them on when you're done."

"Dagmar, thank you so much for your help," I said. "I am really so grateful." I glanced around the tent. I felt like some grand maternal gesture was in order, a hug or a gift of some sort, but what did I have? Money? I needed every borrowed euro I had—but for my daughter's safety? For gratitude? I reached into my purse but Dagmar was already looking back down at her phone, scrolling and showing her friend something on the screen, and Ashley saw me and shook her head with a quick, vehement *No, Mom. Don't.*

"Okay, then." I exhaled awkwardly. "Ash, do you want to gather up the rest of your things?"

Ashley looked at me, helpless, about to cry again. She held out her hands, then let her arms flop at her sides. "These *are* all my things, Mom. I told you. This is all I have left."

Chapter 18

"THE GOOD THING ABOUT LESVOS? Here, everybody knows everybody," Thodoris said. Ashley hobbled between us, her arms draped over our shoulders like a casualty of war. He helped her down into the backseat of his taxi.

His brother Yannis, Thodoris explained, was married to someone named Nikolina, who had a godmother, Vassiliki, whose brother Cosmo was married to Helen—blah, blah—I quickly gave up trying to follow—the names alone were epic—somewhere in his daisy chain of Greek relatives, there was even an Aunt Eurydice. But one of them, it turned out, lived in Skala Sikamineas and had a next-door neighbor named Dina. And Dina, it turned out, had a spare room.

"Usually, she rents only to journalists. But I explain to her, you are a mother with a sick child. You are very nice older woman from Michigan who is a friend of Stavroula's uncle. Okay, I maybe stretch the truth a little. But Dina, she says yes."

"Oh, Thodoris," I said swooningly (though a tiny voice inside my head did balk: *older woman?*).

Thodoris held up his hand. "It is eighty euros a night. Cash only. This, I think is too much. But I cannot argue. This price, she is okay for you?"

I supposed it would have to be. Besides, what the hell did I know? Euros might as well be Monopoly money. When I'd withdrawn four hundred from the ATM at the airport that morning—the absolute limit—all that had registered was *Oh! Pretty!* The bills were peach-colored, pink, and baby blue, like favors at a bridal shower. Mostly, I was just relieved that Joey had been able to replenish our account fast enough so I could access some backup funds before flying on to Lesvos. I'd learned the hard way: Always best to travel with extra bills stuffed in your bra.

My plan now was to get Ashley healthy enough to travel, then book us on the first flight back to Athens. Have the US Embassy there issue her an emergency passport—and *vamoose!*

I could only hope that the medicine I'd brought from America would do the trick—and quickly. If her fever didn't break soon, I'd have to get her to a doctor. And from what I was learning, this would not be easy. There was only one hospital in Lesvos—back near the airport—and the medical services throughout the island, such as they were, were already stretched to breaking. Plus, I'd need to find food and shoes and clothes now for my daughter, too. And some way to contact Joey and Austin on a regular basis.

As I watched Thodoris take a fresh bottle of water out of his trunk and uncap it for Ashley, it occurred to me that there simply wasn't enough money in the world to pay him what he was truly owed, either.

For a moment, I was so overwhelmed, I leaned against the side of the taxi, breathing in and out, in and out. *One step at a time, Donna,* I told myself. *Just like AA.*

The dark, clayey room was off a small porch in the back of Dina's house. A zinc sink jutted out of the wall. Metal storage shelves held jars of atrophied paintbrushes, chair spindles, and dusty plastic flower arrangements. On a table made from two sawhorses was an electric teakettle and an old, cathode-ray television. Noodles of flypaper spiraled from the ceiling, though the assortment of flies zipping around were a testament to how purely decorative they'd become. The whole place smelled faintly of turpentine and solvent and cigarettes and mildew.

Most disturbingly, however, was that Dina had hung an array of her own, original artwork from hooks across an entire wall of pegboard. Her subjects of choice appeared to be kittens, Greek sailors, and clowns.

Still, a sleeping area had been carved out with a rag rug and a narrow daybed pushed against one wall. Dina had set up a cot beside it, so that the room could now sleep two. She showed me the small, unfinished, grouty bathroom. Because she spoke no English, she pantomimed that we'd have to turn on a water heater bolted to the wall every time we wanted to shower.

Then she handed me two keys, said something elaborate in Greek, and vanished.

"Oh God," Ashley moaned. She flopped down on the cot; it promptly collapsed beneath her. "Ow ow ow ow ow!" she howled, clutching her elbow. In a moment, Dina hurried in, apologizing in Greek. She hoisted the bed back up and checked a gizmo on the frame to ensure it was locked in place this time and pounced on it herself just to make sure. By then, however, Ashley had already rolled onto the other bed—the daybed with its iron frame—and lay there moaning and gasping. Dina returned with a large bottle of water and a fistful of assorted tea bags and a pomegranate. She pointed to the electric kettle, then fled again.

And there we were. My daughter and I. Alone and together on Lesvos installed in someone's hastily converted storage room costing 80 euros a night, staring at a collection of oil-painted clowns. "God," Ashley groaned, motioning to the wall. "Those really aren't helping." I knelt by my suitcase and dug out the Tylenol and the hydration tablets and the Cipro I'd gotten. Dutifully, Ashley took them. As she lay back on the narrow bed, I perched beside her and stroked her damp hair with the same vigilance I'd had when she was six with the chicken pox. "Ash," I whispered, as calmly as I could, "just one thing, before you drift off."

"Mmmm?"

"I need to know. Did somebody hurt you? Were you assaulted, or sexually—"

Her eyes fluttered open. "Oh, God, Moooooom. Really?" Weakly, she shook her head. "I just really, really need to sleep is all, okay?"

Remembering that there was a plastic thermometer in the first-aid kit I'd bought, I dug it out, tiptoed across the room, and poked it into Ashley's slackening mouth. Only after it came out reading 99.5 Fahrenheit could I finally, finally, exhale and doze off a little myself.

After I awoke, I rinsed out Ashley's clothes in the zinc utility sink and hung them out on the porch railing to dry. The sun arced higher, bleaching the yard beyond our window sage and white.

Once Ashley herself got up, showered, and swaddled herself in the threadbare towels Dina left us, I made some tea using the odd electric kettle. We installed ourselves outside on the crumbly little back porch.

She nibbled weakly at some of the crackers and packages of Weetabix cereal I'd stolen in bulk from the breakfast bar at the airport hotel in Athens . . . and the two of us looked at each other, stunned to find ourselves together on the other side of the globe, listening to the scrape of the waves and the moored boats dinging in the distance . . .

And finally . . . only after all this, did my daughter clear her throat and swallow and slowly begin to tell me what had happened.

She'd been unhappy in London. "The city itself is awesome. But my housemates, Mom? I mean, just once, I asked them 'Why do British people always *talk* with English accents but *sing* with American ones?' It's a totally legitimate question. But after that, they were horrible to me. It was like a zillion micro-aggressions. One guy, Eric? Whenever he saw me in the kitchen, he'd start mimicking the way Americans talk, going super-nasal, like, 'Oh my God, Ashley, like, isn't this, like, *totally faaaan-tas-tick!*" She picked up her cup indignantly. "I never even *use* that word, Mom.

"And they're all alcoholics. Every night, they go through, like, a liter of wine. They buy it in these boxes from Waitrose."

She turned for a moment to watch a cat slinking through the grass below us. As she did, her towel loosened; her clavicle was so bony, it looked corrugated.

"I was just so *lonely,*" she said. "And then, at the same time, I kept seeing all the horrible stories about the refugees. Fleeing the war in

Syria and the Taliban and ISIS. It's all over social media. But also, oh my God, they show so much more on the news here in Europe than they ever do in the US! Here, Mom, they actually show live-streaming videos of, like, innocent people getting mowed down by artillery fire in Aleppo, and guys being beheaded by ISIS, and all these rubber rafts full of families capsizing in the sea. You saw the photo of the father with the drowned little baby, right? It's like that every day. It's horrible!"

I looked at my daughter.

"Oh, c'mon, Mom. How did you not see that?"

She widened her eyes. "And the governments aren't doing anything! They're saying this is the biggest humanitarian crisis, since, like, World War II. But no one's mobilizing to help. No one's granting these people asylum. Except maybe Greece. And Germany. But in Britain, they won't even let teenagers cross over from France because they're afraid they're 'terrorists.' So, there are all these kids from, like, Africa and the Middle East camped out near the Chunnel in Calais, in France. These poor kids, they've done nothing wrong except, you know"—she rolled her eyes— "they're black or Arab, so, like that's a 'crime'? And they're, like, *my age*, Mom! And they have nothing! No parents, no money—nothing!"

Ashley was so weak and dehydrated, her voice cracked. As she spoke, though, the passion and pain reanimated her face. As much as I'd felt like slapping her for getting herself into this mess, I also felt a niggling sense of pride. My kid: You certainly couldn't say she didn't care about the world.

"And I was thinking about how your grandparents fled the Nazis, and Dad's were Polish immigrants. I mean, could you imagine if, like, they'd had Twitter or Instagram back then? It'd be the same thing." Sniffling, she drew the towel tighter around her and glanced at her clothes drying on the railing.

"If you want," I said, "I can lend you something to wear."

"I'm okay for now. It's good to feel totally clean for a change." She took a belabored sip of tea. "So then, okay, in my seminar there was this Danish girl, Pernille? And she was also really upset about the refugee crisis and wanted to do something. So first, we found this Scandinavian humanitarian group online, but it turned out that they wanted you to be at least twenty-six and maybe a lifeguard. So then Pernille was tweeting with these German anarchists. And they said they were helping to run this refugee camp on Lesvos and needed volunteers. So we were just like, oh my God, we are so there. *Now*."

I couldn't help it. Crossing my arms, I leaned back in my chair. "And you never once thought to tell your dad and me? Or your housemates?"

"Mom, I told you. My housemates were, like, these drunken British douche bags."

"Your father was calling and calling because he was trying to FedEx you your meds. And guess what? Nobody in London knew where the hell you were, Ash. In fact, they hadn't seen you for days. He practically had a heart attack. He was ready to contact Interpol."

"I was going to tell you," she said. "Eventually."

"*This* is how you go about saving the world?"

"Mo-o-om!" She shot me a wounded look of protest. "Can you just not be so judgy for just, like, a minute?"

"No. I cannot 'not be so judgy.' I just flew halfway across the globe for you."

She looked down. "I knew if I told you, you'd be completely against it."

I squeezed my tea bag out over my cup, then dropped it on the side of the saucer.

"Oh my God." Ashley sat up suddenly. "What happened to your face?"

"Nothing. An accident." I coughed. "So how did you wind up with no money and no passport and no clothes?"

She squirmed in her chair and rotated her wrists in the serpentine way she did when she was trying to be evasive. "Um, it started, I guess, on the boat?"

"Boat? Oh good God." I sat forward. "Tell me please you weren't helping to smuggle refugees across the Mediterranean."

"No, Mom. Jesus. The *ferry*. From Athens to Lesvos. It's, like, thirteen hours. That's how Pernille and I got here. We thought, like, it would be totally culturally insensitive to fly. I mean, here are all these refugees arriving in rafts and dinghies, but we're just going to *jet* to the island? So we took the ferry in solidarity."

I was unable to hide my irritation. The one-hour flight from Athens had cost me 58 euros. The thirteen-hour boat ride, on the other hand, had cost 144 euros. I knew this because it was one of the disputed charges flagged on our emergency Mastercard. Joey and I had gone over them, item by item, as I sat anxiously waiting for the flight out of Nashville and we tried to piece together what might have happened. Someone had charged a passage for two people plus a vehicle on the Bluestar Ferry Line in Greece.

"You brought a car over?"

For a moment, she looked confused. Then she said, "Oh. Yeah. No. *That.* Well. That's sort of the other part of the story." She glanced at me apprehensively. "So, like, waiting in line at the ferry terminal to buy the tickets, I kind of met this guy? And he was totally hot, and I thought he was just, like, really sweet. And really funny and smart. He was from Serbia, but his English was amazing."

Okay, here we go now, I thought, sitting back. *The real story.*

"His name was 'Poz'—okay, that was his nickname. But he was, like I kept thinking, just *a total Poz.* He looked like a cross between Adam Levine *and* Macklemore, except with way better hair? And so, we're talking in the ticket line, and he said he used to be, like, this aircraft mechanic for the Serbian military. But now he was working on making documentaries. And also, launching digital platforms for all of Eastern Europe. And it turned out, he and his friend were going to Lesvos to volunteer, too."

"Wow," I deadpanned. "What a coincidence." I couldn't help adding, "And that does not remotely sound like a pickup line whatsoever." (Though the East German judge, I had to concede, gave him an eight.)

Ashley leaned forward, seeming not to hear. "So Poz and his friend, they had a car with them that they were going to use to distribute all these supplies to the refugees when they got here, but just when they were about to pay at the counter, they discovered that they didn't have enough cash on them to bring it over, or their card didn't work or something, which meant they couldn't go at all, so I sort of figured, since they were going to be volunteering with the refugees, too—"

"That your dad and I could just foot the bill for everybody."

"Jesus. It wasn't like I wasn't going to pay you back." She let her head fall forward in a mop of wet hair. "Mom, I'm feeling really horrible right now, so if you're just going to criticize everything—"

I sighed. "No, go on. Keep telling me."

"So, okay. That night, on the ferry? Poz and I, like, totally hooked up. It was so romantic, Mom, it was like out of a movie. He had this sleeping bag, and we were out on the deck under the stars. And we were making Vine videos on our phones together, and telling each other about our families—his sister and his mother—oh my God, it was horrible—he said he never tells this to anyone—but they were killed in the war—and when I told him that I was going to work at this camp run by anarchists on the north coast, he couldn't even believe it because it turned out—"

"It turned out, that's where he was going to be a volunteer, too."

"OMG, how did you know?" Ashley regarded me with genuine astonishment. "So. Poz and his friend, they gave us a ride up here. Which was amazing because, otherwise, we'd probably have had to hitchhike. All the buses and taxis were full. So when we finally got to the camp, Pernille went off with her German anarchist friends, while Poz and I slept out on the beach. I had my backpack with me, because the first thing they told us at the camp was to keep an eye on our belongings at all times. And Poz, he even helped keep an eye on it, like, when I had to go pee. So *totally* sweet, right? And, oh my God, Mom, being with him on the beach, it was like, even more romantic than on the ferry, because now, we were like these two international rescue workers together— these two lovers from two different worlds in, like, the middle of this global crisis."

I looked at her and sighed. Of course she'd think that. It was such a cliché, it was a cliché of a cliché. It was almost as much of a cliché, in fact, as a middle-aged woman tracking down her old high school boyfriend on Facebook and attempting to rekindle a hot teenage romance with him. Talk about hormone-addled romantic fantasists. How could I blame my daughter? Apple: tree.

"So. Let me guess," I said, not unsympathetically. "You slept with Poz out on the beach, and while you guys were having this great international romance, some of the refugees robbed you."

She looked down sheepishly. After a moment, she said, "Basically."

I took her hand and squeezed it. "People are desperate here, sweetie. Thodoris told me to be careful. The refugees have lost everything. So if a bag is just sitting there—right in front of them..." I wanted to say, *I know all too well what it's like to be desperate, and hungry, and frightened, and homeless, with maybe all of nine dollars in your pocket. I know all too well now how tempting that would be.*

Instead, I added, "Do you have any idea at all who— Did you even see—"

"Jesus! It's just all a blur, Mom—it's just all— I can't even." She stopped abruptly; her whole face shut down.

"What? What is it?"

She shook her head violently, pressed the bases of her palms to her eyes. "Nothing. Can I just, please, sleep some more now?"

I reached across the little table and squeezed her hand.

"Just—your passport. Did you report it stolen?"

Ashley jerked her hand away. "What? Are you kidding me? Mom. You think anyone here cares? They have so many bigger things to deal with." She picked up her teacup and set it down roughly. "The last thing I want to do here is go to the cops."

"I understand that," I said. "Believe me, I do. But if your passport is missing, that's a big deal. You need to file a report."

"Jesus, Mom. What could I possibly say, 'Oh, I was just here volunteering with a bunch of anarchists at that 'unofficial' refugee camp'?

Like that wouldn't have gotten me into even more trouble maybe? Or 'Hi, I know I have absolutely no money or ID or belongings or anything, but trust me, I'm American'?"

She glared at me. "I couldn't prove anything to them, Mom! They could've thought I was just another refugee trying to sneak into the EU without papers! For all I know, they could've decided I was from, like, Iraq or Pakistan—or someplace else where the people don't qualify for asylum—and they could've deported me to Turkey or someplace!"

"Okay. C'mon now," I said gently. "Ashley. You don't exactly look Pakistani or Arab."

"How do you know, Mom? How do you know what a 'refugee' really looks like?" she said with surprising violence. "You haven't been here! There are people getting off these boats who could be any of us! Just take away the headscarves! There's not some special 'refugee look'!"

"Okay. Look," I sighed. "Please. Take it down a notch, will you? We're both exhausted." I cocked my head at her and took a deep, long breath and closed my eyes for a moment. "I'm not attacking you. I was just asking whether you'd reported the passport, is all."

She glared at me, still defensive. But her face started to break like an egg. Suddenly, she didn't look nineteen anymore nearly so much as nine. "Well, I didn't call the police, okay?" she said tearily. "Mom, I called *you*."

After she took some more medicine and went back to sleep, I just sat outside on the balcony, stunned, feeling the sun and unfamiliar wind on my face. I was worn out by worry, relief—all of it. I'd forgotten just how exhausting my daughter could be. Now that my fear had subsided—and she was in living color before me again—I could afford the luxury of getting good and furious at her. Halfway around the world I'd raced, at a moment's notice, because she'd been careless with her backpack while hooking up with some boy on a beach. Really? I wondered, too: Were all teenage girls this melodramatic with their mothers? Frankly, I wasn't sure. I'd never had the opportunity to be a teenager with my own mother for very long.

It was morning back in Michigan. If Joey had slept at all, I imagined he'd be wandering around our kitchen, unshaven in his ratty blue bathrobe, repeatedly checking his phone, glancing at the clock, anxiously feeling around in the freezer for some frozen waffles. It was important to get the news to him as fast as I could. I poked around my bag for a paper and pen. BE BACK SOON, ASH, I wrote. DON'T GO ANYWHERE!!! I MEAN IT!!! XOXOX MOM

Finding computer access in the small fishing village was challenging, but eventually, the proprietor of the one hotel in town—who had heard about my plight somehow—word got around fast—Thodoris was right— everybody here *did* know everybody—he took pity on me and let me use the computer in his office. Skype wasn't loading, so I sent Joey an email.

Subject: The eagle has landed.

She's okay, Joey, I typed. **I got her.**

She's skinny and sick to her stomach, but still sanctimonious, so she's still Ashley, right?;-) We're in a room here on the island that actually reminds me of home. (Specifically, the basement.) Her fever is down & she's eating crackers. As soon as she is well enough to travel, we'll fly to Athens. Tell Arjul: THANK YOU AGAIN.

Also, can you/Austin scan & email copy of Ashley's birth certificate? (Should be in file cabinet in kitch desk, second drawer on left, green folder marked KIDS' BIRTH CERTIFICATES.)

My new phone doesn't work here. Will call as soon as I have Skype and internet, but service is weak everywhere, they say.

Lesvos feels like the end of the earth. This refugee thing is INSANE. Really SAD. Who knew? Our kid: She knows how to pick 'em! More later.

I hesitated for a while trying to figure out how the hell to sign off: Best? Love? XOX? Just my name?

Nothing felt right. An estranged couple reuniting when their child was in danger was the stuff of made-for-TV movies. It couldn't be sustained indefinitely, and we both knew it. One problem rarely erases another. Now, I didn't even know how to close out an email to my husband. It made me unbearably sad.

Finally I settled on:

With relief—and exhaustion,

D.

Then, unable to help it, I added:

p.s. She may still be in better shape than you and I are in right now.

Then:

p.p.s. As soon as she's all better, I'm swear I'm going to kill her.

Then:

p.p.p.s. For any third party reading this, that last line was a joke.

Stepping back into the sunshine, I supposed I should try to get some sleep myself. A group of thin African and Middle Eastern young men climbed past me up the hill carrying filmy plastic bags heavy with food containers and fruit and bread. Strangers in a strange land, fending as best they could for themselves. I looked at them and felt a sudden pang of recognition. Above us, on a wrought-iron balcony dripping with bougainvillea, a gray-haired Greek couple sat on folding chairs, watching the square impassively as if it were a piece of theater. *Yeah*, I thought suddenly, *I know what that feels like, too*. Standing there was like being in a dream in which I was everyone at the same time.

Even more surreal was the tavern that had been closed that morning. Now its outdoor café was full to capacity. A pale Swedish couple in anoraks sat compiling a list of supplies with a team of young Greeks. Two women draped in black hijabs and robes glanced around uneasily, frosted bottles of Coca-Cola untouched on the table before them. Four German men straddled their chairs like hobbyhorses, drinking beer and laughing. At the adjacent table, a clutch of British journalists hunched intently over a laptop, camera bags and electrical cables piled at their feet.

Beyond them, light shone over the sea like a glaze. White fishing boats quivered on the water. The air smelled of sea salt and pine. Looking around the little village, filled with the melodies of different voices and languages, I was struck by the beauty of it, how all the pale stuccoed houses with their royal-blue trim and ocher roofs seemed to correspond with one another, so that they existed in harmony.

Then, I saw the life jackets. Piles and piles of discarded orange life jackets heaped by the side of the little fenced-in yard beyond the park benches. Heaped on the dock of the little marina. Orange life jackets strewn about the roadside and bobbing in the water like hideous swollen tiger lilies, undulating back and forth with the tide. And piles of shredded black and green rubber rafts. Dark, matte plastic, like body bags.

And garbage.

So much garbage. The road, the shore, the beach dotted with it like a pointillist painting.

Where could it have all come from? It was a tsunami of trash. And then I realized: That was exactly right. The water. The boats. Until that moment, I'd only equated refugees with scarcity. But forty people fleeing on a raft still bring as much as they can to survive. Seemingly hundreds of water bottles lay crushed in the dirt and scattered between the rocks. Colored plastic bags, bloated with air, floated in the tide like jellyfish. Sandwich wrappers and personal identification papers— smeared with blue ink—and diapers and used tissues and lost bottles of sunscreen and scarves and tampons and receipts and plastic combs and empty potato chip bags. Bobbing along the shore: a yellow toothbrush. A cheap sodden baseball cap. A Pokémon phone case.

I had walked this same route earlier that very morning, but now, it was completely transformed. Or had I simply not noticed? Perhaps I'd been too focused on finding my daughter. Or perhaps, in the time it took Thodoris and me to find a room to rent, and for Ashley to shower and sleep, a whole new fleet of rubber boats had landed in Skala Sikamineas, spilling some of their contents and people into the sea? But how could that many people have landed in such a short period of time? Surely this had accumulated over weeks, months.

Maybe Ashley's passport or some of her belongings could still be unearthed among the debris. Though I suspected it was a long shot— maternal wishful thinking—I started scanning the ground as I walked.

A lone plastic woman's shoe. A broken pair of pink plastic sunglasses. An abandoned denim vest, soiled and tattered among the rocks. And then, what stopped me cold in my tracks: a sopping wet, pale-blue baby blanket flecked with bits of seaweed. And lichen.

I was Jewish mostly by heritage. Certainly, I'd had no religious upbringing. Yet I'd still had drummed into me like a prayer, like Torah, the number *Six million*. So many Jews murdered during the Holocaust seemed impossible to fathom. How could how such a vast amount of humanity ever be rendered real?

Through shoes. Eyeglasses. Suitcases.

The summer we'd taken the kids to Washington, DC, we'd seen it in the museum: Here was Isaac Birenberg. Here was his suitcase.

That drove it home.

Now, as I scanned the debris on the beach of Lesvos, every fragment transformed from a piece of trash to a person, to the story of someone fleeing for their life—a mother, a teenager, someone who played cards, who liked to dance. Whether they had made it or drowned was unknown.

And so many.

I could not look away. I followed the garbage trail farther down the road. Wrappers. Shoelaces. A newspaper. A scarf.

Some volunteers on the shore were picking up the refuse bit by bit, depositing it into industrial-sized garbage bags. I tried to stay out of their way, but then someone yelled in a thick German accent, "Hello! Hello!" Dagmar and her girlfriend. I walked over.

"Hey, thanks again," I said. "You really helped my daughter in her hour of need."

Dagmar shrugged. On her wrist was a red-and-black tattoo of a phoenix. It looked slightly infected to me. "It is no problem. A lot of people here at the camp get robbed."

"Still. I appreciate it."

She squinted up at me. She was not much older than Ashley. Nor was her girlfriend or the other trash-pickers on the shore. They were mostly kids in their early to mid-twenties. Babies, really. Newborn adults.

"I am only sorry we put her in quarantine. But if the refugees get this sickness, it is a very big problem. If they cannot eat. If they are throwing up and shitting all the time—"

"I understand." I looked at the trash bag Dagmar was holding. She looked at me. It seemed only right. "May I?"

I began picking up the detritus with them, erasing the evidence of the arrivals and the tragedies—preparing the beach, I sensed grimly, for the next wave of refugees.

When we'd finished, there was a shared sense of equilibrium restored—and exhaustion. A sadness hung over me, too. We lugged our bulging bags across the tiny town square to a large trash receptacle behind one of the taverns. "Usually, we try to put the bags in the bins closer to the camp," Dagmar said, heaving hers into the container, which was nearly filled to the top. "But today, they are all filled with rafts."

Most of the inflatable dinghies were in tatters, she told me, before the refugees even made it to land. Four dozen people would be crammed aboard a raft designed for twenty—with a weak outboard motor—and simply launched into the sea. If they didn't crash on the rocks, half the time the terrified refugees would destroy the boats themselves as soon as they crossed into Greek waters, because the Turkish traffickers had claimed that the Greek authorities would use the dinghies to return them all to Turkey immediately. For the passengers without life vests, quite literally, it was sink or swim. And many of the women and children, Dagmar said pointedly, had never been taught to swim.

Ashley and Austin had, of course, grown up playing Marco Polo in the lake right behind our subdivision. *Michigan, the Great Lakes State, the Water Wonderland.* Right there on our license plates.

I stared at the rubber skin of a dinghy.

The back door to the tavern kitchen swung open. A burly Greek man with tousled salt-and-pepper hair and a sweat-stained checkered shirt waved us in. "Yassas, yassas, kalispera. Come, come. Parakalo."

"Hey Kostas. Kalispera, Kostas." The volunteers gripped his hands in both of theirs vigorously. The kitchen was full of clatter and steam, an engine running to full capacity. Kostas led us through it to a wooden table wedged between the prep counter and the bar area. A few volunteers quickly foraged some stray chairs and hoisted them over their heads, assembling them for all of us to sit in. I needed to get back to check on Ashley—but I was so tired all of a sudden. My back was sore, my skin exfoliated with wind and salt. The jet lag was hitting me. Then my internal heat lamp came on. I just needed to sit a minute.

Kostas set two enormous carafes of water on the table before us with a stack of glasses. I gulped one, two, three down in rapid succession. I poured myself a fourth. He returned with a large basket of crusty bread—Oh! Food! Thank you!—and another large carafe for us. As he set it directly before me, the afternoon sun hit the beveled glass. A beam refracted off of it in a blaze of gold, the liquid inside winking.

White wine.

Like pale sun. Like liquid music. Philippe, the French volunteer sitting beside me, grabbed the carafe by its neck and began pouring out glasses mechanically and passing them around to all the volunteers.

The wine smelled crisp and lemony with just the faintest, faintest whiff of sharpness beneath it.

"Yamas!" people saluted around me. "Yamas! Santé. Probst. Nostrovia. Chin-Chin." Did I hear someone say "l'chaim" as well? One by one, the volunteers held up their glasses and swallowed, tossing their heads back with abandon, exposing their young, glistening throats to the air.

I looked down.

I set the glass on the table. *Leave. Immediately.* But I remained rooted in my chair and threw my arm over the back of it so I might appear relaxed and casual and not like I was fixating on the wine.

Philippe poured a second round. Everyone toasted again. "Yamas!"

"I love the local wine here," somebody said.

"Yes, it is so light but delicious," said someone else. "I could drink it all day. It would help with the cleanups." It was like a Greek chorus. *Was someone actually paying them to say this stuff?*

I picked up my glass. I could just have a sip. Just hold it in my mouth like a breath. Hell, I'd just put in almost forty hours of panic-fueled travel across the globe to rescue my child. And before that: A night in a homeless shelter. A Tennessee jail. Getting punched in the face. And even just a few minutes ago: I'd nearly pulled out my back picking up some of the world's most tragic garbage. Didn't all of this merit one lousy sip of wine? Why, it barely even looked like wine, it was so faintly colored. For all I knew, Kostas had watered it down completely.

I held it to the light, drew it to my mouth. Perfume. Liquid joy. Think of how fleeting life was. The evidence was all around me.

Don't do this, Donna. You need to stay clearheaded. For Ashley.

"Pas du vin?" Philippe frowned as I set my glass back down.

I looked at him squarely. "I can't." I stood up. "My name is Donna Koczynski, and I'm an alcoholic."

Inga's voice came from the other end of the table: "Oh, that's okay. Stay. We have no pressure here."

A young man in the group named Amir, with a dark puff of hair and a wisp of a mustache, patted the tabletop in front of him. "I do not drink alcohol either. You can drink water with me, my friend."

"Stay, Donna," came a chorus. I looked at the bright assorted faces around the table, open, kind, then at the wine glistening.

A cry rose from the kitchen. Through the archway I could see that a young sous-chef had dropped her knife and was shaking her left hand.

This was excuse and cover enough. "Sorry, folks. Emergency. Out I go." Hastily, I beat a retreat toward the back door. As I passed through the kitchen, I saw the sous-chef sucking on her index finger. Tearily, she picked up her knife again and attempted to resume chopping an enormous pile of garlic. I wanted to reprimand her for not washing her hands, but then I saw: She could not have been older than fourteen. She had no idea what she was doing. Another young sous-chef beside her—eighteen at best—was barely faring any better. He'd managed to peel only three onions, which he hadn't chopped so much as butchered. Glancing around the kitchen at the people bent over their work, I saw a motley mix of old and young, Greek and foreign, working as fast as they could but with wildly varying degrees of ability. Some wore frilly gingham aprons printed with daisies or watering cans or chickens. A woolly-haired older Australian woman I'd seen in the square earlier was wearing one that had a print of Michelangelo's *David* sculpture from the neck down. They were not preparing à la carte, made-to-order restaurant meals at all, but vast quantities of soup, bread, rice, spinach, some in enormous thirty-quart aluminum pots; the cooks had to stand on footstools over the stove in order to stir them with industrial-sized paddles. Some of this food was, in fact, being plated and handed over to the waiter at the tavern. But at the stainless counter along the far wall, an assembly line had been set up to pack it into little aluminum takeaway containers, which were then being hauled out to the parking lot by the dozens in large blue plastic IKEA bags.

I looked at the young girl mincing garlic. She appeared to be on the verge of tears. "May I?" Not sure how good her English was, I motioned to the knife, then pointed at her to go wash her hands in the sink. When she returned, I grabbed a head of garlic and ran my nail along the natural seams delineating the cloves, showing her how to remove them without clawing through all the thick layers of skin. Taking the side of the knife, I lay it flat across a lone clove of garlic, and pressed down firmly until we heard a decisive crunch. "See?" I held out the now-peeled clove to her. By this time, the young guy next to her had stopped futzing with his onions and was looking on, too.

I held up my finger. "Next, we do this." I showed her how to mince quickly and evenly.

"See?" I repeated the technique slowly, then handed her the knife. "Now you try." She looked at me uncertainly. "Don't worry." I smiled at her.

With a look of fervent concentration, she followed what I had shown her, step-by-step. It daunted her to press down on the knife blade, but when she'd minced the clove successfully, her face shone.

"Hey," I called out generally to the kitchen, "is there another knife somewhere?"

The Australian woman hurried past me in oven mitts, carrying an enormous tray of bread, and barked, "In the drawer over there by the sink."

I retrieved a knife and began chopping garlic alongside the young girl. "What's your name?" I shouted over the music.

"Ayisha." She pointed to herself. "What is your name?"

"I am Donna," I said and pointed to myself.

"Donna," she said carefully, in the exacting way of someone unaccustomed to speaking a language, testing it out gingerly. "Where do you come from, Donna?"

"America. Where do you come from, Ayisha?"

"I come from Syria."

"Oh." All the breath went out of me. What the hell was I supposed to say to that? *Oh, that's nice?*

Ayisha motioned to the boy beside her. "His name is Bashir."

Bashir wore little wire-rimmed glasses and had thick brown tooth-brush-bristle hair. I gathered he was her brother.

"Hello, Bashir." We smiled at each other dumbly until something occurred to me. "Merhaba?" I said. "Al Salaam Alekum?"

He smiled suddenly. "You speak Arabic?"

"A little." I tried to think of anything else I could remember from my cooking demos. "Shukron. Ma'ah Salama."

Ayisha giggled, though the boy looked amazed. "How do you learn Arabic?"

"In America, I live near a city called Dearborn. Lots of Arab people live there. Sometimes, for my work, I cook for them."

"You cook Arab food?"

"A little. Kibbeh. Labneh."

"Oh, you make kibbeh? I like kibbeh!" He said something to the girl in Arabic and she smiled at me and pointed to herself, parroting, "I like kibbeh."

We grinned at one another, nodding awkwardly. It became clear: That was the extent of our repertoire. We returned to our cutting boards.

It felt good to mince up garlic. *Smash—fwip!—thup thup thup.* With each press of the knife, I worked out some aggression, some fear. *Smash—fwip!—thup thup thup.*

"Wow, you are very good. You are like a machine," Bashir said.

"Yeah, well. Here"—I pointed to his cutting board—"do you want me to show you the best way to chop an onion?"

Moving over, I demonstrated for him. Eventually, his pace picked up considerably. I chopped onions in tandem with him until my eyes were stinging, then returned to help Ayisha again with the garlic. Through the doorway, I noticed the sun lowering behind the mountains. I needed to get back to Ashley.

At the sink, I rinsed off my hands while the older Australian woman squeezed an enormous bottle of dish soap over an oily tray. "Well, my word, love. You're good," she said, angling the tray under the faucet, reaching for the sprayer. "Are you a professional chef?"

I snorted. "Hardly." I glanced around for a towel of some sort. There didn't seem to be any.

"Hang on. Eleni!" She shouted across the kitchen in Greek. The woman who was Eleni pointed to a dishrag on the side of the stove. "I've told everyone a thousand times to put everything back in its place as soon as they're done with it."

"Are you the coordinator?" I asked.

Her eyes crinkled. "Ha," she said. "Only by default. Kostas and his family are overwhelmed enough." She waved her hand around the kitchen. "This place used to serve sixty diners, tops, during the height of tourist season. Now, we have three hundred to a thousand a day sometimes. They've got nowhere to go until the buses for Moria arrive. We had eighty-eight boats in twenty-four hours once—fifteen hundred people. Right here. In a village of 120 residents. Plus, we feed all the volunteers now. And the journalists—though they pay." She shrugged. "It's unbelievable."

I looked at the team by the doorway, with their hands squeezed into those condom-y food-service gloves that come in a box like tissues. They were assembling takeaway packages of rice, sautéed spinach with chickpeas, and baked cheese.

"Are you an aid worker, then?" I asked.

The Australian gave a hiccupy laugh. "Me? Ha. No, love. I used to work for Queensland Rail back in Brisbane. I retired only five months ago."

"Wow. But you flew all the way here to help out anyway?"

"Oh no. Absolutely not. I just came here on holiday to visit my cousin. To lie on the beach for a couple of weeks, and do my sudoku puzzles, and drink ouzo."

*   *   *

The sky had turned purple, a faint chill settling over the marina. Someone had lit fires inside empty oil drums for the people huddled in the square. The flames flickered against the darkening sky, turning the barrels to lanterns.

Back inside the apartment, I found Ashley sprawled on the daybed, tangled in one of the blankets, listlessly thumbing through a *Hello!* magazine I'd bought during my layover in London. Something about the room looked altered; she'd draped one of the sheets, I realized, over the wall full of sailor and clown paintings. She was wearing some of my new clothes now—a pair of black leggings and a plum-colored, button-down shirt. The shirt was far too big on her and preposterously dark and chic for Skala Sikamineas. It made her look like a little girl playing dress-up. A dirty mug sat on the nightstand, along with a wet little mountain of used tea bags, biscuit wrappers, wadded tissues, empty water bottles, crumbs, and tubes of hand cream and moisturizer from my toiletry bag. Clearly, she was on the mend: She was not only eating again, but making a mess in a room that didn't seem to be capable of being messier.

As soon as I came in, she sat up. "Oh my God, Mom! Where were you? I was totally freaking out."

I had two of the takeaway meals with me in their little aluminum boxes. I set them on the table. I'd hoped Ashley would be capable of eating at least some of the rice and the bread.

"I wasn't far," I said. "Didn't you see the note?"

"Yeah, but, I got up at like, five, and now, it's almost seven. And I don't have a phone, and I couldn't go out to look for you, because you have the key, and I didn't know where you were, or when you were coming back, or even if you were okay."

"Ashley, we're in a tiny village on the edge of nowhere. There are exactly two streets. We have no car. Where would I go?"

She stared at me at moment, "You could've drowned."

I gave a sad little smile. "Only in garlic."

But she made a face and her eyes welled up and her chest started to heave.

"Oh, Ash." My daughter: What she lacked in humor, she certainly made up for in melodrama. I dropped down beside her and squeezed her shoulder. Slowly, I began rubbing her back the way I used to when she was little, aimlessly making curlicues and shapes with my fingers, writing little words in script for her to decipher. We called this "doodling." "Mom," she used to plead when I was tucking her in at night after a bedtime story and about to switch off her Little Mermaid lamp. "Mom. Will you doodle me a little, please?"

"Mmmmm," she said now, closing her eyes. She smelled of the Pantene shampoo I'd bought back in the US. The only light in the room was from a fluorescent tube over the sink. The studio was growing indigo in tandem with the sky beyond the windows. After a moment, Ashley turned to me sleepily.

"So what were you doing in town anyway?"

She readjusted her position, curling up kittenishly with her head on my lap.

"Well, among other things—" I traced a heart and a flower between her bony shoulder blades. "I emailed your dad to let him know you're all right."

She sat up with a jerk.

"You didn't tell him about Poz, did you?"

I looked at her and sighed. *Really?*

"No, Ash. I did not get into the details of your love life. I just told him the trivial stuff. You know, like, that you're alive. And that you're no longer trapped in a refugee camp with no money and no passport and a high fever and projectile vomiting."

She blinked at me uncertainly.

"But of course, since you think the fact that you hooked up with a Serbian airplane mechanic is what's really relevant here," I said, "I suppose I could figure out some way to alert him."

"Hey! Now you're just teasing me, Mom." But she put her head down on my lap again and snuggled in, presenting her back to me again to resume doodling. "The thing is," she said after a moment, "I know that it's retro, and totally feeds into that meme of 'Daddy's little girl' and patriarchy. But for some reason, having Dad know about my sex life just really creeps me out."

"You know, sweetie," I said, exhaling at the ceiling, "I somehow don't think your father minds being spared the details of it either at this particular moment."

"Yeah." Ashley closed her eyes. She snuggled in closer. "He's just not as open-minded and progressive as you are, Mom."

Chapter 19

IT WAS BARELY DAYBREAK when I awoke at Dina's the next morning. After a moment, I gave myself a quiz:

You wake up at five o'clock in the morning in some Greek widow's converted utility room—on a remote island in a foreign country—completely disoriented—and your mind is running like a gerbil on a wheel. What do you do?

    a. *Obsessively watch your nineteen-year-old daughter sleep, monitoring the accordion of her breath for three hours—just like you did when she was an infant.*
    b. *Get up and do something.*

Ashley's forehead was cool and dry; it was safe enough to leave her. Dressing hastily, I left her with a note (and various medicines—and, okay, a pair of my new, embarassingly-large-on-her underwear). Then I hurried quietly down the porch steps and through the vine-tangled garden.

The dawn was enchanting. Oddly, I'd never envisioned tragedies in living color before. It was incomprehensible that they could ever occur in places of astonishing beauty. Back in middle school, watching the grainy film clips of World War II and Vietnam, it was impossible to imagine that maybe, just maybe, the hillsides surrounding Auschwitz were sometimes sequined with wildflowers in springtime, or that soldiers in Da Nang were disemboweled on opalescent beaches fringed with mango trees. Even September 11: The towers were fixed in my memory only in striations of black and white, engulfed in gunmetal-gray smoke.

Yet in Skala Sikamineas, the sun was just rising over the mountains, violet silhouettes against a blush dawn. Trees rustled; the wind smelled of oleander and rosemary and sea salt; the crinkly rhythm of the waves on the pebbled beach in the distance was its own sort of music. As I headed toward the road, the village seemed distilled in peace with its little red-roofed houses nestled amid the foliage like gifts. As I drew closer to the port, the ground grew lumpy with bodies sleeping huddled together on the flagstones. Bodies everywhere, snoring, wheezing, quietly sobbing. Deflated rafts were heaped on the roadside like pelts.

Kostas's tavern appeared closed, but when I walked around to the back door, I could see that Eleni and Cathy and a handful of other volunteers were already scrubbing down the countertops.

"Kalimera. Need some help?" I picked up a rag.

"Please. Parakalo," Eleni said. "Coffee?" Without waiting for my answer, she handed me a cup.

"This is Donna, the woman from yesterday," Cathy announced to the others. I recognized Amir, Philippe, and Dagmar's girlfriend, Inga, among them. "She's the one who prepped ten kilos of onions in a blink of an eye."

"Hardly. You make me sound like a samurai."

"Oh, but you are. You're a human food processor. Lady Chop-Chop," Cathy teased. "That's what we're calling you from now on, love."

Kostas tromped into the kitchen. "Seventeen boats came in last night."

"What?" I hadn't meant to speak out loud. "More people already?"

Kostas's eyes flicked to me, but he didn't bother answering. He massaged the bridge of his nose. "One bus just left, but it means we have, what is the count?"

"The estimate is six hundred ten," said Amir. "Give or take fifty."

Kostas shook his head. "In Molyvos, they got ten, fifteen new boats, too.

So Irina's restaurant, she has no food to spare. I speak to Andreas, over in Vafeios. He says they can bring one hundred fifty, two hundred meals. They start cooking this morning. But the people who just arrive, some have not eaten for two days, they say. The children, they are fainting."

An African American woman with gray hair and red glasses appeared in the doorway. I'd seen her the day before sitting at the café. "Hey everyone. Yassas. For those of you who don't know me yet, I'm Selena. I seem to be coordinating the meal distribution this week. Kostas, Cathy?" She turned to face them directly. "Do we have any word yet from the ministry, or UNHCR, or anyone?"

A conversation ping-ponged between volunteers. No outside help seemed to be forthcoming from any of the international agencies yet. "You're kidding," I heard myself say. "Not even the Red Cross?" We were it? Nothing but a bunch of overextended locals and retirees on holiday and tattooed European anarchists and shmucks like me?

"The local officials here in Lesvos do not even come," Eleni said bitterly. She glared at her husband as if he were somehow personally responsible.

"Come." Kostas led us to a stack of crates. "The farmers today, they bring more spinach. We have onions, garlic. Andreas, he brings feta. But not enough. We will be needing protein."

"Is there any fish?" I nodded toward the port.

An uneasy silence came over the group.

"The refugees won't eat it," said Inga.

"Nor will the Greeks," Selena said quietly. She leaned in, whispering. "Everyone here thinks the fish are poisoned."

I frowned. "From the motor oil in the water?"

"No." She shot a pained look at Amir. "From the bodies."

My coffee cup went heavy in my hand.

Kostas and Eleni began arguing about what to make with the ingredients they had. "We are not making spanakopita today, Kostas. It is crazy," his wife said. "It is too much work. Too much time."

"But soup and rice, soup and rice. Every day. The same thing. *This* is making *me* crazy." Kostas tapped the side of his head. "It is bad for everybody. Bad for morale."

"I think we're all just happy to eat," Inga said quietly.

Amir added, "As long as there is no pork. Food is food. We are all grateful."

"Everyone who comes to Skala Sikamineas should eat Greek traditional cooking!" Kostas said vehemently. He turned to us like a jury. "You do not know our language, but you can eat our food. Greek food is best in the world."

Spanakopita. Good God: Did anyone have, say, six or seven hours to kill in a kitchen obsessively rolling filo dough and de-stemming spinach and watching a clock? Back in Michigan, I'd attempted to make spanakopita myself a few times to demonstrate the Privileged Kitchen's Silicone All-Purpose Pastry Brush ($8.95 in either lime green, mocha, or paprika!) and its best-selling patented No-Stick Bakery Pans ($15.99–$32.99, depending on the size; dishwasher-friendly!). The filo dough alone required an insane amount of rolling and kneading over and over—really, it was like an aerobics class—and once it was done, you had to carefully layer together eight sheets of it, buttering each one. And then the filling itself was a whole other enterprise. I'd used the Privileged Kitchen Choppity-Chop Chopper ($49.99) on enormous bags of prewashed, prebagged spinach. But even with these shortcuts, in the end, spanakopita proved way too elaborate and labor-intensive for demonstrations. I'd had to come up with a much faster alternative.

"I have an easy pita bread recipe. It doesn't even use yeast, so it takes no time. We could just make pita and stuff it with the spanakopita filling instead," I suggested.

Kostas frowned. "You mean we make *sandwiches*?"

"Well, pita *pies*."

"Ha," said Selena. "Spanako-pita."

"That is not the traditional Greek way."

"True," Cathy interjected. "But Kostas, they eat pita in the Middle

East. So for the refugees, it would be a little bit of home, but with a Greek twist. That might be a nice way to welcome everybody."

"Okay. Lady Chop-Chop," Kostas said as he pointed at me. "You're in charge of pita pies then. I show you flour."

"Hang on." I'd only planned to be in the kitchen an hour or so. I needed to get back to Ashley.

"Can you do three, four hundred by noon? We need as many as you can make. Now," Kostas said, turning to the others, "Amir and I, we need three strong people to help carry boxes."

I looked at the ovens warming, then at the lumps of sleeping bodies beyond the kitchen. Kostas had let the refugees with children sleep inside on the floor of his tavern. The days were sunny, but the nights cold.

Fuck it. Yeast-free pita wouldn't take very long to teach. "Okay, folks," I said in my shiny, Privileged Kitchen demo voice, "who wants to make pita bread with me?"

Inga and a half dozen others assembled.

I'd like to say that I simply showed them how to make the bread, set the kitchen in motion, and voilà. But has anyone in the history of the universe ever cooked like that? Hell, the first time I ever did a demo at the Bloomfield Hills Mall, I'd set my hair on fire. And I wasn't even drunk.

All the measurement utensils in Kostas's kitchen were metric. And the oven was in Celsius. Plus, for all my experience in America, I had no idea how to communicate to people who were not native English speakers. Apparently, I talked way too fast. Apparently, I was also a little exhausting.

It didn't help that I kept glancing at my watch, then up toward Dina's, either.

And so, I fucked up the first test batch. The second batch was not something you'd want to serve to people who'd just barely survived drowning at sea, either. Finally, though, with input from the whole group, we got it right. Eleni and I set up a prep team for the pita, while

Kostas and his team hauled in crates of spinach, onions and garlic, and buckets of feta.

"Lady Chop-Chop, can we get you over here now, love?" Cathy called from the prep counter. "Would you show these kind people here how you cut up all those onions yesterday?"

A line of volunteers stood at the ready with cutting boards and knives of various sizes and quality. Ten minutes, tops: I'd just have to do enough to get a rhythm going. As I began to demonstrate the French way to cut onions, a man appeared; he'd slept in the tavern. He had light brown skin and a thick black mustache and a woeful, insistent gaze. What held my attention most, however, were his long, slender hands, covered with tiny burns and scars—and the fact that he was dressed, incongruously, in a suit jacket but plastic flip-flops. Seeing me, he motioned, first to himself, then to the cutting boards.

"You want to help?" I made room for him beside me. We were running low on knives; I gave him our last one.

Smiling, bowing his head slightly, he picked up the knife and went *thwup-thwup-thwup-thwup*, then scraped the chopped onion into the collection bowl with a single, graceful motion. One, then another, then another. The others stopped to watch.

"Wow. You're really good. What's your name?" But he just smiled at me uncomprehendingly.

"Do you speak Arabic?" I said. "*Merhaba?*"

He shrugged apologetically, then held up his hand implying I should wait. Disappearing into the restaurant area, he returned with a boy who looked to be ten or eleven, wearing muddy jeans and a bright athletic shirt reading ARSENAL. "Hello," the boy said in a singsongy voice. "My father says you speak English. He does not. He only speaks Pashto, Farsi, and Dari."

I laughed. "Oh, *only* three languages." The boy, however, did not seem to understand I was joking.

"We are from Afghanistan," he said. "Where are you from? Are you Greek?"

"No. I am American. My name is Donna."

"She's 'Lady Chop-Chop,'" Cathy called out, plunking down another crate of onions, then heading back down to the pantry.

"Oh, because my father," said the boy, "he would like to thank all Greek people. He would like to tell all Greek people that he is so happy that we are safe here in Greece."

"When did you arrive?"

He looked confused.

"Oh. My family. We walk."

"Excuse me?"

"We walk from Kabul," he said very matter-of-factly.

I stopped chopping and looked at him. "You walked from Kabul to *here*?"

"We walk from Kabul to airport," he said.

"Oh, I see," I said with a smile.

"We fly to Tehran. Then from Tehran, we walk to Turkey."

Tehran was in Iran, wasn't it? How far was that from Turkey? It had to be hundreds of miles. I stared at him dumbly.

"It take three months because we walk over mountains but can only go at night. Or they shoot at us. And my sister, she get sick. We walk across Turkey. Then, from Turkey, we take boat here."

I put down an onion. "I'm so sorry," was all I could think to say.

"Why are you sorry, my friend? We are here. We are safe now. My mother. Last night, she sleep on floor here. This morning, she wake up. She say, Massoud, for first time in two years, I sleep well. For first time in two years, I dream."

The whole time Massoud and I were speaking, his father was chopping onions single-mindedly. Tears were streaking down his cheeks and catching in his mustache. Wiping his eyes on his sleeve, he said something to Massoud to translate.

Massoud said to me, "My father, he is so happy to be cooking again. Back in Kabul, he have restaurant."

Massoud's father's name was Safi. Between the two of us, we got the volunteers prepping like a well-oiled machine of sous-chefs. As it turned out, we didn't need any words to communicate at all.

As soon as I could, though, I wrapped up two pita pies and hurried back up the hill to Dina's. I could imagine how distraught Ashley would be if she'd already woken up. As I climbed the steps to the porch, I saw, guiltily, that our landlady had left breakfast for us on a paint-smudged tray on the rickety little table outside. Beneath a netted dome to ward off the flies were slices of bread, fruit salad jeweled with pomegranate seeds, containers of Greek yogurt, two soft-boiled eggs. *Well, at least someone here won't starve*, I thought grimly.

The door, to my surprise, was open. Inside, the utility room had the stale, yeasty smell of a sick room, mixed with the mildew from the walls and a frenzy of flies already swirling overhead. Yet Ashley was awake, newly showered and animated, lying with her feet propped up on the rails of the daybed, talking happily into a bright little screen. My useless American smartphone had somehow come back to life.

"Hang on," she said to it. "Hey Mom, I'm Skyping Mia. Wanna say hi?" She flashed the phone in my direction. I caught a glimpse of black hair and eyes, a hand waving halfheartedly in a rectangle. Mia was Ashley's best friend back at the University of Michigan.

"You got my phone to work?" I sat down heavily on the edge of the trundle bed and pulled off my boots.

"Yuh-uh. When Dina came with our breakfast, I asked if she had an adapter for your charger. And there's Wi-Fi here. The password's taped to the outlet. You can't make calls on this. But if there's Wi-Fi, we can get internet." She turned back to the screen, where Mia's voice was saying, "Yeah, so now, we're all signing this petition, and the department chair is totally freaking out."

"Oh my God. Shut up. I can't believe Blake said that in the first place. That is so totally sick."

"Ashley," I said.

She must have sensed my annoyance, because she said quickly, "Hey, sorry, Mi. I think I have to go."

When she hung up, she tossed the phone on the bed and stretched and yawned extravagantly.

"Well, you seem better," I said.

"Oh, totally. Oh my God. I am like a whole new person." Standing on one foot, she reached behind her and grabbed her ankle, then extended her other arm until she stood poised before me like an exotic bird. "I hope you don't mind, I ate some fruit salad already and the fresh orange juice."

"No, no, that's good. Can you manage an egg or some of the yogurt, too, maybe? You need protein, Ash."

She wrinkled her nose. "Vegan, remember?"

I looked at her and sighed. "I brought a spinach pita-pie for you. I can vouch that the bread doesn't have any dairy in it."

She took the pie off the counter and wandered out onto the porch behind me. I sat down at the little table and reached for the soft-boiled egg in its cup and began to tap it hard—too hard—with the side of the spoon.

I looked down toward the marina. All the little fishing boats did, in fact, remain moored. What were the locals going to eat if all the fish was, in fact, poisoned?

Ashley tore open the pita and poked at it suspiciously.

"Sorry, Mom, but this whole thing is, like, tainted with feta."

Making a face, she scraped out the spinach filling disdainfully, then raked the tines of her fork through it to ferret out the little cheese cubes and quarantine them to one side.

I had the overwhelming impulse to grab her plate suddenly and break it over her head—wasn't breaking plates a Greek tradition, in fact? Well, maybe this was how it really started—not with a wedding celebration or Zorba the Greek—but with some indolent teenage vegan picking feta cheese out of her spinach pie. The last time I'd smashed a dish had been the morning I'd caught Joey with his mistress. The ceramic pineapple utensil holder: It had been so satisfying to hurl it against the wall. Then I saw myself again, beating Joey with the fish spatula. During not one of these times had I been drunk. Even sober, I could be dangerous around kitchenware.

I was a woman capable of great violence, I realized. It was hot within me, part of my intrinsic genetic fabric, lurking just below the surface. I had never really thought of myself this way before. But there it was. Was it the loss of my mother—or my crazy, aggressive father—or just part of *me*, my being alive? Who the hell knew. But how could I not have recognized it before? All that punk rock, with its belligerence, the slam-dancing and spitting, the screaming into a microphone. I sure as hell wasn't a folksinger. I sure as hell wasn't Barbara Mandrell. Even that night in the Tennessee jail, threatening those meth-heads. I was a perimenopausal woman performing yoga on the floor, but they'd seen something in my eyes that they recognized and drew back from.

I sat back in my chair. "Wow," I whistled.

"What?"

That night at Zack's, too. When Janine had punched me in the face, I'd stumbled back and doubled over. But then, I recalled suddenly, I hadn't simply stepped away. Instinctively, I'd straightened up and lunged back at her, smacking her on the shoulder, feebly pulling her hair. How had I forgotten this? There was a reason I hadn't pressed assault charges. There was a reason I had been speeding away from Murfreesboro.

"Hey Mom?" Ashley was, in fact, eating the cleaned-off pita bread now, tearing it off and shoving bits in her mouth. "I checked online, and there are flights back to Athens from Lesvos five times a day. I'm not sure we can get one this afternoon. But do you think maybe tomorrow?"

"Excuse me?"

"I was thinking. Maybe, after getting a new passport, instead of going back to London, I could return to Michigan with you instead? I don't know if U-M would take me back mid-semester, but we could see. I could room with Mia, she says."

I set my spoon down. I gazed at my daughter. "We're not going back to Athens, Ashley." I reached for a piece of bread, broke it.

"What?"

"I had to pay three nights up front for this room. And you seem to be a lot better now. So we're going to stay put for a little while."

"Are you serious?" Ashley set down her swatch of pita. "But Mom. I was just, like, really, really sick. I'm still totally weak."

"Well, you certainly seem well enough now. Well enough to eat, and to figure out how to get internet service. And to make plans to protest back in Michigan."

"But?" She stared at me. "I don't even have a passport or ID here! Mom, trust me. That is *not* okay in this environment."

I picked up another piece of bread, tore it off, dipped it into the egg yolk. "I emailed Dad and Austin asking them to scan a copy of your birth certificate. So that should help."

"Are you kidding?"

"You're hardly the first person to have her passport stolen, Ash. Kostas told me that if we file a report with the police nearby, they'll give you a document you can use as ID here until we make it back to Athens."

"Seriously?"

"Dealing with the police isn't my first choice either. But we'll be able to stay here at least and keep volunteering. I don't have a lot of money, but this seems a worthy cause, doesn't it? We'll finish what you started. *Together.*"

"But I don't even have shoes, or hardly any clothes. I've had only one pair of underwear for six days."

I looked at her oddly. "I'd thought you'd want to stay."

She glared at me, her face going red. "Yeah, but I haven't eaten in like, days, and I don't have my meds—"

"Well then," I said flatly. "I guess we'll both just be in recovery."

"Mom! That's not funny."

I picked up my spoon and set it down with a clatter. "No, it's not funny, Ashley," I said. "It's not funny at all. But you were the one who wanted to come here. You were the one tweeting about this for, like, months—and you were the one who snuck off to Greece without telling anyone. So guess what, sweetie? You've talked the talk? Well, now you're going to walk the walk, as they say."

She looked at me with open hatred. "Oh my God. You're forcing me to stay here, now, like a hostage? You're punishing me?"

"Wow." I stopped. "*I'm* punishing *you*?" My hands were shaking. "You scare the living daylights out of us—your father and I have to borrow thousands of dollars from Arjul—so I can fly halfway around the world at a moment's notice to get you out of quarantine? In a refugee camp? Oh, and make sure you have medicine? And clothes?"

"Okay, what I meant—"

"And the whole time, we are worried sick about you? Your dad and I are wondering, 'How high is her fever? Could she go into a coma? Who robbed her? Was she beaten up? Or worse?' But I guess you're right. I guess I'm just 'totally punishing' you. I'm an absolute monster."

Now it really did take all the self-discipline I possessed not to throw something—and there was so much junk, so many willing objects in that damn utility room.

"But Mom. It's just..." Ashley began weakly. Yet she knew she didn't have a case and she stopped.

"It's just *nothing*." I snatched up the phone and my bag and the card Thodoris had given me with his number and email scrawled on the back. "Take something out of my suitcase and get yourself dressed. *Now*."

Chapter 20

AFTER MY DEALINGS IN Dickson, Tennessee, the last place I wanted to visit—anywhere—was a police station. The one in Molyvos, at least, looked like a retirement villa with a terra-cotta roof and a few cats mewling around. I half expected a Greek grandmother—a *ya-ya*, as Thodoris called his—to wave us inside and offer us a few dry cookies on a plate.

Inside, a powder of boredom had, in fact, settled over the place. As soon as Ashley and I walked in, the one officer on duty jumped up from his desk, overly solicitous, and began straightening his shirt.

"I am sorry, my English, she is not so good." He introduced himself as "Officer Vanis," then offered Ashley a seat as if he were a maître d'. "Please, *parakalo*. Would you like coffee?"

Okay. Clearly we weren't in Tennessee.

He asked Ashley a few polite questions concerning her stolen passport and wallet, jotting down her answers on a lined notepad in Greek. "I am very, very sorry," he said, shaking his head. "Lesvos has always been very safe island. But now, with all the refugees, many people getting robbed. My neighbor, some refugees take clothes off her clothesline. Pants and socks, they steal. She sees one man wearing her husband's shirt."

He looked at Ashley sympathetically. "We can make raids of camps, check papers, try to arrest, but too many people. Too many people coming and going to catch the criminals. The ones who robbed you, do you maybe know if they are from Iraq? Pakistan? Syria?"

Ashley looked down at her lap, then at me. She fixed me in an unreadable gaze.

"It wasn't a refugee," she said almost inaudibly. "Refugees didn't steal my stuff."

"Ash?"

Officer Vanis frowned. "You know this for fact?"

She gazed into the middle distance now. "It was this guy I met on the ferry. A Serbian. Him and his friend. They came with a car. They took some other people's stuff, too. And a box of medical supplies from the camp."

At first I thought maybe my daughter was attempting to deflect the blame, shield the most vulnerable population on the island. But no. I could see it in her face. *Of course.* The Balkan Romeo. It made total sense now. I should've figured it out sooner, in fact. Where the hell was my brain? Suspended somewhere in the airspace between Memphis and Lesvos, I supposed.

"Your boyfriend, he robs you?" Officer Vanis looked at Ashley, his face transforming into something less forgiving. I could feel him reassessing her, us, his judgment accumulating. *Oh no you don't*, I thought.

"For what it's worth, Officer, he sounded like a real operator," I interjected. "He pretended to be a volunteer, targeted my daughter, romanced her—"

"Jesus, Mom. Really?"

But Officer Vanis had already sized her up: her clothes, her age, her femaleness, of course. Already, we'd gone from being tourists to "whore" and "mother of whore."

He frowned. "You have name of this boyfriend?"

"Um, Poz?" She rotated her wrists.

"That is it?"

Ashley's face reddened. She stared at the floor again.

"It could happen to any of us, Officer." I gave him my most winning smile. "You know what it's like when you're young. When you think you're in love."

I held his gaze as if challenging him to a duel. But smiling, still smiling. *See, Joey, this is what we women go through.*

Though his disapproval was still on full display, the officer sighed and massaged his own neck and looked over at his dusty computer. "I can make for you official report. For customs here at airport and for American embassy. But?" He shrugged in a way that made it clear that neither Ashley's belongings nor Poz would ever be tracked down. "You have to be careful," he scolded. "Bad people come here to take advantage. They steal from the volunteers. Make big black market for passports." He turned to me. "They steal from refugees, too. Even at sea. Pirates stop the rafts, tell the refugees they will drown everyone if they do not hand over all their valuables. So everybody, they come and steal from everybody. So do not be so friendly with strange men. Do not wave your purses and jewelry around. You girls must be very careful, do you understand?"

Jewelry? Girls? With beleaguered motions, Officer Vanis printed out the report, stamped a copy, signed it, and handed it over to us. "Enjoy Lesvos."

When we got back outside, Ashley chewed her lip and stared down at the ground. She looked as if she was about to cry.

I snorted. "Well, that wasn't at all sexist or condescending." But Ashley didn't even smile faintly. It was clear now that there was still a lot she was withholding from me, but I couldn't force the information out of her. Certainly not there, not then. We were living together in a utility room in a Greek village with exactly two streets. There would be time. "Shall we at least get you some clothes?"

Ashley glanced around miserably. "I can't believe that we're just going to go shopping now."

"Yeah. Well." Molyvos was a charming medieval town; its cobbled streets, which wound all the way down the mountainside to the sea, were dotted with ice cream parlors, handicraft boutiques, and souvenir stands with bins of garish T-shirts and plastic swimming shoes. But as Thodoris drove us in along the town's waterfront, we'd passed scores of refugees who'd just arrived, trudging up from the harbor with the remains of their possessions.

"It's like on the airplanes, Ashley," I sighed. "They always say to put your own oxygen mask on first before helping anyone else put on theirs."

She crossed her arms. "Jesus, Mom. How many times are you going to keep telling me that? You say the same thing over and over."

I came to a standstill in the middle of the street. "You know some-thing," I said suddenly. "You can just keep wearing Dagmar's flip-flops if you want."

"You'd like that, wouldn't you? To keep humiliating me."

"Excuse me? I just stuck up for you back there, Ash. I didn't berate you for not telling me before that Poz was the one who stole your stuff."

"Well, you're berating me for it now." She chewed her lip, refusing to look at me. After a moment, she added softly, "I just feel so *stupid*." She twisted her wrists around, "And now, like, I just don't want everyone thinking that we're all, like, 'Kardashian,' when everybody else here has nothing."

"*You* have nothing, Ash. You have no underwear. You have no shoes. It doesn't get much more 'nothing' than that. Trust me." I shook my head. "Nobody's going to mistake you for a reality star."

When we finally finished with our purchases and reunited with Thodoris at a café, I plopped down beside him and pressed my fists to my temples. As soon as Ashley headed off to the bathroom to change into her new clothes, I groaned, "Don't let Dimitri grow up to be a teenager. Just skip that part if you can."

"Ah, teenagers." Thodoris raised his coffee in a toast. "There is a quote. *They cut their teeth on our bones.*"

"Funny. My husband says practically the same thing. Of course," I added, "he is a dentist."

"Your husband," Thodoris said in a way that betrayed his curiosity. "He is still in America? Or does he wait for you in Athens?"

"He's home. In Detroit. With our son."

"Ah. So he is good father. How long have you been married?"

I squinted out at the sea. "Too long."

"Oh?"

Taxi drivers: They were like bartenders for sober people. A small bird soared and looped above the marina. I fixed my gaze on it. I heard myself say suddenly, "Everyone always says when they get married, 'Oh, I want to grow old with this person.' But the thing is, I somehow never really understood that meant we'd actually *age*. And our needs would change— Or how I would feel..." My voice trailed off.

Thodoris looked at me. "Stavroula and I, we fight about the best things in our life—our house, our son, our vacation. We fight about these more than the bad things. Like her father being sick? That, we never fight about. But Dimitri's christening? Now, she is inviting twenty more relatives."

He stared into his coffee for a moment. "Love, you think it is easy. That you just feel it so it will do the work for you. But it is complicated. It is very easy to misunderstand someone."

To my surprise, my eyes started to tear. "Sorry." I fanned myself. "I'm just very emotional."

He handed me a paper napkin to blow my nose in.

"Before I fall in love with Stavroula, oh, I am in love with Vasso. We are teenagers, so, all day and all night. Vasso, Vasso, Vasso. I am crazy in the head. Yelling up at window, sneaking onto beach, big fights, like Greek drama, yes? Then, I am in love with Stavroula. I am not so crazy, but I feel like I come home. I feel like my heart gets bigger, like I want to be good man. Then, we have Dimitri, and I feel whole new level of love."

"Yeah, I felt that too, with my kids." I wiped my eyes quickly with my napkin. "Though I can tell you right now, at this very moment, I am not loving my daughter so much."

"Yes, well. She is teenager! But you fly halfway around the world for her."

"Yes," I said. "That I did."

From within the restaurant, Ashley finally emerged in a pair of cheap drawstring pants and the new T-shirt we'd found on sale and the "50% Off!" powder-blue hoodie with GREECE spelled across it in an arc of white letters.

"Thanks, Mom." She handed me the shopping bag with the clothes I'd lent her stuffed inside.

"Sweetie, you look nice. Those clothes look good on you."

"It's my new look." She plunked down into her chair. "I'm calling it 'Totally cloaked in guilt.'"

Back at Dina's, she flopped facedown on the daybed again.

Standing over her, I sighed. I thought about what Thodoris had said. "Sweetie." I settled down beside her. "Do you want me to doodle you?"

A groan emanated from the pillow. "Augh. No. My stomach just really, really hurts now."

"Is it cramping again?"

She shook her head and rolled over reluctantly, shielding her eyes with her forearm. "I just want to sleep," she said to the ceiling.

"Well. Okay. But before you do," I said gently, "I'd like a little more information, please. I'd like us to talk before I head out."

Ashley propped herself up on her elbows and squinted at me. "What have you been doing all the time, anyway? You're, like, never here."

I pulled my hair back, knotted it, secured it with a band from my wrist. "Just making myself useful. It's a really bad situation here. You were right."

"Oh my God. So now *you're* out on the beach rescuing refugees?"

"No, Ash. I'm—"

She sat up. "I can't believe it. Even my mom."

"Excuse me?"

She flung herself down on the bed again and stared back up at the ceiling.

"Ashley. What's going on with you? I know you're not telling me something. What really happened with Poz?"

"I told you. It was a blur."

I sat down beside her. "Did he drug you? Is that why you're so sick? Did he have a weapon of some sort?"

"I told you. We were just on the beach."

I sighed audibly. When my son was quiet, it felt like *quiet*. Like he had nothing to say. Or was concentrating. Or was asleep. Yeah, okay, there was more to him than that—I was sure of it, in fact—which was why I was worried—all that slipping off and weird chemical fumes and that whole creative life of his that only occasionally burst through his surface like an iceberg. But Austin's silences felt like *silence*, simple, straight-forward: blank pieces of paper and purified air. Ashley's silences were the exact opposite. They were never so much silences as *moods*. Weather systems. An entire emotional language crackling like radio static. You had to know how to interpret it, how to palpate beneath the surface.

This silence now was prickly and full of turmoil and obfuscation—but also longing. It was waiting. This was a silence that said "Leave me alone," but also "Please stay" and "Please make me tell you."

"Ashley, please," I said.

After another beat, I added gently, "I'm worried. Just help me understand." Slowly, I took her hand. She didn't yield, but she didn't resist, either. I began to doodle the back of it very, very lightly. "Ash," I said quietly. "I've done all sorts of stupid and embarrassing shit myself lately. Believe me. We all lose our wallets and our phones from time to time."

"It's not that," she sniffled. "I just— It was just really awful."

"Oh, honey, tell me. I'm your mother."

Slowly, she rolled over and faced me. "Promise you won't judge?"

I nodded.

I prompted gently. "So you were on the beach. With Poz."

She sighed and looked down. "And, well, I told you, we weren't exactly sleeping."

"Yeah, that part I got, Ash. Were you, at least—" So much for not judging.

"Yes, we were *safe*. Jesus, Mom. That part, I made sure of. But the thing was?" Reluctantly, she sat up and rearranged herself on the daybed, drawing her knees up, her thin back propping against the iron frame.

"One minute, it seemed like we were alone on this section of the beach, and it was totally romantic. But then, like, all of a sudden, it was total chaos. I mean, organized, but still. All these people came running down and there was all this weird, whispery shouting, like, '*Boats, boats,*' and someone else was ordering, '*Turn off your phones so we can signal,*' and then, it was totally pitch-dark, and just one person nearby was doing Morse code with their flashlight across the water, and there are these flashes of light coming back, and these lifeguards appear—and volunteers, with water and blankets. It's my first night—I don't know anything—so I'm all like 'What can I do? What should I do?' And I want to help and I'm even excited I'm finally here, and I'm finally getting to help, you know? Some people are putting together these foil wraps that athletes sometimes get after a marathon, because it's cold at this point, and if the refugees get to us, they're going to have hypothermia. So I start helping with that."

She hugged her knees tighter and stared straight ahead. "I just have to tell this really quickly, okay? Otherwise, I won't be able to. So. There's all this commotion, and around then, I lost track of Poz, though I thought he was still nearby, helping these guys with these ropes. And then, all of a sudden, all these people start running. So I'm, like, running with them—we're running down the beach, I don't know where exactly—and one of the guys in charge has us, like, get in the water, and grab each other's arms like this"—she held up her arms to demonstrate—"to make this human chain, and we're supposed to, I guess, wait for the lifeguards as backup, to help any of the people from the dinghies who can't make it to the shore."

She shakes her head, though her eyes are far away now. "The water's not that deep—but I still have my jeans on, so they're soaking wet, and my tennis shoes, too. I took them off when I was with Poz but then put them back on when all the volunteers came, and I didn't really have time to tie them well—so they're filling with water—though one of the girls next to me who's barefoot goes, 'Ow. Shit. I think I just cut my foot.'

"And so we're standing there trying to listen to what's going on, and all I have on is my yellow T-shirt but no jacket, so I'm freezing, and then someone on one of the teams radios and people start shouting, 'Move, move! Go left!' And somehow, I guess because they've all done this before, everybody goes one way toward this splashing, but I'm sort of just standing back up on the beach. I don't know what happened, Mom, but suddenly, I just stop. Because, like, some of the boats have started to come in now, and there are all these people running past me up onto the shore, and staggering and falling, and all of a sudden, it hits me that I'm, like, in a war zone. I am, like, a part of a war. Maybe not the actual battle, but, like? Suddenly, here are all these actual people coming up on the beach. And I can see them now, because they're turning on *their* phones. And Mom, I can hear the shouting, the crying, even the sound of—" Ashley's eyes filled up; lines ran down her cheeks. She covered her face. "There were people who weren't making it—you could hear—there was this horrible screaming—And then, I was just running, Mom. Like, just running I don't even know where.

"And then, of course—" She blinked, sniffled bitterly, threw up her hands. "I barely even know where I am—or even what happened, I just feel really, really awful. I'm shivering and sweating and nauseous—that's when I finally realize. All I have on my feet are these wet socks. I lost my shoes somewhere in the water. And my phone's not in my back pocket anymore, either. And then I look around for Poz, and he's just *gone*. And then, I find out, so is his friend. And their car. And my backpack with all my stuff in it that he said he would help guard. And I just knew, Mom. I did. And then, like, duh. Sure enough. Some other people at the camp, too. Volunteers. All their bags were gone, too. And the box of medical supplies."

"Oh, sweetie."

"It was a total nightmare. And if I hadn't met him—"

I reached out to stroke her cheek, but she flinched and twisted her head away.

"And now, I can't believe you're forcing us to stay here," she said. "When I just want to go home."

Climbing off the bed, she stalked into the grungy bathroom and slammed the door—though it was misaligned and bounced back open slightly and wouldn't quite shut all the way, so she had to slam it again. I could hear the lid of the toilet seat clamp down, her sitting down on it angrily.

"Ashley? Ashley, c'mon," I said.

I waited and waited. Yet I knew what *this* silence meant. A pity party—with a Crockpot stew of righteous anger. I heard the pages of *Hello!* magazine snapping back. There was nothing more to be done at the moment. I picked up my bag and my phone and the cheap souvenir apron I'd purchased in Molyvos. On it was a picture of a mermaid and a cartoon map of the island. LOVIN' IT IN LESVOS! it said in mock Greek letters. "You know where to find me," I said.

Local farmers had trucked in cases of tomatoes, peppers, cucumbers, red onions, all dew-washed and paint-box bright. The makeshift kitchen staff was now preparing Greek salad on an industrial scale.

"Hey, Lady Chop-Chop is back," Cathy said. "Not a moment too soon. We've got a new crew in here that can use some training."

I glanced around. "Where's Safi?" The tables inside the tavern had been moved back into place. They were filled again with diners— refugees, journalists, volunteers. The only evidence that people had slept in the restaurant was a large plastic tarp pulled over a pile of blankets behind the silverware station.

"He and his family left an hour ago. They finally got onto a bus to Moria."

"Oh." I felt a stab of grief. I hadn't even gotten to say good-bye, to wish him well.

"Fingers crossed," said Cathy. "Safi has a brother in Germany, so they might have a chance."

I thought of Safi with his graceful chef's hands and ten-year-old

Massoud with his earnest smile, hoping to get asylum in the country my own grandparents had fled.

"Well, Godspeed," I said quietly. Amir was stacking boxes of milk on the counter by the coffee machine.

"Hey Lady Chop-Chop." He fist-bumped me. "Merharba."

"Merharba."

At first, I'd thought Amir was one of the anarchists. But Selena had told me no, he was a refugee from Aleppo. A newlywed. His bride had drowned on their crossing from Turkey. He'd been in Skala Sikamineas ever since, serving as a translator, helping out wherever needed, keeping vigil over the water, unable to move on. He tickled the children, played YouTube videos he'd saved on his smartphone of *World Wide Wrestling* bloopers to make them laugh, sang around the fires at night in the square. Yet his eyes looked like cigarette burns. He could not be older than twenty-two.

"Today, on George's roof, my friend, we see lots of activity on the coast," he informed me. George was a fisherman across the street. He and Amir had set up a telescope on his roof to monitor the Turkish coast and anticipate arrivals. "Many boats will come tonight."

"Okay, then," I said. I pulled out a cutting board.

"Okay then, my friend." He looked at the knife on the counter, the basket of onions. He tilted his head at me strangely. He pointed to my eye. "You are okay? Somebody hurt you, my friend?"

It took me a moment to realize that my concealer had worn off. My bruise was now lemon-lime. I shook my head. "Just an accident. Nothing at all."

"Ice, she is good. So is honey." He smiled weakly. "That is what my wife, she used, when we run out of medicine." With a small shrug, he turned away quickly and headed out to the harbor to help prepare for rescues.

All these people unmoored in the world, so vulnerable and alone.

Even my own children. There was so much of their lives I didn't know anymore. I kept thinking about Ashley that night on the beach. If she hadn't gotten robbed—or sick—I might never know now that she was even on Lesvos. And Austin, with all his mysterious comings and goings back home. Was he adrift? I should've figured things out. I should've known more.

I ducked out of the kitchen. Up the street at the hotel, I got the Wi-Fi password from the receptionist and settled myself on the steps with my phone. It was morning in the US now. The connection was weak, so I used only the audio on Skype.

"Mooomm?" Austin sounded sleepy. I pictured him in his room so far away, sitting on his bed in a grimy T-shirt, sorting through a mountain of clothes. "Hey. 'Sup?"

"Hey sweetie," I said as brightly as I could. I pinched the sides of my nose by the tear ducts.

"You guys see the real Parthenon yet?"

"Excuse me?"

"Like, not the one in Nashville."

"Oh. No, not yet."

"But Ashley's okay? I scanned her birth certificate."

"Yeah, she's okay." I exhaled. "Listen, Austin. How are *you*?"

I heard the kissing sound and metallic clink of the refrigerator door opening, ketchup and orange juice bottles rattling against one another. He was having breakfast. "I'm okay. Hey Mom. When you were in jail the other night, like, which one was it?"

"Excuse me?"

"When you made your 'one phone call,' Dad said the line got disconnected, so he didn't know where you were. He had me do a Google search of all the jails near Nashville. So I was just wondering."

The things that interested a sixteen-year-old boy. "I spent one night in the beautiful Dickson County Jail in Charlotte, Tennessee, Austin."

I heard him close the refrigerator. "Whoa. That one got pretty decent Yelp reviews, actually."

People were rating their jail time on Yelp?

Two young boys exited the mini-mart beside the hotel. They passed me speaking Arabic, their flip-flops caked in dried mud. The taller one was balancing a six-pack of bottled water on his shoulder.

"It was pretty funny, actually. I posted it on Instagram." Over the line, I heard the soft rustle of a cereal box shaking.

"Austin, you know something? The reason I got arrested was because I had your Adderall on me. The cops in Tennessee thought I was selling it. They charged me with 'Possession with intent to distribute.'"

"Oh my God, Mom. LMFAO. That is, like, *insane*." I heard a clink, a spoon dinging against the side of a cereal bowl. "I mean, that's like busting you for Red Bull."

"Well, actually, no. Adderall has the same basic molecular structure as crystal meth."

"Seriously?"

"Austin. Sweetie. You're not selling it to your friends or anything, are you? Not even, casually, like, once in a while for a test?"

"Uh, no?" he said warily. "My friends have their own Adderall."

I stared up at the impossibly blue sky. I took a deep breath. "And you're not, like huffing or anything, are you?"

"*What?*"

"A lot of times, when you've come home late, or I've been in your room collecting laundry, I've smelled these chemicals, and—it's like your sister—she's supposed to be in London, but then I find out she's in Lesvos—"

"Jesus, Mom. Why are you being like this? I'm not doing drugs. I'm not being Ashley—"

"I don't know where you are half the time, Austin. And this world, I'm seeing, it can be a really precarious place."

"Well, I don't know where you are half the time, either, Mom. Like, are you at a chicken-wing-eating contest? Or playing guitar in Nashville? Or suddenly in prison?" He said this with more than a little anger. "Are you even coming home?"

I felt my eyes tear up. "Sweetie, I just don't want to be a bad mother, you know, who forgets to pay attention. I don't want you to feel lost, or to think you can't come to me."

"Okaaay."

"How's your *Odyssey* rap going?"

I heard a faucet jerk on; Austin's voice was suddenly obscured by a static of water, then a clatter of silverware. "Uh, Mom, I'm, like, about to miss the bus."

"Oh. Oh, okay."

"Try to have a good time in Greece. My English teacher says it's awesome." His voice was gentler now.

"Okay, Austin," I said. "I love you."

"Love you, too, Mom," he said quickly.

There was an abrupt, chiming blip. After he hung up, I sat there on the steps tapping my phone against my knee. I heard a distant voice calling out something in Greek, the mournful dinging of fishing boats bobbing in the marina. *Love you too,* he'd said.

Slowly, dabbing my eyes with my apron, I dialed Brenda's number over Skype.

"Hey, milady," she said, picking up on the third ring. "Did you make it to Greece?"

"Wow. You really are psychic."

"Well, you're the only person who ever calls me on my landline."

I heard a metallic rattling in the background.

"Is this a bad time, Bren?"

She gave a fluttery laugh. "No worse than any other. I just got off a night shift in the ICU, and Eli just informed me that he's supposed to bring twenty-three enchiladas for his class luncheon today. They're doing a unit on Mexico, apparently."

"Oh good God. Twenty-three?"

"The school sent an email, I guess—"

"Two words, Bren: 'frozen food.' Get a couple of boxes of El Charrito chicken enchiladas, stick 'em in a pan, doctor 'em up with some extra cheese, and voilà. Trust me. That's how I got away with school potluck lunches for years."

"Wow. And you're a top culinary ambassador! Okay! But this isn't why you're calling. How's Ashley? Did you find her? Is she okay?"

"Well, if 'driving me crazy' means she's okay, she's okay. She wasn't assaulted in any way, which is a huge relief. Her fever seems to be gone. But even for her, she's emaciated."

"Did the drugs help?"

"Yes. Thank you so much for that, milady." Before I left Memphis, I'd called Brenda to apologize—and, well, just to talk. She, of course, was thinking clearly in ways that I was not: "Ashley's trapped in a refugee camp?" she'd said. "Okay. Make a list, you're going to want lice shampoo, scabies medication, hand sanitizer, Lomotil, dehydration tablets. Emergency antibiotics—just in case." She'd insisted on dialing in a prescription for Cipro to Walgreen's in Memphis—in my name this time! Totally legit!—for me to pick up before my flight out that evening. Since she'd once lived in London, she even advised me about British over-the-counter medications I could pick up during my layover at Heathrow, if need be. Of course, the pharmacists there at the terminal spoke English, too. But having the recommendations come from Brenda, and hearing her voice, was enormously comforting. And if Alonso Jimenez had mentioned to her that his Propecia had gone missing from her medicine cabinet, well, she didn't say.

Now I said, "Oh, Bren, we're in the middle of this global crisis. Boats and refugees are literally washing up at our feet. It's heartbreaking. It's surreal. But Ashley and I are still bickering like a mother and daughter in a shopping mall."

Brenda gave a bark of laughter. "Sorry," she said after a moment. "Sweetie, what did you expect? Look at me and my mom."

I moaned. "How *is* your mom, Bren?"

"Oh, Dr. Peebles Sr. is still her same charming self. Yesterday, I brought her a gorgeous bouquet—peach roses, stargazer lilies. She looked at me and said, 'You never did have good taste.'"

"Jesus, Bren," I joked. "What's wrong with these women in our lives? Could they just be a little more civil to us while we're helping them? It's a good thing we're not all stuck in one of these rubber rafts out here. Can you imagine?"

Brenda laughed. "My mother would be like, 'I'm sorry, lifeguard. But that's an ugly wetsuit you're wearing. Get that thing away from me!'"

"Ha! And my daughter would be like, 'Is that life preserver made from any animal products at all, because if so—'"

We both cackled.

"It's human nature." Brenda sighed. "Being rescued can be humiliating. Some people lash out."

"But Ashley called *me* for help."

"So did my callers. I saw this all the time as Madame LaShonda Peyroux. I told you how nasty some of them got afterwards. Hey," she said suddenly. "Speaking of predictions. Now that Ashley's out of the woods. We never did talk about it in Memphis. But Donna. Did you find him?"

I squinted toward the harbor, the cobalt Aegean, the amethyst coast of Turkey beyond it. Nashville felt like a wholly different dimension now. There was no one around, but I felt myself redden. "Yeah," I sighed, scratching the back of my head. "Yeah. I found him all right. Though you probably knew that."

"And? Well?"

"He's stockpiling dehydrated chicken fajitas and ammo in his bedroom closet. He hasn't paid his taxes in a decade, and his ex-wife slugged me in the face. But the sex was great and he swears that he loves me. So what could possibly go wrong?"

"Wow." She stifled a giggle.

"Oh, and did I mention? He drinks like a fish. So, put on some Prince for me when you do the 'I told you so' dance."

Just then, I heard shouting in the distance, followed by the sound of an outboard motor. The proprietor of the hotel ran down the steps past me and toward the marina. I saw figures moving beyond the trees. A commotion. A boat, it seemed, had come in. I didn't know whether to run toward the port or away from it. Given what Ashley had described, I wasn't sure how much I myself could handle. I hadn't signed up for any of this.

"Brenda, I think I better go."

At the marina, I saw Kostas and his brother had pulled in a dinghy that had been deflating at sea. No one had drowned. Some of the newest arrivals were already following Philippe and Inga down the road to the camp. Some huddled in the town square in shock, trying to remain unobtrusive as they gathered their bearings. Some headed directly up the hill for the shuttle buses to Moria. Others, improbably, found seats at the waterfront cafés and settled into tables like tourists who had just disembarked from a pleasure cruise and were now in the mood for a little alfresco lunch.

What else do you do in those very first hours when you arrive in a foreign country as a refugee or an immigrant—especially if there are no loved ones to greet you, to take you under their wing? I watched families trying to reassemble into some form of normalcy after weeks...months...years, even, of travel.

Clearly, more food was needed, but back in the tavern, I found the kitchen nearly empty; Kostas was still out with his boat. There were only a few staff now, all of them staring at the crates of produce, seemingly at a loss. No one was in charge. And, I realized, there wouldn't be. There wasn't much authority to be found in Skala Sikamineas. The world had turned its back on the village, leaving the 120 townspeople and thousands of unexpected refugees to fend for themselves. Many of the so-called anarchists who'd come to volunteer here? They were re-sponding to lawlessness, not promulgating it. They didn't feel compelled to wait for anyone's official permission to step into the breach. Work needed to be done, and they just did it. Those were the rules here: Make them. No one else would.

Who the hell ever thought anarchists would be the ones restoring law and order and saving the world?

A young blond woman with a nose ring and a lanky man with a reddish goatee were struggling to dice bell peppers. After I helped them avoid chopping their own fingers, I showed two sisters from Pakistan— refugees? Yes, refugees—the most efficient way to dice tomatoes. Then I demonstrated to some local teenagers how to peel cucumbers so they didn't cut their wrists. As the salads were being assembled, I demonstrated to everyone at the station how to best slice lemons, strain the juice into the bowl, add pinches of salt and herbs, and whisk it all furiously together with olive oil. "See," I explained as I tilted the bowl, "You get it emulsified like this."

Two Spanish volunteers had just shown up. "Hey guys, can I put you with me over on onions?"

"Ah, so you are Lady Chop-Chop." One of them grinned. "We hear about you in the camp."

"You are so fast," said the other. "You are like on television."

Yet as I began to peel away the fine, papery purple skin, the very fragility of the onion's wrapping overwhelmed me. The translucency. The delicacy of it. Why was everything beautiful and miraculous in this world so breakable, so easily crushed? The knife shook in my hand. I bent over with my hands on my knees, trying to catch my breath.

All I wanted to see was my daughter. What she had witnessed. What she had been through alone. I had a horrible premonition that when I returned to our room, I would find it locked. And that she and her things would be gone.

Dropping my knife, I yanked the strings of my apron and started to pull it off.

Then, I saw.

She was leaning against the little framed archway between the kitchen and the bar, chewing her lip, glancing about warily with her arms crossed in a way that suggested she had been there for some time.

We gazed at each other. A dark fusion. At that exact moment, Dagmar flung open the back door. "Four more boats arriving. Any volunteers?"

A sturdy young blond woman trooped in behind her with a white nylon rope coiled around her arm. "Has anyone here seen Kostas? Or Amir?"

"They're on their boat," voices chorused from the stove.

"Oh. Ashley. You are still here. Are you feeling better?" Smiling, the blond girl gave my daughter a quick, awkward half-hug. "Do you want to come to help on the beach?"

Ashley glanced at me. The girl, I deduced, was her classmate Pernille. My daughter twisted her wrists around uncertainly. "Um. The thing is?" She shifted her weight from one leg to another. "I think, I have to stay here and help my mom?"

Some of the new arrivals stood up, adjusting their clothing, eager to volunteer. A journalist picked up her camera and followed. The restaurant started to clear out as people followed Pernille and Dagmar to the wharf. It was a relief to see others go. *Please, don't let there be another tragedy,* I thought.

In the now-empty kitchen, Ashley sidled up beside me. "So, like, do you need me?" she said quietly, looking down at the half-chopped onion bleeding red on my cutting board.

I handed the knife to her. "Here. I'll go find another."

Slowly, I saw, she began making lengthwise incisions carefully across the onion as I'd demonstrated.

"Like this?"

For a couple of minutes we stood side by side, chopping onions quietly in tandem. We each began to sniffle, blot our eyes with our wrists. At the sink, we splashed cold water on our faces, then regarded each other puffy-eyed.

"Thanks for staying behind to help," I said.

"Yeah, well." She kicked at a flake of wine-dark onion skin stuck to the tiled floor. The new tennis shoes I'd bought her were cheap Converse knockoffs, but rubber-toed and solid. "You *did* come all this way, so."

I shook my head. "You know, Ash," I said quietly, "I can't imagine being in the middle of what you saw when I was nineteen. And totally alone in a strange land."

She wiped her nose, "Well, I was with Poz. And Pernille sort of."

"No. You were alone. And you were really brave, Ashley. Correction. You *are* brave. Brave and compassionate."

She blinked up at the ceiling. "I don't feel brave."

"Look. You saw a gross injustice in this world. And unlike 99.9 percent of the population, you crossed a sea to do something about it. That is a big fucking deal."

She snorted. "Yeah. But then, I get played by this guy. I get robbed and sick and I'm totally useless. That night on the beach? *Even* before the people were drowning. Mom, I was, like, totally paralyzed. I just froze up. I didn't do anything. I was just this pathetic *volun-tourist* standing there—" She made a bug-eyed zombie face. "Now, everybody knows what a baby I am. Nobody else here needed their mommy to rescue them. Nobody else here needed to have their mommy take them to the police station and buy them clothes like they were seven years old."

I tried not to laugh. I gave her a comic, incredulous look. "Nobody else here needs to be rescued, Ashley? Seriously? We're in the middle of a refugee crisis."

She couldn't help it; she looked down and smiled a little.

"I just feel so stupid and helpless," she said after a moment.

"Oh, Ash." Reaching over, I brushed a single strand of hair out of her eyes. "Everyone here feels stupid and helpless. The lifeguards. The volunteers, the Greeks, the refugees. All of us. It's a shit-show. Everyone's overwhelmed. Nobody here is a savior. Nobody's a hero. Fuck. Look at me. I'm just picking up trash and chopping onions. We're all just managing to do whatever we can." Grinning, I threw up my hands. "Welcome to anarchy."

Slowly, Ashley looked at me. She started to laugh. *You owe me $20, Joey.*

"Of course, if you ever pull a stunt like this again, I will likely kill you myself," I said. "But I am incredibly proud of you."

"You are?"

"Of course! Hell, when I was your age?"

"C'mon. You were a total punk badass, Mom."

I shook my head. "Ashley, this is the first time in my life I've ever been overseas."

We stood facing each other. A current of electricity seemed to crackle between us.

"Hey look," I said suddenly, rolling my shoulders. "Sort of off topic here, but this needs to be said. It's long overdue." I touched her cheek. "I am so sorry for ruining your thirteenth birthday party, Ashley. To this day, I cringe thinking about how I humiliated you. Mocking that gift from your friends. If I had a time machine and could go back and redo only one of the many horrible mistakes in my life, that would be it."

Ashley looked at me, then down at her feet. She let out a long, slow breath. "Thanks." She tilted her head slyly. "But you know, you were right, actually. Not what you *did*. But a $300 tracksuit? With 'Juicy' written across your ass like you're some sort of corporate billboard? How totally degrading and sexist is that? I can't believe I ever wanted that. It was, like, kiddie porn."

"Oh, sweetie. You wanted to be glamorous. And fit in."

She shook her head violently.

Wiping her nose again, she pushed herself off from the edge of the sink. Suddenly, she hugged me. Fiercely. A tight, full-body grip, completely surrendered, burying her head in the crook of my neck, her arms squeezing my waist like vines, our limbs fusing. It was the most enveloping hug I'd felt from her since she'd started puberty, in fact. It was a hug, I realized, I had dreamed of for years. Grasping her, I hugged back.

After a moment of snuffling, she murmured into my neck, "I can't believe they're calling you 'Lady Chop-Chop.' though. That is *so* lame."

But as she said it, I could tell she was smiling.

Still, more boats came. Like my daughter, however, I found I couldn't bear to go out to the beach. I didn't know how people like Amir could do it. Just one drowned child, and I'd shatter. I knew my limits by now. Or, maybe, at forty-five, well, I just didn't need to prove so much anymore. Or maybe, I was just too fucking tired.

At night, I found myself dreaming: Austin and Ashley and Eli and Lexie and Thodoris's baby, Dimitri, were washing up on the beach—one by one—like water bottles at my feet. The man in Las Vegas lay prone and purple-blue on Kostas's kitchen counter amid the onions waiting to be chopped. Ayisha and her brother Bashir were screaming, being forced back into a punctured raft and cast adrift back to Turkey.

The next evening, after Ashley and I finished chopping vegetables, we soaked our aching hands and wrists in ice water, then helped Selena and her crew pack up hundreds of meals in IKEA bags. These were too heavy to carry even the short distance, so a man named Stratis drove us to the camp.

The grounds were lit with only a few strings of outdoor bulbs powered by a noisy portable generator. The stench was much stronger now than it had been two days before. People were camped everywhere.

The anarchists had established a harsh but necessary system. Only one meal per person, and everyone who received food had to have a little checkmark put on their wrist with a Sharpie. Food lines were set up. The anarchists, oh, they were big on order. They were positively OCD. I fucking loved them! As Ashley and I distributed the meals in the dark, though, it was still a struggle. We had to take turns holding the flashlight. We learned how to say "hello" in Farsi from an Iranian family, only to find ourselves then serving groups of Syrians, who spoke only Arabic—then Pakistanis, who spoke only—who knew?—Urdu. Women grasped our wrists and pointed desperately to their children, pantomiming hunger. How did we say no to a pregnant woman? A man with a broken arm? The little children thought getting a checkmark was a game, but the adults were humiliated. I didn't blame them. If anyone had tried to put a mark on me back at the homeless shelter in Memphis? I might've opted to go hungry. Or slugged them.

One elderly man grabbed my hand. "You are mother and daughter?"

He bowed. "I am sixty-six years old. I was doctor in Syria. I lose every-body. All my children. Everyone I love. Thank you for feeding me. Allah smiles on you. Praise Allah." I found this even harder to take than the people who cursed us.

When we finished, Ashley and I walked out of the camp robotically, our faces slack, the IKEA bags like spent parachutes in our hands. Following the pale beam of my flashlight, we staggered down the road back to Skala Sikamineas and climbed the hill in silence back to the little weedy path that led up to our room at Dina's. A single weak bulb lit the porch outside, a few flies gyroscoping crazily around it.

I unlocked the front door and switched on the light. The studio was ablaze in eye-searing, blue-white brightness. Dina had mopped the floor that morning (and very pointedly removed the bedsheet draped over her masterpieces). The scuffed tiles smelled of lemon and vinegar. Ashley and I stood in the doorway and took in our room, the daybed and cot with their pilling aquamarine covers, the riotously colorful kittens and sailors and harlequins dancing above them. We looked at the glassed-in fuse box near the utility sink—the big ugly sink, with its own running water!—and the red tab for the hot water heater sticking out like a tongue. Beside it was the bathroom—the bathroom!—its toilet truly a throne—perched beside the newly renovated shower with its hopeful, unfinished tile work.

A porch. A bathroom. A room with two separate beds—one for each of us—just for us. So much goddamn luxury and space.

Ashley dropped onto her mattress, her head in her hands. "I can't even," she said.

I murmured something that came out sounding like, "Mwuuhuhh." My arms and back were so sore, I could barely pull off my hoodie once I unzipped it. It was chalky with filth; it looked twenty years old. So did Ashley's brand-new pants and tennis shoes. I shuffled over to the hot water switch and flicked it on. "Do you mind?" I said hoarsely.

She shook her head. "I just feel like all of the food I've ever refused to eat in my entire life is going to come back to haunt me, Mom." She tilted to one side like a tree being felled and just lay on her bed.

I stepped stiffly into the shower—relentlessly hot. As I squeezed a dollop of shampoo into my palm, I was overwhelmed by all the mothers and children I'd seen huddled on the ground outside, not far from where I now stood in a little protective stall, soaping myself up. I began to shiver. I turned up the water, but I couldn't stop shaking. I began to heave.

What if you're the only ones on the airplane who even *have* oxygen masks?

When I was finally washed and recomposed and swaddled in a towel, I emerged from the bathroom. Ashley was still sprawled in the exact same position that I'd left her in on the daybed, like a statue, a catatonic. But her head cocked the way a cat's might suddenly, listening to something.

"Shhhh." She motioned toward the balcony.

Outside, faintly but very distinctly, coming from the town square, we could hear a chorus of voices rising and falling in waves like water. Clapping. The haunting beat of drums.

"What is that?" she whispered.

"They're playing music in the square. Selena told me they do that sometimes."

"Who?"

"Everyone." I looked at Ashley, then at Aggie, propped up in the corner. "Let me get dressed," I said. "Let's go."

Chapter 21

AN AMERICAN WOMAN, WHOSE own grandparents fled the Holocaust, finds herself in Greece helping the refugees of her own era. I supposed there was some symmetry to this—some of the "balance" Thodoris talked about. If my journey were, say, an epic poem or a picaresque novel, perhaps this was how it should end: With me playing guitar at night with the refugees around the oil-drum campfires on the shimmering beach. With Ashley and I spending our sun-bright days together chopping farm-fresh vegetables, baking heart-shaped loaves of pita bread, and grilling fragrant lamb in the big kitchen with a motley team of other volunteers. We'd be working alongside each other not just as mother and daughter—but as two women at different stages of life who nonetheless have a new, abiding respect for each other. We'd be laughing and sharing little in-jokes as we minced pearly cloves of garlic, and our hands grew redolent of lemon and thyme, and we managed to make our own, small contribution toward nourishing a battered, brutal world.

But of course not. On our third day of cooking, Ashley sliced her left finger dicing an eggplant—there was blood everywhere—you'd have thought we'd have slaughtered an entire lamb on that kitchen floor—and she began freaking out—and okay, I, as Lady Chop-Chop, was not as coolheaded as I should've been, either—yes, it was my kid—and I was exhausted and stressed—but also, she wasn't fucking listening to me in the first place when I told her not once, but *three times*, thank you, to *halve* the eggplant first—you don't just set the whole thing on the cutting board and begin hacking away at it with a cleaver—that's like trying to sever a giant purple lightbulb, for fuck's sake. Eleni bandaged up Ashley's finger with the first-aid kit and a freshly boiled dishrag—good luck getting a doctor in Skala Sikamineas—even before the refugee crisis, a medic came around to the village maybe once a week (a wheezing geriatric with a leather medical kit circa 1958, according to Eleni). So while Ashley was being tended to—and gulping a glass of orange juice to keep from passing out—I ended up yelling something like, "Just how fucking hard is it to follow a basic recipe, Ash?" while she hollered, "Jesus Christ, Mom. You are such a total kitchen fascist. Thanks a lot for all your kindness and sympathy. I could've bled to death right here and all you care about is your fucking eggplant"—after which, the argument quickly devolved into a general cataloging of every single niggling grievance we'd been stockpiling over the course of almost a week of living together: *If you paid as much attention to cooking as you do to your hair?—Well, Mom, I wouldn't take such long showers if you didn't fucking snore all night—Oh! Don't blame me for the fact that you're not sleeping, Ash. It's because you're up all night Skyping Mia and Instagramming. Why not take a little responsibility for your life for a change, will you?—Oh my God. Why did you even have kids in the first place, Mom, if you didn't want the responsibility of us?—Oh, now you want me to take responsibility for you? A moment ago, you wouldn't even listen to me tell you how to cut a fucking vegetable—*

Blah, blah.

As ridiculous as our fight was, oddly, it seemed to defuse the tension for the people around us. There is nothing quite like watching a parent argue with a teenager—a no-win situation if ever there was one—to make everyone else feel relief that this, at least, is not *them*. Although few of them could understand our words, the refugees, in particular, seemed to welcome our bickering as a form of delightful entertainment. After months of living in sheer terror and being treated as either criminals or victims, they seemed reassured—even tickled—by the idiocy of a mother and her teenage daughter shrieking at each other over a butchered eggplant. It suggested that they were, in fact, someplace safe for the moment, that life might, in fact, become mundane and insipid once again. A middle-aged woman in a hijab even winked at me across the restaurant, tilting her chin knowingly at her own petulant, teenage daughter.

Afterward, however, Ashley stomped off with Pernille, Dagmar, and Philippe to pick up trash, a black plastic bag slung over her shoulder. In the kitchen, Kostas and Eleni had gotten frozen ground beef in bulk, and the challenge was to get it all thawed for the massive amounts of moussaka we were cooking. After the eggplants, I was in charge of the béchamel sauce. I never thought that "béchamel sauce" would play even a minute part in a refugee crisis—at first glance, it of course seemed obscene—yet Kostas stuck to his vision.

At the end of the day, my daughter found me still in the kitchen, rinsing off the last of the utensils. The ovens were cooling. Selena's crew had started slicing up the great pans of moussaka into little rectangles, transferring them into takeaway containers for the camp and eating some themselves.

"Hey," Ashley said quietly. Her face was flushed with heat, her oaky hair bleached to copper. She squeezed and unsqueezed her left hand, checking to see how her finger felt beneath its balloon of gauze. The first-aid tape was filthy.

I dried off my knives, set them aside. "How is it, sweetie? Do you need to change the dressing?"

She shook her head. "Maybe just the tape. It doesn't hurt, though." She chewed her lip, kicked at a floor tile with the toe of her tennis shoes. "Sorry about this morning. I was seriously PMSing."

"Yeah. Well," I sighed. "I'm perimensing. So."

"Is that a thing?"

"It is now."

Wearily, we helped pack up all the food. Again. Then distributed meals with the team inside the camp. Again. Then returned to our studio feeling heartbroken and guilty and drained. Again. Yet when I came out of the shower this time, I found Ashley sitting alertly cross-legged on the couch.

"Mom?" She rotated her wrists. Gingerly, she peeled back the bandage to examine her finger. The cut had been longer than it was deep; already, the skin appeared to be shiny and puckering. "How long were you planning on having us stay here? I'm just asking because originally, in London, I figured I'd come for two weeks. If I miss class more than that, I might have to retake the whole semester."

I sat down beside her on the edge of the couch. I looked at the dark sky beyond the balcony.

Ashley sighed. "I mean, I wish I could stay longer." She knitted her fingers together coyly. "It's just that, I'm thinking that maybe it wouldn't hurt, you know, to actually get my degree. Seeing as I can't even cut up an eggplant."

"Oh, Ash, that stuff happens in cooking all the time. Good God. Look at *my* hands." I held them out.

"Yeah, it's just, I'm thinking I might want to change my course of study to include a foreign language? I mean, everyone here—the volunteers *and* the refugees—they all speak at least *three*. All I've got is two lame semesters of high school Spanish." Picking at a blister on her palm, she frowned. "How am I going to help the world if I can't even talk to it?"

I smiled. "Well, there are different ways of communicating."

"Yeah, sure. I mean, you're a chef, so you can communicate through food, which is universal. And Dad is a dentist. Everyone on the planet has teeth. And Austin has his park, which is construction, which can be done anywhere. But what skill do I have, exactly? Tweeting?"

"Austin has a *park*?"

Ashley clamped her hands over her mouth. "Oh shit." She sighed. "Well. Now you know, I guess. Austin and a bunch of his skater friends? They've been sneaking downtown to one of those burned-out lots in Detroit. They've been converting it into this skateboard park. With a half-pipe, and graffiti art. They're supposedly building all these ramps and things. I think they may be working with a local church. And doing a Kickstarter crowdfunding thing."

"Austin?" The kid who, until about a week ago, was essentially a deaf-mute?

"Yeah." Her lashes fluttered. "He didn't want you guys to know, because he was sure you'd totally freak out about him going into the city all the time. But Detroit's having this renaissance, and Rodrigo and him, they're, like, building this playground from scratch. It was their own idea. They started it."

"I thought he and Rodrigo were doing a hip-hop version of *The Odyssey*."

"I dunno. Maybe that, too?"

"Does your dad know?"

"Nuh-uh. Otherwise, he wouldn't let Austin borrow his car. Also, you know how Dad gets with projects and stuff. He'd probably just get totally obsessed and try to make it some sort of weird father-son thing. Austin just really wanted to do it himself, I think."

Well, that explained the aerosol and turpentine stench in my son's room, his soiled clothes, his caginess. But good God: Every single person in our family had a secret fucking life now.

But, oh: How I had underestimated my own son!

I regarded Ashley. She was still birdlike in her boniness, but her face was rose-gold from the sun, her arms and calves taut with young muscle. She would be all right. Better than all right, in fact.

I laughed. "You know, when I was a teenager, I was just sneaking out to get drunk and have sex. You and Austin, you sneak out to help refugees and build playgrounds. That's not bad. Not bad at all, Ash. Wow." I sat back. "You're doing your old man and me one better, that's for sure."

Snorting, she waggled her bandage like a finger puppet. Apropos of nothing, she sang in a falsetto, "*I'm all about that bass, no treble.*"

"Really?" I said.

She began giggling and snorting. "Sorry," she said, waving her hands. "I'm so tired now, I'm punchy."

"Well then," I said. "Let's finish out the week here, then get you back to school."

But me? What the hell was my next step?

At four o'clock that morning, I finally gave up on trying to sleep. The village was eerily still, though somewhere, a dog was baying plaintively, and from inside the walls of our studio, I could hear the relentless *tick-tick-tick* of the water heater. Tiptoeing out onto the balcony, I eased the louvers shut behind me. I took out my phone. The Wi-Fi outside was just strong enough, and I plugged in the cheap earbuds we'd bought in Molyvos. Logging onto Skype, I hit the Call icon. It rang and it rang, but finally that slurpy, digital chime came, and there he was. On-screen. It was the first time we'd seen each other, face to pixelated face, since the afternoon in our kitchen.

"Hey," I said.

"Hey," said Joey.

For a moment, we just sat there, regarding each other on our screens. He was in our basement, I saw, in his "man cave" alcove, his face awash in aquatic light, as if he was in one of those old-fashioned, ultraviolet tanning salons they used to have in the fifties. From the little box in the corner of my phone, I, in turn, looked like an inmate again, this time primed for interrogation; the lone porch bulb overhead was merciless, cleaving my face in chiaroscuro.

"So," said Joey.

"So," I said. With his reading glasses slid halfway down his nose, I couldn't see if there were any bandages left on it. "You okay?"

He shrugged. "You?"

I swallowed. "It's really intense here, Joey." I added, "All these people, with their families. Trying to save themselves on these little plastic life rafts. I've never seen anything like it."

He nodded. "Ashley okay? How's she holding up?" There was a slight delay in the connection, I realized; he seemed to be hesitating more than he probably was. "I appreciate your email updates."

"Yeah. Well. With the time difference, it seems the best way."

We sat there. We nodded. I kept looking down. He kept glancing away, chewing his lip the way Ashley always did.

"Is Austin home?" I asked finally.

He shook his head. "Nah, nah. He's over at Rodrigo's. They're performing their hip-hop *Odyssey* tomorrow, so."

"Hey, how's that going? Is it any good? Shit," I said. "I was supposed to help teach him guitar."

"Yeah, well, you've been busy, Donna." His voice stung with accusation. He looked at me murderously. Then he added more softly, "I think they cut the guitar anyway. When I heard it, Rodrigo was just doing that thing with his mouth."

"Beatboxing?"

"Yeah. Kid's pretty good, actually."

"Joey, have you noticed them disappearing a lot in the afternoons?"

He narrowed his eyes. "Austin and Rodrigo?"

"Ashley told me something," I said quickly. "It's not bad. It's just that apparently, Austin and Rodrigo and some of their friends have been going downtown after school."

"Bloomfield—"

"No, Detroit. Ashley says that they've been working on a secret project for months now. They've taken an abandoned lot downtown and are converting it into a skateboard park. They're putting in a half-pipe, a playground. They're building it all themselves, I guess, but she also said something about them working with Rodrigo's church?"

"You're shitting me." He leaned back. "Jesus fucking Christ. Any more bombshells this family wants to drop on me? You're having an affair and doing porno and getting arrested, one kid dropped out of school to run off to fucking Lesbos without telling anyone, to do God knows what with a bunch of Syrian anarchists—and now the other kid is what? Like, an undercover urban developer? Building a secret skateboard park in downtown Detroit? How the hell is he even financing that?"

"Uh, Kickstarter, I think Ashley said?"

Joey looked up at the ceiling and opened his beefy arms. "What else, God?"

I couldn't help it. I started to laugh.

Releasing his arms, he let them fall to his sides and shook his head incredulously, though not without an appreciation for the absurdity of it all.

"They're good kids, Joey."

He ran his hands through his thinning hair and made a scrubbing sound like *Brrugguhahuhh*. "Yeah," he said softly. "I know."

After a moment, he added, "Better than their parents."

"Ha. I told Ashley the same thing," I said. "I told her that when I was nineteen, hell, I only snuck out to get drunk and have—"

I stopped. Joey's eyes bored through the screen straight into me. I looked down at my lap.

"It's that same guy, isn't it?" he said with bitterness. "I recognized the tattoos from your yearbook."

"Listen. Those photos, Joey. You were never supposed to see them."

"So, are you with him, now? Is this a thing?" His voice cracked.

I shook my head violently. "No. Not at all. Augh. No. It wasn't about him, Joey. It was just—fuck. I just wanted, just one more time in my life to be—to feel—young—desired—*different*. You, of all people, should get this."

Slowly, furiously, Joey nodded, his eyes fixed in the middle distance somewhere beyond his screen.

We were both weeping now.

"You started this, Joey," I said. "Not me."

He said with vehemence, "I just—every time I think about you in those photos, Donna, I can't see anything else. I just want to vomit."

"Well, how do you think I feel? From the second I saw you in our kitchen with that horrible mistress. Betraying me. *Mocking* me. What you were doing was bad enough, but *who* you were doing it as? Are you kidding me? I was nauseated, Joe. I still am. I cannot un-see that, either."

"But it wasn't about *you*, Donna. Don't you get that? Zsa-Zsa's like *my* alter ego—"

"Well, what if I dressed up in some hideous parody of a dentist—or a Polish Catholic—Joey, and hired people to playact with me behind your back? And you saw me totally getting off on *that*?"

We stared at each other plainly now, at the full shipwreck of us. We sighed and wiped our eyes and each looked away.

"Would you have still done it," Joey asked, "if I hadn't been, *you know*—"

Wow: He couldn't even say it.

"I don't think so. Who knows?" I added after a moment. "Maybe."

We just sat there. In the background, where he was, I heard a timer go off. Beyond the balcony in Lesvos, the first few birds of morning were starting to sound.

"Well?" he said. "What do we do now?"

You'd think that confronting the world's extremes and tragedies in real time—being among people who were fleeing war and terrorism—who'd had to make the horrific, calculated decision to sail across the Aegean with their children in an overstuffed inflatable boat instead of risk being blown to smithereens in their apartments or machine-gunned down in their streets or sold into sexual slavery by ISIS—you'd think that all of this would somehow mitigate my own petty, quotidian concerns. And yeah, okay, absolutely: Stuff I'd once obsessed over like outdated kitchen appliances—or the snarky finality of Colleen Lundstedt's response to me in Memphis (**Donna, I believe it's better to give a "Prodigal Daughter" tough love rather than an "emergency loan."**—So much for "family")—or whether Mr. Noodles was on the right dosage of meds from his doggie shrink. All of these things just evaporated in their own ridiculousness.

But they did nothing to mitigate the fact that when I saw my husband over Skype, nervously picking at his cuticles the way he always did, I still had the impulse to reach through the screen and slap his hand away. The world's crises did nothing to alleviate the intense irritation I knew I'd continue to feel whenever he sang, "Oh, I want a snack" to the tune of "The Blue Danube" while rummaging interminably and noisily through our refrigerator while I was trying to work.

More to the point, handing out containers of eggplant to shell-shocked refugees on Lesvos did nothing to erase the images in my head of Joey in all of his Pleasure Chest finery, on his hands and knees with his mistress in our kitchen. Global horror could do nothing, in the end, to alleviate the private anguish and betrayal and domestic absurdity of life in suburban Michigan. All these miseries simply coexisted. Comparing my misfortunes to the greater misfortunes of others did not, in the end, relieve the stabbing pain in my gut. Maybe it was just me—maybe I was as weak and bourgeois as my daughter had once accused me of being. Or maybe pain was just pain was just pain.

Experiencing the world as I was now, though, did make me want to be less careless, less willing to dismiss and discard love so casually.

I shook my head.

"I don't know, Joey," I said plainly.

We'd just have to see.

The next night, several boats came ashore early in the evening. Ashley and I did not witness their arrival. By now, we'd firmly established (okay, barricaded) ourselves in the kitchen, focusing on what we could do without freaking out. But to our great relief, everyone aboard the dinghies arrived dry and intact. Their landings were some of the joyous ones. People cheered and clapped and hugged the Greeks spontaneously. When Kostas and the other café owners lit their fires in the oil drums for people to warm themselves by, another impromptu music session broke out. A volunteer named Igor brought out a tambori from Spain, and two refugees from Senegal, Amadou and Ousman, improvised drums out of overturned buckets. Sam, from Ethiopia, had carried a wooden flute with him over thousands of miles; and two new volunteer girls, Simone and Paula, broke out kazoos. Eleni began singing with Amir. I hurried up to our studio and returned with Aggie.

You would think I'd find a niche playing guitar right there around the campfires with the other volunteers and travelers (the word "refugees" felt tragic and faceless now). But after I started to pluck out "Leaving on a Jet Plane" anemically (I had, it seems, become a one-hit wonder), the lyrics seemed far too heartbreaking—punishing, in fact, for people who had actually left their loved ones and did not know when they'd be back again—plus, who were we kidding? My playing stank—and so I found myself handing my instrument over to an Argentinian named Francisco. Before he set off to backpack around the world, he'd trained for several years as a classical guitarist in Buenos Aires. Although the Rogue Dreadnought was beneath his skills, he played long, intricate, hauntingly beautiful Spanish ballads and arias. Sometimes he would pause his strumming as he sang, so that his voice was suddenly a cappella, angelic and reedy and otherworldly, lifting up over the metronome of the waves like one thin note of hope. The entire village would stop, transfixed. Then, after letting the plaintive cry hang in the air, he would launch gustily into the opening, definitive bars of "You Ain't Nothin' but a Hound Dog," and perform a truly spirited/ridiculous impression of Elvis Presley. He could seemingly play anything, and the little children loved him, hanging over his lanky shoulders, tugging at his beard, begging for more.

As the evening wound down, he handed me back the guitar. "Muchas gracias, señora," he said and bowed.

I waved my hands in refusal. "No. Keep it."

"Oh, no, no," he said. "I couldn't possibly."

"You have to. Trust me. It's yours."

"Aw, Mom," Ashley said as we climbed back up the hill together. "I can't believe you just gave him Aggie."

"I only owned it a couple of weeks, Ash. It's not exactly an heirloom." I snorted. "Besides, the last thing I want to be is some middle-aged woman talking to her guitar case."

I did find myself, though, wanting to stay on in Lesvos. But I was not naive. Nor independently wealthy. Yeah, Skala Sikamineas was cheaper than the US, but I was a forty-five-year-old with a mortgage, and monthly health insurance premiums that cost more than my first car, and one kid in college and another on his way, and Joey and I had to pay back Arjul. And the stupid doggie shrink—and now whatever medical expenses Joey had run up beyond our insurance—thanks to his being on the wrong end of my spatula— Well, I supposed, whose fault was that? And depending on whatever happened to our marriage? Certainly, if nothing else, we needed both money and time.

In my punk rock heart, there also lurked a cynic who bristled at using volunteer work abroad as any sort of solution for a midlife crisis.

Surely, I knew better than that.

Detroit itself had soup kitchens. And homeless shelters—and God knew, I now had an intimate, Yelp reviewer's knowledge about what might best serve them. All those ghost gardens on abandoned estates: Maybe I could team up with Austin to convert them into more play-grounds for children (though I suspected he'd be even more mortified by the prospect of this than of playing my Stratocaster: M-o-n-om!), Or, I could just get off my high horse and help other alkies like myself for a change.

Who the hell knew? There was more than enough to do back home.

Though at the moment, I *was* certainly needed right there in Greece; I was part of the Kitchen Chorus, a member of the Trash Band. After taking Ashley to get her passport replaced, I could stay on just a little longer, couldn't I?

Emailing Joey, I asked him to investigate what I'd need to do to cash out part of my Privileged Kitchen 401(k). There would be penalties and paperwork, no doubt—blah, blah—but I wanted to explore the options I might be lucky enough to still have. It didn't matter whether Brenda was Nostradamus or not: She was right. The world needed much more than some white lady driving around in her Subaru ruminating over a lost love based on a tarot card.

Time to roll up my sleeves and get the fuck down to work.

*   *   *

And so I did. The next morning, Ashley and I cleaned up the town square together, methodically picking up debris from the night before. Crushed aluminum cans caught the morning light like prisms. Colored candy wrappers and shoelaces and bits of torn clothing confettied the water's edge almost prettily: You just shouldn't look too closely. It was high tide, and the waves came up almost to the road. A handful of young Afghan teenagers, desperate to have something to do, were helping as well, shoving one another and laughing as they scooped up empty water bottles. We paced up and down the flagstones, filling our garbage bags piece by piece. The life jackets, we piled in one heap by the stone wall.

The breeze had picked up. It ruched the cobalt water, sunlight darting over it like quicksilver. I closed my eyes and inhaled. I could smell that wonderful briny scent of the sea, mixed with eucalyptus and rosemary.

Suddenly, the proprietor dashed down the hotel steps right past us, a pair of binoculars bouncing against his chest, shouting to his neighbors in Greek. I heard a growl and sputter of engines, then saw the fisherman Georges starting his boat. A woman and her son emerged from the mini-mart, also shouting, carrying cases of bottled water.

At the far end of the pier, Kostas and his son, Alex, were heaving up an anchor. Volunteers ran toward them holding armfuls of salvaged life vests.

Philippe, Dagmar, and Amir were getting into position at different points along the seawall, peering through binoculars.

"How many?" Philippe called.

"Three, but I cannot be certain!" said Amir.

"Is the coast guard there?"

Selena came up behind us, accompanied by three Middle Eastern teenagers. "I found some translators," she panted, pressing her hands to her knees as she tried to catch her breath.

"Hello," one of the young men said. "You need translator for Arabic, my friend? My name is Ahmed. I tell my father to come as well. Last night, he rescues five people on our boat with us."

"Is your father a lifeguard?" I said.

"No, he is electrical engineer."

Two other boys appeared. "Ma' Salaam. I am Omar, and this is my brother, Mustafa. We can speak Farsi, Dari, and Pashto."

"Okay." Selena glanced around, assessing. "Plus, we've got French, Spanish, German, English, Portuguese, Wolof, and Greek. That better do it."

I heard the pulse and chug of an engine, men shouting across the water. Other men began running. The flagstone pier hooked around the port. In the curve of it was a rocky outcropping. Perched atop this was a tiny white stucco church—the village's famous Temple of the Mermaid—a singular outpost and beacon above the sea.

"Ashley," I said. We grabbed each other's hands. Emerging from behind the temple now like a magnificent bird, like a resplendent parade float, a sky-blue fishing boat came into view on the water towing a large inflatable raft crammed with passengers, women and men and children bundled into orange life vests and thick scarves, sitting stock-still, their arms rigid against the ballast, seemingly too terrified to move or even breathe for fear of upsetting the boat.

As soon as they saw the waiting marina, however, the children on the dinghy began to cheer and shout and point, and a few adults started applauding, and one of them, a middle-aged man upholstered in a navy-blue life vest, forgot himself; overcome with relief and joy, he half stood, shouting to the sky, "Allah Akbar!" For a few heart-stopping seconds, the entire boat lurched back and forth, and a collective scream went up from the passengers and witnesses alike as the boat tilted and a bundle bandaged in plastic tumbled off it and it slid into the sea.

Yet the dinghy was parallel to the stone pier, and a dozen Greek hands grasped it and pulled it in against the wall, securing it fast. Amid great yelling, I saw Selena pull Ahmed and Omar along, shouting, "I've got translators! I've got translators!" Three drenched figures stood shivering in the fishing boat, shrouded in blankets; Eleni was helping them onto the pier like a footman. Only then did I see that Kostas and Alex had just returned with a second dinghy in tow. This one, however, had already taken on water, dragging heavily behind their fishing boat like a wet diaper; in fact, a few of the passengers had already spilled out into the water beside it, clinging to the deflating vinyl, paddling and kicking furiously, their faces fixed in terror.

An older man who'd already alighted onto the pier, his face bracketed by eyeglasses in heavy tortoise frames, kept pointing to the ground and shouting, "This is Europe? Are we in Europe? Please? This is Europe?" I watched a woman in a pink chiffon headscarf yank her two small children, an older girl and a younger boy—*Salt and pepper*—down onto their knees beside her—first in prayer, then to literally kiss the flagstones.

Ashley and I were helping to hand out water bottles—there wasn't time to think—we were just doing—the passengers gulped them down in three or four greedy swallows, though a few poured it over their heads like an anointment.

"Does anyone here know CPR? CPR? Anyone?" Cathy was shouting from Kostas's fishing boat. "Please, someone!" Inga and a burly young Greek man started running down the pier. "CPR! CPR!"

It was only as I watched them leap into the boat that it struck me: *Fuck. I know CPR.* I'd used it barely two weeks ago.

"Hey!" I hollered, waving. "Hey!" Yet my legs refused to move. For a moment, I felt so disembodied, so bifurcated and dizzy, I wondered if I wasn't having a stroke. Finally, finally, I felt myself lurch forward, pushing my way through the crowd on the pier—Good God, *watch me slip and give myself a concussion*—but I shouted, "I know CPR!" I shouted and slid down into the hull of the fishing boat, nearly twisting my ankle in the process. "Who is it?"

Inga looked over her shoulder at me. She and the Greek man were crouched over a wet body, prone on the bottom boards of the boat. She brought a single finger to her lips and her eyes were unreadable. I clamped my hands over my mouth. An Arab man knelt beside the figure, clutching the white hand, shaking his head, silently weeping in that openmouthed way where the voice catches at the back of the throat and sounds like a car stalling.

I dropped to my knees.

"False alarm," said Inga. She raised her eyebrows at me.

The Arab man coughed apologetically. "My brother, he does not have a heart attack." He emitted that raspy staccato sound again. "He is only drunk."

He wasn't weeping; he was laughing with incredulity. He shook his head, trying to contain himself. "My brother. He is devout Muslim. He never takes a drink in his life." Sniffling, he dabbed his eyes. "But in Turkey, we hear so many bad things about the boat trip, my brother, he is so frightened, in Izmir, he buys little bottle of vodka. Pours it in his canteen. Says it is water. Drinks it all the way here. First time in his life having alcohol. As soon as we land here in Greece, what does he do? He is falls down drunk."

"Exactly how big was the bottle he bought?" I asked.

The man calipered his fingers.

"That's not enough to kill him from alcohol poisoning."

The Arab man chuckled. "No. But my mother? Please, do not tell. If our family hears Mohammed is drunk, he will be the first person not killed by bombs in Aleppo, but by his mother in Greece."

I rejoined Ashley on the waterfront, laughing. I started to tell her about the drunken man when a voice bellowed from a rooftop, "Boats! Boats!" *There were more?* A couple of Spanish lifeguards bounded into view from beyond the trees. High up in the distance, on the edge of a rock, someone was signaling frantically. Three dinghies were suddenly approaching the coast far down the beach to our left; one going at full speed, bouncing along in the water. Another seemed to be having engine problems. I could hear the asthmatic wheeze of a dying outboard motor. The third, cutting in toward the shore at an angle, was much closer, but already, it was starting to list. You could see the people on it beginning to scramble and panic.

It happened so quickly, it didn't fully register. Their bottoms scraping against the rocks, the boats were bobbling up to the shore now, and some of the refugees who had made it were slipping and staggering up onto the pebbled shore, clapping and crying, taking selfies with the life-guards and the volunteers to celebrate their landing. Someone shouted in English, "We're safe! We made it! Praise Allah!" It was a sudden, surreal party. People were throwing off their life vests and dancing around a little bit. But then Ashley grabbed my arm, hard. "Mom!" she cried. And then we froze. I heard it too. Howling, the most anguished, chilling wails I had ever heard. A young woman was keeled over in the sand, shrieking, "*NO NO NO.*" "She says there's a baby! Does anyone see a baby?" someone shouted. And then there was splashing and shout-ing and total pandemonium. Two other men—volunteers or refugees—emerged from the sea, bellowing, carrying a man whose body was so pale and purplish, it was almost iridescent. He was limp and heavy, like a bag of wet cement. And another man was brought out of the sea, his mouth and his eyes wide open as if he were still screaming at the sky. And then. Then a little girl in a flowered dress, no more than ten years old.

"Mom, Mom." Ashley was sobbing into my neck, clutching me fiercely. I clamped her face in place in the crook of my shoulder, trying to shield her—to shield both of us—from seeing, my eyes squeezed tight, my pulse furious in prayer. *Please, God. Please, no. Make them live again. Make this not be happening.*

A moment earlier, the Aegean before us had seemed calm and empty. But now, again, we heard the relentless cry—"Boats! Boats!" Ashley and I looked at each other, seized with alarm. *More? How could there be more so quickly?* Her face went pale; she glanced frantically toward the village, as if calculating distance. "Deep breath, Ash. We can do this," I said, though my own heart started punching. But I'd decided: There was no more running away for either of us.

An air horn bleated. Fishing boats were starting up in the marina, though given where the new boats seemed to be approaching from, I knew that Kostas and his men would have to maneuver around an outcropping of rocks before they could reach the dinghies. More Spanish lifeguards had pulled on their swimming shoes. Without hesitation, they plowed directly into the water, slogging through the waves until it was deep enough to dive. Then they plunged like a school of dolphins, swimming with astonishing speed toward the dinghy.

"Make a human chain! Make a human chain!" someone shouted, and suddenly, I glimpsed Igor and Inga and the dreadlocked Swedes and Amir, and a few of the Senegalese refugees from the night before with Amadou, then Alex and Eleni running and the Afghan teenagers and the Greek with the expensive sunglasses. Ashley and I barely had time to exchange glances before we were separated and swept up by the group— "Ash, you got this!" I shouted, my words borne away in the wind—as my arms were linking through other arms, people grabbing each other, still more people joining, all of us lunging toward the water in a crazed zigzagging line, weaving and swaying as if performing a folk dance.

I felt the frigidity of the sea before my brain actually registered that I was in it. I hadn't expected it to be quite so cold, nor so deep, and the stones underfoot managed to be both slippery and jagged at the same time. The water seeped down into my absurd New Jersey Turnpike boots and up the legs of my jeans. My left arm was hooked through Selena's, my right through that of one of the teenagers from Afghanistan, who smiled at me with incredulity, shivering. Ashley was in the line parallel to mine, a few positions back from me, one arm linked with Francisco, the other with Inga. We were both being pulled forward by our teammates deeper and deeper into the water. "Ashley," I shouted.

She shrugged her shoulders helplessly, her face flush with fear but also, I saw, resolve—the same terrified determination she'd had as a small child, pedaling furiously, Joey running behind her, cheering her on. "I guess we're doing this," she shouted back. Our lines slogged deeper into the water a few more feet, then halted at the signal of one of the Spanish volunteers coordinating with the lifeguards. She showed us how to join and cross our arms, gripping each other's wrists for stability to form a human bridge. The lifeguards had seized the dinghy and were now paddling furiously as they swam back toward the shore towing it in. I heard a commotion of splashing and shrieking; people in the dinghy were tumbling into the water as the rubber collapsed farther beneath them. Yet it was shallow enough now that after they plunged, they discovered they could easily stand. As they struggled to get their balance on the slippery rocks, they started yelling in languages I did not know, raising their hands to the sky and motioning and gesturing. More and more refugees were now voluntarily sliding off the boat into the water on their own, helping one another off, holding each other's hands as they wobbled up the last few feet to the shore.

And then I saw the baby. The mother, sobbing and terrified at the helm of the raft, did not want to surrender it to the lifeguard, but the dinghy, still taking on water, was starting to give way beneath her. With a sob, she finally held out her arms beseechingly and relinquished her infant, then leapt off the boat. One lifeguard placed the baby gently into another lifeguard's wet arms, and then it was passed in its tiny wool blanket like a secret, like a firefly clasped between a child's cupped hands, from one set of arms to the other down the entire length of our chain. I was positioned across from one of the dreadlocked Swedes. As soon as it came to us I was filled with panic—Good God: *please, don't let us drop it, don't let us drop it*—but also, too, with awe and a fierce, animal desire: I wanted to snatch the baby to my breast and encircle it in my arms and dash up onto the beach with it by myself. Instead, however, treating it with the fragility of a robin's egg, the Swede and I together placed the baby carefully into the attending arms of the Afghan boy and Igor beside us, who then passed it carefully along to Francisco and Dagmar.

When the baby was finally redeposited into the arms of its mother on the shore, a huge, sonorous cheer went up. Refugees and volunteers alike began laughing crazily with relief, fist-pumping, throwing back our heads to the sky and hooting "Woohoo!" and "Allah Akbar!" and "Gracias a Dios!" And maybe, because in the middle of life's tragedies, there is often some absurd nugget of humor—a gift from an ironic god—several of the children on the road, swept up in the gloriousness of deliverance, still dripping wet in their life jackets, started running back into the water, falling down comically and splashing each other, delighting in what had terrified them just moments before.

"Get back in place," Selena shouted. "Everybody get back in place." The second dinghy motored in. It moored in the shoals to our left, and we all slogged over toward it in the sunshine, holding fast to one another, trying not to slip. Yet something did not go as planned, because all of the passengers tried to alight as soon as the motor stopped, and the lifeguards were suddenly overwhelmed, and refugees everywhere were dropping into the water, then struggling back up onto their feet, and some of them were so happy, so happy and thrilled to be safe, that they started hugging the volunteers—or maybe they were still terrified—so they clung to whoever they found, and the chain fell apart and people were splashing and thrashing and cheering, some of them dancing, some of them weeping, and all was chaos.

The light was blazing over the Aegean now, as bright and crazy as mercury. My arms were no longer linked through Selena's, or anyone's, and I felt myself slip. As I stumbled backward deeper into the water, I heard Ashley shout, "Mom!" She was on the edge of the shore, holding a tiny girl in a life jacket. I waved and smiled, though I was fighting to regain my balance. The tide was getting rougher. There was a drop-off in the seabed. Waves generated by the third dinghy and the fishing boats tumbled in now, slapping me from behind, jouncing off my shoulder. My cheap sunglasses fell off and started to sink. A wave broke over me fully, leaving me ravaged with salt on my tongue.

A few feet away, a woman in a sopping headscarf flailed toward me. I flailed toward her, paddling with my arms through the chop as best I could, trying to keep standing. I reached out to grasp her at the precise moment she reached out to grasp me; we clung to each other, our cheeks pressed together, our wet shirts swirling around us, entwining us in fabric. Each new wave lifted us up off the seabed, splashed over us, then set us down gently as it receded.

I heard someone laughing, her voice pealing against the sky, trilling over the octaves in a caw of pure ecstasy. I saw my daughter shimmering distantly on the shore, waving frantically. "It's okay. It's okay!" I shouted, as another great web of sea foam exploded over us. We squeezed our hands together, and it broke around us in a million dazzling shards of light, and again, I heard that wild, clear note of laughter, and again we went under.

Author's Note

Although this is a work of fiction, the refugee crisis in Greece and around the globe is very real; it is, in fact, the largest humanitarian crisis since World War II. This novel is set in 2015 and inspired by events that occurred in Lesvos and elsewhere in Greece at that time. Since then, however, the crisis has only continued and conditions for the refugees have only worsened. Although boats still arrive in Greece, EU borders have effectively shut down. Refugees are now finding themselves trapped on the islands and in camps for years. Facilities intended to house them for just a few days have turned into virtual prisons. Indeed, Moria, which was first established as merely a weigh station on Lesvos, is now being called, at the time of this writing, the worst refugee camp in the world. People are confined there indefinitely without shelter, running water, electricity, toilet facilities, heat, blankets, or a modicum of safety.

Much humanitarian aid is being provided by nongovernmental organizations and volunteers like the ones depicted in this novel.

If, after reading this book, you feel compelled to help, here are a few small, well-established, effective organizations doing vital work on the frontlines in Greece. They regularly need volunteers and monetary donations. You can learn about them here through their websites:

Advocates Abroad: advocatesabroad.org
Dirty Girls of Lesvos: dirtygirlsoflesvos.com

Drapen I Havet (Danish for "A Drop in the Ocean"):
drapenihavet.no
Lighthouse Relief: lighthouserelief.org
Project Elea: projectelea.org
Samos Volunteers: samosvolunteers.org

There are countless others—and not only in Greece. But these, at least, are a start.

Acknowledgments

I am grateful to so many people for their help and support throughout the writing of this book.

First and foremost, I bow before my agent, the Phenomenal Molly Friedrich, and my co-agent, the Incomparable Lucy Carson. They fell in love with *Donna Has Left the Building* and committed to this novel in its earliest stages; they have been tireless advocates and readers ever since. Thank you for your literary savvy, dedication, frankness, wit, professionalism, and exquisite care. It is a joy and privilege to work with you both. I owe a special debt of gratitude as well to Heather Carr of the Friedrich Agency for her smarts, conscientious feedback, and warmth.

And then...there is simply not enough poetry, live gospel music, or hyperbole in the universe to adequately convey my gratitude to my editor, Millicent Bennett. Millicent, if I could be reincarnated as Cole Porter, I would come back and write a classic song about you to be played throughout the ages. You are the proverbial tops. Your editorial brilliance astounds me. You brought inexhaustible faith, energy, and insight to this book and envisioned it in its entirety even when I got lost in the sentences. I cannot imagine writing this without you. A million *grazie milles, ragazza*.

I am continually grateful for all the support and attention I've received from the publishing team at Grand Central Publishing and Hachette Book Group USA—including, but certainly not limited to—Matthew Ballast, Staci Burt, Karen Kosztolnyik, Brian McLendon, Meriam Metoui, Caitlin

Mulrooney-Lyski, Michael Pietsch, Luria Rittenberg, Ben Sevier, Charles McCrorey, Michele McGonigle, Thomas Louie, and Karen Torres.

Ellis Avery, Elizabeth Coleman, Brigette Delay, Susan Dalsimer, John Seeger Gilman, Valerie Lack, Eric Messinger, Karen-Lee Ryan, Desa Sealy, Adam Smyer, and Linda Yellin: Thank you for so willingly being my readers, sounding boards, and champions.

Maureen McSherry, you deserve deification for all the love and support you've given me. Thank you for your astute multiple readings, extensive editorial advice, beach time, wisdom, and, most of all, enduring friendship.

A huge thank you as well goes to Dr. Rachel Seidel, Josh Sherer, Paul Stefanski, and Veronica Vera for their professional expertise that informed aspects of this story. I am also deeply indebted to two of Tennessee's top attorneys, J. Michael Shipman and David Louis Raybin, for their legal counsel and for taking the time in particular to illuminate for me Tennessee's drug policies and search and seizure laws.

A heartfelt *danke/merci/grazie* to the staff of the Cambrian Adelboden—to Anke Locke and Stephane Gheringer in particular—for continuing to give me a "room of one's own" and keeping me well cared for while I completed this manuscript.

To my parents, David Gilman and Ellen Gilman, for simply being my parents—and not asking too many questions.

I am profoundly grateful to Andreas Ashikalis, Simone Plassard, and Paula Johanna Pleuser of Project Elea at the Eleonas Refugee Camp in Athens; the Mariola Family at the Aphrodite Hotel in Molyvos, Lesvos; and Nikos Molvalis in Vafios, Lesvos for their extraordinary work and for sharing their stories with me. Also to Francisco Gentico, Malen Garmendia Gomez, Santiago Jatib, Isabel Reardon, Emily Wilson, and the countless other volunteers and coordinators in Athens. To Thodoris Birbas and Vasso Stavropoulou for being my family in Greece.

Alas, there are not adequate words to thank the refugees who have taken me into their lives. Most of them will have to go unnamed here to protect their privacy and due to their precarious status in the world.

However, I am honored to acknowledge my friends and interpreters, Masoud Majidi, Ahmad Zafar Hotak, and Mohammad Sohrab Safi for all that they have done.

My character Donna remarked that none of us are heroes. However, I do have a hero in real life. My beloved husband has been my champion—and a tireless reader who has gone above and beyond the limits of human kindness and patience with me for as long as I've been writing books. Bob Stefanski, you are my rock, my engine, my greatest love, and a balm for my soul. You make me possible. Thank you, *mon mari*. This one is for you, too.

About the Author

Susan Jane Gilman is the bestselling author of three nonfiction books, *Hypocrite in a Pouffy White Dress*, *Kiss My Tiara*, and *Undress Me in the Temple of Heaven*, as well as the novel *The Ice Cream Queen of Orchard Street*. She has provided commentary for NPR and written for *The New York Times*, *The Los Angeles Times*, *Real Simple*, and *Ms.*, among others. She has won several literary awards, and her books have been published in a dozen languages. You can visit her through www.SusanJaneGilman.com